S0-ABC-991

7/21

By ELLE E. IRE

Vicious Circle

STORM FRONTS
Threadbare
Patchwork
Woven

Published by DSP PUBLICATIONS
www.dsppublications.com

ELMONT PUBLIC LIBRARY

ELLE E.
IRE

WOVEN

DSP PUBLICATIONS

Published by
DSP PUBLICATIONS

5032 Capital Circle SW, Suite 2, PMB# 279, Tallahassee, FL 32305-
7886 USA
www.dsppublications.com

This is a work of fiction. Names, characters, places, and incidents either
are the product of author imagination or are used fictitiously, and any
resemblance to actual persons, living or dead, business establishments,
events, or locales is entirely coincidental.

Woven
© 2020 Elle E. Ire

Cover Art
© 2020 Tiferet Design
http://www.tiferetdesign.com/
Cover content is for illustrative purposes only and any person depicted
on the cover is a model.

All rights reserved. This book is licensed to the original purchaser only.
Duplication or distribution via any means is illegal and a violation of
international copyright law, subject to criminal prosecution and upon
conviction, fines, and/or imprisonment. Any eBook format cannot be legally loaned or given to others. No part of this book may be reproduced
or transmitted in any form or by any means, electronic or mechanical,
including photocopying, recording, or by any information storage and
retrieval system, without the written permission of the Publisher, except
where permitted by law. To request permission and all other inquiries,
contact Dreamspinner Press, 5032 Capital Circle SW, Suite 2, PMB#
279, Tallahassee, FL 32305-7886, USA, or www.dreamspinnerpress.
com.

Mass Market Paperback ISBN: 978-1-64108-249-5
Trade Paperback ISBN: 978-1-64405-448-2
Digital ISBN: 978-1-64405-447-5
Library of Congress Control Number: 2020937845
Mass Market Paperback published July 2021
First Edition
v. 1.0

Printed in the United States of America
∞
This paper meets the requirements of
ANSI/NISO Z39.48-1992 (Permanence of Paper).

As always, this work is dedicated to my soulmate/ spouse. There is no one in my life who knows me as well as you do and encourages me to be the best I can possibly be. Thank you for helping me embrace my true self. Thank you for believing in this dream so that I would continue to write when I wanted to give up. I love you.

Acknowledgements

THIS IS a rather bittersweet moment for me writing these thank-yous. For as long as I can remember, this series, and especially the character of Vick Corren, have been haunting my thoughts both waking and dreaming. I can picture her clearly, in no small part because of the amazing work of my two cover artists—Nathalie Gray who did the covers for Threadbare and Patchwork, and Anna Sikorska who finished the series with the beautiful art for Woven. I can also hear Vick in my head, always nagging me to get her story out there, and I'll confess, she hasn't yet shut up, so while I'm taking a break from Storm Fronts, there may be more for her to do in the future. It saddens me to see the trilogy come to an end, but a character like Vick never sits still for long.

I want to thank my amazing editorial team—Gus Li, Camiele White, and Brian Holliday for putting up with all my misplaced commas and hyphens and triple-checking for continuity errors. I am so grateful to have had them along for the entire series. Their support and enthusiasm, along with their suggestions, took me in directions I hadn't originally planned, and I know the trilogy is better for their influence. Any remaining errors are all mine.

Thank you to Naomi Grant for her promotional wisdom and everyone else at Dreamspinner Publications who has had a hand in getting this series out there.

Thank you to my writing group: Amy, Evergreen, Gary, Joe, and Ann for their ongoing advice and for keeping me sane throughout the publishing process. Thank you to those readers who have contacted me or left reviews to express your enjoyment of Vick and Kelly's adventures. Those words mean so very very much and make me want to write more and more. In particular, thank you to authors Arielle Haughee and MB Austin for your praise and support.

Special thanks to my agent, Naomi Davis, who believed in this series from the very beginning and continues to believe in me as an author.

Thank you to my daughter, Ana, for cover art opinions and never-ending eagerness to read the next book.

Finally and most of all, thank you to my spouse for car-ride brainstorming sessions, random what-ifs, last-minute read-throughs, and all the love and support an author could ever ask for. None of this would have happened without you by my side.

CHAPTER 1: VICK
INTERFERENCE

I am tired.

I STUMBLE toward the Storm's military transport ship. The ramp seems to waver and buck as my boots climb it, though I know it's solid and still. The hatch stands open, Lyle's massive form framed in the entryway and backlit by the interior lights casting his already dark exterior into shadowy blackness.

"Corren, great job today. You kicked some serious ass. That psychopath won't be hurting kids ever again," he says, his bass tones falling over me like a thick blanket. Warmth, comfort, companionship. These tonics wait for me in the shuttle, if I can just make it another few steps, though the one person I need the most isn't onboard.

A smaller form appears behind Lyle—Alex, our tech expert. "Yeah, and you did it in record time according to the Undercover Ops records I hacked. Mission spec for this job was another week at least. Hunt the bad guys, take 'em down, get home for breakfast. No one has beaten their estimates as bad as you just did." Alex didn't know the Storm *had* an Undercover Ops until five months ago when they "invited" our team to join them. Even VC1, my ever-present, brain-inhabiting AI, hadn't been able to confirm their existence, and she makes Alex look like a kid playing with a toy circuit set. But from the inside, they both have a lot more access to intel, including data that U Ops probably doesn't want us to have yet, if ever.

An image of my new handler, Carl, appears on my internal display, his broad chest and tree-trunk legs barely covered by a cheerleader's uniform. Meaty arms and hands the size of my skull wave pink-and-white pompoms before the entire picture vanishes.

Yeah, the boss will be pleased. The Fighting Storm's decision-making board will be pleased. The accountants will be pleased. Everyone who has any kind of power within the Storm's infrastructure will be fucking ecstatic.

Yippee for me.

I'm two steps from the lip of the hatch when I stumble, nearly falling off the metal ramp to hit the landing field tarmac six feet below. It wouldn't do serious damage, but it would hurt, and I place my next foot with extreme care.

"Hey, you all right?" The concern in Lyle's tone touches me in places I hadn't known I possessed until Kelly, my life partner, helped me reconnect with them.

Damn, I wish she was here, but then again, I don't. I'd be a heartless, cruel bitch to bring an empath into a kill zone.

When I trip a second time, Lyle closes the small distance and catches me, grabbing me by both shoulders and hauling me upright. With his face mere inches from mine, his frown is impossible to miss, shadows or no shadows. "You don't stumble."

In other words, I'm programmed for optimum agility.

I stop that line of thinking, my own growth and Kelly's influence curling tendrils of guilt in the pit of my stomach. Such thoughts not only belittle the individual human I am, even with the implants, but also make unfair assumptions about Lyle's perception of me. He and Alex both have worked hard at overcoming the predominant mindset that I'm a machine in an organic casing (and even that's cloned version 2.0), a walking biological computer, a robot with a pretty exterior. If they can accept me as a person, a friend and teammate, rather than property, then I can damn well give myself the same treatment.

"This is our third assignment almost back-to-back," I remind him. "I'm… tired."

But I shouldn't be collapsing on boarding ramps. The implants' job is to maximize my energy reserves, keep me to all outside appearances fit and focused, and I'm not. *What's going on?*

Exhaustion, mild dehydration, emotional trauma. In other words, the usual.

I swallow a bark of laughter at that last comment. VC1's droll humor becomes more and more like my own every day, but my non-AI partners will be even more worried if I start laughing out loud without an obvious stimulus. No, not a stimulus, a *reason*. An obvious reason. Sometimes I worry the more human VC1 becomes, the more machinelike the rest of me gets.

I push that concern into a dark emotional corner with all the rest in order to focus on my current dilemma. *Why aren't you doing anything about it?*

Because you are now in a position of safety and security. I have been moderating your physical and emotional stress for several days. My own systems are not taxed. You are in no danger of redlining or overload or burnout—

I close my eyes and exhale. No, I don't want to burn out ever again. Dying that way once was more than enough.

—but I, too, have limits, as you are well aware. It is imperative that I allow your biological infrastructure to heal naturally when time and situation permit. It gives me an opportunity to perform maintenance on my own functions while preventing you from becoming overly dependent upon my assistance.

Which means you've pulled out your support and I'm about to lose consciousness.

Precisely.

Wonderful. That thought and the tightening of Lyle's hands on me are the last things I remember before the universe goes dark.

I'M IN some sort of research facility, long metal-walled corridors stretching out before me and

branching in multiple directions, door after door breaking up the endless walls on either side. Some of them
are open, revealing white-coated technicians perform-
ing a variety of experiments or typing furiously at their
desk comps. I'm wearing an identical lab coat over
gray pants, my white canvas shoes covered in plastic
protectors, but the uniform feels odd, out of place, like
it should belong to someone else.

Medical personnel pass me as I hurry along, most
ignoring me, their faces locked in masks of concentra-
tion, though a few smile and raise a hand in greeting.
I return the gestures, but again, they feel performative,
fake.

At the end of the hall is a larger set of double doors
with a red light above them. I fish a keycard from my
lab coat pocket and wave it over the electronic lock.
The photo on the ID card depicts a blond male, but I'm
in a female body, dark hair cascading over my shoulders. I have a second to wonder where I got the card
before I hide it away again. The light flashes green. The
doors part.

I'm in a launch bay. Lots of ships of varying sizes.
Lots of activity. The bay doors stand open on the far
side, the glimmer of a force field indicating why everything and everyone isn't being blown out to the open
starfield beyond.

Asteroid. Or moon. I'm not sure where I am in the
greater picture.

"Doctor?" a man in a pilot's uniform—a Sunfire
pilot's uniform—asks, approaching me at a brisk clip
from one of the smaller spacecraft. "Can I help you with
something? You science types don't come in here much."

I pause, for the briefest moment uncertain how to
proceed. Then I meet him halfway, placing a hand on

his shoulder and guiding him back toward his ship, into the shadows it casts in the otherwise well-lit bay. "Yes, there's a problem," my voice says, but it's strange to my ears, not quite my own, but still mine. It lacks inflection, sounds like the me of years ago, right after my accident in the airlock. Once we're out of sight of any other workers, I lean in, keeping my pitch low. "We think you may have brought back a virus from your last mission."

The pilot straightens, surprise turning to indignation in his ruddy features. He runs his hand through dirty-blond hair, brushing it away from his reddening face. "I keep a clean ship. And me? I never skip decon cycles like some of the other guys."

I nod, conveying earnest sympathy with my eyes even if it's missing from my voice. "Regardless, scans suggest something attached itself. To your hull."

"My—" He turns away to stare up at the exterior of his sleek fighter craft. Fast and heavily armed, heavily shielded. Perfect.

The second his back is turned, I'm in motion, wrapping one arm around his throat and giving a sharp, brutal twist. His neck pops. He slumps backward. The body should be heavy, but it's nothing to me. I drag it behind the landing struts, use my lab coat to cover his flight uniform, and remove his gun belt and laser pistol. I strap it on over my gray slacks, tucking my black T-shirt into the pants. I take his boots, leaving the canvas shoes in an empty shipping crate. No one will notice the corpse until I've lifted off in his fancy ship. The burners from my engines should char it nicely. They might not be able to positively identify my victim for days.

And I'll be long gone.

I'm searching for something. No, someone. Some-one to ease the anger, the fear, the... incompleteness. I have to find her.

Though I don't know how I know it, I'm certain my sanity depends on it.

I WAKE up in a bottom metal bunk, gasping for breath, disoriented until the vibration of a ship in motion transmits to my sleep-fogged brain.

What the fuck was that about?

I have nightmares all the time. But that? It felt real—more real than usual. It felt like *me*, like a memory more than a dream. But that sort of calm cold-bloodedness, even toward an enemy Sunfire merc, sends icy sweat dripping down my spine. I'm not like that. Even when I have to kill, I have regrets, feelings, guilt.

I suffer.

This me felt nothing at all.

And that aching emptiness, that sense of not being whole. Definitely not me. I have Kelly. She's everything I need.

I freeze, my muscles tightening, my breath stopping in my chest. It. Felt. Like. Me. *I'm* not like that, but....

I review the already hazy dream images in my head, which in itself is confusing. My organic brain transfers my thoughts instantly to my implanted brain. VC1 stores the memories in perfect clarity. This is why nightmares are more difficult for me than others, why bad experiences cause me more problems for longer periods of time than normal people's. This is why she sent my worst memories... elsewhere.

When I first woke up as a clone, there were doors, lots of doors, in the research facility, but they were shut and locked. It wasn't the same location as the one in my dream, but I had wondered then, and I'm wondering now—

"Are there other clones of me? And is another one awake?" I ask aloud in the otherwise unoccupied cabin. *And is she completely, utterly, entirely insane?*

A wave of disorientation hits without warning, my vision swimming, my head spinning. Nausea churns in my gut before I can squeeze my eyes shut against the unexpected onslaught. *What the hell?*

I am sorry, VC1 whispers through the migraine setting in behind my eyelids. *There are things you cannot know. Things I must prevent you from knowing.*

Why? I'm blacking out again. Remaining conscious is like swimming upstream in a flooding river.

One of my primary directives is to protect you. If you knew there were other clones, you might take unnecessary chances with your life. You might assume you would be "reborn" even once resources have run out. Expensive resources, which applies to another of my directives, to minimize waste for the Fighting Storm.

But if there's another me *awake right now…*

She is not an immediate threat. One directive overrides another.

Once again I am reminded that VC1 is not perfect, that no programming is without glitches and bugs. Another clone, awake, dangerous, is definitely a threat to me, at least indirectly. She could blame me for her actions, though those actions and her half-formed goals are fading even as I think about the possible ramifications. The pain blossoms into blinding agony, my brain feeling as if it's collapsing in on itself, and I know with certainty that VC1 is erasing the memory from her storage.

When I wake again, I'll recall the bad dream in the same vague, undefined, fleeting way any human being would remember a nightmare before it vanishes entirely from my thoughts.

The irony is not lost on me that *this* is one of those rare moments when I wish I weren't so human.

I SHAKE myself, dispelling the remnants of a strange bad dream, and glance around. Standard furnishings for Storm shuttles like the one I was boarding when I passed out, so I know where I am, and I haven't been out long. Or have I? It's a two-day flight back to Girard Moon Base, so....

Four hours, thirty-seven minutes, twenty-two seconds, VC1 supplies to my unasked question.

You need to stop interpreting my thoughts as inquiries. Seriously. Sometimes I'm just being hypothetical.

You did not wish to know how long you were unconscious?

I stop. Yes, I did want to know. So why did her fulfilling my unspoken desire annoy me so much? Some people would (and did) kill for that kind of service. *I guess...* I begin, feeling my way through my emotional response, which was never a strong suit even before the accident that made me part machine... *I want to have the right to voice my request, internally or externally, rather than you assuming what I need. When you jump into my thoughts it's... rude. It makes me feel less human.*

A pause while she processes that information. Then, *I will endeavor to be more... polite. However, I stand by my continual observation.*

And what's that?

Human beings are strange.

That earns her a smile I'm sure she can feel. Reaching up with one hand, I place my palm flat against the bottom of the upper bunk so I don't cold-cock myself. Then I swing my legs over the side to sit up. The cabin swims in my vision. Something partially damp but mostly stiff falls to the floor—a small face cloth. One of the guys must have laid it across my forehead when I fainted.

Right. I fainted. Wasn't going to live that down anytime soon.

The other two bunks attached to the opposite bulkhead are also empty, so they're giving me my space. It's a nice gesture, considering the long flight and the limited privacy on one of these shuttles. Either that, or they want to be alone too.

Two months ago, Alex finally confessed his romantic feelings for Lyle. Fortunately for everyone on the team, Lyle felt the same way. Unfortunately, they've been going at it at every opportunity. They try for discretion, but… they fail a lot.

I shake off that lovely image and take in my condition. I'm dressed in the clothes in which I boarded, so that needs dealing with. I've been wearing the same set of standard-issue office wear—white button-down shirt and tan slacks, comfortable boring faux leather brown shoes—for two days. My gear's stored in one of the footlockers bolted to the deck at the ends of the bunks. I need to feel like me.

These days, I rarely do.

Shower first. *Is it available?*

The sanitation facility is unoccupied, VC1 responds.

Good. And she waited for me to ask this time. Baby steps.

I stagger to the hatch leading into a bathroom made as small as possible by the shuttle's designers. Yeah, Carl and I are going to have some words about our accommodations.

Even with VC1's assurances, I wait for the hatch to open all the way before glancing inside. It wouldn't be the first time I walked in on Lyle and Alex. If I forget to ask VC1, she lets me do it. I think it amuses her. But the space is thankfully empty.

I peel off my undercover business casual wear and leave it lying on the floor. Then I step under the automatic spray in a stall the size of a gym locker. Ice picks drive against my skin, telling me even though the guys aren't here now, they were recently. They always use up all the damn hot water, and I can't imagine how they fit in a space this small.

Images pop up on my internal display.

Oh. Geez, come on! Knock it off. I can't not see what's in my head. Won't be able to unsee it later, either. *You promised to wait for a direct request*, I remind VC1.

I promised to try.

"Fuck you," I mutter under my breath, but there's no heat in it. Still no heat in the water, either, but the pressure's good, and it relieves some of the tension in my muscles while the chill clears my head.

Which has the unwanted result of bringing the events of the past week into sharper focus.

The civilian space station orbiting Jupiter had been reporting children going missing for months. (Where did children go missing on a freaking space station?) Occupied mostly by gas miners and their families, along with the usual gamut of support businesses and their employees and a security force, the station possessed an excellent surveillance system and scanning tech. They needed the most cutting-edge equipment to detect pockets of revigen—the latest in a number of recently discovered gases determined to be effective fuel sources for interstellar craft. So, they knew the kids weren't being spaced. They would have detected the bodies, even in pieces. And yeah, wasn't that a lovely thought?

An image of severed limbs, small ones, *tiny ones,* forms in my internal view. I wish this were one of VC1's sometimes twisted metaphors, but no. These I witnessed first-hand when I tracked down the coworker in the station's mining accounts division who'd been acting suspiciously.

I press my palms flat against the shower's tile wall, the water beating down on the back of my neck, willing the image from my inner sight and failing to dispel it. Instead, they keep coming.

I spent a week playing number cruncher—not difficult with VC1's assistance. I learned his mannerisms, talked to him, *befriended* him, though being anywhere near him made my cloned flesh crawl. We had the right guy. I knew we did. His odd, darting glances, his focus on any children outside the duraglass windows of the cubicle complex, the way his hands tremored and his tongue darted out to lick his lips whenever he saw someone under the age of twelve.

When I followed him to his hidden torture chamber buried deep in the maintenance access tunnels of the station, he was holding a little girl's detached foot in one hand while he held her still-alive, still-screaming body down with the other one.

I retch, gag, and spit bile onto the shower floor. It swirls down the drain with the pouring water. Doesn't much help that the kid lived, that I blew the psychopath's fucking head off. I had to watch that too. And there were so many others. So many more *parts* and *pieces* lying about the forgotten space.

VC1... can you... help?

VC1 gives me the same answer she's been giving after every mission for Undercover Ops so far. *The receptacle where I stored your other unpleasantness is no longer accessible to me. I continue to seek a better method for blurring these images as if they were merely stored in your organic brain tissue, but reducing my capacity for memory storage is limited and proving... difficult. It also would be painful for you if I attempted to do so.*

Again so soon, I think to myself and wonder why that thought occurs. I push it away.

In other words, she's having a hard time dumbing herself down. Yeah, I can see where that would be an issue for a sentient computer, not to mention there's probably some programming in there that requires her to store everything. Sentient or not, we're both restricted by our makers.

I'm shivering now, my breath coming in quick, short gasps, goose bumps flaring over my naked flesh—my unscarred, naked flesh. My *cloned* flesh, unblemished until I sustain some unavoidable injury. My breathing borders on hyperventilation. I fight to even it out and marginally succeed. If I don't find a distraction, an emotional outlet soon, I will redline the implants.

One plus about being part machine—with a comm unit embedded in my skull, I can initiate communications from pretty much anywhere, including in the shower, where other technology would suffer from water exposure.

Closing my eyes, I mentally instruct the unit to connect to Kelly's personal comm. If she's not available to talk me down, it's going to be a long journey home.

CHAPTER 2: KELLY
LONG-DISTANCE RELATIONSHIP

Vick is struggling.

WHEN MY comm buzzes with Vick's identification pattern, I'm not surprised. It's early in her current mission assignment, but she surpasses Undercover
Ops' expectations on a regular basis, and she always
contacts me at the end of each trip out. It's the timing
that has me starting, sitting straight upright in my bed
back in our Girard Base quarters, fumbling for both the
comm and the light at the same time and finding neither
with my clumsy hands.

The one item I do locate is the touch-sensitive
bedside clock. Its numbers illuminate when I make

contact with it, glowing at just the right brightness so as to not blind me in the otherwise pitch-dark bedroom—3:17 a.m.

"Damn," I breathe out loud, though no one can hear me.

I'm not cursing because she awakened me. I'm cursing because I know she wouldn't… unless something is very, very wrong.

I locate the still buzzing comm by the light of the clock, its sound harsh and grating in the otherwise silent room. Well, okay, Girard is never silent. Gravity generators hum. Air recyclers whirr. But after so many years working here, I've finally gotten used to the background noises I thought I'd never adjust to.

I wrap my fingers around the communicator and hit the Connect icon, then tap the speaker symbol, sending her signal through the double speakers wired into the headboard of our bed. We have sets of them in each room of our quarters. It's easier than trying to hold the device to my ear, and I can be doing other things while speaking to her.

Sometimes intimate things, especially when she's away for a while. VC1 ensures everything remains encrypted and untappable, and we have steel walls, so no passersby can hear me from the hallway. My lips quirk upward a little, but I sober fast enough.

"Hey, Vick… what's going on?" A yawn splits my inquiry in half. I clear the phlegm from my throat. "Are you all right?" My hands twist in the sheets. She's not. I know she's not. We're too far apart for an empathic connection, but my psychic skills aren't my only ones. I can read behavior patterns (and deviations from them) quite well.

"Kel? Why do you sound— Fuck, what time is— Shit." A pause, then much softer, "I'm sorry."

I frown. She hasn't activated visuals. Vick's comm may be deep in her skull, unlike mine, but VC1 simulates a standard unit's visual capabilities by accessing whatever camera pickups might be present, which is virtually everywhere on most civilized worlds. So, either she's someplace *un*civilized, or in a bathroom where even the military doesn't usually place cameras, or she doesn't want me to see what sort of shape she's in. I do detect water running in the background and an echo in her voice, so, shower?

"You know I don't mind," I reassure her. "If you need me, I'm here."

"Doesn't matter. Should've checked the time difference. Slipping," she growls.

I absorb the emotion in her tone, not empathically but analytically, and reach a quick diagnosis. "Panic attacks don't keep timetables. How bad was it?"

She knows I'm referring to the mission, not her current attack. That isn't over yet. "Bad," she admits. "Kids. Dismembered kids. Still alive dismembered kids...." Her voice trails off.

I pull my blankets to cover more of my suddenly freezing body.

"You don't want me to go into more detail than that," she says.

"If you need to, I can take it." I'm not certain I can. I'll have nightmares. But I'm not porcelain. Some pain is worth taking. My gaze drops to the ring on my finger, glittering green gemstone surrounded by tiny diamonds. "You've seen gruesome things before."

"I shot him point-blank. No warning, no trial."

"He was murdering children."

Vick's conscience powers her ability to do what she does. Since being drafted into Undercover Ops, they've tilted her moral compass. I don't like it, and I don't like them. But where Vick goes, I go. And as she reminds me often, she is doing good. So beyond the trauma, what else is bothering her?

"Spill it, Vick. There's more."

A pause. "You can't read me from there," she says with faint surprise, which tells me I've hit the mark.

I wait her out in silence.

"Just nightmares," she admits, rewarding my patience.

"That's not all." She's too worked up for this to be the usual nightmares. Too much tension in her tone, too many hesitations while she tries to find the words.

"I can't remember the details. But—" Vick blows out a resigned breath. "—Kel," she continues, and I detect a faint tremor uncharacteristic of her, "do I still have a soul? Did I have one when I was just part machine? Now that I'm a clone, is there anything left of the actual me?"

"Oh, Vick." Back on Elektra4, when she first came to me in her new... form, she'd had to convince me she was still her. It took her all of about five minutes. From her posture to her mannerisms to her word choices, I knew her, and when we touched... the empathic bond between us reasserted itself like another lightning strike. "No matter what... edition, no matter what U Ops makes you do, you are you. And you have the most beautiful soul I've ever seen."

Her only response is a relieved sigh, then, "Thank you," and the connection drops.

CHAPTER 3: VICK
DELICATE INTERACTION

I am ill-equipped.

"I CAN feel it. You really don't want me here, do you?" Kelly accuses, hands planted firmly on her slim hips, lips pursed in a pout that would be fucking adorable if it didn't precede our unavoidable upcoming argument. It's been a week since I had to call her en route home from the last mission. This is a new one, what should be a less stressful assignment, except for one thing. Kelly's with us.

Lyle and Alex take this as their cue to scurry out of the cockpit of the transport I'm piloting.

Cowards.

I turn back to the controls, feigning a need to concentrate more fully on our approach to the small moon
that is our destination—a hidden slave-trade operation
on the rock's surface not unlike the secret base my father lived in, though they are some lightyears apart.

Kelly laughs, though there's no humor in it. "Don't
try to fool me. VC1 could fly this thing by herself, and
we both know it."

"Indeed," comes VC1's familiar yet inflectionless
response through the overhead speakers.

You are not helping, I admonish her.

Her chuckle carries much more emotion than her
words.

Okay, then. I mentally turn everything over to my
AI symbiote and swivel the pilot's chair to fully face
my life partner. Her eyes flash in anger, so I focus on
the ring on her finger instead, a testament to our life-
long, if not legal, bond.

Machines can't get marriage licenses on Earth's
Moon. Dead women can't get them on Earth. In other words, our partnership will remain purely symbolic
until Kelly's politically connected mother can convince
one of the governments to change its laws.

I have lots of love and respect for Kelly's mother. I
still believe she doesn't have a chance in hell.

I draw my attention to the more immediate
problem.

Technically, I could lie to Kelly and deny her accu-
sations. She can't discern untruths for certain unless we
are in physical contact. However, lying to her has never
turned out well for me in the past, and I don't expect
that to change.

"No," I say, going for forthright. "I don't want you
here now, or on any of the Undercover Ops missions."

I spare a glance at her face, regretting it when her glare narrows. "This isn't like the others," she says. "It's not...."

Even she can't say it, but I hear it easily enough. *It's not an assassination.* The team has been with our new division of the Storm for almost six months, and the four missions I've completed with them so far have all been fatal for my targets. U Ops wasn't foolish enough to force Kelly to go with me, considering what she'd feel from my murder victims.

Not murder. Assassination. And always for good reason. They do extensive research before accepting contracts, VC1 interjects.

Whose side are you on?

Yours. Always. I am attempting to make your career path more palatable.

It's not working.

She shuts up.

Turns out my conscience, which always struggles with killing, even when done from a fair, face-to-face, defensive position, cannot handle shooting people from a distance or stabbing them in the back or pulling a weapon on someone whose trust I've gained.

My hard-earned mental stability began to slip, hence the reason why—

"Vick. You need me on this one."

Yeah, that.

Her tone has lost its edge and I risk another glance—softened features, sympathetic eyes. We can have a conversation now.

It's not that Kelly's unreasonable or anything, but sometimes I wonder if being calm, collected, and stable for everyone else makes her more volatile when she does get angry. I don't want to make her angry. I try so hard not to.

"I know," I say, attempting to placate her. "It's just not something I want you to see."

She frowns, a wrinkle forming between her eyebrows. "I'm not following you."

I drop my elbows onto my knees and rest my chin in my hands. A stray auburn curl tumbles in front of my right eye, and I stare at it a long moment before recognizing it as my own. I brush it away, more violently than I intend, pulling it in the process. "Geez, I don't even look like myself." I wave my arms about, frustrated by my lack of ability to explain what I'm feeling.

Nothing new there.

Kelly frowns further, then comes to kneel beside me on the carpeted deck. The civilian shuttle we're using has all the luxury extras: high-end shielding, illegal military-grade weaponry, shiny new furnishings, and of all things, deep blue carpet. My boss, Carl, assured me it was the current rage among slave traders.

She catches my hands and pulls them down to rest on my lap. "Come on, Vick. Help me understand. I can feel how agitated you are, especially when you look at me." Her gaze bores into mine. "One thing at a time. What does your hair color have to do with any of this?"

"It's not mine," I say. I gesture to my whole body, dressed in what amounts to a dark gray business suit cut to fit my curves. Masculine black dress shoes press indentations into the sea of plush navy at my feet. "None of this is mine." Especially not the hair.

Kelly, at least, looks like herself, though her hair is pulled back into a tight bun. She's wearing black spiked heels, a very short, straight skirt that barely covers the upper half of her thighs, and a low-cut, filmy white blouse leaving little to the imagination. Every bit of the costume screams both sex and assistant—in everything. She's agreed to it to be there for me. I don't know how to deal with that kind of loyalty or my kind of guilt in response.

"Clothes can be changed. Hair can be dyed back and restraightened. You had to do something to disguise yourself. You're a little too well-known as a merc."

Yeah, VC1, aka Vick Corren, is becoming a name to fear, according to the Storm's intel. And my picture has been circulating through some of the darker networks. Hence, the clothing choices and auburn, slightly curled long hair.

I can't cut it. I don't think even Kelly knows the extent of that aspect of my manufactured appearance. Either that, or she's caught that detail in my file and doesn't ever mention it. My hair is a synthetic construct, since much of my skull is metal. Even though I'm a clone, the scientists and medical personnel had to make room for my implants, which meant removing a large section of my skull and more than half the brain within it.

The irony is not lost on me. My clone would have had a normal brain, duplicating my genetics. But to transfer my personality, my knowledge and memories to it, the clone had to have implants. To have implants, they had to damage me in exactly the same way the bullets in the airlock had. To live, I had to become a machine again. I'm told it's much more precise and neater than the damage caused in my airlock accident, but I refuse to look at the scans.

I have enough nightmares, thank you very fucking much.

However, that means everything that was built into me before the cloning is still built in. Including the hair. It takes dye and curl easily, which is convenient, but it doesn't grow. If its length is shortened and I should change my mind and want it back at some point, well, I would have to go in for a pain-in-the-ass procedure to replace it to make it look… natural and have it stand up to a DNA scan. I have to do that often enough anyway due to damage on missions and such. I'm not going to ask for it.

Add to all this a set of aqua-colored contact lenses over my mechanical eyes, and, well, "I feel like I'm cheating."

Kelly blinks. "I'm sorry?"

"Cheating. Not playing fair. It's bad enough that I'm pretending to be their business associates, distant relatives, *friends*, but I don't even look like me. In my head, I'm not facing them as VC1 or even Vick Corren, which is already hiding my skill set—"

VC1 lets out an amused snort.

"—instead I'm presenting myself as a nonthreat. It gives them no reason to suspect, to begin to defend themselves. If they could put up some kind of fight, I'd probably still win, but at least then—"

"It would be self-defense."

I nod, the fucking curls bouncing against my cheeks. "Yes, and it wouldn't be so damn… easy. I'm winning. I'm cheating to do it, and that fucks with my head." I turn hopeless eyes to her, the burning in them threatening to become something much more embar- rassing. I blink it away. "Does that make any sense?"

Through our bond, through our physical contact, I read her surprise at my admission. It's growth of a sort, being able to admit weakness out loud, or shame, or guilt. She'd know it, feel it anyway, but to say the words, that's a rarity for me.

Standing, she climbs into my lap and wraps her arms around my neck, resting her head on my shoulder. Her fingers find my hand again, toying with the ring she gave me, a smooth black titanium band inset with three equally flat bright blue gemstones. Smooth and flat so as not to catch on anything when I fight. Blue because she's determined that I do, in fact, have a favorite color despite my denials of caring about aesthetics. She knows me better than I know myself.

I'm glad, now, that Lyle and Alex fled. It allows me to be affectionate with her without the rise of discomfort that a public display would cause.

"It's not cheating," she whispers, her breath tickling my neck. "It's an attempt to keep you safe. Anything that protects you is something I'll support. And as for easy... well, it might be easy *for* you, but it isn't easy *on* you. It bothers you, and it should. When it stops, when it becomes as simple for you to forget as to commit, *then* you should worry, about your sanity and your soul."

Except that I never forget anything. Not without it being erased from VC1's memory, and I have forbidden her and the doctors back on Girard Base from doing that. With the exception of Rodwell's rape, I resent any memory taken from me, even the bad ones. If I am going to do immoral things, then I *should* suffer. At least for as long as any normal person would. That's when the scales of my self-measured justice become unbalanced and cruel.

Kelly's reminder that I *am* suffering and not just strolling through my life without care does help. I'm not some kind of monster, at least not yet. That doesn't solve my other problem with having her along on this mission.

Kelly sighs. "There's more," she says, seeing through me. "What else?"

I pull my hands from hers, raising them in frustration. "Isn't it obvious? Of all the missions to send you on, it had to be the one where I'm posing as a slave buyer. And worse, you as my assistant. My *slave* assistant." With everything that title implies.

"It's not like we'll be giving public demonstrations or anything."

I close my eyes. Maybe, maybe not. My research says things can get out of hand very quickly in this sort of environment and make the Purple Leaf sex club back on Girard Moon Base look like a toddlers' playground.

My team will enter the slavers' base of operations under the guise of being buyers at an imminent auction, Alex and Lyle posing as our bodyguards in this charade. The goal? To map out the installation via VC1's technology, then send the schematics to U Ops' strike forces holding position just out of scanner range. They will extract us, or we'll extract ourselves. Then they launch an attack, wiping out shield generators, weapons centers, and the leaders' quarters while hopefully avoiding areas where the slaves are held. Once the base is taken, they free the slaves and obtain data revealing where the operation's other bases are located so they can deal with them later.

It's a multiplanetary initiative, our fees paid by a cooperative of governments who've lost citizens to the slavers but have been unable (or unwilling) to annihilate them themselves.

"If I'm going to maintain our cover," I say, the muscles in my jaw clenching, "I will have to do whatever they expect of their buyers. I'll stall and avoid as much as I can, but in the end, I'll have to do things I don't want to."

In other words, I'm programmed, no, *brainwashed* as Kelly insists because programming is too inhuman, to not let this mission fail if it's in my power to prevent it.

"One more good reason to have me here," she says. "I can run interference for you, make up excuses for why you aren't participating in all the 'fun.' I'm not going to let them force you into a situation you can't live with."

I'm still not thrilled with her presence, but I shoot her a grateful look.

"And the smaller ones we can't avoid?" she continues. "I know it won't really be you. It will be Valeria Court." Kel grins at the ridiculous alias, but U Ops suggested that having a name vaguely similar to my own would make it easier to remember. The manufactured persona with complete and impressively trackable records is a slave keeper/buyer from the opposite edge of the outer rim worlds who has traveled across the known universe hoping to purchase something more "exotic."

Gah! Someone, not something. I'm already beginning to think like a fucking slaver.

Kelly will keep her own first name and a last name of Laroe, since her real surname, LaSalle, would turn up her diplomat mother in a background check.

She reaches out to caress my cheek, fingertips trailing along my jawline. "Vick Corren, however, is unwaveringly faithful." Her lips find mine, and I allow my mind to forget my concerns for a few pleasurable moments. They don't last.

Unwaveringly faithful. Yes. But to whom? Kelly or the Storm? No matter what I want, I know which one will always force itself to the forefront. I hope our relationship can withstand it.

CHAPTER 4: KELLY
PERSONA

Vick is.... Valeria.

WHILE VICK and I are kissing, Alex chooses that moment to open the hatch and pop his head into the cockpit. I feel his embarrassment before I turn, confirming it with the red flush crawling from the neckline of his black T-shirt to his forehead.

"Um, sorry, I just wanted...." He breaks off, pointing at a thermocan of Amp-Ade in the copilot seat drink holder.

Vick looks from him to the can and back again, her own flush and the faint yellow aura around her revealing her own discomfort with the interruption. She reaches across, takes the can, seals it, and hurls it at the doorway, catching him square in the chest with it.

"Oof! Hey!" His offense is fake, his pained smile apologetic.

"Next time, chime or knock first." Vick's annoyance is not fake.

I rest a hand on her shoulder. She calms under my touch. Lyle appears behind Alex. "Final approach, folks. Remove anything out of character for a slave-buying team and let's do this thing so we can go home."

Vick stands, leaving VC1 managing the piloting. We give each other the once-over while Alex and Lyle do the same. Her gaze lingers on my left hand. I cover my ring with my right palm. "No."

She smiles, but there's only sadness in it. Shaking her head, Vick pries my fingers away, then slips the engagement ring from me. "A slave owner's assistant engaged to that owner would be too hard a cover to sell, and you know it." She takes off her own, the pair clinking together in her hand. There's a lockbox on the flooring beside the pilot's chair. It takes her a moment to uncode it, place the rings inside with great care, and seal it again. Alex and Lyle slip quietly out the hatch.

"Will that be enough? What if they break into the ship?"

She shakes her head again. "They won't. It would be an extreme breach of etiquette."

My brow furrows. "Criminals have etiquette?"

Vick huffs an amused laugh. "The organized ones do. Always wanting people to think better of them while they do the worst. We're guests here. Overriding our ship security, then the cockpit hatch, and then the lockbox would be unforgiveable and send the wrong message to all the other buyers. No one would do business with him, regardless of what he found. He won't risk it with us or anyone else." She pauses, staring at the box. The aura around her shifts from light to dark. "When this is over, I want to finalize things between us. As much as we're able. A quiet ceremony. Friends. Family. Even if it won't be—" Her voice catches.

I wrap my arms around her, holding her to me from behind. She's trembling.

"—real or legal," Vick finishes.

Every ounce of love I have for her I project through our bond. It returns to me a hundredfold. "It may never be legal," I tell her, "but it will always be real to us. Always."

"Incoming transmission," VC1's monotone interrupts through the cabin speakers. "A Mr. Jacks requesting our identification packet. Sending now."

The shuttle's forward viewscreen shifts to show our vessel approaching a scattering of prefab buildings on the small moon's surface, enclosed duraglass walkways connecting them to one another, their squared-off edges blurred by a protective shield dome encasing them all. Tractor beams pierce the darkness around the installation, locking on to our vessel and guiding us toward a widening opening in the shield. The largest building, with massive steel doors, gapes open, ready to swallow our entire shuttle whole.

Vick sighs. "Go ahead and cut the engines," she tells VC1.

The almost subliminal rumble beneath our feet subsides.

"Well, we're in it now. They've got full control," she says, sinking back into the pilot's chair.

"Jacks is… requesting… visual communication with 'Madame' Court." No monotone this time. VC1 is amused.

Vick snorts and leans toward the visual pickups and the smaller screen built into the forward console. "Put him through."

I blink. The warmth has vanished from her voice. It's all hard edges and complete control. Her expression settles into sharp lines of disinterest and displeasure. I place myself at her right shoulder, deferential and ready to act upon any request she might have of me.

A face resolves itself on the screen, depicting a man who's seen more than a few hard knocks and survived them with defiance, cruelty, and aggression. Straight, neatly trimmed brown hair, lightly lined features for someone well into the second half of his lifespan, but with a jagged scar running vertically down the right cheek and forcing one of his piercing brown eyes into a perpetual squint. His lips curve into what he probably thinks is a smile, but it comes off more like a sneer that seems to say, "I've got you exactly where I want you."

"Ah, Madame Court. Or is it Mistress Court?" he asks with a wink of his good eye.

"Either suits me, depending on my mood, which, at the moment, is shit. It's been a long trip, Jacks. My staff and I are eager to settle in. What's this about?"

Jacks stiffens, pulling back from the screen as if affronted. Or afraid. A smile threatens, and I smooth my features. In or out of character, Vick has that effect on people.

He frowns. "Your reputation precedes you, and you're living up to it."

"Then you know I'm here for business, not to play name games. Are you letting us land or not? There are other places where I can shop for what I'm after." Vick folds her arms across her chest.

"No need for that." Jacks waves an apologetic hand at the screen. "But hopefully you and your staff—" He nods to me at Vick's shoulder. I suppress a shudder. "—will have time for both business *and* pleasure. My auctions are events, not quick displays of flesh on a block. We do things differently on this side of the rim. Consider it more of a festival than a shopping trip. Tonight, after you're settled, you'll be my guests at a dinner in the buyers' honor, something to show how much I value my clientele. And I have some new merchandise that bears testing out on the right audience."

"I'm not interested in being your lab rat, Jacks," Vick snaps.

He ignores her. "Land your vessel in the open hangar. When you get the green light, proceed to disembark. An escort will meet you there and show you to your quarters. Jacks out."

The screen darkens. I let out a long sigh, but Vick remains ramrod straight in the pilot's chair. Tension radiates off her in waves.

The tractor beams pull us into the hangar and settle our shuttle on a marked-off landing pad not far from several other opulently appointed (and some garishly decorated) craft. The gigantic doors seal shut with a resounding bass clang of thick metal on metal. After a few more moments, indicators on the control console switch from red to green, informing us that the bay is pressurized and contains gravity and breathable atmosphere.

Across the bay, a much smaller hatch opens and a team of eight armed guards in forest green uniforms, our escort I assume, strides toward our ship, outnumbering us two to one. "Not unexpected," Vick mutters. Her mouth forms a grim line. At least their weapons aren't drawn, though their hands hover near their holsters.

"There is something wrong here," comes VC1's voice from the speakers, her even tone revealing none of the concern her words convey. "Now that we are within their shields, I can take much more accurate readings of this facility. The power consumption, not to mention the number of biological life signs I am detecting, are far insufficient for the population this installation is re-ported to contain. In fact, the buildings themselves ap-pear to be nothing more than mere facades. Beyond the exterior walls there are no designated rooms, no fur-nishings. Some appear to be storage facilities manned by a skeleton crew, but most stand empty."

Vick and I exchange a look. The escort guards have arrived at our boarding ramp, which lowers with a distant rumble of machinery and a hiss of hydraulics.

"What does it mean?" I ask.

"It means our intel is fucked." She pauses, con-sidering. "Can't change course now. Can't call in the reinforcements until we're certain the slaves aren't here somewhere and we attempt to set them free or they'll die in the crossfire. Let's get out there and figure out just how fubar this is." The auburn curls and blue eyes do nothing to soften Vick's growl of frustration as she heaves herself from the chair. Her hands pat down sev-eral places on her clothing concealing hidden weapon-ry. We can only hope the signal scramblers sewn into the lining of her suit will do their job better than U Ops' intelligence officers.

She slams her palm against the hatch lock and exits the cockpit before it slides fully open. I trail behind her. What have we gotten ourselves into this time?

CHAPTER 5: VICK
UNDER NOT OVER

I am confused.

LYLE AND Alex meet us at the top of the ramp dressed in matching black boots, cargo pants, and T-shirts. They wear their weapons openly, a back holster between the shoulder blades for Lyle, a much more accessible thigh holster for Alex, their pants pockets bulging with other lethal and nonlethal accessories. They'll have other items hidden on their persons as well, if they're doing their jobs the way the Fighting Storm taught them.

Our luggage already rests at the ramp's base, deposited there while Kelly and I sorted things in the cockpit, I suppose. One of Jacks's guards signals for an autocarrier, and the flatbed robotic device leaves its charging station against one wall and trundles over. The guard loads the bags onto it, taking care with each item, so we're still falling into the "guest" category. Our covers haven't been compromised, no matter what other weirdness is going on.

A second green-garbed guard, this one female, sends an inquisitive glance up at us, then flashes a smile past me at Kelly. It vanishes at my hard look.

"Let's join the party." That's our agreed-upon code for "drop fully into character." Lyle takes point, then me, Kelly, and Alex at our six. I'm not thrilled with the formation. I'd much rather lead, but I'm the wealthy slave buyer. I keep private security. I don't get my hands dirty. Not in that way.

We process down the ramp, striding into the swarm of forest green, who take up circular positions around us. The autocarrier rolls along behind us all. "Welcome," the lead guard says. "I'm Felix, head of security here. You are permitted to keep your own people with you. They and only they may go armed." He passes a scanner wand over myself and Kelly, confiscating the pistol I had beneath my jacket—not military issue, not very powerful, and intended to be taken from me. They would expect me to be carrying. I don't want to disappoint.

"You'll get this back when you leave," Felix says, offering an apologetic smile and handing it off to another guard, who drops it into a bin beside the ship and locks the lid down. He turns to Lyle and Alex. "Your weapons go with your luggage for now. No one is allowed to have them en route." He pulls their pistols and tucks them into a pouch, which he plops on the autocarrier with our bags. "If anyone starts any trouble inside, Jacks will deposit all of you outside the shield and let you suffocate." It's all said with a polite smile, matter-of-fact rather than threatening. "Once you enter the complex proper, you'll each be fitted with a locator beacon. Don't remove it. As long as it remains green, you're in a common area. If it goes yellow, you've stepped into a transition section and should retrace your steps immediately. Red means you're in a restricted zone. If you get that far, you're already considered in violation of the house rules and subject to expulsion beyond the shield."

"Doesn't Jacks have any other forms of punishment?" I ask, sarcasm evident.

Felix glances over his shoulder to make eye contact. "No."

Wonderful.

"I'll provide your assistant with a full list of the do's and don'ts around here, but those are the most important ones to remember. Anything you need, have her contact Markel, Jacks's secretary. You may not get it, but you can ask."

Our group continues across the landing bay's concrete floor, bootsteps echoing in the huge chamber and bouncing off the high ceiling. A maintenance team flutters around one of the other yachts, scrubbing the hull, refueling the tanks, and stacking boxes of dried foods beneath the ship's ramp for later storage aboard. One of our female escorts, the one who'd smiled at Kelly, notices my interest.

"We'll resupply your ship before you leave," she says. "The service is free with any purchase."

Which would be a nice perk if I didn't know that purchase would be a *human being*. I'm unraveling the intense feelings of anger… no, all-out hatred boiling under my cool exterior. I'm essentially a slave to the Fighting Storm. Of course I'm taking this mission even more to heart. Should have figured this out sooner, but while I've made a lot of progress, I still struggle with pinpointing what I feel and why.

Then there's the little matter of the slaves themselves not being where they're supposed to be. "You want to tell me what's really going on here? Because my… scanning equipment showed a handful of warm bodies. Where are your staff and your… merchandise?" I force the word out, the minute pause undetectable to everyone but my team. Lyle gives me a quick glance over his shoulder, his face unreadable, then returns his attention forward.

The woman smiles again, bright white teeth shining and blue eyes twinkling, like an advertising holo. "You must have some damn good equipment. I'll have to talk shop with your tech support. Don't be alarmed. You'll understand shortly. I promise you, you'll have a fine selection to choose from. I'm Petala. I'll be the liaison between our people and your private security team." She gives Alex and Lyle a little wave. Lyle ignores it and walks on. Alex waves back with a grin.

He and I will have words later.

Or maybe not. Gaining Petala's trust will help us move about the slave facility with more freedom, and I already know Alex's sexual preference wouldn't include her. He's playing the game. Good boy.

An image of me patting a large shaggy dog on the head, the dog's collar tag reading "Alex," appears on my inner view. I shake it away.

The autocarrier has gotten far ahead of us. At the end of the bay, a pair of double doors slides apart. The carrier glides inside, and they close behind it. I hope our luggage makes it to our rooms unmolested.

We reach the doors ourselves, which part at our approach, but it's not a hatch to another room or even a corridor. It's a freight elevator, its deep, empty interior of plain metal walls and flooring utilitarian and unadorned in any way. The autocarrier is gone, already dropped off on whatever level it was headed for. Lyle follows the lead guard, Felix, inside along with several of the other local security. I halt before my boot crosses the threshold.

"Vi—Valeria?" Kelly asks, bumping into me from behind. She comes around to my right side and places a hand on the sleeve of my suit jacket. "Something wrong?"

She thinks I'm balking at getting on an elevator. Too close in structure and feel to an airlock, and I still, despite years of separation from my first death in one, have issues with those. For once, that's not it.

I take a deep breath and make eye contact with Felix, who has turned around at the holdup. "This hangar has no second floor." I glance up to confirm, though I already know. It doesn't. It's the height of several stories, but it's all open space except for a couple of catwalks, and the elevator doesn't go there. "Where will this take us?"

Felix shows his teeth in a challenging smile. "Hop in and see."

Not like I have a choice. I force my leaden feet forward and end up in the center of the car, surrounded on all sides by the various guards. Kelly sticks close, her shoulder in contact with mine, but beyond that, the lift is large enough that we aren't packed in like a box of ammo.

The doors seal shut with the softest *whoosh/bump*, not like the loud *thunk* of an airlock. Felix steps to the controls and presses a sequence of buttons. The elevator drops.

And drops.

And drops.

It's not fast or violent enough to upset stomachs or cause panic, but the vibrations through the flooring tell me we're in constant motion as the seconds tick by. A lot of seconds.

I exchange glances with Alex and Lyle, both of whom are shifting their feet. Lyle swallows hard. Alex checks his wrist chronometer, then checks it again.

"This isn't a gravlift," Alex comments, resting his palm against the nearest wall. "The vibrations aren't consistent. Cables?"

Felix nods. "Old school, yeah. A gravlift wasn't compatible with the shielding. Besides, Jacks prefers to make use of existing equipment when he can."

In other words, he's taken his facility from a previous owner, and he's a cheap bastard. Got it.

It's all in the moon's core, I think at VC1. *The entire slaving operation. That's why no one ever registered their power signatures, why it was so hard to find until an informant told one of the hiring governments.* I pause when we stop and the doors slide apart, revealing a rough-hewn tunnel, the walls of which are the same forest green as the guards' uniforms. A musty, moist odor assails my nostrils, not unpleasant, but not at all what I expected. Flickering sconces holding bulbs simulating flamelight hang at wide intervals extending far into the distance. They turn the entire scene into something out of an ancient Egyptian tomb or castle dungeon catacombs more than a modern installation. The hall bustles with activity: servants, no, *slaves* carrying trays of food and drink, some other obvious buyers dressed in whatever is trending for their homeworlds' elite no matter how ostentatious, and more of the ever-present security in their matching forest green. But there's a difference. The slightly lighter green trim on their uniform jackets gives off a subtle glow under the subterranean lighting, making their imposing presence easier to spot. While we disembark, one guard removes his jacket and folds it over one arm. The shirt beneath, as well as his pants and boots, do not have the same luminescent piping, meaning local security is seen when it wants to be and can "go dark" in the multitude of shadows if the need arises.

Oh, that'll be fun when this mission goes to complete shit.

"How are we breathing?" Alex asks, his voice a squeak like a bat in the darkness and at complete odds with his role as bodyguard, or as a merc for that matter. I roll my eyes at him. He tries again. "I mean, up top you had shields holding in the atmosphere, but down here—?"

Felix gives us a proud smile, spreading his arms out to indicate everything around us. "Actually, the natural atmo isn't sufficient to sustain human life, but we're adding in the additional oxygen we need. The shields extend deep beneath the moon's surface," he explains. "This was a mining facility before DigCorps abandoned it, and Mr. Jacks stumbled upon it while searching for a new place to operate from. Most of the original equipment was intact, just a few minor repairs needed and we were good to go. Don't worry. We have backup generators, and you'll find bins of emergency rebreathers in every tunnel." He points to one now, a white wooden container with an image of a standard oxygen mask emblazoned in red on the front. One tap on the lid and it would dispense its contents from a chute on its side.

But how far apart are these dispensers? Do they hold enough masks for the entire population here? Have they been maintained?

I glance at the uneven rocky walls of the now-too-narrow tunnel. Servers and guests make contact with me as they brush by in the tight space. A constriction settles in my chest and throat. Why do the rocks feel like they're closing in?

"We're fine, Valeria," Kelly whispers beside me. "Deep breaths. You're okay."

Oh. Fuck. This I don't need.

When I joined the Fighting Storm, I had zero claustrophobic tendencies. My death by airlock changed that. VC1 might have sent the worst of my memories, the Rodwell rape, to some other data storage location when I became a clone. But I've still got all my other traumas. Lucky me. The discomfort with enclosed spaces hasn't been too severe of late, nothing I couldn't push through, but….

Is the guard right about the shields? I ask VC1, forgetting the man's name. Felix. It's Felix. Shit. If I'm not careful, I'm going to blow my cover.

Then again, the slavers would probably expect one of their buyers to be more claustrophobic than a battle-edged, fully-trained merc.

Sigh.

The guard is correct. The shields extend well below our current level of the former mining operation. Their maintenance is… adequate. They have backup generators in place and the systems appear to be functioning efficiently. If it will help, I will leave a remnant in their computer to monitor it. It will also enable me to better map the facility for our purposes.

Right. VC1 can divide herself to perform a variety of functions at once, so long as I'm not situated too far from any one of her… pieces? Tendrils? Whatever, so long as it works. *Do it*, I command, then add, *please.* I will not treat my computerized symbiont the way the Storm treats me most of the time. I won't. Knowing my secret partner is on it, I manage to fill my lungs on my next inhale.

Beside me, Kelly's shoulders untense. "Better," she says, patting my arm.

"Why don't we proceed to someplace a little more… open?" Felix suggests, grin firmly in place and waving an arm for us to follow him. I don't miss the fleeting panic in his eyes.

Guessing it won't look good for him to freak out one of Jacks's most affluent customers.

Petala holds up a hand for us to pause, then produces four wrist bands from a pouch at her belt—the promised locater beacons. She fastens one on each member of my team, saving mine for last. A sensor in the band's center glows green, making it look more like jewelry than a security device and reminding us that we are in an approved area. Once mine is securely in place, she gestures us onward.

In motion once more, we tromp along the tunnel, Petala placing herself on my left and cautioning me to watch my head for low-hanging stalactites. The smell of dank dampness increases the farther we walk. I brush my fingertips along the rock wall. They come away wet. I dry them on my suit pants with a disdainful growl in keeping with my Valeria persona.

Petala keeps up a constant stream of tour-guide-like chatter, pointing out mining equipment sitting idle in some of the side tunnels, explaining the use of a laser drill to remove gemstones with so much precision as to not damage them in any way. When one of the drills starts up mere feet from my position, I jump at the sudden shrill whine and deep grating like gravel caught in a blender.

Oh yeah, Vick. Smooth and in control. That's you.

"We still do a bit of excavating in our off-hours," Petala says, smiling. "There's not enough here for commercial excavation, but most of the guards have squirreled away some good-sized stones to start a retirement fund."

"That sounds like fun," Kelly pipes up when I don't respond, my voice caught in my throat. "You should offer drilling excursions to your buyers."

"Oh, don't worry," Felix says with a wink. "Our buyers find plenty of distractions during their visits here."

On that note, the tunnel ends, opening into a much wider space—an enormous cavern soaring so high over our heads and so far out to the sides that I can't discern a distinct perimeter in the dim light. Our path continues forward onto a wooden platform extending about twelve feet before it abruptly stops and drops into inky black nothingness.

CHAPTER 5: KELLY
RIVER STYX

Vick is nervous.

WE PAUSE at the edge of the wooden platform, me crowding Vick to keep her moving. She doesn't want to reach the end, and considering our path seems to drop into the great beyond, I can't blame her, but our guards show no concern for our, or their, safety.

At least her claustrophobia has abated.

If anything, I've developed a touch of agoraphobia. I don't like dark corners I can't see into—a paranoia that's increased since my exposure to Vick—and the emptiness on all sides except behind gives me the creeps. I put a little more space between myself and

Vick's body. While I need her to walk forward, I don't need our physical contact to transfer my fears to her. She has enough going on in her head as it is.

The platform is wide enough for four of us to walk abreast, and instead of Lyle and Alex being first and last, we find ourselves side by side. We're a team. No matter what the Storm assigns us, we're a team. And it's nice.

As we reach the end, Lyle points across the emptiness. There's a light—a tiny circle of wavering light, though it's growing in size as it comes closer. Soon enough the light reveals a large raft-like structure attached to it, empty except for one male figure guiding it with a lever at the front. A soft whirring echoes off the distant walls and ceiling, a motor of some kind.

Vick slips between two of Jacks's security to the edge of the platform, then peers down.

"It's a lake. A gigantic fucking lake. In the middle of a moon," she says, voice breathy with awe.

I move beside her. Now that there's more light from the oncoming raft, I can make out hundreds of tiny darting forms beneath the formerly smooth, now slightly rippling surface of the water. The light reflects off the iridescent scales of the fish, turning the entire body of water into a midnight sea of shooting stars. It's fascinating, hypnotic, and—

"Beautiful," Vick whispers.

The emotion in her voice stuns me, and I'm reminded of how very far she's come in her emotional regrowth. The back of her hand brushes mine as we stand beside each other, my skin tingling with the urge to take hers and hold it, but that would be out of character at this moment. Realizing she's slipped a bit herself, she steps away from me, straightens her posture, and places her hands on her hips, more like a businesswoman surveying a possible purchase than a gawking tourist.

Or a hopeless romantic.

My heart surges. I stifle the need to grin like a fool and school my expression into one of professionalism—the perfect assistant.

"How did they get here?" she asks.

"The miners who originally worked here had the lake stocked so fishing could be a recreational activity. Not a lot to do between shifts down here," Felix says, playing tour guide. "The current staff takes advantage of it sometimes as well. And they're quite tasty, though chemicals in the water mean you have to cook them in a detox boil."

"Yum," Vick mutters under her breath.

The raft bumps gently against the dock platform. The operator opens a swinging portion of the railing that runs around the entire craft, and we all step aboard, taking places along the rail and wrapping both hands around it. Even the local security grabs hold.

"Does it get rough?" I ask, a slight tremor in my voice. I've been on rocky boats. Neither I nor my stomach enjoy them. As I speak, the operator backs us up, turns us around, and sets us off toward a distant, invisible shore.

Petala glances at me over her shoulder from where she stands on the opposite rail. "Um, no. But we do have some, shall we say, overeager wildlife. Nothing carnivorous," she hastens to reassure me.

Oh good. I'm having flashbacks of octosharks. A shiver passes through Vick's frame beside me. She still has nightmares about that encounter, when two of the eight-mouthed creatures nearly tore her limb from limb in the ocean on Infinity Bay. I guess that incident was too recent for VC1 to eliminate when she transferred some of Vick's worst memories elsewhere.

I continue to wonder where that "elsewhere" is, and so does Vick.

Regardless of Petala's assessment of the danger, all four of our team members stare into the dark waters of the cavern's lake, trying to spot anything aggressive before it spots us. Or eats us, for that matter. But it's peaceful, the tiny albino fish circling around the raft in large clusters of shimmering brilliance. My shoulders relax. Vick shifts her stance away from the one I recognize as "ready to fight" and into her "at ease" pose, still prepared to snap back to attention at a moment's notice, but more observant than wary.

I'm guessing we're about halfway across the body of water. If I narrow my eyes, I can just make out the outline of something flat jutting into the lake from an opposite shore—the landing dock, and beyond that another tunnel mouth leading farther into the installation. There's movement too, a number of indiscernible figures milling about, waiting for the raft to take them to where we came from. Some of them stop and wave, an odd gesture for people I assume to be guards or servants, but I give a faint wave back. There's also sound, like… shouts of welcome? I can't make out specific words in this echo chamber, especially with the raft's sail flapping so loudly in the… wind?

Lakes surrounded by shields in the center of moons don't have wind.

And the raft has a motor, not a sail. So what—?

A chorus of shrieks like a cross between the gemstone drill and otherworldly banshees reverberates off the unseen cavern walls, and I realize those on the opposite shore aren't waving. They're gesticulating wildly and pointing.

"Watch out!" Felix and Petala shout in unison, lowering their heads. We follow suit, but not before something catches in my hair, yanking out my businesslike bun so that my blond locks tumble around my face, blinding me. Then we're all swarmed by a mass of flying things, dozens and dozens of scaly bodies brushing over my skin, snagging the fabric of my professional attire. I shove my hair aside, focusing on leathery wings attached to foot-long lizard-like creatures in metallic colors of red, green, gold, and silver, shiny in the raft's light.

They would be lovely if they weren't attacking us.

There's a yell of surprise from behind me, and I whirl. Several of the creatures are working in tandem, talons gripping the shoulders of Vick's suit jacket and her skin beneath. Small trails of blood show through the material—nothing life-threatening but certainly painful, reinforced by the hint of red in her emotional aura, and I raise my shields to avoid the empathic echo. The creatures must be stronger than their size would suggest, their wings powerful enough to have her over a foot off the floor of the raft. She's got a hold on the handrail, but one of her hands slips as I watch so that she's tugged upward at a sideways angle.

I grab the person beside me, Petala, shaking her. "Do something! I thought you said they aren't carnivorous."

"They aren't," the guard says, pulling her pistol from its holster, a strange plastic-coated model I'm not familiar with. Not that I'm a gun expert. That's Vick's area. But this one is like nothing I've ever seen before. "This behavior isn't normal. If they bother passengers at all, they buzz the group, maybe pull a little hair or some clothing, and fly off. They're just territorial."

"How territorial?" I growl, getting in her face.

Her mouth sets in a grim line while she adjusts her weapon, searching for a clear shot. "If they truly feel threatened? Deadly so. But they live on the cavern ceiling and in narrow tunnels along the lake walls. We shouldn't be considered a threat...." Petala trails off and shakes her head.

I turn back to Vick. Alex and Lyle each have one of her legs, and they're pulling her downward, but it's a tug-of-war with the lizards actually gaining height and more joining them every moment.

What I don't understand is why Vick doesn't do something. She's dangerous as hell, and I'm betting she has more weapons secreted on her than the one they confiscated in the landing bay. Why isn't she fighting back instead of depending on—

Oh. Right. A businesswoman isn't supposed to be a trained warrior. And her weapons would be concealed in the lining of her clothing for later use once we drop our covers. She doesn't want to reveal them now, doesn't want to give us all away before we've even begun to accomplish our goal, and I wonder how much is her own desire and how much is her brainwashing to finish the mission at all costs.

I stare at her face, frustration warring with determination in her features, the gray hue of her emotional turmoil almost black in its complexity. She hates helplessness. She hates relying on others.

Especially when those others aren't succeeding in saving her.

CHAPTER 7: VICK
INFRASTRUCTURE

I am a target.

I'M WONDERING which of my prime directives wins out in a situation like this—the one that says I must finish the mission or the one that allows me to protect myself to prevent the loss of expensive Fighting Storm equipment.

The two are not mutually exclusive, VC1 reminds me. *It would not be out of character for a slave buyer to have concealed weapons on her person.*

No, it wouldn't. Except that if I reveal them, I'll likely lose them. And these are the expensive toys made from composite metal alloys that won't register on scanners. Regardless, as I'm lifted higher by the swarm of tiny flying lizard-dragons, and my left hand also loses its grip on the rail, my right slips inside my suit jacket and fingers the loosely sewn covering on the hidden inner lining compartment.

Alex yanks hard on one of my legs while Lyle grips the other in his viselike hands, and still I'm being dragged over the railing. If these things manage to drop me overboard....

The water is toxic with elements from the moon's core. Not fatal but corrosive if not treated quickly. You do not want to end up in the lake.

That's all I need to hear.

I rip the fabric covering free and slip the palm-pistol into my hand, preparing to draw it on the tiny beasties when another, louder tearing sound freezes my arm in place. The shoulder seams are separating from the arms of the suit jacket, threads severing at the joints. Both arm pieces snip apart at the same moment, and the lizards holding me screech with victory as they pull the body of the jacket—along with strips of my collared shirt and two chunks of shoulder skin—away from me and fly off with it clutched in their glinting metallic talons.

I fall and am caught by Alex and Lyle, the three of us tumbling in a heap to the raft's deck, the palm-pistol clutched in my white-knuckled fingers. I'm aware of rapid shuffling movement around us and a further blotting out of the ambient light while Jacks's guards form a protective dome over our crouched bodies.

My relief is short-lived when Kelly's bare legs aren't among those in trousers blocking us in on all sides.

I work my free hand loose from the tangled limbs and yank on the nearest pantleg. Petala's face leans down into my line of sight. She activates a handlamp and lights our human body cave within its real counterpart. "Where's my assistant?" I demand.

"Just behind me. I've got her. Don't worry."

"You'll forgive me if I'm not entirely confident in your abilities to keep her safe," I growl. The raft's engine increases in volume, and the craft rocks side to side as it gains momentum. "Are you telling me we could have gone faster all along?" I'm almost shouting, but I rein in my anger, keeping my tone more like an irritated CEO at a multimillion-dollar company board meeting.

"We go slow to avoid catching the lizard-dragons' attention." Her gaze narrows on me. "But no point in that now. You've already caught it. Come clean," Petala says, eyes narrowing on my closed fist, her light glinting off the palm-pistol clutched within it and barely visible. "What else were you carrying in that jacket of yours? How much metal? And what have you still got on you?" She leans back, gazing upward, then ducks down to close our huddle once more. "They're not leaving. They almost never go after anyone in particular unless that person is carrying a significant amount of metal. Lizard-dragons like metal. There's quite a bit of ferrousalcate in their scale structure. It's what gives them that shiny appearance, and they line their nests with any bits of discarded metal they can snatch and steal."

Kelly pops her head between another guard's legs to catch Petala's last few comments. She glances up at someone's crotch, flushes deep red, visible even in the dim light, and shifts her position so she's now between two different guards' outer thighs, her own knees on the deck. Behind her, a couple of strangely muted laser pistol pulses tell me the other guards are still trying to chase off the flying swarm. Their weapons sound odd, as if they are made of something other than metal, and under the circumstances, I guess that makes sense. A pitiful, high-pitched screech is followed by the plop of something hitting the water beside the raft.

I consider Petala's question. A cold, empty pit forms in my stomach.

"I've got some personal arms sewn into my pants and boots," I admit, allowing myself a sheepish smile. It's a truth. It's just not *the* truth. "If someone had warned us, I might have made different choices."

"If you'd followed the rules, you wouldn't have needed the warning," the guard counters. She shakes her head, then grins. "Tell you what. You let us patch you up when we reach the dock, and transfer a couple hundred credits into your escorts' accounts, and we won't mention to Jacks that you can't follow instructions. Deal?"

"Deal," I mutter. I signal to Alex to make that happen, and he pulls his datapad from a cargo pocket, frowning all the while. It's a simple matter to use the dummy account we've got set up under Valeria Court's name to distribute the funds. I'm too distracted by inner thoughts to argue or haggle.

Kelly reaches out, her hand landing on my thigh, her expression concerned. She's picking up on my despair, reaching the same conclusions I have.

The dragons didn't want my jacket. My shoulders just gave them something easy to sink their talons into, and most of the weapons left on my person are small.

But my skull. My skull is mostly medical-grade steel fused with a little remaining bone structure. Very little.

They wanted, and still want me because I'm more machine than human.

We bump the opposite dock before I can sink into a full-blown depression, Kelly's presence the only thing keeping me on an outwardly even keel while my internal emotions whirl and flash and collide in angry, violent, screaming impacts of stomach acid, painfully tight muscles, and cold sweat. My human shield stands back, allowing me and Alex and Lyle to rise to our feet. I turn to the bow. The dragons hover in a glittering cloud a few yards offshore, hesitant to come closer to so many humans in one place.

And many there are. A dozen sets of helping hands pull us from the rocking raft to the stable dock. I nod my thanks, surprised when they release me and my knees buckle. I have to grab for one of the mooring pylons or risk falling into the water.

Lyle and Alex are on either side of me in an instant, shoring me up by providing strong shoulders to lean on. "You okay?" Alex asks under his breath.

"Yeah," I manage. "And thanks for not letting go out there. Wasn't in much mood for a swim."

Lyle touches my arm briefly, then steps away when he's certain I've found my footing. "We've got your back. And the rest of you. Just figure out how to finish this job."

Without us all getting killed goes unsaid.

There's a wooden box on the dock painted with the universal symbol for medical aid. I'm betting there was an identical one on the opposite shore, but I didn't take notice of it.

Yes, there was, VC1 assures me.

Well, at least they're prepared.

Petala unlocks the box with a touch of her own personal locater bracelet to the lock, making me wonder what else the devices do. She removes a second, smaller container, also wood, and sets it beside me, gesturing for me to sit down. Wood boxes. Of course. Because the lizard-dragons would have been attracted to the standard metal ones. I really should have picked up on that oddity sooner. Too busy gawking at the lake.

While Petala strips off the ragged sleeves of my lost jacket and peels away the tatters of shirt clinging to my shoulder wounds, I ask her, "What about the drills? And the breather receptacles? Those were metal, weren't they?" VC1 flashes me an image of one, made of wood, but still. No mining operation could function without metal-based machinery, not to mention the shield and artificial gravity generators.

The guard shrugs, her hands moving quickly and efficiently to clean, seal, and bandage the wounds. They don't look too bad, from what I can see by craning my neck around to watch her. I've lost about two inches of flesh on each side, but VC1 provides an internal scan showing me no nerve or muscle damage and no significant blood loss.

"They like the lake area," Petala explains when she's finished, answering my earlier question. "They eat the fish. They live in the alcoves and short tunnels around it. We never see them farther out."

Good. Though I'm wondering how my trip back across the lake will go. But that's a problem for later. I have a mission to complete before I worry about the local fauna.

Petala speaks rapidly into a pocket comm unit, my enhanced hearing picking up something about replacement clothing, and a few minutes later another guard arrives carrying a dark suit jacket not too far off from the one the dragons took. I slip into it, hiding my wounds beneath. It isn't of as fine a material as mine, and the color complements but doesn't exactly match my trousers. It's also a more masculine cut. Still, it's a passable substitute and shouldn't raise questions.

"You keep spare clothing around for your buyers?" Kelly asks before I can. She and Alex reach down to give me a hand up from the dock.

Another shrug from Petala. "Let's just say that when guests are caught breaking the rules, Jacks doesn't let them take their belongings with them outside the dome."

Kelly pales beside me while a new shiver makes its way along my spine. I'm wearing a dead man's jacket.

An image of a shabbily dressed figure standing at a crossroads appears in my internal display.

Beggars and choosers. Right. I get it.

Making certain my entire team witnesses the definitive action—yes, I'm in control, this isn't throwing me—I fasten the front jacket button and settle the fabric more evenly on my shoulders. "I'm ready. Let's go."

CHAPTER 6: KELLY
ROLES TO PLAY

Vick is distracted.

THE GUARDS deposit us in a two-bedroom suite with reminders to monitor our personal locator bracelets if we should choose to explore. I'm surprised they don't forbid wandering about, but I guess when you have the threat of asphyxiation on your doorstep for stepping out of the approved zones, you don't worry so much. There's a gym facility down the corridor/tunnel and a communal lounge area with snacks and beverages beyond that.

Our accommodations are luxurious, opulent, and tacky all at the same time, with the central living room and the two bedrooms carved straight from the core stone, and velvet wall-hangings in reds and blacks hiding the rock itself and giving the illusion that there could be windows behind them. Maybe that's to counter the claustrophobia of the space. Even I have the urge to rush out of doors, see the sky, breathe nonrecycled air. My walls are up, but Vick's got to be suffering far worse. It's illogical. We live in our own enclosed environment back at Girard Moon Base. But there's something about being surrounded by rough stone rather than the pristine, modern, solid steel that makes everything feel like it's caving in. Literally.

While Alex and Lyle scan the rooms for bugs and cameras, I head straight for the environmental controls and raise the temperature by several degrees. Shield or no shield, these caves are chilly and would be worse without the wall hangings.

Vick makes for the garbage incinerator by the main entry. She shrugs out of the suit jacket and the remains of her shirt, stuffs them inside, and slams the lid shut. The device gives a satisfactory whir while it breaks down the composition of the dead man's clothing. Shaking herself like a wet dog, she locates the luggage in the center of the seating area, presses her palm to the genetic codelock on her brand-new designer-label suitcase, and yanks out a replacement shirt and dinner jacket that coordinate with her pants. Despite the journey, they're wrinkle-free, thanks to a fabric-flattening mist produced by the carrying case itself. It costs a small fortune, but a slave buyer wouldn't quibble about such things. I wonder if the Storm will let her keep it once the mission is complete.

Like in the corridors, the dim lighting also assists in fooling one's eyes, but it adds to the medieval castle-like setting and creates shadows that shift and deceive. More than once I catch Vick darting glances into corners and peering hard where there's nothing to see.

Her paranoia is on overdrive.

"We're clean," Alex announces, he and Lyle returning from opposite bedrooms. Lyle concurs.

"VC1, what do you see?" Vick asks, glancing toward the now active vidcom unit set up on a desk against the side of the gathering space.

"This unit is secure," not-Vick's voice responds while Lyle shifts his feet at the sound of her speech coming from the embedded speakers. "This is an internal communications system only—incapable of off-moon transmissions. Given time, I can link it to the slavers' more advanced system for a much farther reach."

Lyle pulls his personal comm off his belt and studies its screen. "No long-range signal on these down here either, though we can reach each other. Not like that's a surprise, but we can't contact our orbital backup."

I nod. "Make the connection, VC1. How long will it take? And can you keep it undetectable?"

"Approximately six hours." The monotone takes on a decidedly offended note. "And of course."

I grin. Nothing like offending a sentient computer.

"Sorry," Vick says, grinning as well. "I shouldn't doubt your skill set."

Alex approaches the vidcom, looking at first one speaker, then the other, as if he's not quite sure how to address it. "Hey, um, VC1? Would you mind if I, well, watch what you're doing with the comms? I mean, can you show me and talk me through it? It would be so cool if I could learn to do that."

Vick and I exchange a shocked glance, her eyebrows almost reaching the top of her forehead. I read her pleasure in the turquoise glow that surrounds her. Acceptance, both for her and VC1—something she's sought for far too long.

"I would be... happy... to instruct you," VC1 responds from both speakers, earning even more surprise from the rest of us. Sounds like Vick isn't the only one who craves being a complete part of the team.

Alex drops into a chair in front of the vidcom, happier than an overworked empath in a null zone. The screen activates, filling with scrolling symbols no one else in the room can follow, so we don't try. Instead, I take my own luggage—mundane, commercial gear made for the masses (and business assistants) and start for the larger bedroom Vick and I will share to change for the evening's "festivities."

"Oh," Alex calls, eyes never leaving the screen, "will it be all right if I stay put tonight, then? Or will you need me at dinner?"

Vick considers for a moment. "Should be fine," she says at last. "We'll have Lyle. And it wouldn't be unusual to rotate the two of you so one is always well-rested. Just make sure you actually get some rest and don't stare at the vidcom all night."

"No worries!" Alex waves a hand over his shoulder, then leans in toward the display.

I shake my head. He won't be sleeping anytime soon. I hope we won't require any backup.

CHAPTER 9: VICK
SHOWTIME

I am on.

A CHIME sounds through the mining installation, followed by an announcement that the reception
is to begin in fifteen standard minutes. All of us except for Alex make final preparations and head for the
door. Alex is so engrossed in whatever VC1 is showing
him that he doesn't even notice us getting ready. Before opening the suite door, I hand Lyle and Kelly a
couple of the Storm's antitox tabs, designed to counter
the effects of all alcoholic beverages and most narcotics. They chew the tablets, faces scrunching up at the
sour taste. I don't bother. VC1 is my antitox, far more

efficient at monitoring my chemical makeup, sensitive to a wider variety of substances, and faster than any deterrent drug.

We step into the exterior tunnel, where Petala and a guard we haven't met wait to escort us. Petala inclines her head toward the suite's closing door. "Where's the cute one? Alex, isn't it?"

Guess Alex's smile and wave really did impress her. Lyle growls softly beside me. I hope his jealousy won't be an issue going forward. To Petala I say, "He's taking a sleep-shift. He had piloting duty, and it was a long flight."

Petala doesn't even blink at that explanation. She turns and leads the way, the other guard, male, taking up the rear position behind my team. I'm not thrilled with the formation. I'd much rather have Lyle there, but I'm not in charge and need to get used to it.

Lyle does fall back in step beside the guy so they're both covering our six. They strike up a friend-ly bitch session I wouldn't be able to hear without my enhancements about unreasonable hours, demanding bosses, and inadequate pay, all designed on Lyle's part to build camaraderie between them. I internally nod my approval. Our Undercover Ops division might not meet my moral/ethical standards, but their training is impres-sive. Lyle becoming "friends" with Omar, whose name I've also picked up from their chat, means Omar is less likely to shoot at him without asking questions first when the mission shit goes down.

The farther we walk, the more crowded the tunnel becomes, other buying parties leaving their own guest quarters with additional local security as escorts. The mood is jovial, lots of friendly chatter and eager antic-ipation for the festivities. Soon we're packed wall to wall, and I focus my attention on taking deep breaths and not succumbing to the lingering claustrophobia.

Kelly pulls off the datapad clipped to her belt and scrolls while she walks, her high heels click-clacking on the stone floor. With the added height, she's almost as tall as I am, the stilettos accentuating her shapely calves and thighs. I clear my throat and look away, glad the dim light hides my sudden blush.

"They've messaged over the auction schedule of events," Kelly says, a soft chuckle in her voice.

Damn, she caught me checking her out. But hey, it's in character. And honest.

"Dinner reception tonight, along with an unveiling of some new product they're pushing. There'll also be a 'meet and greet' with some of the prospective merchandise during the meal."

I can hear her distaste, but anyone who didn't know her well wouldn't detect it. Also, I'm not fooled. She's reciting the timetable to distract me, but it is at least minimally effective.

"Wait," I say, making eye contact while we continue walking. "That 'product' was mentioned earlier, but I thought they meant the slaves. Is there something else?"

Petala glances over her shoulder. "Mr. Jacks dabbles in a few other pleasure-centered areas: aphrodisiacs, sex toys and accoutrements, even lingerie." She focuses on Kelly, studying her curves almost as intently as I was. "You'd look great in some of his people's designs."

"Thanks!" Kelly says, bright smile in place. "I'll keep it in mind."

I suppress a growl of my own. Guilt seeps in. She wouldn't be here except for me. And while I know she's an adult and can make her own decisions, I still wonder every day whether it's her love for me keeping her by my side or the bond that ties us together.

We reach an archway leading into a much larger chamber, and for a moment I fear another raft ride/drag-on sightseeing tour, but when we make it through the crowd, it's an ordinary enough cavern, wide and spacious and laid out for a banquet. Long, narrow tables crisscross the expansive space with enough seating for more than a hundred, all facing a stage on the far side. Scantily clad slave servants come and go via one of a number of narrower tunnels. I'm guessing those lead to kitchens and beverage prep areas. The slaves slip between the tables, delivering platters of food and drinks to those already seated. Their smiles are strained, and zeroing in with my exceptional vision, I note the heavy makeup hiding shadows around their eyes and numerous scrapes and bruises. Jacks has guards stationed at intervals along the walls and two flanking the stage, their expressions serious and focused, arms crossed over their chests, monitoring both the slaves and the buyers in equal measure.

A soft, citrusy-sweet scent wafts on the recycled air pumping in through shafts in the ceiling. It covers the musty odor of the caverns, but there's something else….

VC1, what are they drugging us with?

It is a mild mixture of pheromones designed to turn humans' thoughts to copulation. Nothing that cannot be overcome with knowledge and willpower. The antitox should take care of the others.

Turn humans' thoughts to copulation? I parrot back at her. *With a description like that, you should write love poetry on the side.*

VC1 huffs and goes silent in my head.

Great. I've offended the AI.

Petala guides us to what appears to be a VIP table, right up front with the best view of the stage. "Your security can stand to the side, or if you prefer, he may sit with you, as may your assistant," she informs me.

I give the other VIPs, seven men and one woman, a quick once-over. The woman has kept her male assistant taking notes at her side. She's older than I am by at least twenty years, maybe more, dressed in a modest evening gown of black velvet that covers her from neck to ankle. Not a bad figure, but her age is showing in her eyes and face. Her graying blond hair is pulled back in a severe bun. There's something vaguely familiar about her, like I know the face but it doesn't go with the rest of her. Since she doesn't even glance up at my arrival, I guess she doesn't feel the same about me. Her assistant gives me a nod and goes back to his datapad. The men have no nearby entourage. They're telling bawdy jokes, slapping each other's backs, and clanking their glasses of ale in anticipation of the upcoming "show." Nothing about them seems threatening.

I exchange a look with Lyle, tilting my head toward the nearest wall of the cavern. He nods and retreats, taking up a stance beside one of the other guards where he can keep an eye on me and Kelly and the rest of the room.

"I'll keep my assistant with me," I tell Petala. Where I can watch out for her. Kelly's looking a little glassy-eyed, her antitox tab not yet counteracting the pheromones.

Petala nods, pulling out seats for each of us in turn. I'm on the end of the table, which is perfect if I need to make any fast moves, with Kelly tucked between me and the other woman's assistant. A couple of the men lean over to greet me down the line, raising their glasses in a welcoming toast before returning to their conversation.

Good. I'm not here to engage. I want this prelude over with so I can return to our suite and slip out to map the installation, find where the slaves are being housed, and hopefully get that information back to our operatives waiting in ships just outside scanner range so we can wipe this hellhole off the fucking universal map.

There's a light tap at my shoulder. At first I think it's Petala with some last-minute "dump you outside the shield and die" warnings, but when I turn, she's gone, replaced by a very attractive redhead in a shimmering green miniskirt and bikini top barely covering her ample assets. "I'm Cate. I'll be servicing... serving you tonight," she says, a wink suggesting her verbal slip was anything but. "What can I get for you and your assistant?"

I study her further. Young. Very young. My stomach drops. She's maybe seventeen, if that. Minimal makeup, no bruises or scrapes, not an ounce of fat on her, but not half-emaciated like some of those circulating through the rear of the cavern. The VIP guests have the most attractive of the merchandise waiting on them. "My assistant will have ice water. I'll take whatever you have that's expensive and goes down smooth," I respond, lowering my voice to an in-character, sultry purr, the double entendre clear. Giving her a wink, I add, "Surprise me."

Cate lowers her lips to my ear. "I'm hoping to do just that. Word among us is you're a good owner. You treat your people well." She tilts her head toward Kelly, tapping away on her datapad and smiling to herself, also in character.

Yes, that's the persona Undercover Ops created for me. Hard-as-nails businesswoman, very particular about my purchases, but when it comes to my slaves, I may keep them, but I care. It's supposed to be a carefully guarded soft spot, one we've "let slip" so the prisoners here won't avoid me and my team if we're engaged in trying to rescue them.

The reality is, there are no "good" slave owners. By definition, they are inhuman, lacking empathy, which, I guess, given my mechanical tendencies, should make me perfect for this role. The Fighting Storm probably considers themselves "good owners." They feed, clothe, and house me, tend to my constant expensive medical needs, even pay me a salary, though most of that goes back to them to offset the costs of my implants.

But I can't leave. I can't choose. Legally, I can't love. They would say I'm incapable of it.

Cate's hand slips from my shoulder to brush the top of my right breast through the dinner jacket fabric, jarring me from my dark thoughts. "Choose me and I'll make your fantasies come true." Her breath tickles my neck. I suppress a shiver of pleasure, giving myself a mental kick.

Kelly already fulfills whatever fantasies I have.

Do something about the fucking pheromones, I tell VC1.

She chuckles in my head, but a moment later I feel more in control.

"Like I said. Surprise me." I shift away, waving Cate off, and she gives a pretty little pout, then heads for the nearest access tunnel.

Kelly bumps my other shoulder. "Pricelist," she says, passing her pad to me. "Cate's in the upper sixth.

Youth, virginity, and pleasure training are the top criteria here."

I check out the numbers, an involuntary whistle escaping my lips. Her price is more than my entire team's combined yearly salary. Meanwhile, Kelly is running her hands over my jacket, then slipping them underneath to my shirt front.

Undercover Ops selects my wardrobe these days. They think I wear this sort of thing well. I was wearing something like this the night I tried to propose, the same night I tried to kill myself before lightning did the job for me.

Kelly freezes midpetting, no doubt remembering the same things I am. I don't need her to say it. I read it in her face. She eases her hands away.

"You're getting high off what they're sending through the air here," I say to distract her. "I need you to stay with me."

"I'm always with you," she grumbles, but now she's focused.

Cate reappears and sets a generous glass of amber liquid beside my plate while passing Kelly her ice water with her other hand. Another server, male and dressed in a pair of super-tight shorts with his chest bare, holds a tray of salads and soups, depositing one of each for all the VIP table members.

The lights go dimmer, spotlights activating on the stage before us, while the servants vanish into the shadows. The boisterous chatter and clinking of glassware hushes when Jacks himself parts more red velvet curtains and steps to center stage, every beam striking him from four different angles.

He's shorter than I expected from our shuttle's vidscreen interaction, but stocky and muscular, that facial scar turning his grin into something between roguish and grotesque. His good eye sparkles with pleasure—probably thinking of all the credits he's going to make over the next few days.

If I have anything to say about it, he won't keep even one.

"Gentlemen and ladies," Jacks says, an unseen amplification system projecting his deep bass throughout the entire cavern, "welcome! Tonight, you are my guests, not my customers. Enjoy my hospitality. Preview the auction's offerings both on and offstage." He gestures to some of the waitstaff milling about. "You are, of course, welcome to make a preemptive purchase by depositing double the asking price through our automatic payment system, if someone catches your fancy. Remember, to ensure you get the one you most desire, you'll need to take bold action."

Several loud beeps sound in the echoing chamber, coming from the datapads now out and in front of almost every buyer present, or their assistants. On Kelly's screen, a couple of the midlevel slaves' names turn red, a line crossing them out and the word SOLD appearing beside them. The higher-end ones remain in the black. Bold action or not, the wealthier, more discerning guests don't jump to spend thousands of credits.

"Excellent." Jacks rubs his hands together. "Now, for you more indecisive types...."

The crowd chuckles in response. I swallow bile.

"Enjoy this presentation and *demonstration* of the most exquisite collection of human merchandise this side of the known universe. Allow me to present Saarah and Hodei."

The lights go down. Jacks steps behind the curtain. Kelly's hand finds my thigh beneath the table and clenches, though whether that's yet another residual of amorousness or she's expressing the tension we both feel, I can't tell. The linen of my trousers prevents the channel of two-way emotion transference from opening completely.

On the stage, dark figures rush back and forth setting up props of some kind, then scatter out of sight. Low, sensual music plays over the sound system.

I fold my arms on the table and take a deep breath, schooling my expression into one of moderate interest, my unspoken message clear: work hard if you want to sell me something. Come on. Impress me.

On with the show.

CHAPTER 10: KELLY
SEDUCTION

Vick is a professional.

I DIG my nails a little deeper into Vick's thigh,
conveying that this isn't lust. It's nerves. She glances
sideways at me, lips tight, jaw muscles taut, eyes revealing nothing. But her hand falls over mine beneath
the table, prying my fingers free and wrapping them in
her own. She gives a little squeeze, sets my hand back
in my own lap, and withdraws.

Someone reaches over my shoulder to remove my
untouched soup bowl, now cooled, and shifts my salad
plate from the side to the center. I hear it scrape the base
plate, but my eyes are focused on the stage and what

inhumane display is about to take place upon it. To my right, the server named Cate takes up a position directly behind Vick while other attractive servants/slaves do the same behind the other VIPs, but not the assistants, myself and the small man on my left. I guess we don't warrant that kind of attentiveness.

The spotlights come up and the audience lets out a cheer and applauds. Some of the less refined stomp their feet, whistle, or bang their glasses against the tables in a barbaric display, though most of the VIPs are fairly quiet. A naked woman appears at each end of the stage, one blond, fair-skinned, about my height and build, meaning above average breasts, narrow waist, wide hips. The other is deeply tanned, tall, muscular, with smaller breasts and long, straight, dark hair that reaches all the way down to tease by covering them, the deep pink nipples just peeking through. They're both young, though not as young as Cate, but their eyes are aged, telling a story of haunted seriousness, a tad glazed like they're more drugged than their audience.

Sweat beads on the tanned one's upper lip and forehead. Our seats are so close I can see tremors rippling through those taut muscles, like she's resisting whatever it is she's about to do and losing that fight. I've seen Vick like this, struggling to overcome her brainwashing, fighting to turn down missions she is too exhausted or stressed to be taking on, and failing.

The blond's trembling seems more born of fear than fight, and indeed when I let my walls down just a tad, I can see the deep purple hue of her fright surrounding her, though it's mixed with a generous helping of lavender lust. It's always seemed odd to me that two very different emotions would reveal themselves in such similar colors. I've never seen them together before. I wish I wasn't seeing them now. Because the only reason I can come up with for such disparate feelings in the same person is drugs.

Not only are the two women slaves on display for sale, but they've been given something to compel them to show off more than their bodies for the pleasure of the gathered crowd.

I'm glad I haven't eaten anything. Otherwise I might lose it right now.

A third light comes on, illuminating the center of the stage, where a large bed has been placed facing the gathered assembly.

Oh. Wow.

This is what Vick tried to tell you, a tiny voice whispers in my head. *She tried to protect you from all this, but you insisted she needs you.*

She does need me. Just maybe not right here.

If I focus all my attention on the numbers on my pad and ignore the stage, I'll get through this. I scroll some more, not really seeing anything, but keeping my eyes lowered. The sound system picks up the rustling of skin against a mattress, then flesh brushing flesh. There must be microphones embedded in the damn headboard to capture such subtle sounds. Regardless, my mind is oh so helpfully filling in visuals for what my ears hear, even though I refuse to raise my head.

I glance to the side where Vick watches the stage, expression composed, eyes analytical—every inch the prospective buyer evaluating pricey merchandise. No sign of eagerness or arousal. Nothing to give away a particular interest that might encourage Jacks to raise his opening bids, because Jacks is indeed watching the watchers. I spot him beside the stage at floor level.

He's fixated on the VIPs, making notes on a pad of his own. And—

Beep. On my pricelist the listings for Saarah and Hodei jump by over a thousand credits each.

Jacks knows his business.

The rustling coming from the hidden speakers shifts to heavier breathing and the occasional soft moan. Murmured approval from the audience picks up in volume.

Don't look. Don't look. Don't look.

Instead I lean back, checking out the competition as I suppose a good assistant might do. The male on my left, working for the woman on his far side, is doing the same. We exchange a tight smile before he returns his attention to his datapad. His employer, the only other woman at the VIP table, appears anything but pleased. Odd. She's not analyzing or appraising like Vick. Instead, she's sitting ramrod straight, shoulders tight, muscles tense. Her expression suggests she's just eaten something sour, but the salads contained no citrus. Dark, deep shadows around her eyes accentuate the lines of age on her face. I lower my shields for a second, internally recoiling at the anger and strain within this woman.

She also looks familiar somehow, like I should know who she is but can't quite place her. I'm about to raise my shields and ask Vick what she thinks when there's another, stronger sense flaring up amidst the sea of lust and wanton desire surrounding me. It's rage and aggression and a desire to satisfy a sexual frustration so intense that it treads close to murderous.

No surprise that a combination like this would be present here. Many, if not most slave buyers would project that toxic mix of emotions. What's surprising is how well I'm reading it, even if I can't identify the source. Whoever is projecting so strongly must share some small percentage of a brainwave match with my own patterns for me to detect it without physical contact.

I jerk my head toward Vick, focusing on her to defuse the violent emotional onslaught while I get my mental shields in order. She meets my gaze with her impassive one, eyebrows rising just a tad in a mix of confusion and concern.

Behind her, Cate adjusts her standing position to face away from us, giving us some minor semblance of privacy.

Vick's hand lands on my shoulder. She leans toward my ear, her warm breath tickling my neck. My muscles tense. It takes a concentrated effort not to recoil from her touch, so much did the brief contact with that other mind throw me off-balance. Through our connection, my senses tell me Vick's calm and composed, though worried about me. I read it all in the shifting colors surrounding her. The rage and desire to do harm I sensed moments before fade into the background, then vanish.

She must pick up my tension through our bond because her lips shift into a frown. "You all right?" she asks.

I shake myself, struggling for focus. I peer into corners, then around and behind us at the rest of the crowded cavern, but I can't trace the specific source of what I felt, not with so many other distractions and my mental walls back in place.

On top of everything else so horribly wrong with this scenario, somewhere in this repurposed mining facility there's a mind fixated on what I can only describe as psychotic, vicious action.

It's terrifying. But it's not our assignment. And Vick doesn't need to be worrying about unrelated problems when she's in the middle of a delicate mission. When we take this operation down, this new problem will hopefully be eliminated right along with it.

I force a wavering smile. "There's a lot of emotion in here. It's a little overwhelming even with all the shield practice I've been doing these last few months." It's true. Undercover Ops has specialists on retainer for everything, including empath experts who've been working with me, preparing me for something like this. I've learned as much in my field as Vick and the guys have learned in theirs.

It still isn't enough.

Her hand tightens in what is meant to be a comforting squeeze, though it's all I can do to not tense further. "I can send you on an errand if you need a breather," she says. "Lyle will be here."

I shake my head. "It's fine. I've got it now."

She gives me a slow, unconvinced nod. "Okay."

Shields or not, her trust, support, and faith in my abilities flows through our bond. It would be the perfect response if it didn't also bring a stream of suppressed desire along with it. Heat pools in my core, at odds with the chill I'm fighting off. The result is a violent shiver that runs all the way down my spine to my toes.

It's timed perfectly with a cry of release from one of the women on the stage, followed by a roar of applause and cheers from the assembled buyers.

Oh, it's going to be a long night.

CHAPTER II: VICK
DEBBERT

I am in trouble.

Is she really all right? I ask VC1 once Kelly relaxes, by increments, into her seat. She's avoiding looking at the stage at all costs. Despite my concern, I suppress a smile. Given that the two women in the display bed are currently shifting to a sixty-nine, that's for the best.

The frequent enigma of Kelly LaSalle is one of a growing number of things we have in common.

I almost choke on the sip of expensive rum I'm in the process of swallowing. Kelly glances my way, but I wave her off and set the glass aside. Yeah, for all I know her, I don't understand half of what I should about Kelly. It's almost comforting to realize the AI is as much in the dark as I am.

I catch myself drumming my fingers on the table-top and still them. This display is typical of what our intel has told us about Jacks, but I wish they'd get on with things. The sooner I'm out of here, the sooner I can sneak away and locate all the installation's critical areas. Then I can report to our invasion team and leave this hellhole behind.

It's becoming warm in the cavern, and not from the effects of the view. I shift a little, tugging at the collar of my fresh dress shirt. There's a soft orange glow emitting from flat metal panels hung in the upper corners of the space—portable heaters to ward off the moisture and chill of the stone. Not necessary at the moment. The crowd is producing plenty of its own heat.

"May I remove your jacket?" Cate asks from her attentive position behind me.

Prickles run over my neck and the back of my scalp. I hate having anyone out of my direct line of vision, and this entire setup is playing on my paranoia.

"Yes, thank you," I tell her, remaining in character. She eases the heavy fabric from me, then hangs it across the back of the chair. Her hands return to my shoulders, where they take up a firm but relaxing massage.

"Um—"

"Please, allow me. It's part of the services Mr. Jacks provides."

There's a note of desperation in there. Will Jacks punish her if he thinks she's not treating me properly? I'm trying to skirt the edges of my adopted persona, accepting as little physical attention as possible for both Kelly's and my sake, but I don't want Cate hurt more than she already has been by being here in the first place.

Jacks remains off to the side of the stage, but he is watching us. With an inner sigh of resignation, I stop arguing and hope Kelly knows it's not something I want.

"Interesting choice," I comment to distract myself from the expert kneading of the knots in my neck. "Two women. Not complaining."

Cate laughs. "Yes, Mr. Jacks made us familiarize ourselves with all the VIPs' sexual preferences." She leans in again. "I am well aware you enjoy female company."

I swallow hard. Kelly tilts her head in our direction but doesn't make eye contact. Oh, I'm going to hear about this later.

It is an insightful and calculated choice on the part of Mr. Jacks. According to the data I have compiled, ninety percent of the men in attendance prefer women. Ninety percent of the women here prefer women. By having two women on the stage, he is pleasing almost everyone in the room. Very few heterosexual women or homosexual men dabble in sex slave ownership. It is not a tendency they have, though there are rare exceptions.

I'm guessing VC1 means the woman a few seats down from me, but honestly, that woman doesn't seem to be enjoying any aspect of this fucked-up extravaganza. I wonder what she's doing here at all.

VC1, can you run a facial recognition scan on the other female buyer at this table? I know her. I'm sure I do.

On it, the AI replies.

Cate leans in closer, presumably to apply more pressure to her massage but also serving the dual purpose of brushing her almost bare breasts against the back of my neck. Her skin warms in contact with mine, an erect nipple tickling as it passes over my taut tendons.

Onstage, Saarah shudders through another impressive orgasm, her entire body going rigid, her spine arching off the bed in a perfect arc. The audience heaves a collective sigh. I wonder how much is real and how much for show, but Kelly flushes a deeper shade of pink, and Jacks strides up the steps to the center of the raised platform.

"Well," he says when he is blocking the audience's view, "that seems like an appropriate time for a short intermission."

A groan rises up from the crowd along with some hisses and boos, like we're all watching a circus or a sporting event rather than two women being forced to have intercourse in front of a couple of hundred strangers. Cate steps away to refill drinks, offering an appeasement for the interruption, leaving me to focus on the object of my anger.

I hate this man. And if the opportunity presents itself, I'm making certain he never survives to go before a court for his crimes. Too many chances he'll be released on a technicality. No, this ends here.

The glass in my hand cracks with the pressure I'm exerting on it, a tiny fissure running down its side. I stare at my white-knuckled grip.

Fuck. Kelly thinks I still have a soul. I have my doubts.

"Breathe," Kelly says, covering my hand with her own, whatever was bothering her earlier put aside because I come first in her world.

Thanks to the Storm's programming, she must always come second in mine.

Jacks isn't the only one I'd like to eliminate.

"I hope you're all enjoying the presentation." Jacks gestures behind himself at the two panting, sweat-glistening women on the bed. "Sorry, there's no preempt on these two. You'll have to wait for the auction to bid on one or both of them."

Another general groan.

"I promise, there's more entertainment to come. But first, dessert!" He throws both hands up in the air like the referee in an airball match, and from around either side of the stage, two lines of scantily clad servers appear bearing trays laden with bowls of rainbow-colored fruits and confections.

I blink at the untouched plate of some sort of fish and vegetables in front of me. When did that get there? And how long has it been sitting?

Best damn soldier in the Fighting Storm, my ass. That kind of distracted, anyone could have crept up on me and done some serious damage, or worse, gone after Kelly. I need to get my head on straight.

You were distracted. Being human, understandably so.

My eyebrows rise. Is VC1 attempting to… comfort me?

I also have the information you requested. The other female buyer at this table is Clara Hothart, Secretary of the Treasury for Earth's One World government. She is wearing a wig, and her makeup is intended to age her by approximately ten years, but that is her identity.

And that just made my job here a whole helluva lot harder.

I lean forward and cast a casual glance her way, but she's paying me no attention, her narrowed eyes glaring at Jacks on the stage as if she could bore a hole through his forehead.

What the fuck is she doing here? Is she an actual buyer? If so, then the disguise would make sense. An elected official to the known universe's most powerful government would not want to be identified here. But if that's the case, why isn't she more interested and entertained?

I follow her gaze again, to Jacks, and then beyond him… to the girls on the bed.

While I run the possible scenarios through my head, a server sets a bowl of diced fruit in front of Kelly. She digs in, probably since she also hasn't eaten much and she's using the food as a distraction.

I need background on Saarah, I tell VC1, selecting the girl closer in skin tone and facial features to Secretary Hothart. *I have a very bad feeling.*

You are not a precog, VC1 reminds me, *but I am following your thought processes, and I share your… bad feeling.*

I snort but stop myself. If I can have feelings with all my mechanical parts, why can't she?

Cate doesn't let the server deliver my dessert. Instead, she takes it from him, using it as an opportunity to reach around me and brush her lithe arm across my breast once more. She sets down a small dish with a single pink-cellophane-wrapped candy resting upon it. The other VIPs receive similar treats in varying colors, while the other assistant also gets fruit. I shift around in my seat. None of the other buyers have these either. It must be something very expensive and rare, not worth wasting on the lower-tier customers.

"Try this," Cate purrs in my ear. "I think you'll enjoy it." Prickles chase each other across the back of my neck.

I unwrap the dessert, the cellophane crinkling in my fingers. Inside is a single piece of what appears to be chocolate, dark and rich, with a pink dot at its center. The men at the table are popping them into their mouths, but not before I spot blue dots on theirs. Secretary Hothart's also displays a pink dot. She doesn't bother eating it, but rather pushes it away on its tiny plate.

Different candies for the men and the women? Seriously? Is Jacks that sexist?

I place the confection in my mouth, the bitter sweetness bursting over my tongue as it melts too fast to be mere chocolate. There's something else, a touch of tart, a bit of spice, flavors I can almost but not quite isolate as it fills my senses in one quick burst, then fades.

I wait for VC1 to fill in the missing ingredients for me, but she's silent. Maybe she's finally learning not to provide unasked for information after all.

"Well," I mutter, "if he ever decides to quit the slave trade, he could make a living as a chocolatier."

I roll the wrapping into a tight ball and discard it to the side while I become aware that Jacks's gaze has sharpened on my table even further. His eyes dart from one of us to the next, watching, studying… waiting.

For what?

VC1… I begin as heat rises in my stomach and works its way outward in an ever-increasing spiral pattern, up into my breasts, tightening the nipples even harder than before, and down, lower, spreading to my.... My thigh and vaginal muscles clench in response, in protest. My heartrate picks up its rhythm.

What the actual fuck?

I have the answer to your inquiry, VC1 informs me.

VC1, I try again. I have more urgent needs than background info.

She ignores me. *The one Jacks calls Saarah is in fact Cynthia Hothart, Secretary Hothart's only child.*

For a moment, my physical issues are forgotten. I sit up straight, noting with a different part of my brain that the men down the table are shifting in their seats, back and forth, side to side. More than one masculine hand disappears beneath the ornate tablecloth. Their attendants step up behind them, leaning down, whispering into their ears. Some of the VIPs close their eyes in apparent bliss.

I pull my attention back to my AI's latest news. *Why didn't we hear anything? A kidnapping of that much political importance would have made every newsnet in and out of the Sol system.*

Every merc team would have made a bid to attempt Cynthia's rescue. It would have been the biggest payday of the year for whomever got the contract.

Likely it has something to do with the fact that Cynthia disappeared from one of Los Angeles's premier BDSM nightclubs.

Ah. Yeah. I can see where Hothart might have been reluctant to let that bit surface, and too self-centered in her concern for her career and her daughter's reputation to put her daughter's life above those things. *Idiot.*

So now she's here, incognito, to do what? Rescue her daughter by herself?

I take another quick look at her assistant, fussing with his datapad in one hand and a fork for his fruit bowl in the other. Now that I study him, I can make out the outlines of muscles beneath his oversized suit jacket, the way his eyes dart from the pad to Jacks to the corners of the room and back down again. He's a hired soldier, in a much better disguise than his employer.

I wonder which outfit he works for.

I'm about to ask VC1 to do a search on him too, when Jacks gives a wave of his hands to the two women behind him, Saarah who is not Saarah, and Hodei. The girls fall back into their sixty-nine, a screen dropping down behind them and hidden cameras highlighting every touch, every caress, every heave of their breasts.

Between my legs, moisture pools. I swear I can feel Hodei's sinuous tongue on my own lips, teasing, tasting, slipping between my folds to probe deep inside me and—

"Kelly," I manage, voice croaking. My fingers grip the edge of the table. She turns to me, eyes widening at whatever expression I'm presenting. "I'm—" I can't finish the thought. On the stage, Saarah/Cynthia groans, her back arching off the bed, her own tongue losing its place between Hodei's legs above her.

I arch too, right into Cate's palms that have found their way over my breasts. A low groan works its way free of my throat.

What was in that candy? I demand with my last bit of coherent thought.

I'm going to have an orgasm, I realize, the pressure building and building inside me with only one way to go. Right here, right now, in full public view of everyone at this barbaric event.

I cannot identify several ingredients within the dessert's mixture, VC1 replies. *And therefore*, she adds, pounding the final nail in my lust-filled coffin, *I can do nothing to counteract it.*

CHAPTER 12: KELLY
GRIT

Vick needs me.

GREEN AND lavender, discomfort and lust, swirl around Vick in great clouds, the feelings themselves so powerful they seep through my strongest shields. Not angry or aggressive like the strange source I detected earlier, just desperate. A moan of need escapes her. She flushes red and clamps her jaw shut, eyes squeezed tightly closed, then snapping open as another colorful wave of desire rushes down the length of her body.

I pick up the abandoned pink cellophane wrapper by her plate, giving it a pointed look, then meet her eyes for confirmation.

She nods, unable to speak. The muscles in her jaw pulse with the effort not to moan again.

I need to do something.

I have no idea what.

All along the table, the other buyers are in similar states, shifting, rocking, clothing rustling as hands beneath the tables hurry the feelings to their inevitable conclusions, but they don't display Vick's panic. Why should they? This is what they're here for, after all. Instead, they're laughing, smiling, pulling their servers into their laps and grinding against them while the slave servants paste fake grins on their faces and mutter soft encouragements.

"I see my most important guests are enjoying their special treat," Jacks says from the side of the stage where he's retreated so as not to block the view of the girls writhing on the bed. "Pleasure Candy. That's what we're calling it. A new sex enhancement drug encased in the finest of confections made by Harold Linzman himself."

My eyes widen. Harold Linzman is famous on Earth for his exquisite chocolates. His family have been chocolatiers for at least seven generations. Every piece is handmade and outrageously expensive. I wonder if he's in on the drug deal with Jacks or if they are simply incorporating their concoction into his sweets. If it's the former, I may never indulge in a Linzman chocolate again.

All the datapads in the room give a choral beep. "If you'll consult your pads, that is, when you have a free hand available…." He chuckles. The VIPs chuckle with him, except for Vick and the other woman at the table. "You'll find I've sent you an order form for Pleasure Candy. We're still doing some fine tuning

on the potency. The female dosage can be a little…
over-intense, so it will be a few weeks before shipping
commences, but you can place a preorder as soon as
you'd like."

I don't take my eyes off Vick to check the pad. I'm
sure it's ridiculously costly.

"Sorry I wasn't willing to give free samples to everyone," Jacks continues, waving to the "lesser" buyers in the rear of the cavern, "but you can witness the
effects yourselves and imagine what my front-row customers are experiencing." As if to punctuate his words,
one of the men shouts in ecstasy, then falls back in his
chair, limp and exhausted. "Whatever arousing stimu-
li they are exposed to, either visually or audibly, they
feel it themselves. Imagine the possibilities!" Jacks
gestures at the women on the bed, now with multiple
fingers buried within each other. "All alone? Traveling
for business? No entertainment available except for
what you can bring up on your vidscreen? Sex shows
not doing it for you? No worries! Pleasure Candy will
ensure you achieve the ultimate release every time."
He sounds like a professional actor in an infomercial.
"Regardless, enjoy my gift for now, and the rest of
your evening, and ladies," he says, leaning forward
to focus on Vick and the other woman, oblivious to
Vick's discomfort or the fact that the other female buyer hasn't eaten her dessert but rather has it tucked in
the folds of her skirt, "don't resist the need. We're still
tweaking the mixture for feminine hormones and other
chemical makeup, but for now, the more you resist, the
worse it gets."

Jacks gives another signal, this time to staff members on the periphery. They scurry out of sight, and a
moment later, the lighting in the cavern dims to a much

more intimate level. It makes the women on stage stand out even more, but it also subtly hides the actions of those at the head table.

It signals an opportunity.

First things first. I gently but firmly reach over and take Cate's wrists in my grip, tugging them away from Vick's breasts. The nipples beneath Vick's dress shirt protrude so prominently, I'm certain she must be experiencing pain at their hardness and sensitivity. Cate pouts at me and parts her lips to argue, but I shake my head. "This is *my* job," I say, putting steel behind the words. "If she chooses you, it will become ours, but for now, it's mine. Valeria doesn't enjoy public displays with strangers." I glance past Vick's shoulder toward the tunnel where servants have been going for drinks. Lyle is there, his gaze scanning over our heads, not focusing on us, not watching what Vick would call this massive clusterfuck. "Get her something strong to drink. Stronger than that," I say, gesturing at Vick's empty glass. "She's going to need it when this ends."

I wish I were a precog and could know how that ending will go.

Cate turns and heads for the adjacent corridor, Jacks following her departure with a scowl on his face. I worry what this will mean later for the servant, but I have more immediate problems.

The green of discomfort swirls around Vick, emerald darkening to deep forest, testament to her worsening condition and struggle against the drugs in her body. I touch her cheek with my fingertips, the skin flushed and burning with heat. "It's going to be all right," I tell her. "*This* is why I'm here. But I'm not doing anything without your consent." It's a bit of a lie, and we both know it. I'd do something without her consent to save her life, to protect her, to stop her pain, but this is none of those, not yet, anyway. "So, do you want me to help you?"

For a long moment, emotions war with each other, crossing her face one after another: anger, desire, frustration, need. She nods once, a sharp, decisive movement. Still, I have to be as sure as I can be. "Is that the drug talking or you?"

"Me. I need my focus back," she grinds out through clenched teeth. "If you help, it will be... faster. I hope."

I slip from my chair, crouch beside her, and crawl on hands and knees beneath the table until the draping white tablecloth hides me from outside view.

The uneven stone flooring and loose pebbles dig into my knees, my skirt riding up high on my legs. I place my hands on Vick's thighs; the muscles beneath her trouser fabric tremble in response. She's hanging on, but barely. I can almost hear her in my head. *Get me through this. Get it over with. Please, please make this stop.*

There are no true telepaths, or so my professors at the Academy told us every term. Sometimes the bond between empath and subject is so intense it feels telepathic, but you are extrapolating what you think they'd say from your emotional impressions. That's all.

Bullshit. I know what Vick's thinking. I know it and I have to help her.

I tug until she's at the edge of the seat. My fingers fumble with her zipper, then slide it down with a soft hiss. A few yanks and her shirt comes free, allowing me to slip my hands to her taut, heated stomach. I'm all ice to her fire, and shivers travel across her abdomen at my touch. Parting her legs takes effort. She's fighting her own responses, but I am relentless. The table shakes above me, her elbows hitting the surface as she braces herself.

In my skirt pocket, my comm buzzes—three short vibrations, one long, Morse code for the letter *V*. *V* for Vick. I've never liked that she uses that as her contact identifier. It's always felt so... mechanical, but she insisted. Sometimes I think she *wants* to be part machine, like she doesn't know herself without that part of her identity.

Maybe she doesn't. It's a battle we may fight for the rest of her life.

Of course, this caller could also be VC1, who uses the same code when Vick is incapable of speaking for herself and there are no other convenient options.

Exhaling heavily, I slip the earpiece out and tuck it in my right ear, the fingers of my other hand working their way down into Vick's trousers until they reach her wet heat.

I've always been good at multitasking. Time to put that skill to a real test.

CHAPTER 13: VIEK HUMILIATION

I am ashamed.

Pick up the comm, Kel. Pick it up, pick it up. Fuck! Another wave of arousal heat crashes through me, harder and stronger than the last. Cate's no longer massaging my breasts, but I feel lips and tongues on my nipples, swirling, teasing, tugging, biting. Against my will, my eyes remain fixed on the stage where Saarah/Cynthia is doing exactly those things to Hodei, who thrashes her head from side to side in apparent torturous bliss.

Beneath the table, Kelly has my trousers unzipped, the waistband folded downward to give her as much access as possible without revealing me to my table-mates, not like they're paying any attention anyway. My enhanced hearing picks up the buzzing of the comm signal I've sent via the implants. If I can hear it, she damn well should too. Why doesn't she fucking answer?

Her thumb slips beneath the elastic of my underwear, slides lower, lower, then brushes my clit. I jerk upright, banging one knee on the underside of the hard wood table. Damn, that's gonna leave one helluva bruise, but the pain brings more clarity. I blink and focus. I can't fight, but my flight response is kicking in with full thrusters. I need to calm the fuck down.

"Vick."

Kelly's lowered, sultry voice carries over my internal speakers, fills my head with a warmth that has nothing to do with whatever drugs Jacks has given me.

"Breathe, Vick. You're okay."

I want to shake her. "I am definitely not okay," I subvocalize, my teeth clenched. "I need you to—"

"I know what you need." She gives a soft laugh. "Believe me, I know."

Right. Everything I feel, she feels. Muted, yes, especially if her shields are fully up, but I'm affecting her too. "I'm sorry. I fucked up."

"Not your fault. You didn't know."

No, but I shouldn't have eaten or drunk anything without having VC1 check it out first. I've grown too dependent on the AI's skills, counting her to neutralize anything harmful to my system. I need to remember she is not without limits.

Kelly's other hand slides up my trouser leg, over my thigh, then splays across my bare hip, applying pressure to hold me better in place. Well, at least I shouldn't be banging my knee again. It's still throbbing from the first time.

It's not the only thing that's throbbing.

My pulse seems to have settled between my legs, the low, steady beat of raw want pounding and echoing in my skull. Kelly's thumb shifts lower, between my folds, finding the slick wetness there and spreading it over my lips, my clit, making everything so sensitive I want to squirm out of my own skin.

I need this. I just wish I didn't need it here.

I tear my gaze from the stage, amazed at how much effort that takes, and study first one exit tunnel, then another, judging distances, traffic flow, how many people between me and the nearest dark corridor. I'd have to zip up, move my heavy chair, navigate around servers. Hell, my leg muscles are trembling to the point where I'm not certain I can even stand, let alone powerwalk my way out of here. I can't run away to some dark hallway with her.

Kelly's thumb moves in circles over my slick clit. I bang the other knee.

Yay, they'll match.

I swallow a sob of frustration. "Kel. You're making me—"

She pauses, her thumb no longer in contact while I hear her shift her position.

All hell breaks loose in my body.

A wave of aching arousal rolls through me. My hips jerk, trying to force the connection between me and her hand, then jerk again like I'm having some kind of erotic seizure. The drugs tear at the layers of my inhibitions, stripping them away like paint remover on a weathered fence.

I have about a half second to wonder where that analogy came from, a flash of a childhood memory of me helping the landscaper outside our Kansas home. So weird to have access to everything now.

Then another pleasure-pain wave hits and I can't think about anything else.

Do something! I beg my symbiotic partner.

Still analyzing, she returns, and I swear she sounds strained. The toll on my body is affecting her too.

I feel like I'm dying.

"I'm here, Vick. I'm here for you. Don't fight it," Kelly says over our still open comm connection.

The pleading in her tone comes through loud and clear. She wants to do this. I'm not forcing her actions. She's not embarrassed. Of course, she's also hidden from almost everyone. Still, I can't help feeling like I've put her in this horrible, degrading position, treating her like all the other enslaved men and women in this cavern.

I'm responding when a third figure steps onto the stage, a male this time, wearing tight black briefs and nothing else. From the bulge, he's large there like the rest of him—tall, muscular, deeply tan… and carrying an actual whip.

A combination of boos and cheers ripples through the audience of slave buyers—those who enjoy this sort of thing and those who don't. I accept that many find it arousing, tantalizing, but I fall firmly into the *don't* category.

A surge of mixed emotions: hope, worry, confusion rush through me. I'm not into BDSM. Never have been, especially after my ex-girlfriend surprised me with it on our last night together, followed a few years later by Rodwell's rape.

Pain incurred in the line of duty, helping others, bringing criminals to justice or ending them altogether, is welcome pain. But I get enough of that. Off duty, I want gentleness. There's so little of it in my life.

A twinge of panic and a quick flashback to that awful rape leave me panting, the blood draining from my now chilled face, but it stops there. I remember the assault with the remaining organic pieces of my brain, but I'm no longer tortured by the sight-sound-smell-feel clear-as-if-it's-happening-now replay that my implants used to subject me to before VC1 transferred that memory elsewhere.

"Vick. Don't go there," Kelly whispers over the comm.

I won't. It's not my unconquerable tormenter anymore. I owe VC1 more than I can articulate.

My current worry is what kind of effect watching a whipping will have on me, factoring in Jacks's see-it-experience-it drugs.

The male flicks a switch on the whip's leather grip, and I realize it's no ordinary variety. It's vibrating, electrified, a crackling blue aura of energy tracing down the long leather tail. I'm analyzing the voltage when he flicks his wrist, a minimal movement up/down, the rest of his arm held straight and still. The sizzling leather licks out like a serpent's tongue, landing squarely on Saarah's exposed hip, molding itself to her curves. Its tip reaches just between her legs before he snaps it upward and away.

The effect is immediate and intense—a combination of mild electric shock and vibrating heat curling across my skin, causing all my stomach muscles to tremor, then ending at the juncture of my thighs, right beneath Kelly's waiting hand. Not painful, but so stimulating. And *oh god* it's good.

I suck in a sharp gasp, releasing the breath on a shuddering exhale. "Now, Kelly," I subvocalize. "Touch me now."

She doesn't argue. Her thumb retakes control of my center, moving faster and faster, applying more and more pressure.

It isn't enough.

The need builds, pounding at my walls, growing and growing with a force I have never known before. Yes, Jacks does need to do something about the female variety of this fucking drug. It's building, but it isn't releasing, like thousands of gallons of water rising behind a floodgate with nowhere else to go. I get a mental image of metal holding it in, straining and bulging outward, expanding and stretching but not breaking through, and this visual is mine, all mine, not something VC1 is using as a metaphor.

I can't stand it. I squirm in my seat, unable to keep still even if I wanted to, but no matter how much I concentrate on Kelly's tantalizing actions, I can't let it go. Something won't allow me to let it go.

The mixture is imbalanced, VC1 supplies. *My analysis suggests that it works in male chemistry but is not as effective with feminine biology. It will continue to arouse you, but you will need more than the drug to achieve the relief it forces you to seek.*

Oh, that's just great.

"Kel," I whisper into my internal comm, "I need more, Kel. I can't—" The pressure rises higher. I hiss out a breath. "Fuck, it hurts."

"I'm not sure what else I can do," she answers, voice out of breath and bouncing around in my skull.

It's an echo chamber in there, all other thoughts driven away except Kelly and my physical responses to the drug and her touch. "For more, I'd have to reveal you, and I know you don't want that." She pauses. "At least you won't want it later, when whatever you took wears off."

She's right. I know she is. I'm already in for it with my insecurities and self-esteem issues, and Lyle is watching this entire display, for fuck's sake. He has to have some idea of what's happening between my legs where the tablecloth hides my partner. But at this moment I'd let Kelly strip me naked and take me on top of the fucking table, I'm so hot.

There's more shuffling and shifting at my feet, Kelly maneuvering into what I hope will be a position to push me over the edge. "I'm going to cut this connection," she says. "I have an idea. Trust me."

"Okay," I growl back. I trust her. I do. With everything I am and will become. There's no one else I trust the way I trust Kelly, even after what she did to me all those years ago. A faint click sounds as she drops the call.

I take slow, even breaths, or at least that's what I try to do, but they shudder out of me in audible gasps. I make the mistake of glancing up, the whip holder bringing his weapon down once more between Saarah's legs. Jacks stares at me from the side of the stage, watching, evaluating my responses. I'm a test subject, an experiment.

I guess I always have been. Why not once more?

Kelly's fingers find my waistband again and pull it out from my body, then slip something cool, hard, and plastic into my underwear, parting my lips to let its smooth surface rest against my most sensitive parts.

What the hell?

My inner eye recreates the shape of it, forming a picture of it in my mind, identifying it just as the comm unit vibrates between my legs… and doesn't stop.

Oh.

Kelly's got it on some kind of constant alarm, set to vibrate only, no sound, though I can just make out the buzzing with my enhanced hearing. It's intense and everywhere, large enough to hit all the places I need it to where her fingers couldn't reach.

As hot and aroused as I am, it doesn't take long.

My eyes close. I lean back in my chair and struggle to take deep breaths. When this happens, I don't want the attention of the entire cavern on me.

Even so, when the orgasm hits, it hits so hard I go rigid, my neck and buttocks the only parts of me in connection with my seat. It's a fight to remain silent, teeth drawing blood as I bite my lower lip. I don't quite manage it, letting out a faint whimper of relief while the aftershocks course through me.

I drop down and slump over the table, barely aware of the cessation of the buzzing sound and Kelly removing her comm. She crawls out from her hiding place, straightens her tight skirt, and retakes her chair, carefully not making eye contact with me.

My fingers fumble across the table, wrapping themselves in a trembling grip around the now-full glass Cate must have dropped off at some point. I dart a look over each shoulder before downing the pricey whiskey in a couple of shaky gulps. No sign of the servant-slave. But that doesn't mean she didn't see my response to the entertainment before giving me a modicum of privacy.

When I glance at the stage, Jacks is still watching, a smug, knowing smile on his lips. No pretense of privacy there.

Before this ends, I am going to wipe that grin off his face. Permanently.

Chapter 14: Kelly
Aftermath

Vick is regrouping.

"I'M GOING to kill him," Vick says for the third time. It's quiet, under her breath, but I glance up and down the narrow tunnel leading to our temporary quarters in the slave complex. A few other buyers, their clothing askew, hair mussed, and in general disarray, walk in front and behind us, but they don't react. I spot the second female VIP from our table, without her assistant, coming out of a side corridor. She gives us a quick, curious look and hurries on her own business.

Lyle brings up the rear of our trio. He rushes to catch up to me while Vick strides ahead. "She needs to calm down," he whispers for my ears only.

"Working on it."

"Work on it faster," Lyle says. "She's got that temper of hers just beneath the surface. It's controlled now, but if she doesn't bury it deep, she's gonna blow our cover."

We've both seen the full extent of Vick's temper. Last time she used it to not kill but utterly destroy Rodwell, the bastard who raped her and killed her father before she could reconnect with the last remaining member of her family. Her use of fatal force went way beyond what I'd ever thought her capable of, way beyond what *she* ever thought she was capable of. She hasn't forgiven herself for those monstrous acts, regardless of the provocation, and if I don't reach her, she'll do it again.

What Jacks did to her back in the main cavern, well, the other buyers wanted it, and Valeria Court would have wanted it. But Vick isn't really Valeria Court. Other members of U Ops sign up for this knowing that they may be placed in horrible situations. Vick knows too, but she has no choice, and I know she wouldn't have joined the Storm's ultra-secret department if she'd been given any say in the matter. So where does the blame really lie? The Storm sent her in. Jacks essentially forced her to orgasm against her will, but her persona would have been willing. I'm the one who facilitated it, but…. Crap. Will Vick blame me as well?

I study her emotional aura, the blackness swirling around her, all the colors of anger, guilt, embarrassment, and faint hints of fading lust mixed into one dark cloud. There's no indication any of it is directed at me, but empathic talent is far from an exact science. Quickening my pace, I move to stride beside her. It's not easy, given her longer legs, but I manage by almost jogging down the tunnel. Her jaw is set, eyes narrowed, expression fierce.

"Vick?" I ask, voice tentative. "Are you mad at me?"

The question stops her cold. Literally. Lyle's boots scrabble on the stone floor as he skids to a halt to avoid crashing into us both. Vick whirls on me, shock fighting with her furiousness.

"What? Why would I be mad at you?"

I wave a hand vaguely back the way we came. "Because I… I made you… it was me who—"

Lyle's cheeks flush pink. He turns around and strides a few paces away, studying the nearest oxygen mask dispenser with intense interest.

Vick catches my flailing hand in her own, tugging it gently down between us. She pulls us over to the wall, leaning me back against it. Then her mouth comes down on mine. Hard.

Her kiss is fierce and desperate, displaying all the desirous remnants I detected earlier. Her tongue snakes its way between my lips, finding mine and claiming it, and the rest of me, as hers. I'm losing myself in the kiss when there's another burst of familiar feeling, that aggressive, dangerous, deadly pattern of thought I picked up on in the cavern. At first I worry it's coming from Vick. Her fury at Jacks is intense, and we're in close proximity. Very close proximity. But that maniacal edge to it isn't hers. She's had her borderline insanity under control for a long time now.

I open my eyes, unaware of when I closed them, and spot a female figure ducking around a curve in the corridor. A slave? A guard? Regardless, a peeping Tammy, and one who wanted what I or Vick was getting.

Through our bond, Vick must pick up on my sudden discomfort. When she pulls away, I'm breathless, my blood pounding in my temples and the residual lust I absorbed from her making me shiver where I stand.

"Sorry," she says, panting, breaking eye contact. A few buyers chuckle as they pass us, then hurry on to their rooms. "Sorry," she says again. "I just... I'm still... shit." Vick takes a moment to compose herself, then makes another attempt at coherent speech. "The drug isn't all out of my system. No, I'm not mad at you. You did what I asked you to. You even waited for my permission. And honestly—" Her lips quirk upward in a brief grin that sends relief coursing through me. "—if we'd been anywhere else and you'd asked me to experiment, I would have enjoyed it. Aphrodisiacs aren't my thing, but this was... impressive, though the mixture still needs work. I just hate not having choices. I never have them. I'm not mad. At you."

I consider telling her what I felt and saw, but we have more immediate problems to resolve. "You need to get over being mad at all," I tell her. "For the slaves' sake. We can deal with it later. I promise. For now, you can't let yourself be distracted."

She laughs softly, without humor. "You mean *more* distracted. Yeah, I know." She gives herself a shake. "I know," she repeats. Her expression shifts to something I can't identify. "I thought *you'd* be mad at *me*."

My eyebrows go up. "For what?"

"Well, I mean, I caused you to be in that position. Yes, I know it was the drug," she says, putting up a hand to forestall any argument from me. "But I was careless, assuming VC1 could handle it. And then, well, I needed mechanical, um, assistance to—"

"Whoa. Stop right there." I place a finger over her lips, quieting her. "Seriously, Vi—" I catch myself. "Valeria. Considering your reputation for playing the field against both teams, I'm kinda stunned by some of the things you never tried."

She remains silent, waiting for me to explain. I can't help rolling my eyes at her.

"There are tons of reasons why someone who really wants a pleasant sexual experience might not be able to, well, achieve one: stress, tiredness, you name it and it can interfere. There's no shame in employing a little automated stimulation."

Vick gets a funny look on her face. "Is this something you're into?"

I lower my voice to a sultry purr. "How do you think I get through those nights when you're away on missions without me?"

Her mouth gapes open.

Reaching out, I close it for her. "Oh, do we have things to explore when we get home."

"Yeah, definitely." She grins and waves Lyle over. "Come on. Let's do this."

We make it back to our quarters without another incident. When we step through the doorway, Alex looks up from where he still sits at the vidcom and waves a weary hand.

"You were supposed to sleep," Vick scolds, though there's no ire in it.

"Only broke through their communication scramblers and shields a few minutes ago," he says. "VC1 is amazing. She bypassed three security systems, rerouted their transmissions to both clear us a frequency and cover all our signals, and matched our voice patterns to three of their senior guards' to make it look like those guys are betraying Jacks if our messages get intercepted." His expression when he stares at the vidcom screen is one of undisguised fondness.

"Thank you," VC1's voice says from one of the speakers. She sounds surprised. And pleased. More emotion than her words normally convey.

"Excellent job, both of you." Vick heads for the bedroom the two of us are sharing. "Let our backup know to be on the alert. I'm gonna change and do some reconnaissance."

"Vick," I call, stopping her before she can step through the doorway, "are you sure you're up to this right now?" I keep my tone gentle. I don't want to embarrass her further or set off her anger again, but if that drug is still affecting her....

"I'm okay. Wired, actually. Seems to be an aftereffect."

I open my shields, studying her emotional mix. She's right. Her energy levels are very high. A trace of lust lingers but is fading fast. The anger has receded.

"If I get what I need," she continues, well aware that I'm analyzing her, "we're calling the reinforcements in before daybreak, or whatever passes for daybreak on this rock, and we're ending this now."

I lock eyes with her. She meets my gaze steadily, calmly. I nod once, acknowledging her competence. "What time is it, anyway?" I ask, lacking Vick's internal chronometer and not finding one attached to a wall.

"About three forty in the morning," Alex provides. "According to the daily schedule I found, there's a skeleton staff working overnight, including a much lighter guard shift and some of the unpaid workers—"

"You mean slaves," Vick corrects him. "Call them what they are. They're why we're here."

"Right," Alex says, flushing. "They've got some slaves working in the kitchen areas doing food prep for breakfast at nine, and a few more on call for anyone who wants... services... during the night."

Ready and waiting sex workers. My fists tighten at my sides, and I will myself to unclench them. Vick's earlier anger is rubbing off on me. I follow her into the bedroom, where she's rummaging through her suitcase, pulling out her all-black tactical suit. She strips and slips it on. The loose-fitting bodysuit hangs on her until its special fabric compresses, shrinking around her limbs and torso to form-fit her perfectly. Normally she'd add a layer of flexible armor over it, but if she's caught in that kind of gear, it will give her away as a merc for certain. As it stands, she looks like she's wearing some sort of sex-play catsuit—a plausible explanation if it fails to keep her hidden in the shadowy tunnels.

"I'm fine," she repeats, as if expecting me to argue further now that we're in private.

Or maybe she's trying to convince herself. I hope she's really okay. She's getting better and better at hiding some of her stronger emotions from me, dampening them down beneath her implants' suppressors. Without connecting fully with her, I can't tell for certain, and that would imply a lack of trust.

"Focusing on the job helps me ignore the last of it. Besides, if I don't do this now, we'll have to wait another full day. They triple the security in the daytime."

She's right, of course. There were a lot more guards patrolling the tunnels when we first arrived. But there's more to it. Her urgency flashes around her in gold sparks. "What else is going on?"

Vick sighs. "Right. You don't know. It's that other woman buyer, the one two seats down from you at dinner." She draws a deep breath. "She's Clara Hothart."

It takes a moment for the name to click. When it does, I gape at her. "Wait, One World's Secretary of the Treasury Clara Hothart?"

"Yeah," Vick says, strapping on a utility belt with several compartments and a knife sheath. She slips a small blade inside. "And sex performer Saarah is her missing daughter, Cynthia."

Vick spends the next couple of minutes filling me in on how that is possible. When she's done, I help her on with her back holster, check that her pistol's safety is on, and slide it home. It's weaponry she can get out of and discard quickly if she's discovered. Not the best armaments, but something.

"You see why this has to get done fast. With the Secretary here, I've got to look out for her and her daughter both."

"It's worse than that," I say, thinking about our most recent encounter with the government official in the tunnels. "When we passed her, she was heading *away* from the guest suites. And she didn't have her assistant with her."

"Fuck."

I'm definitely spending too much time around Vick, because that was my thought, exactly.

CHAPTER 15: VICK
OUT OF BOUNDS

I am getting this shit over with.

KEEPING TO the shadows, darting from one abandoned side tunnel entrance to another, I make my way down the main corridor toward where VC1 best guesses the shield generators and controls might be. One particular chamber is giving off a huge power signature. While nothing on our stolen installation's schematics is labeled "Slave Base Defenses," most areas have names attached, like kitchens, banquet cavern, and guest suites. But there are several large unmarked spaces that have life support running to them. They're a good bet for the generators and prisoner holding. I

just have to confirm my suspicions before I acciden-
tally bring the Storm's weapons raining down on the
wrong spots.

VC1 points out that while the controls might be
nearby, the generators themselves may be above ground
after all since the shields extend both above and below
this moon's surface. That would be the best-case scenario. If they're on the surface, especially if I can shut
them off for a few seconds, the Storm's weapons can
destroy them easily. If they're below hundreds of feet
of rock, we've got bigger problems.

Our ships have lasers that can bore down through
the surface, but it will take time—time during which
prisoners can be moved, evacuated, or killed. Time
during which a defense can be mounted, though Jacks
isn't supposed to have any significant space force.

He wasn't supposed to have an underground hideout, either.

I swallow my frustration over our terrible intel.
There's nothing I can do but roll with what I've got.

Following the map VC1's projecting on my internal display, I take a right at the next branch of the tunnel and stop when something flickers at the corner of
my vision: my personal locater wristband. Instead of
the constant green glow I've become accustomed to,
the light at the center of the bracelet flashes rapidly in
warning yellow. I've entered an area that's off-limits.

Must be on the right path.

There's no sign of the Secretary of the Treasury
anywhere, though I'm keeping an eye out for her.
Wouldn't do to let her get caught in the crossfire.

A flash of movement catches my attention and
I whirl, peering into the darkness with my enhanced
eyesight. Nothing. Maybe one of those lizard-dragons,

though I'm nowhere near the underground lake. Maybe some other creepy-crawly.

Maybe these narrow tunnels are fucking with my claustrophobia again, making me lose my shit. But I can't shake the feeling I'm being followed, watched.

Are they tracking me? I ask VC1. I had her alter the outgoing signal from my locater band when I left the guest suite, transferring it to the sitting room's vidcom unit so that if anyone did a search, it would place me there. But if there's one thing I've learned tonight, it's to double-check.

They are not, she responds, sounding miffed. *Will you be second-guessing me from here forward?*

Yep, definitely miffed. *Only when my life's at stake.*

She shuts up. Guess I hit a nerve. Or a logic circuit.

I turn the bracelet toward the inside of my wrist so I'm not lighting up the corridor like a beacon and continue onward. There's sound coming from up ahead—soft conversation, some shuffling movement.

Creeping forward, I lean around the next bend in the corridor, internally signaling VC1 to map everything I see and pass it on to Alex's data storage. From there he can update our schematics and transfer it to our waiting backup ships.

Two guards dressed in Jacks's forest green uniforms flank a single metal door embedded in the rock face. They're both armed, one with a laser pistol, the other with one of those electrowhips used in the earlier stage performance. A faint shiver of need ripples through me, the last remnants of the pleasure drug reminding me of what that whip can do when applied in just the right way.

I shake it off. If the guard here hits me with his whip, it isn't going to feel good.

"Vick, you okay?" Kelly's voice comes over my internal comm. Of course she felt that touch of lust.

"Fine," I subvocalize back. "Going in. Don't distract me."

"Right. Sorry." She sounds apologetic but not hurt. Good. She's a professional. A professional in a personal relationship with me that goes beyond most couples' connections, but she tries not to let that interfere with our jobs. Much.

I draw my pistol from my back holster. The first shot from my specially silenced weapon takes down the righthand guard. The other gets off one crack of that damn whip, but it bounces right off my tactical bodysuit's slick, protective material. He's used to targets with lots of exposed skin to take the full brunt of the electrical charge, not someone like me.

I could engage in some witty banter about the wisdom of bringing a whip to a gunfight, but we're short on time, so I take him out with a second shot. Five steps bring me to the door and the locking mechanism embedded in the rock wall beside it. I press my palm against the smooth metal plate, giving VC1 easy access. Three whirs and a click and the door slides aside, whining and grating on its track. The sound bounces off the tunnel walls and ceiling, echoing into the distance.

Shit. Think anyone heard that?

This area of the installation is not heavily inhabited.

Well, one can hope.

I have to step over the corpses of the guards to get inside. A small twinge of guilt makes me swallow hard before proceeding, but I brush it off fast. They chose to work for a slaver. I have little pity for their fate.

The second I cross the threshold my locator bracelet's light switches from yellow to red, not flashing, but holding steadily on that foreboding color. I'm where I'm not supposed to be. If I hadn't transferred its data to our quarters and scrambled the signals it sends, a horde of security would be descending upon my current location.

The door slides shut behind me, crunching stray bits of stone as it moves, the sound setting my teeth on edge. Lights come on in the new space, illuminating bank after bank of control consoles. I cock my head, listening, but there's no thrumming of generators, no vibrations through the stone floor, just the faint hum of large amounts of functional technology.

Tonight's luck might be changing.

"The generators are on the surface," I announce out loud, not quite making it a question.

"So it would appear," VC1 responds from a speaker in the corner that she must have disconnected from the installation's PA system. There are old-fashioned, rusted, heavily damaged speakers hanging in corners throughout the mining tunnels—remnants of the former purpose of the place. Given their condition, I'm surprised they function at all.

"Many do not," VC1 adds, tapping into my thoughts. "But Jacks reconnected the system for his own use. It is only activated for emergency drills."

Something tells me it's going to be activated very soon.

I stride to the closest bank of controls, none of which make any sense to me, but with VC1 looking through my eyes, I'm certain she'll know what everything does. I place both palms flat on the console's surface. The tingle of energy rushing down both arms might be my imagination, but when the lights on the controls grow brighter, I know it's not.

Turning around, I lean back against the equipment and wait. No alarms sound, but I've got my weapon trained on the room's only entrance. There are no other tunnels leading from here. If security comes calling, I'll be well and truly trapped.

"Don't trip anything," I mutter under my breath.

"Really, you should have more faith," VC1 says through the speaker. "I am a sentient computer manipulating a much less sophisticated piece of technology. This is... what do you call it? Child's play."

A few more minutes pass. I'm getting antsy, despite VC1's reassurances, when she says, "Done. As we hoped, the generators themselves are on the surface, making it much easier for the strike team to permanently disable them. I have inserted a remnant of myself in this system. This way, when you are ready, I can turn the shields off for a brief time to make them even more vulnerable to laser fire."

I frown. VC1's got a lot of pieces in a lot of places. One at Dr. Peg Alkins's secret cloning base, several in the Storm's Girard Moon Base installation, and who knows how many more? How far can she go before she overextends herself?

I am capable of self-replication, in many ways not unlike this clone of yourself. There is no need for concern, she says in my head as I move for the door.

Not for the first time, I'm glad she's on our side.

I will always be on your side, she says. *Perhaps not always on the Storm's, but certainly on yours. Whenever I am allowed to be.*

Huh. Definitely something to think about later.

Besides, there are other greater issues to consider. Such as, once the shields are off, you will have a very limited window in which to act before the existing life support dissipates.

Yeah, I figured that. The shields don't only protect the slavers' base. They hold in the breathable air, the minimal heat. Everything.

She returns the base's schematic to my heads-up display while I scan, then slip into the exterior corridor. A big red *X* marks the other large cavern where she detects greater numbers of lifeforms and maximum-security protocols in place. Slave quarters.

I pause to collect the electrowhip from one of the dead guards. It's an intriguing weapon, safe to use in almost any environment, with a good reach. After coiling it, I loop it over my left shoulder.

"Alex," I say, triggering my comm. "Let the strike team know it's almost go time. I'm going to confirm the slaves' primary location and then have VC1 take the shields down." I pass one of those breather containers in their wooden boxes along the tunnel walls. Various stages of rot have worn the slats away, revealing the plastic-wrapped emergency equipment inside. These must also be holdovers from the mining operation that built this place. "Make sure the three of you have on Storm-issued breathing gear. I don't trust Jacks's ancient crap."

Not to mention there are insufficient numbers of them, VC1 chimes in.

Um, what?

Jacks has not deemed it worthwhile to provide protective gear for the base's entire population. There are approximately enough for himself, his staff, and his guests.

But not the slaves.

Precisely.

Despite their value as commodities, they are in-
finitely replaceable. Disposable humans.

And I worry about my own humanity.

*Don't you think that would have been a good thing
to mention sooner?*

VC1 huffs. An honest to goodness huff. From an
AI. *That was not an area you asked me to investigate,
and I had other tasks. Now that I am part of the security system, I can affirm that the majority of the breathers are nonfunctional, the functional ones having been
moved closer to staff and guest quarters. The rest are—
how do you say it?—for show.*

"Alex, new plan. As soon as you alert the orbital
team, I want you, Lyle, and Kelly to gather as many
breathers from the guest areas as you three can carry."
I transmit the schematic with the *X* on it to his console.
"Tell Kelly to change into pants and running shoes.
Meet me at the marked location, but approach with caution. I may need backup when everything goes to shit."
Which it will. That's a given. "Approximate ETA—five
minutes, so move fast. Leave everything except your
weapons and emergency gear."

"Got it," Alex replies, a little harried. Good. I need
him to feel the urgency.

I pick up my pace, moving just slowly enough so
I can check my corners, but the extra caution doesn't
stop the body hurtling out of the next darkened corridor
to collide with my torso and take me down, hard.

CHAPTER 16: KELLY
TO THE RESCUE

Vick is under attack.

IT OCCURS to me, even while I run with the rest of Alpha Team toward Vick's location, duffels, satchels, and purses stuffed with breather masks bouncing on our backs and hips, that I should wonder how I can read Vick from this distance. After all, I can't pick up her emotions from across Girard Moon Base. Our empathic bond doesn't reach that far. And yet she's coming in crystal clear to me.

And she's in trouble.

I know the stronger emotions carry longer distances. I also know that softer materials like dirt and rock allow more to seep through them than, say, Girard's steel walls. And there aren't a lot of doors here—tunnels wind in endless directions, all interconnected and most of them open to one another. That might explain it.

I have no more time to speculate as we skid around yet another corner, Lyle's momentum slamming him into the rock wall on the turn, and spot Vick kneeling on the stone walkway, straddling a male figure dressed in clothing similar to her own. It takes a second, but then it clicks—the man is the Secretary of the Treasury's assistant from the banquet. I notice other details. Vick's got one of those electrowhips over her shoulder. I wonder where she collected that. "Who are you?" Vick demands of her captive. "What outfit are you with?"

There's tension behind that question. If it's the Sunfires, we have bigger problems. It took a while, but they finally figured out Vick survived the crash on Elektra4. Well, she didn't really, and I still have nightmares about her painful, if brief, demise. They just don't know she's a clone. Regardless, we don't need the additional complications.

The "assistant" points one sprawled hand in the direction of Lyle and Alex, both with their weapons trained on him. "If you don't mind," he says, "you've got me. And there's a particularly sharp rock digging into my spine. May I sit up while I explain?"

Cultured accent, British origins maybe? Polite, articulate speech.

Definitely not a Sunfire.

Vick eases back and up, rising to her feet. One hand moves to wrap around her rib cage, her face twisted into a grimace. I frown. "You okay?"

"Our friend here cracked one of my ribs. Talk," she growls in the assistant's direction.

"I'm part of OWL."

Oh. Right. Of course he is.

OWL stands for One World League, the protection agency employed by members of the One World government on Earth. My parents use them whenever my mother attends a large public function. They're not mercs, not exactly, since they only work for Earth's politicians, meaning they only serve the greater good, or so they'd like the populace to believe at least. Some politicians are more good than others.

"Then we're on the same side," Alex ventures.

Vick shoots him a look. He shuts up.

Our captured OWL bobs his head in an almost real owl-like manner. "I figured as much, judging from the catsuit."

The cat and the owl. Oh, we're just full of metaphors tonight. I'm betting VC1 is having a field day with the images in Vick's head. Vick flushes an embarrassed pink that fades as fast as it forms—the AI at work, no doubt.

"You can call me Robert. I'm here to put a stop to this operation."

"No. You're not. You're here to get back the Secretary of the Treasury's daughter."

Robert stares at Vick, eyebrows touching his hairline. "Good intel," he says, then nods over at the rest of us. "Bad form. That thundering herd approach of yours is going to bring the entire security squad down on us."

It's our turn to blush, all three of us. "Kelly said you were in trouble." Lyle rubs the toe of his boot on the stone floor.

Vick glares. "In it and out of it. I appreciate having backup, but I *can* take care of myself, you know." She shakes her head. "But he's right. We need to move before they find us."

As if on cue, pounding bootsteps race toward our location. We duck into the shadows of a branch-off tunnel. Vick pulls Robert back against her until we're all out of sight. A team of six guards in forest green runs past us, heading in the direction of the guest quarters.

They know where we came from. They don't know where we went.

When their footfalls fade to silence, we step back into the center of the tunnel. Vick releases Robert, allowing him to stand on his own. "It won't take them long to figure out we aren't in our guest suite," she says.

Robert shakes his head. "And you've made my assignment much, much harder. I need to locate the slave quarters, free Secretary Hothart's daughter, and get out of here."

"You mean get the daughter *and* the Secretary out of here. Oh, and by the way, your boss has gone for an evening stroll. We passed her heading away from the suites. Why the fuck would you bring someone that important on a mission like this?" Vick hands him a pistol she must have confiscated during their struggle.

"Bloody moronic piss sipper," the OWL mutters.

I fight down a smile at the colorfulness. It puts Vick's simple "fucks" to shame. Then again, blunt and to the point suits Vick better.

"I didn't," he continues. "She stowed away on my transport, and by the time I realized she'd done so, I was already in orbit. We had to scrap my plans of going in as a buyer and reorganize ourselves as a team or abort the entire proceeding. I feared Jacks might sell Cynthia if we waited any longer, and we would never find her."

None of us can find an argument for that.

"We're wasting precious time," Robert adds. He sets off at a brisk pace down the corridor.

Vick clears her throat. "You're going the wrong way."

Robert stops, pivots, and places his hands on his hips. "And how would you know that?"

Vick's eyes unfocus for maybe a second. I'm thinking no one else noticed until I catch Alex's knowing smile.

Well, good. Both he and Lyle are learning to read Vick better. And they accept her for who she is.

Robert's comm beeps in the small pouch on his utility belt. He frowns, withdraws it, and stares in silence at the screen. "Base schematics?"

Vick nods.

"The X is where Jacks keeps the slaves?"

Vick nods again.

Robert locks his startled gaze on her calm one. "How did you get such detailed information? We've been trying ever since we discovered who had taken Cynthia. Who the hell are you people?"

Vick smirks, gesturing at the three of us with a sweep of her arm. "They're Alpha Team, the best damn unit in the Fighting Storm. Me? According to the precious chickenshit government you serve, I'm either dead or don't qualify as 'people.' But you probably know me as VC1."

CHAPTER 17: VICK CONTINGENCY PLAN

I am pressed for time.

KELLY SHOOTS me a look at the "chickenshit" remark, but then sighs in resignation. I shouldn't have said that, but, her mother aside, she knows I'm right.

To be fair, I get why there's an issue. I've died enough times, one of which they don't even know about, that my breathing status can be confusing. The "human" part, though. That just pisses me off and reveals them for the cowards they are. Earth doesn't want to contradict the Moon's autonomous government. And the Moon has decided I'm a machine.

Granted, that's in large part because in an official court hearing, I said so myself, but that's beside the point. I did it to save Kelly. Kelly was saved.

Now I want my fucking life back.

Alpha Team trails Robert through the tunnels. He holds his comm-map in his outstretched hand, the rest of us with weapons at the ready to cover him, except for Kelly of course. Her pistol remains holstered. She handles killing devices only when it's essential, and even then, it's like she's holding a dead rat by its tail. More than a few times, I catch Robert casting surreptitious glances back at me, his gaze calculating and openly curious, but my glare turns him around. I'm a team member, not a tourist attraction.

Twice, Lyle and I draw on a servant and have to jerk our gun arms up to avoid firing. Both times, the slave-servant skitters back the way she came, disappearing into the darkness, but not apparently raising any kind of alarm. Word will be quietly spreading that there's a strike team onsite, and that's good. I want the slaves to be ready to fight their oppressors.

This walking is taking a toll on my broken rib, each step jarring the bones together. *Can you do something about the pain?*

My entire left side goes numb, the nerve endings cut off from my brain's sensory system.

Okay, then.

We take a few more turns without incident, then pause at the sound of quiet conversation and the general noises associated with large groups of people. At the next archway, we stop and peer into a cavern about the same size as Jacks's makeshift banquet hall.

The slave quarters aren't as bad as they could be—a wide, open space with rows of beds, each with a small standing cabinet for hanging clothing and a foot-locker for storing a small number of personal items like toiletries and such. A few side tunnels similar to our own lead away at different angles, and I detect water running from some of them, so, likely showers and bathrooms.

There must be about fifty cots altogether, narrow spaces between them allowing for controlled move-ment. Most are occupied, their owners curled into fetal positions, blankets pulled over their heads, thin pillows pressed to their ears to block out the overhead lighting and sounds from their neighbors. A handful are empty, probably belonging to the ones currently "on duty."

The few slaves moving about have glazed eyes and hopeless expressions. Jacks drugs the ones not work-ing. Makes sense, but my jaw clenches. It's harder to motivate stoned people to run.

Four security guards patrol the perimeter—a small contingent for such a large number of prisoners, but then again, with them drugged, scantily dressed, and mostly small and not muscular, it's probably sufficient. Four guards, four of us eager for a fight. I like our odds.

That is, until the alarms go off.

"We're out of time!" I shout, grabbing the guard passing our entrance and hauling him backward off his feet. I slam his head against the closest wall. He drops like the stone he just hit.

Kelly's whimper carries over the blaring din.

"You okay?" I ask, drawing close enough for her to hear me. Robert, Lyle, and Alex barrel into the main cavern, taking cover behind cots and cabinets. Gunfire erupts. An electrowhip cracks over and over again. Slaves scream while metal bedframes scrape on stone, and heavy storage bins topple and crash.

Kelly shakes off her empathic connection to the guard I disabled. "Yes. He's not dead. Thank you for that."

"Sure. No problem."

I intended to kill him. She doesn't need to know it. Not going to examine the impulse too closely. Kelly says I have a soul. Gonna stick with that for now, even if I doubt her judgment.

"Stay put. People are getting hurt, and I don't want you picking up their pain full blast. If we look like we're losing, give us some covering fire from here." I glance at the pistol she now holds loosely. "Might want to take the safety off that thing."

Her smile, even sheepish, warms me inside. She flips her thumb over the switch. "Got it."

I touch her shoulder once in parting, then dart into the room, dive-rolling to avoid a barrage of laser fire and ending up behind a sideways cabinet with its contents scattered across the floor. It's not big enough to cover my entire body, but it will do, and I get off a couple of solid shots, taking down a second guard on the far side of the room. Then I'm scrambling, searching for better protection. I'm racing past another side tunnel when hands grab me and pull me into it, laser blasts following in my wake.

"Thanks," I mutter to the hands' owner while I study the scorch marks on the stone wall just past my head.

I send VC1 a message to shut down the alarms, and the area drops into relative silence.

"Are you here to free us?" a female voice asks.

I turn to the sound and come face-to-face with three naked girls, one holding a towel, the other two dripping wet from an interrupted shower. They're attractive, young, and I've got the remnants of the sex-enhancement drug in my veins. I avert my gaze, fixating on a point on the wall behind them. "Yes," I say, answering the lead girl's question. "Get some clothes on and stay behind me. I'll cover you to the exit tunnel."

VC1, can you interrupt the shield generators now? Also, I need directions to the quickest, easiest way to the surface.

I feel her assent as the schematic behind my eyes shifts to a new perspective—a map detailing a route to a bank of freight elevators designed for hauling large amounts of ore to the above-ground storage facilities. We'll have to cross the slave quarters cavern and take a tunnel on the far side, but that's not a bad thing. Reinforcements will most likely be coming from the guest suites back the way we came, so we're heading away from them.

"Alex," I say into my internal comm, "tell the strike team to begin their run. And make sure they're landing the transport ships as soon as the shields go down for good." I transmit the escape vectors to my teammates.

"Acknowledged," Alex responds, a little out of breath. The gunfire in the main cavern continues. I need to get back out there.

"Stay behind me," I tell the girls when they're dressed, "dressed" being a relative term. One wears a nightie in pale pink that barely covers her ass. The other two have on short skirts and halter tops. No protection whatsoever. I suppress a sigh.

"I should've known you weren't a real buyer," the one in the negligee says. "And here I thought I was losing my touch."

I know that voice. Peering harder at her face, I realize this is Cate, my personal "assistant" during the banquet. I didn't recognize her with her wet hair stringing into her face and everything else on display, forcing me to look elsewhere.

"Your touch is fine," I assure her, blushing when I realize the double meaning of what I just said. "I'm just very taken."

I drop to my knees and crawl into the main chamber. The girls follow suit, and I wince in sympathy. The stone must be cutting into their bare knees, but they've been through too much to complain about the relatively minor discomfort.

"Your assistant, yeah. I figured as much. She was very possessive."

"She can be that." I chuckle even as I target another guard. My shot misses when he ducks. Taking a small risk, I pop my head up behind a cot and survey the situation. At the far side of the cavern, slaves are streaming through the exit and disappearing into the tunnel beyond, Lyle ushering them out as fast as they can move and laying down covering fire. I don't spot Cynthia among them. I do spot several newly arrived guards, about four, joining the two that remain. And just like that, we're outnumbered and sure to become more so.

Robert is creeping between the rows of cots, sneaking up on one of Jacks's security. He takes the guard out from behind, sees me watching, and tosses me a jaunty salute.

Cheeky bastard, but for all his posturing, I'm glad to have him.

I point at the exit where Lyle is waiting. "That way. Go. Keep your heads down and your legs moving."

Waving my hand over my shoulder, I gesture my three charges onward, letting them crawl past me.

At that moment, the ground beneath me shudders and a rumbling boom echoes from the cavern ceiling and down all the adjacent tunnels. The Storm has opened fire on the above-ground generators. The three girls from the shower freeze halfway to their goal, craning their necks to stare back at me.

Is the shield down? I ask my internal counterpart. It doesn't feel down. I think I'd know if—

There's a sudden shift in the air, a pressure imbalance that pops my ears in a painful rush. Then *whoosh.* A howling wind hurricanes its way through the cavern, conflicting air currents crisscrossing from the various tunnels, colliding in the center and upending whatever furniture remains standing. A miniature tornado forms, whirling and picking up everything in its path: beds, storage units, people. It's got one of the guards, but some of the slaves as well, careening them around until they collide with something more solid, most often a rock wall.

Screams cut off as bones crunch. The pressure release eases off. The whirlwind dissipates, dropping lifeless bodies on the floor.

I expected casualties on this mission. I didn't expect death by cyclone.

"We're not in Kansas anymore," my father's voice whispers in my head from beyond the grave, and I'm momentarily overcome by a flood of memories, him repeating the iconic *Wizard of Oz* phrase anytime our family encountered something unexpected. I guess when you grow up in Kansas, Oz references are inevitable, and Dad was more obsessed with the stories than most.

When the wind dies completely, I become aware of an increasing tightness in my throat and chest, each breath coming harder than the last, the exertion of crawling making the need greater and greater. The girls' eyes widen, one clutching at her neck, another placing a hand over her ample breasts. Wheezing turns to gasping. I trigger my internal comm.

"Need those breather masks," I shout, or try to. It comes out as a faint whisper. My vision sparkles at the edges, then darkens with black dots. If I pass out, none of us are escaping.

Movement at the tunnel where we entered sets me to panicking. It's Kelly, already wearing her Storm-issued mask, behind which her face is ghastly pale, and I realize she felt the deaths that just occurred. Nevertheless, she's darting from bed to storage trunk to cabinet, keeping low and zigzagging as I've taught her, wavering a bit, but not losing momentum as she fights her own urge to faint. Several near misses blow apart furnishings to her left and right, and if I weren't already doing so, I'd be holding my breath. She slides in on her knees, skidding to a halt beside me, and yanks a satchel from over her shoulder. After digging around inside, she comes up with a breather and passes it to me.

My oxygen-deprived brain can't make my clumsy fingers close around it. Next thing I know, she's dragging me to her with one hand cupped behind my head. The other tugs the straps of the breather over my hair, tightens them, and adjusts the mask to cover my nose and mouth.

I take a slow, deep breath while she moves to the three girls with me, doing the same for each of them. When she's done, she crawls back to my side.

"Glad you're here," I say, placing my hand over hers so she can feel the truth in it. Her love and gratitude flood me in return. "Good job handling all this."

She beams with pride, though her eyes are teary and her hand shakes under mine.

After I inhale a few more times, my vision clears and I take in the battle zone. The drop in oxygen levels has done us one favor. It's more than leveled the playing field. While Alex and Lyle scramble to get masks on all the slaves and Robert, they leave the guards to suffocate. It's an unpleasant way to go, faces turning blue, mouths and eyes wide open in helpless terror.

Oh fuck. They're dying. They're dying and I've got Kelly beside me, and she's already in bad shape.

I grab and pull her close as she topples against me.

Chapter 18: Kelly
Tunnels of Dark

Vick is stubborn.

I HUDDLE in Vick's strong arms while the guards' deaths wash over me, one by one, some hanging on a little longer than the rest and prolonging my agony. My body writhes. A moan escapes my clenched teeth. Vick grabs the bag I'm carrying, the one with the breathers, and rummages through it until she finds the hypodermic I always keep with me. After rolling up my sleeve, she presses the needle against my skin and pushes the plunger home. It's all happening simultaneously, but it feels like time slows to a crawl before all the medication is administered.

The effect is immediate: a cool rush of calm flowing outward from the injection site to every part of my body and mind. Emotional dampener drugs allow me to remain conscious and function in all but the worst of exposure circumstances. My other senses sharpen as my empathic abilities snuff out beneath the blanket of chemicals. But there is one major downside.

I won't be able to sense Vick's emotions, either.

Well, that's not entirely true. I'll sense them, but more like being hit with a blunt instrument rather than tasting the nuance of her emotional roller coaster. For example, right now I feel a mix of her energized excitement, her fear, and her anger, whereas a moment ago I could differentiate between the energy derived from the current fight, the fear from the asphyxiation of both herself and me and everyone else, and her anger over the slave practices in general. I will also have less range in picking up what she's experiencing. If she leaves my side, I'll only catch the strongest surges.

I don't like being less effective, being a victim of my own power's weakness. But I have to be able to act.

Vick pushes me upright so I'm facing her and peers into my face, nodding at whatever she sees there. "Better?"

"Yes." For certain definitions.

"Good. Let's move. It's going to get worse."

With the guards out of commission, we're able to rise to our feet and walk the rest of the way to the exit on the far side of the cavern. Lyle, Alex, Robert, and a host of formerly enslaved women and men await us there, all wearing functional breather gear. The ex-slaves shiver in their scanty garments. Goose bumps arise on their exposed flesh, and some of the girls' lips are blue.

In the adrenaline rush, I hadn't noticed the temperature dropping, but when Vick exhales her next breath, it fogs the mask she's wearing.

"It's getting colder. A lot colder," I say, surprised by the chattering of my teeth and the unsteadiness of my speech.

"With the shields down, the heat is escaping too fast for the equipment to compensate," Alex explains. "We need to meet our extraction team before we freeze to death."

I glance at the young men and women waiting for guidance from us. "Some of us faster than others."

"Why aren't the alarms going off?" Robert asks. "All this should have brought the entire security team down on us. I assume this is your doing?" His tone is accusatory.

From her frown, Vick doesn't appreciate it. "Yes, it's our doing. So is the strike force that's coming to back us up, and the rescue ships that will carry everyone to safety. And yes, I've shut down the alarms."

Or VC1 has, but she isn't drawing additional attention to her counterpart. As a member of the OWLs, Robert already knows some of VC1's abilities, anyway. Which makes me wonder. "Shouldn't you be aware of this operation?" I ask as we all trudge along the tunnel toward what I hope is a way out. Vick's in the lead. She must know where we are going.

"I've been acting under deep cover for multiple days. I was aware something was in the works, but to be honest, given all the red tape involved in a multigovernment undertaking, I didn't expect it to get underway so soon. Good on you for pulling this together." He tips an imaginary hat.

"Thanks," Vick jumps in. "Now shut up. I'm in contact with the strike team, and if you don't want them shooting up this section of the mines, you need to not distract me."

Robert's eyes widen. "In contact with? Below several hundred feet of rock? How is that even—?" He breaks off at Vick's stern glare and focuses on me instead. "So, if she's VC1—"

"Vick," I correct him.

He has the courtesy to blush. "Vick. Yes, of course. Then you must be Kelly LaSalle, the diplomat's daughter."

I acknowledge his assumption with a nod.

"And the two of you are… together."

I raise an eyebrow. "Yes."

"Pity," Robert says with a rakish grin, then moves forward to assist some of the struggling escapees.

Shaking my head, I smile to myself, even wider when Vick gives me a *look* over her shoulder that says she heard the entire exchange. Nice that she can still become jealous about me after all we've been through.

We continue on. This part of the complex is less-used, more rugged. Fewer lights guide our way, and we're stumbling through near darkness. Things move in the shadows, and down one tunnel I hear a slosh of water and the flutter of leathery wings. Another lake? More flying mini-dragons? Vick says nothing but picks up her pace. A shudder works its way up her retreating back.

After three more turns in the passageway, we reach a floor-to-ceiling pull-down gate beyond which lies a large flat metal platform with railings running around it and an endless stretch of blackness above it. Vick strides to the front, bends down, and yanks the heavy gate upward with seeming ease. "All aboard," she announces.

Under different circumstances there would be pushing and shoving in their hurry to escape, but these poor young men and women are close to freezing, their skin bluish gray, their violent shivering uncontrollable even with their arms wrapped around themselves. They shuffle forward, making room for everyone. It's a tight fit, but all thirty or so of them manage to squeeze inside, along with Lyle and Alex. I push in between them, then notice neither Vick nor Robert is attempting to follow.

I hold up a hand in useless protest as Vick yanks the gate down to click into place at the bottom. "Vick...." It's a warning, and she knows it. She gives me an apologetic smile.

"We haven't found Cynthia or her too important secretary mother. And I have unfinished business with Jacks," she says, straightening the electrowhip over her shoulder. I'd forgotten she had that thing. Beside her, Robert nods.

My heart sinks. "This was your plan all along, wasn't it?"

Even through the emotional dampening drugs, I feel Vick's guilt. "Not all along. I hoped we'd find them along the way. All three of them. But we haven't."

I lower my voice. "They're probably dead, Vick. There's not enough air, little heat, and the strike force—" I'm interrupted by a tremendous explosion back the way we came. The entire elevator rattles around us. If we don't leave soon, we aren't leaving at all.

"All the more reason not to take you with me and expose you to that. I'll avoid the strike zones. I have to try. That girl...."

Her eyes are haunted. I'm sure mine reflect the sentiment. "Please be careful," I tell her, reaching through the segmented metal strips of the gate to clasp her shoulder. She covers my hand with hers. Love flows through the bond, soundly defeating the drugs in my system.

"I will. Besides—" She jerks a thumb at Robert behind her. "—I'll have this idiot watching my back."

"I believe that will be the other way around," he says, starting off the way we came.

Vick rolls her eyes. "See you up top." She tugs free of my grip, jogs off after the OWL, and disappears from view.

Alex throws a metal lever on the railing beside me and the freight platform groans, then rises, first by inches but picking up speed into the pitch darkness above.

Normally, I'd be terrified. I can't see my hand in front of my face. The others are whimpering or all-out sobbing in fear, and that fear flows over and through my core. Vick isn't beside me, keeping me steady.

Instead, I'm grateful. No one can see the tears streaming down my cheeks.

CHAPTER 19: VICK
LOOSE ENDS

I am sorry. For some things.

"YOUR BOSS is making this hard," I mutter as Robert and I put more distance between ourselves and the safest way out. The betrayed look on Kelly's face is imprinted on my mind in its implant-enhanced perfect clarity.

"This was your plan all along."

Not my *plan*, no. But that doesn't mean my bosses didn't have this in mind.

From the moment his greedy, controlling, scarred image appeared on our transport's vidscreen, laying down the rules for our arrival, I thought I was going to kill Jacks. In general, I don't like assassination jobs. This is different.

This is personal. Jacks is never enslaving anyone again.

I glance to my right, where Robert strides with purpose and determination, his jaw set in a hard line that mars his otherwise attractive features. Definitely hadn't planned on doing this with a member of the OWLs as backup.

The bombardment from above continues, though the booms and rumbles echo from farther away—supply storage areas, security team quarters. Dust and pebbles shower us in a gray/brown mist with each distant explosion. The remaining working lights flicker off, then on again. Robert pulls a small but powerful flashlight from his belt.

If I use my eye lamps, I'll scare the living shit out of him. A chuckle threatens to erupt from my throat, but I swallow it down. Better to save that bit of fun for when it's really necessary.

We aren't the only ones in the tunnels, but we are the only ones alive. We pass a number of corpses collapsed against the walls, sprawled across the walkway: staff members, buyers, the occasional slave who wasn't in their quarters when the end came. Those hurt. We knew there would be casualties we didn't intend. We tried to minimize them. But we had to do this in one quick strike before Jacks moved his base elsewhere. The ones lying face-up are the worst, with their blue faces, distended throats, and sightless eyes. More nightmare fuel, like I don't have enough of that already. The facedown victims aren't much better, since any female form bearing a passing resemblance in hair length and physical build to Secretary Hothart or her daughter,

Cynthia, necessitates Robert toeing the body onto its back so he can be certain it isn't either of them.

Every few minutes, he tries his commlink to Hothart with no success, while I maintain communications with the strike force, but the signal is spotty even with VC1's assistance, and the primary messages I can make out between bursts of static, from the boss man Carl, himself, are "What the fuck are you doing?" and "Get the fuck out of there, now."

The direct order should override my vendetta. It doesn't. Which implies that the board implanted Jacks's death as a secret secondary objective even Carl isn't aware of. And now I'm wondering if my murderous intent is my own or a byproduct of the programming.

I am so fucked-up.

I'm attempting to send a curt reply when Robert, who's gotten a turn in the passage ahead of me, gives a startled yelp followed by one of his colorful strings of inelegant yet appropriate curses, this time involving oversexed plant life and flat beer. I cut my connection to Carl and race forward, almost colliding with my temporary partner running toward me.

"What is it?" I ask, eyes narrowed. He's paler than pale, the shaking in his limbs having nothing to do with the cold. The only color in his cheeks is greenish gray, and for a moment I fear he's going to puke on the rock floor at my feet.

I take a step backward, in case.

What could make a highly trained member of Earth's most elite security force toss his metaphorical cookies?

Robert swallows once, twice, his Adam's apple bobbing while mind overcomes stomach matter. "You don't want to know," he manages, voice hoarse.

I disregard the warning and stride past him, turning the corner into a dimmer passageway and almost tripping over the corpse sprawled across the corridor. The lights flick off, then on, and even with my enhanced eyesight, I'm scrambling to adjust. At first I notice nothing more grotesque about this body than all the rest.

Until my vision clears.

In stunned silence, I study the face. The young blond woman is beautiful in a sweet way that embodies innocence. In fact, she looks a lot like— "Kelly," I breathe softly. But that isn't the worst of it, not by a long shot. Someone or something has torn open the skimpy lace-up bodice (a slave, then) and carved deep into each ample breast with something very sharp.

The short skirt also bears rough, hastily made tearing, but I don't follow the damage any farther. My brain registers bloodstains on the victim's lower half, and that's quite enough. I can't help overlapping Kelly's face onto the girl. Bile rises in my throat. I force it down. Embarrassing myself in front of Robert won't help.

It's not her. I know it's not. But the resemblance puts me on edge. I trigger my internal comm. "Kel? You out? You okay?"

Nothing.

Too much interference from the attacking force, VC1 explains.

I nod, more to myself than in acknowledgment. If I want to assuage my anxiety, I'll need to finish my business down here that much faster.

I sense rather than see the OWL move to stand beside me. When I turn, he's staring straight ahead into the darkness of this side tunnel rather than down at the body. "It's butchery. Pre or postmortem?" he asks me, like I would know.

"Do I look like a doctor to—"

Both, VC1 says, her voice bouncing between my ears. *Some before death, some after. And recent. After the loss of atmosphere.* A few feet away, I spot a discarded breather mask with its strap snapped in two and nod.

"The implants say both and not long ago," I tell my partner, who's staring at me quizzically. "Someone down here is a sicker fuck than the rest."

"If it was a person at all. Some kind of cave-dwelling creature, maybe? Those lizard-dragons I've heard talk about?"

I snort in response. He wasn't on the raft with us when we crossed the underground lake. He doesn't know I've got personal experience with the little flying bastards.

I shake my head. "Not animal. At least I don't think so. Those slices in the... torso... are clean and precise. A bladed weapon of some kind." Or really smooth narrow claws, but the lizards' talons were curved, not straight, and we aren't close to the lake, so it wasn't them. The other injuries, judging from the brownish-red stains on the skirt, I refuse to speculate on out loud. I swallow hard, mentally kicking myself for judging Robert earlier. This is definitely puke-worthy, especially with my history.

When something stumbles out of the darkness, I almost shoot it. I jerk my gun arm to the side, then down, and move to help Robert grab the two women hanging on to each other, barely keeping their feet.

"Secretary Hothart! Thank God." Robert eases the older woman to the floor while I take her daughter, Cynthia, by one arm.

"She can't breathe," the girl informs me matter-of-factly, no panic, no concern. Her voice is monotone, the resemblance to VC1's speech making me take a closer look at her. Pale face, blank stare. Her motions are lethargic, like she's on autopilot. It's not the drugs. Those would have worn off by now, especially with all the adrenaline that must be racing through her system. It's the trauma. Good thing her political connections will get her the best treatment money can buy.

I hope it's enough.

"She's right," Robert says, bending down beside Secretary Hothart. "This breather's got a hole in it, and the converter is crushed." He points to a tear in the woman's mask and the dented two-inch-long canister hanging from it.

Moving fast, I retrieve the dead woman's mask, make short work of yanking its torn strap free, and replace it with the strap from the secretary's breather. Then I slip it over her head.

She heaves a few wheezing breaths, settling into a smoother pattern after a few moments. Nodding her thanks, she allows Robert to draw her to her feet. I'm standing between them and the mutilated body behind me, blocking as much of their view as possible. Robert guides them both around the corner, away from the gruesome sight.

"Sorry," I whisper before leaving the slave girl's body behind. "I failed you."

An image of all the rescued men and women going up on the freight elevator fills my inner display.

None of that matters to her, I tell my counterpart.

The display goes dark.

We reach the cavern with the underground lake without running into anyone else alive. Robert and the two women step through the archway. I don't. "You're not coming?"

"Rescue and destruction were only half my assignment," I say through clenched teeth. It's cold in here even for me, but that's not the only reason.

"You're really here to assassinate Jacks."

I nod. One more bit of my soul chipped away. He doesn't need to know it was a last-minute addition. He wouldn't understand how that works. "I need confirmation he's dead. I don't have it." I turn back toward the darkness and the guest and staff lodgings, then pause with an afterthought. "You're gonna need to leave your pistol and anything else significant made of metal you're carrying," I tell Robert. "The lizard-dragons will go after you if you don't."

He raises an eyebrow, his hands fumbling with the ropes tying the raft to the dock. Fortunate that it was on this side of the lake. "You're serious?"

I unzip enough of my stealth suit to reveal the healing scars. "Dead serious."

He leaves his gun with me. I attach it to my belt.

"Thank you for your assistance," he says. "I know the secretary wasn't part of your mission. If you need anything, I owe you one."

An OWL owes me. How about that? "You wanna pay me back? Lean on your bosses to give me basic human rights."

Before he can respond, I jog off the way we came, back into the darkness.

It swallows me whole. The power's down farther in, and I activate my infrared vision. Everything becomes tinged with blood.

Geez, where the fuck did that imagery come from?

VC1 sends me an image of myself with vampire teeth, droplets of red hanging from each pointy fang.

Not the best time for your humorous side, I tell her.

I am still learning the nuances of your human interactions. With practice, I will master them.

I chuckle under my breath. *Yeah, you just might.*

She says nothing else, but I get a sense of pride, almost in the way I feel Kelly's emotions through our bond. This relationship between me and VC1 just gets weirder and weirder.

Continuing down the tunnel, I pause at every juncture to check my corners. Jacks might be dead, but whoever mangled that poor slave is in here somewhere. And I have a feeling the slave boss is alive. If anyone would have quick and easy access to a fully functional breather mask, it would be him, and to hell with everyone else.

I go a few more steps before VC1 says, *My fragment in the installation security system says we have company coming.* Not, "I am detecting another lifeform." Yeah, she is getting more human every day.

"Is it Jacks?"

I can determine motion, but not details. The lighting is too dim.

"Thanks," I subvocalize, then drop into a crouch. My enhanced hearing picks up the footsteps a second later, echoing in odd counterpoint to the ongoing distant explosions and rumblings. I suppress a shiver at the continuing temperature drop and hold position. It could be anyone, so I holster my weapons. When the red-glowing heat signature turns the corner, I tackle it to the ground.

We roll over and over until we slam into the opposite wall. "What the hell?" says the figure beneath me.

I'd recognize that arrogant tone anywhere. "Hello, Jacks."

CHAPTER 20: KELLY
MISSING

Vick is alone.

AS SOON as the freight elevator raises us to the surface of the small moon, Alex, Lyle, and I usher our rescuees through the empty façade buildings to where Storm transports have blasted their way into the landing hangar. Backup teams meet us halfway, picking up and carrying most of the drugged, freezing victims, who can barely take another step. I'm not much better off, but I refuse Alex's offer of a shoulder to lean on. I do accept a heavy parka from one of the similarly dressed mercs, and a fresh breather apparatus.

When we reach the hangar, I head straight for the guest elevator… where three shivering figures watch me approach.

Three. And it doesn't take me long to figure out that none of them are Vick.

I pick up my pace, not pausing until I can wrap my hands around the lapels of Robert's jacket. "Where is she?" I shout into his stunned expression. Yes, this little empath has claws, especially when it comes to Vick. "What happened?"

He tells me, prying my fingers gently but firmly away from his clothing. With each word he utters, my eyebrows rise higher.

"You left her? Alone? You just left her down there?"

The mine is collapsing in on itself. I overheard the mercs talking about it as they passed us. It won't be long before the entire installation is one big underground pile of rubble and dust.

"Your partner is rather persuasive," Robert says. Two medics arrive and take Secretary Hothart and her daughter to a waiting ship. He moves to go with them, but I grab on to his arm. "Really, you need to stop doing that. I merely wanted to fetch a warmer coat and get a replacement weapon. I'm not taking off just yet."

I let him go, realizing my panic isn't helping anyone prepare to go back down there for Vick. I reach out with my empathic sense, but she's too far away. I can't sense her at all. Or she's already dead.

No. Peering at the flooring at my feet, I can just make out a faint blue line that disappears beneath the surface. She's alive. But she might be hurt or captured. And she's alone.

I pull my comm off my belt and try to reach her. Nothing but static answers my call.

If she gets out of this one, I'm marrying her as soon as we return to the base. Legal or not, we're having a wedding. I'm making her mine in everyone's but the lawmakers' eyes. Before I lose her again.

"Let me get some additional firepower. Don't worry. We'll find her," Robert says, reminding me he's still here.

I grit my teeth. If he doesn't hurry, I swear I'm going to punch him the way Vick taught me—no holding back, going for the most damage I can inflict in one blow.

Something whispers that this aggression is unlike me, and I should worry where it's coming from, but I ignore the concern. This is Vick. She needs backup. The Storm and everyone else put so much faith in her skill set, and it's well-deserved, but no one should be expected to overcome such odds all the time. The Storm is supposed to be a team.

Alex and Lyle jog up behind me, having delivered their charges to the transports. Alex has a medical bag and a repair kit slung over one shoulder. They pass a coat to Robert, and Lyle gives him an extra pistol. At least Alpha Team is on this. "Vick go after Jacks alone?" Lyle asks.

"Indeed," Robert admits, shrugging into the insulated parka. He depresses a button on its exterior. Red lines light up throughout the material, extending across the front and back and down both arms.

I stare at him, then find my own button and press it. Additional warmth floods my frozen body.

"Self-heating," Alex explains.

"Where is Vick?" I ask again.

Robert repeats his explanation, admitting that he wanted to go with her. "I'd like to take a few shots at that bastard Jacks myself, but someone had to see the secretary and her daughter to safety, and that duty was mine."

He's right. I know he's right. It would have been irresponsible of him to leave the two inexperienced women to fend for themselves. They could have run into more guards on the other side of the lake from where Robert says he left Vick, or on the elevator, or even up here.

"I did send the raft back to her," he says. "Or I sent it in that direction. It's got a deadman's pedal, but I held it down with a chunk of stone. It should bump the opposite shore and run onto the rocks. With her strength, I'm sure she can manage a push-off."

If. If. If. If she's not hurt. If the raft doesn't just stop in the middle of the water. If the entire complex doesn't collapse before she can get away. I make an exasperated sound, then stomp off a few feet away to regain my composure.

After giving me a minute, Alex eases up beside me. He rests a tentative hand on my shoulder. "She's very capable of taking care of herself," he says, echoing Vick's own words only an hour or so ago. Has it been that little time? "We're going down there, but she'll be fine. Are you okay? You're usually calmer than this."

"I—" What *is* wrong with me? When Vick's in trouble, I'm not calm. I'm panicking on the inside. But he's right. I don't show it like I am now. If it's really bad, my empathy takes me out of the equation altogether and I go into emotion shock. If I can function, I'm cool-headed. So what is going on?

A surge of aggression and frustration blasts me then, like a shuttle's backdraft on takeoff, and I spin around, shaking off Alex's hand and searching the hangar for the source of the powerful emotions. At first I wonder if it could be coming from Vick, but no. The blue thread representing our connection still drops below the taxiing tarmac surface of the flooring, and the balance of feelings… it's similar to Vick's signature aura, but it's not her. It's wrong. It's unstable.

Like what I picked up in the underground installation.

Whomever it's coming from, the emotional output is strong enough to break through the barrier of the dampening drugs Vick gave me.

I scan all the figures milling about, too many to pinpoint the source. Most have the hoods up on their jackets, keeping in as much warmth as possible in the absence of heat shields, and those who don't still have their faces partially obscured by the breather masks. There's no one familiar, though I'm not sure why I expect the person producing those emotions to be someone I'd recognize. Emotional responses aren't connected to physical appearance. And yet….

"Kelly?" Alex says.

I jump. He's right there. I knew he was right there. He still startles me. I need to get a grip on myself or I'll be no use to Vick when she comes back. And she will come back. She always does, even from death, just in varying states of mental and physical health. She'll need me.

Someday she won't. There may not be more clones. Someday, the Storm will send her to a permanent end. What are you going to do then, Kelly? Hmm? You're deep, deep in with her and there's no turning back.

When she does die, you'll die too, even if your body goes on living.

I tell the voice in my head to shut up.

"I'm fine," I assure Alex. "Just worried. When you go back down there, I'm going with you."

He looks like he wants to argue but thinks better of it and gives me a solemn nod. I follow him to the guest elevator and climb aboard with him and Lyle and Robert. The moment we drop beneath the surface once more, the emotional onslaught ends.

So now I have some idea of where my unusual aggression is coming from.

At least it can't affect Vick unless she's in physical contact with me and the source is still in the vicinity. She's not an empath.

Chapter 21: Vick
Karma

I deserve what I get.

JACKS IS armed. So I disarm him. He's out of breath and disoriented from my tackle. Knocking the pistol from his grasp takes little effort. It goes skittering off into the deeper darkness of the tunnel and vanishes from my infrared view.

He's also got infrared goggles on, so I yank them off and toss them aside as well. Don't need him figuring out who I *really* am. I have no intention of letting him leave this facility alive, but I'm not taking chances.

"Valeria," he pants through the breather mask. It comes out as a wheeze. I may have damaged the device or I may have damaged him. I don't much care either way. "Are you angry about the drug sample I gifted you with? Really, Valeria, the men in the room recognized a boon when they received one. People will pay a fortune to feel that good."

"You didn't warn anyone. And your 'formula' isn't calibrated for female biology. It *hurts* women, Jacks. You hurt me. That's not easy to do. And you're going to pay for it."

Jacks struggles against me, then gives a grunt of surprise when he can't shake me off. Yeah, I've got VC1-enhanced strength, an adrenaline burst keeping me in firm control of my captive.

A wave of rage heats my face and roils through my body, my red-tinged vision having nothing to do with my night sight. I think of the captive men and women and slug him in the jaw. I picture their glazed, drugged eyes and obedient compliance and punch him in the gut. I remember the look of lustful intensity while he watched the drug's effect on me, grab him by the hair, and slam his head into the stone floor.

He shouts with pain. Something warm and sticky runs over my knuckles, forming a darker puddle in the wavering shadows around his face. His grip on my arms slackens, not that it had affected my range of motion before, but his hands fall away to drop to his sides with dull, meaty thuds.

The strings of lights lining the tunnel ceiling flicker on, blinding me for half an instant before I can switch off the infrared view. I stand, one boot on either side of his torso, staring down in ultimate judgment. He's still conscious, but his gaze wavers, eyes blinking too fast like he's trying to clear his vision and failing.

I think of the insufficient safety measures in place in this godforsaken hole, the lack of enough breathers for everyone, draw back one boot, and kick him in the ribs. They crunch beneath the impact. He screams in agony. My mind registers the sound, but my emotions are far, far away, buried beneath my suppressors that at some point I ordered on full.

I picture the cold, dead eyes of the other buyers, eyes probably not unlike my own right now, but I'm too far gone to consider the implications—the way they analyzed each curve, bulge, blemish, imperfection, gave them numerical values, calculated their worth. What should they bid? What bargains might they strike? And Jacks, raising and lowering his asking prices as he evaluated his semicaptive audience and his fully captive merchandise.

Uncoiling the electrowhip from my shoulder, I step to the side and give it a few practice cracks against the stone walls. The sound snaps Jacks to attention, whatever damage I did to his skull shaken off as his eyes narrow at me. He makes half a move to rise, groans, and flops to the floor.

It takes several tries to get the hang of the unfamiliar weapon. Leaning forward or back, moving my feet, all result in the end of the whip falling harmlessly to the stone like a man's flaccid member, with no visible or audible impact. Same thing goes for too much wrist motion. It takes a smooth arc of my arm to produce the desired *crack* of sound, and my heart beats faster, excitement at my success coursing through me, with each echo of it.

Once I've got it, I flick the switch on the whip's handle and light it the fuck up.

Jacks moans in despair while his eyes trace the flicker of blue-white electrical energy moving along the length of tightly wound leather. I stand at his feet and remember.

Crack—for the way your dick hardened when Cynthia felt the touch of one of these weapons. I land the first blow across his torso right where I broke his ribs. Jacks howls. *Crack*—for how the whip made *me* feel, under the influence of his enhancement drug. The weapon strikes his tearstained cheek, forcing him to jerk his concussed skull away. His eyes widen, then close. I kick him to regain his attention.

And finally, *crack, crack, crack* at the juncture of his trembling legs for making me beg Kelly to bring me to orgasm, forcing her to degrade herself on her fucking knees beneath the table in the dining cavern, whether she saw it that way or not.

Never, ever would I have wanted to put her in that sort of mental and physical position. Never, ever will I forgive the man who did put her there.

He screams and screams, writhing beneath the whip's electrified caress, pain warring with pleasure, back arching so his wounded head presses hard into the stone. Blood pours. Blood pools.

"Stop, please, stop." Shivers run the length of Jacks's body. "I'll pay retribution. I'll cut you a special deal. Any of my stock."

"Your stock is dead," I growl, not recognizing the sound of my own voice. "Your *human beings* are dead."

"Not my fault," he argues. "I didn't launch this attack."

My hand freezes, whip held aloft, ready to bring down once more. *No. I did.*

Most of them, the great majority of them, survived. They are safe. Above ground. With others in the working breathers finding their way to the remaining elevator even now. VC1 slices through my hesitation, her voice snapping me into focus. *You did not enslave them. You did not bring them here. You did not hold them against their will. You are not to blame for those who died. Do not let the fact that you possess a human conscience dissuade you from ending a man who does not.*

All the images hit me in a rush, slaves and sex, lightning and Rodwell, airlocks, explosions, and beneath it all, my helplessness to change a single goddamned thing, my impotence, my bondage to the Storm. My utter lack of choice.

I flick the switch to a higher setting, moving the whip from the power output of a pleasure-pain sex toy to a true torture device. Jacks screams again and again, his eyes never leaving the play of electrical fire racing up and down the cord. When the sound of his voice annoys me, I press my boot on his throat, cutting off his air from the mask he wears. Then I unleash the whip upon him.

If Kelly could see me now, I would terrify her.

I don't know how much time passes. I should. My internal chronometer is infallible when I'm functioning, but I'm not really functioning, am I? All I know is that VC1 eventually cuts through the haze of blind rage I've plunged into.

Stop. You need to stop. He is dead and has been for three point four minutes. Your actions are a waste of useful energy.

I will my arm to cease its motion, but the whip touches down twice more before I succeed. I'm out of breath, panting into the breather, the whine from its cannister telling me I'm overtaxing its abilities to produce enough air for my heaving lungs.

My vision clears, focusing on the destruction I've wrought upon the body.

A bizarre calm settles over me. With extreme precision, I flick off the power and coil the whip, then loop it over my neck and shoulder. I step to the nearest wall and brace myself against it with one forearm. My other hand removes the mask from my face so I can heave the contents of my stomach onto the stone.

This is worse, so much, much worse than what I did to Rodwell. Worse than whoever attacked that slave girl Robert found. It's like something took over my mind, my body, my—I won't think "soul." How can I possibly have one after what I just did? How am I any different from that monster dismembering small children that I took out a few weeks ago?

Those children did not deserve what was done to them, VC1 murmurs in the back of my mind.

I risk another glance at what remains of Jacks and swallow hard. *No one deserves what I just did, either.*

I would disagree. However, I do not possess your human perspective.

I'm not sure my current perspective is entirely human.

Violent tremors wrack my body. Not the cold. Something much deeper, primal. I can't move, and VC1 takes control of my arm and forces me to replace the breathing apparatus over my mouth and nose before I suffocate. *Am I redlining?*

My medical analysis display appears in my inner sight, seven of the ten indicators well into the red zone. And VC1 is no longer verbally responding, meaning she's overtaxed and needed elsewhere.

Another tremor rocks me, and it takes a moment for me to realize this one is external. The entire cave system shifts, tossing me against one wall, then to the floor like a dog's discarded chew toy. I throw my arms over my head, protecting myself from a shower of stones, shattered lightbulbs, and a security camera come loose from its ceiling clamps.

A new terror grips me, almost as bad as my horror over my actions—I'm about to face one of my worst fears. I'm going to be buried alive.

The freight elevator. Is it still reachable?

No verbal response, but a blurry image of the service lift, crushed, its gate thrown into the corridor, comes up on my internal display. VC1 must have captured the shot through one of the few remaining working security cameras.

I'm going to have to use the primary guest elevator.

I stagger down the tunnel, taking the turns more by feel, careening off the walls to remain upright as I race time to get to people who can help me—Kelly and the Storm's medical personnel. Thoughts come in dramatic polarized waves, slowing me, then propelling me forward. What will Kelly think of me when she connects, when she *feels* the horror and terror of what I've done? Will she finally see me for the monster I am? Which step is one too far for our relationship?

I slow down.

VC1 pushes me on.

Static erupts in my head, communications attempting to break through interference and layers upon layers of rock. Kelly or Carl or one of the other Storm mercs trying to reach me.

Or something else. VC1 sounds strained.

Why would she push herself to communicate right now? She must be struggling just to keep me alive.

It may reduce your stress if you understand the cause of your actions. Reducing your stress would be helpful to me.

I know the cause. I'm a horrible excuse for less than half a human being. But she has my attention, what's left of it. Gritting my teeth, I tell her, "Go on." Speaking out loud helps me focus, at least a little. I'm almost to the lake. Not sure what I'm gonna do when I get there. Robert took the raft. If no one has come to back me up, I'm really screwed.

There are... transmissions... from an unknown source. Tracing has proved unsuccessful. They may be influencing you.

Or it might be wishful thinking, if an AI is capable of such. I shake my head. It makes me dizzier, and I trip on the uneven surface, stumbling three steps before I regain some balance. "Nothing's influencing me. I do violent things. I have nightmares and hallucinations of doing more violent things. Sooner or later, I was gonna cross the line again."

Will this be the line Kelly won't be able to pull me back from?

CHAPTER 22: KELLY
HELPLESS ABANDON

Vick needs help.

THE GUEST elevator reaches the bottom of the shaft, depositing us where we began this crazy mission, except the scene below is much worse for wear. There's power, which is nothing short of miraculous, but the explosions, even distant as they are, have shaken many of the hanging lights loose from their wires. Their shattered bulbs cover the tunnel floor in diamondlike glittering sparkles, catching the glow from the lights that remain.

There are bodies here too. Corpses that, according to Robert, weren't present when he and the secretary and her daughter ascended only moments ago. One guard's unbreathing figure lies with his arm out-stretched toward the lift's controls. He must have died knowing that he was within inches of his salvation. My natural empathy cries for him, even with him being our enemy, though my psychic ability picks up no trace of his emotional state at the time of his death. It's been too many minutes, and I was too far away for the impact to reach me.

"What happened?" I ask as Robert and Lyle use their strength to flip the body. He's wearing a breather. There's no sign of external injuries.

Alex bends down and removes the mask from the bluish-tinged face. He swings the medkit off his shoul-der, removes a scanner, and aims it at the body. I look away. "His breather failed," Alex says. "Well, it ran out of power. These older models don't hold a lot of charge, and considering the poor maintenance Jacks was sup-plying, all the ones down here are probably running out about now. They were designed to get people to the sur-face and a ship with its own artificial atmosphere and no longer than that."

I experience a moment of panic for Vick, then re-member that I gave her a Storm-issued breather that should be fine for several more hours.

Except she's not fine. The dampening drugs are wearing off. Adrenaline makes me burn through them faster, and I've had a lot of that. My senses are prick-ling at the back of my neck. Goose bumps rise up and down my arms beneath the parka, though I've got the built-in heater turned up to full. "We need to hurry," I tell our group.

Lyle opens his mouth to argue but thinks better of it. He's probably remembering Vick's irritation when we showed up to "rescue" her from Robert and she had it under control. But she's not in control now. I'm certain of it.

Without waiting for agreement, I set off at a brisk pace along the corridor toward the lake, not even bothering to check corners or use caution. If the breathers are all failing, I doubt anyone will be putting up any resistance at this point. To my satisfaction, the men fall into step behind me. I wonder if Vick feels this way about being in charge.

My unease increases all the way to the end of the still and silent dock. Though we have minimal light on our side of the lake, the opposite shore is shrouded in complete darkness. Somewhere in the distance, heavy crashing sounds echo over the water.

Alex presses one finger to his ear, frowns while listening to whoever is on the other end of his comm unit, and shifts his attention to us. "The boss broke through the interference. The entire installation is caving in on itself. Scans say we've got twenty, maybe thirty minutes to retrieve Vick and get out."

I nod, then stare across the water. Nothing. No sloshing or splashing, no calls for help, no bobbing lights to indicate she's on her way. But my anxiety is spiking in response to hers, and the blue glow of the line that connects us burns bright and fierce, stretching over the glossy black liquid surface.

Then, "There!" Alex shouts. He's pulled a set of macrobinoculars from inside his jacket, and he's got them trained on something out on the lake.

I strain my eyesight to spot what he's seeing. Nothing… nothing…. Two pinpricks of light appear, at this distance a millimeter apart, but I know what they are—Vick's eye lamps.

"What the—?" Robert says, incredulous. "Are those her... eyes?"

"Deal with it," Lyle growls, cracking his knuckles. "She's ours."

Even in these dire circumstances, I can't suppress a smile at that.

A few moments later, the blurred shape of the raft crawls into view, a single figure at the helm, crouched down low, keeping close to the rail, no other sign of life aboard. I wave my arms. We all do, but she doesn't return the gesture, and I hope it's because she's too intent on guiding the craft across rather than due to some injury she's sustained.

When she's a little closer, about halfway, her stress and guilt become more than I can literally stand, and I allow myself to sink to the wood of the dock, Lyle's hand on my shoulder. She's done something. Something she feels horrible about, or something she perceives she should feel guilty over. Vick's always been heavy on the self-punishment and blame even when she doesn't deserve it.

I've also seen her lose control.

It then occurs to me that if topside can reach us, I should be able to contact Vick, so I pull my comm and flip it open, transmitting to her personal code. She answers on the first buzz.

"Kel? That you?" She sounds tired, worn out even, but not in pain.

"Yes," I say on an exhale of relief. "We don't have much time. Can that thing go faster?"

A pause, and I spot some slight movement on the raft, the beams cast by her eyes shifting with her motion. "No. Even if it could, I don't want to attract attention."

I frown. Everyone else is dead. Attention from—oh. The flying kind. Right. "Wouldn't they be dead without breathable air?"

"They're native to this moon. We're not entirely without oxygen, by the way. It's just thinner than we can take, but not the lizard things. They were here before the mining company opened this facility, and they'll likely last long after we're gone."

Sometimes I wonder if there's anything Vick's AI doesn't know. "Are you okay? You feel off to me." I don't want to be more specific than that. Until I can touch her, I can't be certain.

The longer pause gives me all the confirmation I need. "I'm better than I was," she admits.

I take a deep breath. "Are you redlining?" *Are you in overload?* I want to ask, but I'm afraid of her answer.

"Three out of ten systems. Was worse before. I'm stabilizing. Things were bad for a while. VC1's taking care of me. I… I took care of Jacks."

Ah, so that's it. She's killed him. Likely in some very aggressive, more so than necessary, way. That would explain her guilt. She always worries about me too, how I'll perceive the things she does, and I admit, her methods are sometimes shocking to me. However, anything she's done to that bastard isn't going to make me judge her. "It'll be okay. Whatever happened, I'll help you work through it."

There's a catch in her voice when she says, "I know you'll try."

Okay, I don't like that response at all.

I'm coming up with encouragements when Vick's raft moves fully into the range of the lights around the dock. Movement above and behind her catches my attention, small shadows flickering against the darker ones. It doesn't take me long to figure out the source. "Vick, watch out!" I shout into the comm. My cry echoes across the expanse of water, howling "out— out—out" until it fades away.

Vick's head jerks up, redirecting her eye lamps, the beams finding a dozen or more glittery flying bodies in reds, greens, and golds. She throws her arms over her head, protecting herself as best she can, as the entire flock of them swarms down in one swoop, talons extended, wings pulled back.

To all of our horrors, they latch on, digging into her clothing, skin, hair, whatever they can grasp.

Then they lift her.

There's no one to hold her down. No Lyle with his powerful arms to grab her and pull her back to the raft. She manages to draw a pistol, and gets off a couple of shots, but I can see the damage they're inflicting, streams of red on her hands and face and scalp, torn flesh that makes me want to turn away, but I can't look from the terrifying scene before me.

The raft rocks as Vick's boot hits the railing. She's trying to get a toe around it, but she misses by inches. Her wild shots strike two or three of the lizard-dragons, their shrieks piercing like screaming banshees. Her struggling twists and turns shake one loose, then another, the injured no longer able to maintain their hold.

They drop her. Into the murky water of the underground lake.

CHAPTER 23: VICK
DEPTHS OF DESPAIR

I am well and truly fucked.

I HIT the water with a splash that cuts off when my head goes beneath the surface. But that doesn't mean it's as silent and calm as it should be. Kelly's muffled screams carry in distorted echoes to my enhanced hearing. An odd crawling sensation like pins and needles on steroids prickles over my face, neck, and hands—every inch not covered by my tactical bodysuit. Where the lizard-dragons have torn my skin, the water stings, then burns, and I swear I detect a hissing from each and every injury like someone's pouring acid into the wounds.

That is essentially correct. As I explained when we first crossed this lake, the water is corrosive. You need to get out of it as quickly as possible. VC1's got my bioscanner on my heads-up display, showing my systems that weren't already taxed creeping into the red zones.

A snarky reply comes to mind, but I'm too busy flailing and kicking for the surface to think it at her. The ravenous little beasties followed me into the lake, and they're tearing at me still. Who knew the fucking things could swim? My clothes, thin as they are, weigh me down, my heavy boots pushing at the water that seems thicker than what I'm used to. But it's also more buoyant, and my efforts bring me up fast.

The lake is mineral rich.

Is a science lesson going to help me? I ask, gasping when my head is above the surface again. It's psychological. The breather mask kept feeding me oxygen even underwater.

Likely not.

Then shut up.

I swim for the raft, a few feet away. The lizards pursue me under the water, biting at my feet and torso. I shove at them with one hand while reaching for the edge of the raft with the other, my legs churning to tread water. When my fingers wrap around the wooden flooring of the watercraft, I get my first glimpse of the damage to myself.

Muscles, tendons, even the white of bone in a couple of tiny patches are visible through the eaten-away skin on the back of my hand.

"Oh… holy fuck," I breathe, feeling the blood drain from my face.

My face.

Oh my God.

It's really just my left cheek that I feel. The other side is numb. Is that VC1 blocking my ability to feel the pain, or is the entire right side just... gone?

No input from my AI counterpart. *You've picked a helluva time to master the difference between a thought question and an actual inquiry,* I grumble at her.

I believe mastering when it would be harmful to answer such questions is a worthier goal.

Under the circumstances, that's an ominous response. No time to think about the ramifications just yet. My right hand is no better than my left, but they both obey my commands for now, and I claw my way onto the raft, which hasn't moved from when the flying terrors lifted me off it. Some kind of deadman switch that brought it to a halt without its operator. I lie on the uneven wood surface, panting, the lizards circling in the water, preparing for another strike.

Give me octosharks any day.

Something lies dark and coiled on the deck in front of me. I stretch out a hand, wincing at the ragged strips of flesh hanging from it, and wrap bony fingers around the handle of the electrowhip. With my thumb, I flip the switch to the weapon's highest setting. Blue sparks crackle up and down its length. I can't manage my feet, but I rise to my knees, swing the whip backward, and smack it against the lake's surface as hard as I am able.

Flash. Blue-white concentric rings of electrical energy expand outward from the point of contact. They pop and sizzle, catching the remaining dragon-lizards in their increasingly widening spiral. The acrid scent of ozone assails my nostrils, along with a not unpleasant aroma of cooking meat—a cross between gator bites and frogs' legs, the memory of which I pull up from some high school Spring Break Florida trip. A moment later, seven charred reptilian bodies float to the surface. The few that survived take flight and flee into the darkness of the caverns. I flop back onto the wood floor of the raft.

You need medical treatment, VC1's voice intrudes on my semiconscious drifting. My internal comm buzzes and buzzes in my skull like angry bees about to sting. It's Kelly, trying to reach me. I want to open the connection. I can't remember how.

Can't concentrate, I tell my AI counterpart.

You are in shock. You must focus.

Am I in overload? I don't think I am. The heads-up display shows me redlining in a number of my systems, but nothing life-threatening.

The damage is extreme... but for the most part cosmetic in nature. Still, it will have an impact if left untreated. Your reactions are primarily psychological, which I have had much practice at balancing. However—

I'm losing it.

Indeed.

Why doesn't it hurt? There's no pain. I'm tired. Really tired. And cold. I was shivering, but not anymore, and something tells me that's a really bad sign. The numbness I noted earlier is spreading across my face and up my arms from my damaged hands, but from what I saw, I should be screaming in agony.

As with your broken rib, for the organic injuries, I have blocked your pain receptors. With regard to the synthetic flesh that covers portions or your skull, the simulated nerve endings have been destroyed.

Destroyed. As in... what? I lift my arm from the deck, my hand at the end of it like an aftermarket

addition—I can see it, tendons and bones and sem-
ishredded muscle, but it might as well be a Halloween
decoration for all I recognize it as part of me. It responds
to my commands, but I can't feel it at all. Regardless, I
raise the semiskeletal fingers toward my face—

You do not want to do that, VC1 warns.

No monotone this time. Her internal voice promises dire consequences if I explore any further. A primal
instinct responds to that warning. I slowly change the
direction of my hand, instead letting it lower to a foot
pedal beside my head. The weight of my limb presses
the pedal down. The raft's idling engines rev higher,
propelling it once more toward the shore where my
team waits to rescue me.

Background noise resolves into shouting, which
clarifies further into words of encouragement and concern. "Come on, Vick!" "Just a little farther!" "That's
it. You've got it. Don't let up on the pressure."

I close my eyes, the raft rocking from side to side
until a dull thud tells me I've hit the dock. Hollow footfalls pound toward me, then stop. Everyone's talking
at once, Lyle calling over his comm for a status report
from topside, Alex asking to be let through since he
has the medkit, Kelly, upset because what she's feeling
from me doesn't make sense, Robert running his usual
stream of imaginative expletives.

The raft rocks harder while my team steps aboard.

My friends fall silent.

My eyes are closed, but I can feel them around me,
staring down at what must be gruesome damage.

Kelly breaks first, uttering a half gasp, half sob.
There's a thud when she hits the deck on her knees, her
hands finding my arm and holding on tight. Someone's

gagging. I think it's Lyle. There are several wet plops as he vomits into the lake over the side of the raft.

"Oh… fuck me now," Robert breathes from my opposite side, too shocked to be creative. "Is that metal? Is she a robot, then? That wasn't what our intel said. Does she feel pain?"

"Shut up," Kelly snaps. "No, she's not a robot. Of course she feels pain… only… she isn't right now. I don't know why."

The beep of a mediscanner sounds close to my left ear. "VC1's got her receptors turned off. Good thing," Alex says. "This looks a *lot* worse than it is."

"Well that's a relief, because she looks like fucking roadkill," Robert mutters. There's a loud slap.

"I told you to shut up," Kelly says.

Go, Kelly.

"Can it, or I'll throw you overboard and we'll see how *your* body handles the acid lake," Lyle adds.

"Actually," Alex says, moving the scanner up and down the length of my body, making the beeping move farther away, then closer to my head again, "her organic tissue is more resilient to the corrosives. It's the… bio-engineered flesh that's breaking down. We need to get her out of here, and we need to do it discreetly."

Right. Because while most members of the Storm have a general impression of what I am, few know the extent of it, and almost no one outside of our mercenary organization has any clue at all about me. Even I haven't seen what I look like beneath the pretty trappings. All photoscans taken during my initial surgeries have been blocked by security tight enough that my AI can't get through it.

I have a feeling I'm going to see it soon, though.

A shiver runs from the back of my neck down my spine.

"We'll have to put her in stasis. We can't let any medical teams but hers work on her. No one else knows... her eccentricities," Alex adds.

Meaning that I'm a clone, an entirely illegal life-form, and that if anyone beyond my inner circle figures that out, I'll be put to death. Of course, if that happens, I'll probably wake up again in another cloned body in the Storm's hidden research facility, and this whole process will begin anew. Knowing what I know about dying, it isn't all that comforting a thought. I return my limited attention to my more immediate issues.

I don't want to, but I'm overwhelmed by a sudden morbid curiosity. I reach for my face again. Kelly applies more pressure on my arm, holding it down. "Don't, Vick," she says, voice full of sympathy. "Let us help you first."

I force my eyes open, the right one whirring a bit in the socket, the cushioning tissue having been eaten away. It takes some effort to focus on her strained smile and tearstained cheeks. She's holding it together, but it's a fight and she's losing. I hate that I'm putting her through this. When she looks me in the face, she flinches.

She catches herself and schools her expression, but it's too late. I saw it. She's horrified and disgusted by whatever I've become.

No. What I've always been, just buried beneath a pleasing façade.

I close my eyes and turn away.

Shut me down, I tell VC1. *Put me under. Whatever you need to do to knock me out. It'll make things easier to maintain anyway.*

Seconds later, the world falls away.

CHAPTER 24: KELLY
HORRORS

Vick is terrifying.

VICK'S BODY slumps against the raft flooring, her taut muscles slackening as she loses consciousness. I shoot a concerned glance at Alex, but he isn't paying attention to me, all his focus on the mediscanner in his hands. Since he's not panicking, I take a deep breath and let it out, seeking internal calm.

I'm not finding it.

The damage to her exterior is extreme, mostly to her face and head, though her hands have suffered as well. The entire right side of her skull is now uncovered burnished metal, a protrusion of circuitry where the ear had been, crossing forward over her right cheek, then patchy bits of fake skin that eventually rejoin organic flesh slightly more than halfway across her nose and mouth. Her right eye has no lid, no covering at all, but it's dulled like a faint haze covers the lens, indicating its inactivity. The left one is closed. She must not have been able to tell the difference, that one could actually close and the other couldn't, or she would have been reaching for that too.

Thank God I didn't allow her to touch her face.

A few remaining strands of hair have dropped to cover the mechanism of her right eye. When I go to brush them away, they tear off in my hand, along with a swath of artificial scalp, revealing even more metal replacing the crown of her skull as well. I stare at the fake flesh, then with an involuntary cry, hurl it away from me into the lake.

Lyle's hand falls on my shoulder. "Steady, Kelly," he says. "They'll fix her."

Fix, not heal. Staring at the atrocity of humanity lying before me, I can't bring myself to correct him.

No. This is Vick. No matter what she looks like on the outside, it's her heart, her spirit, her soul. And she's going to need more convincing of that than ever before, especially if she catches a glimpse of her current condition.

I push to my feet. "Let's get moving." To punctuate my statement, more rumbling crashes sound from across the lake, closer than before.

Robert and Lyle lift Vick's unconscious form, Robert taking the feet and Lyle the shoulders. I note that the OWL keeps his eyes on her undamaged legs the entire time.

"They're prosthetics," I admonish him as we step from the raft and plod down the dock. "Her eye, her ear. If it were an arm or foot, you wouldn't think twice about it."

Robert frowns. "It's her entire bloody skull, and from what I understand, most of her brain. And yes, I'm thinking twice. At what point does she become something other? She wants basic human rights. What if she's no longer basically human?"

"If you weren't helping to carry her, I'd punch you," Alex mutters.

"If I really didn't give a damn, I wouldn't be helping to carry her," Robert shoots back. "Look," he continues as we tromp toward the guest elevator, "I'm not saying she isn't entitled to rights. I'm just questioning her status." He glances at me. "Don't think I didn't see you flinch away when you looked her full-on in the face. It's not an easy thing to take."

Damn. I'd hoped he hadn't noticed, that Vick hadn't noticed, that her losing consciousness at that precise moment had been a necessity, not an avoidance tactic.

"It was a human reaction," Alex says to me. "You couldn't help it. No one could have. She'll understand. She'll forgive you."

Vick will. But she won't forget it. She'll add it to her ever-growing list of reasons why she isn't good enough for me. I rub the inside of my ring finger with my thumb, the absence of the engagement ring even more palpable. Vick's questions about a soul, and now this. I worry she'll talk herself right out of marrying me.

I need to reconvince her, and I need to get her through this.

We reach the lift and file aboard, the interior lights coming on and the doors sealing behind us. This is much more comfortable than the freight cage I went up in earlier. Sensing the endless walls passing on either side and knowing just how far down we were was an unnerving experience I don't wish to repeat. But when Alex hits the controls, nothing happens.

"Um…," he says, pocketing the mediscanner and pulling a diagnostic device in its place. A moment passes, then he's using a multitool to strip off the metal panel and toss it aside.

The car rattles with another not-distant-enough cave-in. Lyle's comm unit buzzes. He balances Vick's upper body on one knee and answers it. Several terse grunts later, he clicks off. "Five minutes. We've got five minutes to get the hell out of here before the whole thing collapses."

"No way I can get this thing moving in five minutes," Alex warns. He laughs without humor. "It's on a safety override. Seems its onboard systems think the mine shaft is too unstable to ascend."

"We're all gonna die if it doesn't," Lyle says.

"It's not sophisticated enough to convince."

"No, but VC1 is." I move closer to Vick's inert figure. Lyle has a firm grip on her now, he and Robert holding her flat and even. "VC1," I address her, feeling foolish. "Can you take control of the lift?"

Robert blinks at me. "Who are you talking to?"

Before I can respond, the tiny screen on Alex's diagnostic device flashes once, twice, then words scroll across it.

IF I DIVERT MY FOCUS,
SHE WILL REGAIN CONSCIOUSNESS.

No need to explain who "she" is. "If you don't, we're all going to be buried alive," I say to the air.

No more words appear, but several indicator lights within the elevator control panel light up, then flash in random sequence. The metal surrounding us creaks. A grinding sound echoes through the compartment along with the rattle of a shower of pebbles and rocks striking the roof of the car. Then we're moving, crawling really, but making our way up the shaft toward the surface.

Vick groans, then lets out a sharp gasp and struggles against the hands holding her. "Down. Put me down," she manages.

The guys comply, propping her to sit upright against the side of the car. I'm moving to her when another jolt rocks us, throwing me against the elevator's wall. Robert staggers into me. Lyle and Alex steady each other; Vick slides into the corner, giving a yelp when she hits. From above us, there's a loud *crack* and a metal *twang* and the whole car tilts sideways at a terrifying angle. The grinding sound increases in volume. We're still rising but moving even more slowly than before.

"We've lost one of the cables," Alex shouts over the din. "Just need the last one to hold a little longer. I think we're close."

A creak is the only warning we have before the overhead lighting comes loose from its fastenings, swinging down on a single set of hinges. Lyle shifts to brace himself like a human tent over Vick's huddled figure, his arms rigid against the corner walls above her. The light bar breaks free and crashes to the floor in a shower of sparks.

Darkness. Noise and darkness. No way to tell how far we have left to go.

"Kel?" Vick calls into the empty air. "My eye lamps aren't working."

"It's okay. Don't worry." And then we stop.

For a second, I think this is it. The lift has failed. We're stuck, and soon the collapsing shaft will send us plummeting to our deaths with an immediate burial beneath all the rock and stone.

A bell chimes, its high-pitched tone far too cheerful for the circumstances. The doors slide halfway apart, then halt, revealing the hangar bay sideways to our view since we're hanging at a sharp angle.

"Out. Out now. Move! Move!" Lyle shouts. He scoops up Vick in his powerful arms, getting through the breach first, with the rest of us not far behind them. We take maybe ten steps from the lift before the tearing of metal has us all turning back.

A *snap* like a firecracker going off in our ears. Then the entire thing breaks free and drops away. We catch a fleeting glimpse of the ragged cable trailing after it and disappearing into the darkness. The shaft is too long for us to hear the impact below.

"Oh… fuck…," Vick whispers.

At first I think she's referring to our narrow escape, but when I turn toward her, I see her with her hand to her cheek, or rather, her missing cheek, her good eye wide with horror, her remaining skin so pale it's practically transparent, showing the veins beneath.

Most of the time, Vick keeps her nails blunt. Long, pretty nails, though they can be effective weapons, interfere with practical things like handling knives and pulling triggers. They catch in delicate gear and tear off in painful jagged edges. However, for this assignment, as part of her Valeria Court persona, Vick had grown them out. Now, as she moves her fingertips across the exposed metal of her skull, they send up an earsplitting screech.

I've never heard Vick scream before.

I'm hearing it now.

CHAPTER 25: VICK
UNWANTED INFLUENCE

I am a monster.

I KNOW I'm screaming. I know I'm upsetting Kelly beyond all imagination. She's never seen me like this, even at my worst.

Guess I've hit a new worst.

I know I'm attracting attention. Anyone in the hangar who wasn't already running toward us after the lift broke free and fell is definitely heading our way now that I'm shrieking at the top of my lungs, though I'm growing hoarser by the moment.

Some remaining logical part of me notes that my vocal cords will give out well before my terror does.

I scrunch my eyes shut, or try to. The left closes. The right turns off. My eyelid is missing. Oh God, my eyelid is fucking *missing*. Somehow I manage to scream louder.

Lyle is shushing me, making soothing noises and holding me closer to his chest. I feel Kelly take my hand and pull it away from my head. "Shh, Vick. It's okay. Everything is going to be okay," she says, but her voice wavers. She's not sure. Her uncertainty carries through our bond.

"We need to hide you," Alex says. Something warm and heavy drops over my face. A jacket, maybe.

Right. Hide me. So I don't frighten everyone. So they don't shoot me on sight like the monster I am.

No. Because they don't understand and because your components are classified.

VC1! I'm relieved to hear her. It means I'm not overloading, though I'm sure I'm redlining everything.

You are, she admits.

Can you make me stop freaking out? I can't control it. It kills me to admit that, even if it's only to the AI, but I'm imagining what I look like right now, and it's every nightmare I've ever had rolled into one.

I am maintaining your other systems. You will need to regain control yourself.

Fat chance.

I'm being carried across the tarmac, my screams reducing to whimpers, then occasional moans. Kelly's walking beside Lyle, with a death grip on my arm to keep me from being stupid again. The other arm is tucked between me and Lyle's muscular chest. Even with his strength, he's panting with the effort by the time the sound of his footfalls changes and we clang up a metal ramp into what I'm assuming is the shuttle that brought us here. Was that only last night?

"Gotta get her in a stasis box," Alex says. His steps pick up speed as he pushes past us in the ship's narrow corridor.

A hatch *whooshes* open and shut. Antiseptic smells and equipment humming—the shuttle's tiny medbay. I'm placed on a table, Kelly still holding down my arm. "You can let go," I tell her, throat raw and voice cracking. "I won't do it again." No way in hell am I touching my metal skull again. A shiver runs the length of my body.

She eases up on the pressure but doesn't release me. Not sure if she doesn't trust me to keep my word or if she needs the physical contact. That's fine. I need it too.

Someone lifts the jacket off me, replacing it a moment later with a heated blanket—a stopgap to ease my constant chills while they prepare what I'll need. Off to my left, there's lots of movement, containers opening and closing, hydraulics *hissing* as a stasis pod is opened.

The sound ignites a new round of panic. Stasis pods resemble coffins—tight, narrow spaces they lie a damaged body in, pump it full of hibernation drugs, then close the lid and transport it to a more advanced medical facility. I've woken up in a few of them, lids open. I've never been conscious when I was put inside one.

The moment two sets of hands prepare to lift me again, I fight back, kicking and twisting, muscles shrieking in pain while I attempt and fail to get free. "No. Nonononono." I'm not being rational. I know this is what has to happen. I can't stop myself.

The door to the medbay opens again. "What the hell is going on in here?" A new voice, angry, and one I recognize—Carl, my boss in Undercover Ops. His steps bring him to the side of my table. "Shit, what happened to her?" No anger now. In fact, it's almost gentle. A new set of hands, probably Carl's, join the others in grabbing hold of me. "Drug her first, then move her," he orders. He leans down to my ear. "VC1, you are not to interfere with the preliminary narcotics or the stasis drugs."

"Acknowledged," my mouth says, though it isn't me speaking. My eyes widen; then I remember. Carl is my superior officer. My loyalty programming forces compliance with a direct order from my commander, unless it would place me in harm's way, and no matter how claustrophobic I am, the logical part of my brain knows they're trying to help, not harm me. Carl doesn't even need to use a code. I glare up at my boss.

He returns it with a sympathetic look of his own. "You know I don't like doing that," he says. "But you need medical care you aren't allowing us to give you."

They set me back down on the table, then hold me in place. There's a pinprick on the inside of my elbow, the squirm-inducing sensation of a needle sliding into a vein, then soothing warmth rushes up my arm, down into my chest, up into my head. Things get fuzzier from there. A lethargy like I've never known settles over me. Muscles I didn't realize were taut slacken. My body seems to sink into the table, solid though it might be. I open/activate my eyes. Blurred figures move with purpose around me. A familiar feminine outline hovers to my right—Kelly. Even drugged, I'd know her anywhere.

"Hey," she says, not looking directly into my face. Of course she's not. A tiny chill invades my warmth, quickly chased away by the narcotics. "Better?"

"A little," I say, the words coming out slurred, my tongue too thick for my mouth.

She smiles, amused by my impaired speech. "Sounds like it. Give it a minute more."

Kelly's right. She usually is. After about another minute, I'm floating on clouds, the pain and fear still there but smothered under pillows of euphoria and calm. She studies me, then nods at what she sees or senses.

"Ready to go into stasis now?" she asks, squeezing my shoulder.

"Sure…," I murmur. "Whatever you want." What *I* want is to sleep for days, maybe weeks. I want to forget what I did to Jacks, what the dragon-lizards and the lake did to me. I want all this horror to be a nightmare I'll wake up from. In my current state, it feels like a dream. "Am I dreaming?" I ask, fighting unconsciousness.

She shakes her head, frowning. "Not yet. Soon."

"Damn," I whisper and let them lift me into the padded box. It's soft and comfortable in there, not at all scary like before. I can't remember why I fought this.

Confident I won't struggle, my teammates release me and move around, making final adjustments to the stasis controls before they will close the lid. I miss Kelly's touch, the imprinted memory of her hand on my shoulder still warm and tingly, but she can't come with me where I'm going.

We have a problem, VC1 says, intruding on my haze.

"Mmm, no, we don't," I mutter out loud.

"Vick, you okay?" Kelly asks, leaning over me.

"Fine. Just chatting with the AI."

"Shhh," she whispers, placing a finger on my lips and glancing over her shoulder where Robert is talking with Carl and Lyle. "She's a secret, remember?"

"Right… secret." One that neither Robert nor Carl knows. I'm supposed to keep it that way. Can't remember why, but it's important. I stop babbling. My eyes drift shut/shut down. I'm going under.

Wake. Up. VC1 again.

You are being a real pain in the ass, I tell her. The hydraulics on the stasis box activate. Kelly steps away. The lid locks into place over me. I don't mind at all.

There is an anomaly. I need your human input as to the possible cause.

I sigh, noting on my next intake of breath the sweet scent of the hibernation gases flooding my enclosed space. *Better explain fast. I'm high and getting higher. Any input I give will be highly suspect.* Hah. "Highly" suspect. I chuckle to myself, drawing in more of the gas.

I am monitoring the shuttle's security systems. There is a discrepancy in the weight of the craft between when we arrived here and our current mass.

Mmm. I purposely take in a huge lungful of gas. It tingles in my nostrils, tickling as it goes down my airway into my chest. So good. Everything feels so good. I don't recall ever feeling this good before, and I want more of it. My breaths come deep and even. *That's just Carl*, I tell the AI, trying to hold scattered thoughts together long enough to appease her. I wonder if she can nag me even while I'm in stasis. That would suck.

I have taken Carl's mass into account. This is something more. Not the refueling. Not additional cargo. It is moving.

Something prickles at the back of my neck, and it's not the effect of the gas. *Moving?* I should be concerned. Part of me is, but it's so far detached from the rest that I can't latch on to the feeling or act upon it.

I cannot identify the source, nor am I able to access external means of communication. I cannot inform any other member of Alpha Team. It is as if I am being blocked in some way. When I attempt to focus security cameras on its location, those cameras momentarily cease to function. When I trace the records of the weight shift, those records have been wiped from the ship's memory, and... something is attempting to erase them from my own....

Wait. What? She's telling me there's a computer intelligent enough to tamper with her memory. But that's impossible. The only thing that would be capable of something like that would be... another AI. Or something very near equivalent.

My primary directive programming made a grave error in keeping information from you. Your confidence was misplaced. I am unworthy as a teammate. You are in danger. I must tell you ... that ... I must ...

I stop sucking in the gas, holding my breath for as long as I'm able while my drugged-out mind attempts to make sense of what she's said. Panic fights with the soothing narcotics, but I'm too far gone, too high to come back down. My enhanced hearing picks up muted alarms, the medsensors' response to my sudden emotional upheaval and internal struggle. Outside the stasis box, they must be blaring, startling my team into frantic action. I try to raise my hands to beat against the glass casing, but at some point soft wrist and ankle cuffs locked me into place.

I activate/open my eyes to see Kelly with both her palms pressed to the transparent casing, her face twisted with worry, mouthing to me to calm down, that it's okay. I shake my head, no, but she doesn't understand.

Relax, VC1 says, monotone. *Everything is fine.*

No. It's not. You just said you were being infiltrated, tampered with, that I'm in danger. What were you trying to tell me?

Everything is fine, she says again with no inflection. *I am fine. There is nothing wrong. Sleep.*

They've gotten to her. That's it, isn't it? Whatever she was worried about, it's erased her memory of ever having been concerned, except the remnants of my organic brain remember it. Whatever it is, it can't tamper with that.

You are very tired, and you are damaged. Sleep.

I'm not the only one, I think back at her, but she isn't listening.

The hiss of the stasis gas increases in volume. I wonder who turned it up, my team or VC1. Regardless, I can't hold my breath any longer, and I let it out with a rasping gasp, taking in another full breath of the sleep inducers almost immediately.

My vision blurs, then goes dark. My last thought is to wonder whether I'll recall any of this when I wake up. Assuming that whatever has boarded our shuttle doesn't kill me in my helpless state of stasis sleep.

CHAPTER 26: KELLY
IS ANYBODY THERE?

Vick is in stasis.

WHEN VICK finally lets go and drops into unconsciousness, I sag into Lyle's arms. The medbay alarms die down, then cease their wailing. The rest of us stare at one another in the sudden silence.

"What happened? I thought she was completely out of it. Then she's fighting off the drugs like they're poison." Alex looks to me for answers. I don't have them.

"That… shouldn't have been possible. I gave her a direct order." Carl never takes his gaze off the stasis box, Vick's face now relaxed through the view window.

Robert scoffs. "Hard to obey an order when you're drugged and confused."

Right. He doesn't know. He doesn't realize that VC1 should not have allowed Vick to fight breathing in the gas, that Carl's order would have triggered her loyalty programming unless... I swallow a surge of panic of my own. "Alex," I say, getting everyone's attention with the fear in my voice, "double-check her readings. Is she stable? Is everything all right? She has other chemicals in her system, that pleasure drug of Jacks's. Could there be a bad combination? Could what we gave her be harming her in some way?"

Alex steps to the side of the stasis box, examining the readings that mean nothing to me, but there are a lot of green blinking and steady lights. "No, she seems fine. I mean, as fine as she can be with her injuries, but nothing life-threatening. Jacks's crap wore off almost an hour ago." He sounds unsure, though. Like the rest of us, he knows she shouldn't have fought the way she did.

"Hmm," Carl says, rubbing the stubble on his chin, then covering a yawn. We've all been awake and on duty for too many hours. "Well, comm me if there are any further problems. I'll be on the main passenger transport, overseeing the return of the slaves to Earth and from there to wherever their homeworlds might be. I want Alpha Team to report back to Girard Base immediately and start Vick's medical team on making her repairs."

"You mean healing her injuries," I correct him.

He waves me off. "Right. Whatever. Just do it. I need her functional and on duty as soon as possible." So much for the almost compassion he showed her earlier. Without looking back, he exits the medbay. A few moments later, a chime sounds over the shipwide PA, letting us know he's used the exterior hatch.

"Sometimes our boss is a class-A asshole," Lyle says. He glances down at me. I'm still leaning against him. "You good? Or do you need me to walk you to your cabin?"

"I can manage. Thanks." I push away from his chest, give Vick one final once-over, and head out. He and Alex follow me down the corridor, arguing over who's going to fly us home. With all of us exhausted, normally we'd let VC1 take over, but I don't want to attempt to distract her from monitoring Vick, if she's even functional while Vick is in stasis.

They eventually decide on four-hour piloting shifts with Lyle taking the first turn and Alex heading for his own bunk. Lyle heads for the cockpit. Alex and I walk aft in companionable silence. We reach his cabin first.

"Do you really think she's okay?" I ask one more time.

Alex nods, but it's hesitant. "All the indicators say so, and VC1 would find a way to let us know if something is really wrong."

"But Carl's command—"

"I know," he says, holding up a hand to forestall my argument. "But the scanners show no problems. Maybe VC1 was fooled by Vick's claustrophobia and thought Vick was in actual danger for a minute. Maybe she found one of those loopholes in the loyalty programming Vick's mentioned a couple of times."

I nod, wanting to believe it. VC1 has been searching for a way to set Vick free from her Storm ties, to eliminate the programmed compulsions that make Vick do whatever her superiors ask of her. To the best of my knowledge, though, the AI has been unsuccessful so far.

"Get some sleep, Kelly," Alex says, giving me a sympathetic smile. "I've got her monitors set to alert all of us if anything goes wrong while she's out. I even ran a quick diagnostic on the backups. She's covered."

I nod, stifling a yawn of my own, and let him step into his cabin and shut the hatch. Still, I can't shake the uneasy sense that follows me into my own berth, hovers around me while I change into sleep shorts and a soft T-shirt, and nudges at my senses as I crawl beneath the covers of the lower bunk. I drop my psychic walls and reach toward the medbay with my empathic sense.

Nothing. I sense no emotions from her. I can just barely detect Alex's worry despite his assurances. Lyle reads as exhausted, but a moment later there's a spike in his energy, probably indicating he's taken an approved stimulant for his four-hour stint in the pilot's chair.

I can't tell if my inability to read Vick is due to the stasis field, her suppressors, or something else, but there are so many factors, I shouldn't be concerned. And yet I am.

The blue line that connects us, that signifies the love and affection we feel for each other, is wide and bright, leading from where I lie to disappear through the cabin door. That's a positive sign. When she's severely weakened or in any kind of extreme physical distress, the line fades to a dull bluish gray and narrows as if it were drawn by a pencil rather than a paintbrush.

It's all the comfort I'm going to get, so I let my head drop back onto the pillow and close my eyes. A small twinge of guilt nags at me as I allow my body to relax. I'm permitted a full eight hours or more of sleep while the guys get catnaps. But my piloting skills aren't up to being unsupervised and in full control, so it is what it is.

Before long, I'm drifting off.

My dreams are of Vick. They usually are, and they take on one of two genres—horror or romance.

The horrific ones have me reliving some of our worst moments: the shuttleport attack in North Carolina where I watched her die, or when I very briefly "killed" her in the courtroom on Girard Moon Base, or worst of all, when she died after being struck by lightning. And yes, I'm well aware of the running theme throughout them all. Vick dies. I watch. Or in the last case, I listen. And yet, after going through that with her again and again, I learned my lesson early on. I'm not tempted to block her love for me ever again. Whether I lose her that way or through some final death, the pain and torment will be the same—unbearable. So I will enjoy what we have together to the fullest I am able, for as long as fate gives us.

The romantic dreams, though, they make me want to go to bed early, especially when Vick is off on a mission without me. Ever since Vick's memories of Rodwell and what he did to her had been blurred, she's been much more willing to engage in amorous activities.

With the return of all her more pleasant memories, she's got a wide repertoire of locations, approaches, and positions to choose from, her lack of sex toy knowledge notwithstanding. Since she's my first and only lover, she's taken great pleasure in showing me everything she knows, and those things stick with me.

I'm in the middle of one of the good dreams when something disturbs my sleep. I'm warm and cozy beneath the blanket, worn out from our exertions to rescue the slaves, and I was deep in REM, so I'm pretty groggy when I roll over to see why I'm awake.

The door to my cabin is just sliding shut, a shadow slipping through at the last moment.

Except the guys are either asleep or in the cockpit, and Vick is in stasis.

I throw off the covers and race through the door and down the hall to the medbay. The hatch barely gets out of my way in time for me to avoid crashing into it. I skid into the small room, slipping and sliding in my socks, not having bothered to put on my boots.

Everything is quiet. Vick's stasis box is undisturbed, her passive face relaxed and unlined in sleep. The equipment hums softly, emitting an occasional beep when her vital signs are regularly scanned. There's no indication of any problem. Vick hasn't moved.

I don't have my comm, so I step to the wall beside the door and activate the shipwide intercom. "Lyle? You up on the bridge?"

"Kelly? No, it's me, Alex. I took over for Lyle about thirty minutes ago. You need something? You're supposed to be asleep."

I hesitate. What do I need? "I think I need your tech expertise."

"Well, I can't leave the bridge, but head on up here and I'll try to help."

Three minutes later I'm sitting in the copilot's chair, trying to phrase my request so I don't sound like a raving lunatic. "I was out of it, just waking up. I could have dreamed it," I begin. "But I swear I saw someone leaving my room a few minutes ago. I checked on Vick in the medbay. She's fine. You're here, and—" I lean over and check a readout on the console. "Biosigns place Lyle in his cabin. So what did I see?"

Alex mulls it over. "We're all exhausted. Under-cover Ops is running us ragged, especially Vick. Look, I can check the security footage of your cabin for the last half hour." He reaches forward and fiddles with some of the controls. A vidscreen activates in the lower right corner of the forward viewport. The timestamp shows it as thirty minutes prior. "Here, I'll speed it up."

"Are we always being recorded?" I ask, a little unnerved that there's footage of me undressing somewhere. Or going to the bathroom. Or bathing.

"This is a Storm shuttle. Yes, we're monitored. No one watches it unless there's an issue. And after each mission debriefing, the footage is stored and locked down. You'd need to file a special request to see it and have a damn good reason."

That… doesn't really make me feel better about it, but I can't change it.

We watch the feed in silence. I'm not a restless sleeper. Other than rolling onto my side once, I don't change position during the entire half hour.

Nothing else changes, either.

The door doesn't open. No one enters the room. Then without warning, I wake up, throw off the covers, and race from the cabin. A second camera picks me up in the corridor, and a third catches my actions in the medbay. I look like a crazy person.

"Must have been a vivid dream," Alex says with a sympathetic smile. "You were deeply asleep. Seems normal enough to me."

"Maybe," I acknowledge. Except, no matter which way I turn it in my head, it feels real. Contrary to the evidence, I would swear someone had been in the room with me, and my empathic sense says that someone meant me harm.

CHAPTER 27: VICK
MIRROR, MIRROR

I am disturbed.

OF COURSE I can't just go into stasis and catch up on the sleep I've lost, have a nice, peaceful, restful experience, wake up refreshed. No, that would be normal. By all accounts, most patients come out of stasis well-rested and not remembering anything from the time spent in the box.

Me? I dream. And I do it vividly.

My first sense is one of intense longing, so powerful it hurts like a gaping hole has been cut in the center of my chest. I'm both parched and starving, but not craving water and food.

I want Kelly. So painfully that I feel incomplete without her.

So I go find her.

One minute I'm in the stasis box, my sensory perceptions cut off from the rest of the world. The next, I'm moving along the transport's central corridor, being pulled like a fish hooked on a line. Except I'm not struggling against it. I want to be caught.

I am cautious, though. I check my corners. I'm careful not to trigger any hatches into opening. I have the implants deactivate the security cameras, instead instructing them to show and record old footage of empty passageways, leaving no trace of my being there. It makes no sense. Why am I hiding? I'm part of this team. Am I worried they'll be mad that I left stasis?

Which prompts the most important question. How did I get out of the box?

I'm able to rationalize the answer pretty easily. I didn't get out. I'm still inside, dreaming. But it's all so very real. And if it's a dream, why am I sneaking around? Cameras aren't going to record my dream self.

Regardless, I creep along until my implants inform me that I've reached the cabin Kelly and I had been sharing on our way out to the slave installation. Except I shouldn't need that information. I already know this.

I step into the range of the hatch's proximity detector, allowing this door to open. It slides aside, casting a swath of bright light across the metal flooring. The bunks remain in shadow on the left side, Kelly curled up, facing the wall, sound asleep.

And she's beautiful, the way her thick blond hair flows across the blanket in soft waves, the curve of her body beneath the thin covering, the gentle sound of her breathing in the otherwise silent compartment.

I move to the side of her bunk. The hatch closes behind me, plunging the room into near darkness again, emergency lighting along the walls casting a faint glow throughout the small space. Closer now, I view her face in profile, the delicate slightly turned-up nose, the long lashes, the full lips.

I want… I don't know what I want. But I'm incomplete. I have to make her mine, part of me, fill that hole that's widening around my heart. And I don't know how to do that.

Again, I'm struck by the inconsistencies. I already have her. She's mine. We're bonded by our empathic connection and by love. Kelly says for her it takes on a physical representation, a thick bright blue line that runs from her soul to mine. She's still convinced I have a soul.

I'm still not sure.

Especially right now.

Right now, I have the terrifying urge to shake her awake, force her to open the channel between us, pour my negative feelings into her through that connection—and I have so many dangerous emotions right now: anger, fear, lust. It would overload her, send her into emotion shock, and I. Don't. Care.

Back at the slave base, I couldn't get to Kelly, so I took a replacement, a girl who looked like her, but she didn't *feel* right. She had no gift. She couldn't take my pain. I found no connection, so I carved one out of skin and flesh. When she died, I felt nothing, but the hole widened. The need increased.

I'm incomplete.

I will be whole.

I reach toward Kelly's shoulder, but when my fingers are inches from contact, she mutters something unintelligible, then rolls toward me. "Vick...," she sighs, still deep in sleep. So much love, so much affection in that one word. It hurts. I snatch my hand away. Her eyelids flutter, and I race for the door. The bunk creaks with the shifting of her weight as she sits up, but the hatch slides shut behind me.

Not clear yet. I need a hiding place. The computer in my head directs my attention to the overhead ventilation system. But that's wrong too. It's not a computer. It's an AI, a... friend, and her name is—

Flash. Then pain and more pain. Blinding white lights pierce through my eyeballs, seeking the remnants of my organic brain and lancing it with agony. I squeeze my eyelids shut, wondering when I opened them.

Do not do that again, VC1's voice warns in my head.

I'm disoriented, the last vestiges of the nightmarish dream fading into vague memory. *Where the fuck am I?* Hints nudge my senses: the lack of a ship's murmuring engines, a hard table beneath me, antiseptic smells, humming and beeping medical equipment.

At a guess, I'm back on Girard Moon Base in the Storm's medcenter or some other facility of its like.

You are correct. You are also still damaged, though some repairs have been made, and your timing is inopportune. Your heightened emotional state has burned off the anesthesia faster than anticipated and I am having difficulty returning you to unconsciousness. Between surgeries is not a good time for wakefulness.

I was having a nightmare, I tell her, turning my head from side to side, listening for other clues. *Can't remember the details.* No people in the room. I really have surprised them. But the monitors are beeping faster, and somewhere distant an alarm sounds, muffled by a closed door.

That should not be possible. Stasis patients do not dream.

I'm not typical, I remind her, unnecessarily. If anyone knows how different I am from most human beings, it would be VC1. After all, she's a major part of the difference. There's something else too. Something disturbing that happened right before Alpha Team closed the lid and put me under. But it's all hazy and vague and I can't separate reality from dreams. Whatever it was, it slips from my mind like sand through a sieve.

I blink again, opening and closing my eyes too quickly to see whatever it is VC1 doesn't want me to see, relieved that I now have two eyelids to blink with. So yeah, they've fixed some things. But not everything, according to my AI. I flex my hands at my sides. Some soreness, but nothing unbearable, so those have been repaired as well.

But what about…? Curiosity swells like a rising tide. I wrap my fingers around the edges of the table I'm lying on, bracing myself.

VC1 figures it out a moment before I take further action. *Do not*—she warns, but too late.

I open my eyes and keep them open.

It takes a moment for them to adjust to the brilliant white surgical lighting. It glints off the metal instruments gripped by robotic limbs positioned all around my head—immobile now, but no doubt in use on me within the last hour.

Mechanical surgery for a mechanical being. The irony is not lost on me.

I lift my head with effort, noting the wide view window embedded high up on the wall past my feet. There's motion behind the glass, undistinguishable figures, some facing me, other rushing about doing indeterminable things, but I'm too weak, and my head drops back down with a dull thud.

Movement to my left and right draw my attention there, and I freeze from the inside out.

Mirrors. Two of them on each side, spotless reflections of my ill-conceived miniscule actions. The doctors in the observation booth would use them to view every step of the robotically conducted surgery, checking for precision and error.

I want to crawl under the table, but the damage is done. I can't hide from my own reflection.

My eye might have been fixed, and they've replaced my ear. But that's the extent of the surgeries my med team has performed so far. I can see why the doctors needed a break.

I'm as horrific, as grotesque, as I'd feared. The right side of my "face" glints in the harsh overhead lights, the metal flashing with each small movement of my head. My right eye blinks back at me, seeming out of place in its inhuman landscape of steel. The ear on that side, covered in synthflesh, stands out even more with no hair to hide it and everything around it in varying shades of gray.

My left cheek fared better. The real organic skin on that side is pock-marked in some places, crisscrossed by healing scars in others. When they're done with me, none of this nightmare will be visible, the injuries concealed, the metal buried beneath a "Vick Corren" mask that's fooled everyone, including me, into believing I'm a living, breathing human being.

I knew. I've known since the accident. But I wanted the illusion. I needed it. When VC1 told me she couldn't break the encryptions on my medical records,

I didn't press her to keep trying. Deep down, I didn't want to see.

And now I have.

I take a deep breath that stutters in my chest. A single tear slides over the metal planes of my manufactured face like a raindrop down a corrugated roof.

A robot that cries. The Tin Man with a heart at last. And it's breaking.

Somewhere behind me, a door slides open. Familiar footsteps cross to my side. Gentle fingers take my hand and hold it. "You weren't supposed to wake up until they were finished," Kelly whispers. "I reminded them that you need larger doses, and they listened, but you woke up anyway."

I turn my head away. She lets go of my hand, takes my chin, and turns me back toward her. I close my eyes. "Don't look at me," I croak, sounding like I swallowed nuts and bolts.

"Why not?"

"Because you'll flinch away. Again." I give myself a mental kick. I hadn't intended to mention that slip of hers at the slaver hideaway. But it hurt, and I'm hurting still.

A sigh. Her soft exhalation tickles my one skin-covered cheek. "I didn't flinch because of how you look," she says. "I flinched because of how much it must have hurt you, even with your suppressors running on full, even if I couldn't feel it."

"You're ly—" I stop, unable to make the accusation of falsehood. Her fingertips stroke my chin. We're in physical contact. My suppressors are down. Her love washes over me through our bond, drowning pain and self-hatred, or at least smothering them for a time. I open my eyes and stare into hers. "You're *not* lying."

"No. I'm not. You can't lie to me. It's unfair if I try to lie to you."

I keep staring, disbelieving, but unable to doubt my own senses. More tears follow the first. "Why?" I breathe. "Why do you keep loving me? Why would you want me the way I am?"

"Oh, Vick." She leans down, laying her head on my chest, wrapping her arms around my trembling form. I'm covered in a thin hospital gown and shivering from more than cold. "For one reason, because you don't know how amazing you are," she says, voice muffled against my shoulder. "You're brave, loyal, protective, you encourage me to try the most incredible things, but you're always there, watching out for me." She lifts her head, her breath warm and close to my ridiculous human-looking ear sticking out of my steel cheek. "And you're fantastic in bed."

I sputter, the tears flowing freely now. I could ask VC1 to stop them, but I don't bother. "God, I love you," I say, using my healed hands to pull her closer.

"Like no machine ever could," she agrees. She taps her engagement ring against the one on my finger. She must have retrieved them from the shuttle's safe and replaced mine on my hand once I got out of stasis. "When they're done with you, and you're up to it," she continues, "we're sealing this deal. I'm not waiting for anything else to take you from me. When Medical lets you go, we're getting married, legal or not."

CHAPTER 28: KELLY
MONSTERS

Vick is not herself.

THE WEDDING ceremony I'm hoping for has to wait longer than I expect. Obstacle one is Vick herself. Not that she's opposed to the idea; she proposed to me, after all, but she's been stalling, her self-esteem issues and the fact that it can't be legal getting in the way. My drive surprises her, and I sense she still feels she's unworthy, but my insistence is convincing her little by little. However, she isn't recovering from her injuries at her usual superhuman rate.

Oh, the physical ones and the cosmetic damage have all but disappeared. Thin lines serve as reminders of where the surgeons put her back together, but in a few days, even those will vanish. She looks like the Vick I fell in love with. Her doctors even replaced her auburn curls with her normal long, dark hair. To see her, one would think she's healed. But I can see inside as well as out, and her psychological scars aren't fading at all.

Every time I think she's almost overcome one trauma, another rises up to take its place. Airlocks barely faze her anymore. She can make love to me without flashbacks of her violent rape.

Now it's reflective surfaces. I notice it first in her room in the medcenter, the day the doctors tell her she's being released. Vick dresses by feel, without the aid of a mirror. In fact, she stands facing away from the one hanging by the bathroom door. She pulls her brush from the duffel of toiletries and clothes I brought her and yanks it through her hair in a handful of quick movements, all the while staring into the corner, not at the mirror, and not meeting my gaze.

"Your part's a bit crooked," I say, laying a hand on her arm to slow her down before she rips out all the new strands. Taking the brush, I fix it for her. When it's a perfect line down the center of her head, I tuck the brush away in the bag. "You okay?"

I know she's not. To my sight, she's shrouded in an aura of green discomfort.

"Fine," she grinds out, a bald-faced lie. She knows I know. "I just want out of here."

Fair enough. Vick and medical facilities have a long and painful history with each other. Some terrifying things have been done to her under the pretense of health improvement. But this is more than that.

The Storm restricts her to light duty for her first two weeks back, Vick grumbling about it the entire time. They've got her going over mission reports, giving lectures to new recruits, and conducting training sessions— anything not overly strenuous or emotionally taxing. It's a logical decision, a good plan for most soldiers working their way up to active status, but not for Vick. Her psyche requires constant stimulus as a distraction. Otherwise, she dwells. And when she dwells, the disquiet creeps in.

I worry it's more than the metal making up her skull. She's insisting on sleeping apart in our two-bedroom quarters, though we haven't done that in months. Her excuse? She's restless at night and worried she'll keep me awake.

Translate "restless" to "constant nightmares."

I feel them. Her suppressors don't work as well when she's asleep. She's keeping me awake regardless, but I don't tell her that. She has enough guilt about what she puts me through already. I hide my exhaustion with makeup. Vick doesn't use makeup. She doesn't know how to hide the dark circles that ring her eyes. She's lethargic and unfocused.

"Will you talk to me?" Before she can disappear into her room for another torturous night, I take her hands and pull her down on the couch in the center of our living room. "It's been a week. I want to respect your privacy, but I'm worried. The nightmares—"

Her head drops. She stares down at her lap. "I'm sorry," she says.

"Dammit, Vick. Stop already. I'm not porcelain. You won't break me." Not like this, anyway. She's come damn close before. I don't mention those times. I wouldn't trade them. "It's not your fault. What *is* your fault is refusing to take steps toward recovery. The first one is telling me what is going on."

Vick shifts her position so she's facing forward while I study her from the side. Her gaze darts from one corner of the room to another, flitting about but never settling, carefully avoiding my eyes. Her mouth opens, then closes, then opens again, like she wants to tell me something but can't quite bring forth the words.

Is she being blocked? The Storm can do that. One order from the right person and Vick can't tell me anything they don't want her to. I'm about to attempt some creative questioning when her mouth opens again.

Finally, a whisper. "They're so real."

"What are?" I don't want to push too hard, but I need this information if I'm going to help her.

"The dreams," she says, then turns to me. I suck in a gasp at the bleak hopelessness in her eyes. Manufactured or not, they are expressive.

"Tell me."

She takes a deep breath, lets it out. "I'm... doing horrible things, monstrous things. Kel, I'm hurting people, killing them. Not people who deserve it. Not like on assignments. These are people I don't even know, that I've never seen before. Why? Why would I do that?"

A chill passes through me. I force it away. "You aren't." I take her shoulders and pull her to me, holding her close. She's shaking. Hard. "Vick, they're dreams. You know they aren't real." We've come so far, and now it's like we've lost years' worth of progress over the past two weeks.

"But that's how they feel. Smell, sound, taste, touch, they have them all. Like when VC1 replays a memory for me, except these aren't mine. And they are. I see myself doing these things. I don't understand them, and I can't stop them."

"When did these different dreams start?"

"When we came back to Girard Moon Base," she says, then stops. "No. I think… I think I had one that night I commed you and woke you up by accident, but I couldn't remember it then. I wonder if I've had them even before that."

Wetness soaks into the fabric covering my shoulder. She's crying. I can count on two hands the number of times I've seen Vick cry. Whatever this is, it's cutting her deep.

"And the aversion to mirrors?" I ask.

Vick goes rigid. Damn. One problem at a time. I should know better.

"What aversion?" She tugs herself free and wipes her eyes on the backs of her hands, then scoots away to lean against the armrest, but not fast enough. I already felt the lie.

"You know what I mean. You haven't willingly looked in a mirror since the slaver mission. You dress and do your hair by feel. You keep your eyes down. You avoid reflective surfaces."

She shakes her head, but I reach out and place my hands on either side of her face.

"Vick, you're healed. There's nothing bad to see." Maybe they're connected, the dreams and this aversion. But no. She was having these new nightmares and asking me about her soul before we went after the slavers. What is this? And how do I help her get through it?

Vick raises her hands to my wrists and pulls mine away. "Haven't you figured it out yet? When I look at myself, I always see something bad, even before the toxic lake. It's worse now, but the monster has been there since the airlock accident. The Storm hid it, but it's always been there."

CHAPTER 29: VICK LOOKALIKES

I am protective.

I'M HEADING out of our quarters to give yet another string of lectures on safe weapons protocols when my internal comm buzzes. VC1 shoots me an image of Officer Sanderson. No. *Helen* Sanderson, head of civilian security on Girard Moon Base. The facsimile wears a concerned frown, and I wonder if my AI knows something I don't.

Kelly's still asleep. As support personnel, she isn't required to keep my hours, and I know my nightmares disturbed her last night, so I slip the rest of the way into the corridor, let the door slide shut behind me, and lean against the wall.

Kelly. I'm disappointing her in a big way. So much psychological progress gone to shit. I broke off our talk last night to retreat into my bedroom, and we haven't spoken since.

Vick Corren. Mercenary hero. Girlfriend coward.

The comm buzzes again. *Go ahead and open the channel*, I tell VC1.

There's a click, and I *feel* the connection open. I've asked Lyle and Alex. Regular humans don't detect this sort of thing. They think it's cool.

I don't.

"Hey, Sanderson," I subvocalize, forcing false energy into my tone. "What's up? There a game this afternoon?" Good company, a couple of beers, and some Cirulean grass hockey at the promenade sports bar might be just the distraction I need.

"No games, and I'm definitely not playing," her voice comes back, somber and low. "We've got a situation on the civilian side. It's got my guys baffled, and I could use your and your... assistant's... take on it."

She doesn't mean Kelly. Sometimes I wonder if she's figured out VC1 is more than some advanced technology, that she has a mind of her own. Technically, I shouldn't be working with any organization other than the Storm without the board's permission, but I'm not programmed against it, and I owe her. Besides, I kind of like breaking the Storm's rules when I'm able. It's so rare that I can.

I bring up my schedule on my heads-up display. "I'm free later this afternoon. Where should I meet you?"

A pause. Then, "The Purple Leaf. It's public enough, but they've got those secluded alcoves in the back. Meet me in the same one where we had our one and only sort of date. You remember which?" She stops and gives a short laugh, but there's no humor in it. "Of course you remember. And if you don't, I'm sure VC1 does."

"Um, okay." The Purple Leaf's a sex club. I hung out there a lot before the airlock accident, had a lot of casual sexual encounters, did some crazy shit. I'm not that person anymore. "What's going on?"

"Nothing I can discuss over the comm, even if your counterpart is scrambling it. Just meet me around four o'clock." A pause. "And don't bring Kelly."

I'm about to argue, but the connection drops.

Don't bring Kelly. Which probably also translates to "don't tell Kelly."

Shit.

I'm going to a sex club. Without my fiancée. I'm meeting another woman who also prefers women, and I'm not telling Kelly anything about it. Actually, the more I think about it, the more I'm in favor of that plan.

An image of me digging my own grave appears on my internal display. *Too close to home*, I tell the AI, considering that I did exactly that on Elektra4 not that long ago. VC1 was in control, and I didn't witness any of it, but I know it happened, and it still turns my stomach if I think about it too hard.

Sorry. But you are taking actions that will undoubtedly cause problems between you and Kelly LaSalle.

If she finds out about it, I send back.

When has she ever not *found out about any of your its?*

I sigh, pushing off from the corridor wall and hurrying toward Storm central and the class I'm supposed to already be in the progress of teaching. *Sometimes I wish you were a little less of an AI*, I admit. *Your insights are too damn accurate.*

I will take that as a compliment.

Needless to say, classes do not go well. I'm distracted by Sanderson's upcoming clandestine meeting. The room I'm teaching in has one-way glass across the back—in other words, mirrors. So not only do I not want to look in that direction, the direction of my class of recruits, but I have the distinct impression that I'm under observation. Someone in the Storm hierarchy is keeping tabs on me and my recovery process.

Can you confirm? I ask VC1 while demonstrating the proper way to load an XR-7 Safety Net with its blunted rounds. I don't say what I'm asking her to confirm. I know she monitors my thoughts even if she's gotten better about not acting upon them without being asked.

You are indeed being observed.

Great. I can't imagine what they're seeing is earning me points.

We take a break for lunch, returning to the same room afterward. To make everything worse, there's a power surge about two-thirds of the way through the second training session. The lights flicker, go out for a moment, and then flash back on. The brightness intensifies until the entire room of students is shielding their eyes. Some duck down in their seats, and I have a moment of realization, enough time to crouch behind the podium, before several of the fluorescent bar lights shatter, showering everyone with bits of glass. One arcs a visible jagged streak of electricity from the bulb to the floor, not far from my defensive position. I throw myself out of harm's way, swallowing a shriek of terror, even though I know for a fact that it would have done no more than give me an uncomfortable shock.

It looked like lightning, and that's all my psyche could focus on.

What the actual fuck?

The lights steady. Everything returns to normal. But my hands tremble throughout the remainder of the lesson, so much so that I fumble a box of ammunition and have to chase the rubber-tipped rounds across the tile floor, gathering them up in clenched fists to avoid dropping them again. I wait for the recruits' mocking laughter. It never comes.

Even at my worst, I'm intimidating, my reputation enough to keep them in line. For now.

After class I send Kelly a message that I'm meeting Sanderson for a beer and let her fill in the blanks as she will. Partial truths are easier to sell than outright lies, and I'm quite certain alcohol will be involved in whatever the security chief has going on with the civvies.

The promenade dome is quiet when I arrive on that side of Girard Base. Too quiet. It's midafternoon. Even if the day shifts haven't gotten out yet, there should be more people around, tourists from the settled worlds, spouses of military personnel running errands, and the station school ends classes at 1500. A few teenage couples are necking on the benches at the central hub of the dome, but the usual echoing laughter and loud conversation are missing.

Whatever Sanderson's issue is, it's big.

I pause at the entrance to the Purple Leaf, handing over my Storm ID to the bouncer at the door, letting myself be scanned for weapons. He holds out a meaty palm, and I pass him my personal XR-7, grip first, then slip my matched set of knives from my boots and give him those as well. He in turn sets them on a counter in front of a window where an attractive blond woman tags each one and hands me a claim chit.

Once he's satisfied, he waves me through the archway into the gaudy interior. The holdout pistol in my back holster, the imitation leather lined with sensor scramblers, goes unnoticed beneath my black jacket. No way am I entering a potential danger zone unarmed, and I'm willing to bet most of the other mercs milling around the circular bar in the center of the establishment and lounging on the deep violet plush couches are equally prepared for trouble.

Even here, the crowd is thin. Almost no civilians, only uniforms. A couple of waitresses clad in purple-leaf-covered bras and G-strings lean against the wall, chatting to each other. The manager, a tall, dark-skinned, elegant gentleman in a deep purple suit stands by the bar, arms crossed over his chest, surveying the two-thirds empty room.

I give him a nod and head toward the back, VC1 supplying a reminder of which alcove I'm aiming for, even if there's no way I'd forget. One of the gray-camo-clad women at the bar gives me the once-over when I pass her and offers me a drink, but I shake my head. I'm here to see what Sanderson needs, help if I can, and get the hell out.

When I turn toward the alcoves once more, Sanderson has the curtain to the farthest one pulled aside. She's standing in the archway, watching my approach.

"She's hot," Sanderson comments when I'm within earshot, nodding at the woman who flirted with me.

"She's all yours," I return, feeling a blush suffuse my cheeks. "I'm taken."

That earns me a laugh, though her expression is sober. "Don't I know it." She beckons me into the private seating area, two overstuffed violet couches and a small round table between them the only furnishings. The curtain drops into place, giving us more privacy. Even so, I instruct VC1 to give the space a once-over for cameras and listening devices.

All areas of this establishment are monitored with security cameras, though there are no microphones present, she informs me. No surprise. Sometimes the Leaf's customers get rowdy. The bouncers need to know where things are heating up, and not in a good way.

Thanks, I tell her, never wanting to take her services for granted. Turning to my human companion, I ask, "You want me to put the cameras in here on a loop?" A strange feeling passes through me when I make the offer. Like a touch of déjà vu, though I haven't done that camera trick in a long time. Have I? I shake it off.

Sanderson's eyebrows rise almost to the hairline of her buzzcut. "That's right. You can do that, can't you?" She seats herself on one of the couches, expression going contemplative.

I sit opposite her, my own eyebrows raised, waiting for a response and wondering what the hell is going on.

"Right. I never answered you. Yes, do it. Please." She leans back, crossing her arms over her chest. "Can't believe I'm a security chief violating station security, but desperate times and all that shit." For a long moment she appraises me. I'm about to start squirming under her scrutiny when she speaks again. "Good to see you looking so well, if a little ragged around the edges.

Scuttlebutt said you'd suffered some serious injuries on that last mission of yours."

I shrug it off, not wanting to rehash it. "I'm fine."

Someone raps on the wall outside our concealing curtain, and for a second I wonder if VC1's tampering has been noticed. Then a sultry female voice says, "I have your drink order. May I come in?"

Sanderson gives her the okay, and the sexy blond sets two coasters and frosted mugs of ale in front of us, then departs. I take a long sip of mine, then another, appreciating the chocolate and coffee accents of the porter. It's exactly what I would have ordered if my companion hadn't beaten me to it.

Do you wish for the alcohol to have an effect? VC1 asks. She's found a workaround for my initial programming that used to prevent me from ever becoming intoxicated. She'll never allow me to get stinking drunk, but it's nice that I can feel a buzz once in a while. Still, considering the seriousness of the apparent situation, I'd better stay sober.

Not right now. Maybe when we're done here.

Sanderson chugs a third of her lager and sets her mug down with a soft *thunk*. Guess she doesn't share my concerns. Or perhaps she has too many different things to be concerned about. I study her face with more intent. Dark circles and bloodshot eyes. She's not sleeping.

I gesture at the beer in my hand. "You know me a little too well for someone I'm not dating," I joke, trying to lighten the mood.

"I may need to know you better than that if you're going to help me."

That sobers me fast enough. "Okay, spill it, Helen," I say, invoking the power of first names. "And I don't mean the beer. That would be a shameful waste. What do you need from me that's so secret I'm risking Kelly's wrath to meet you in a sex club without her?"

"Oh, like Kelly would have come here even if you invited her along."

I give her a grin, but I'm not so sure she's right. Since the makeshift vibrator incident during our last mission, Kelly's been hinting that she'd like to experiment more as soon as I'm fully recovered. She even tossed out the Purple Leaf as a possible date night destination, much to my surprise. I won't say I'm opposed to her finding her wild side. My newly recovered memories tell me I have a crazy one of my own. My worry is that she's doing this because she thinks it's what I want, that she's worried about competing with my past sexual partners. But that's a problem for another day.

Helen retrieves a messenger bag from beneath the table and pulls an old-fashioned file folder from its depths. I'm reminded that she has a fondness for things old-school, like her Sherlock Holmes-ian office. Before I can tease her about it, she spreads a set of glossy photographs across the table, careful to avoid the condensation pooling around our mugs.

I don't need to see details to recognize dead bodies—torn flesh, bloodstains; they practically jump from the half-dozen images. "Fuck," I breathe, finding no more appropriate term. I take a longer pull on my beer. "That's a lot of victims."

"Six in the past two weeks. And we can't catch their murderer. We don't even have a lead. That's not the worst of it. Look closer."

I don't want to. I have enough nightmares. But Sanderson is a friend, and I allow myself so few. I lean in.

And recoil, slamming my spine against the back of the couch.

"I know," Sanderson says, shaking her head. "It's uncanny. And it's why I wanted you alone to see this."

Kelly. Every one of the victims looks like Kelly. Not identical, but blond, green eyes, delicate features, at least the ones they have left. Worse than the resemblance, they're all disfigured like the blond in the tunnels of the slaver hideout, faces flayed open on one side to expose the bone beneath.

The similarity to my own recent injury hits like a punch to the gut, and my beer threatens to make a reappearance. But even *that* isn't the worst part of all this.

I've seen these girls before. I've seen them in my nightmares, though one at a time so I didn't make the Kelly connection, but I've seen them. I've seen them, because in my dreams, I'm the one killing them.

Those nightmares didn't just *feel* real. They *are* real. At least the victims. What about their killer?

Without another word I stand and bolt from the table, through the drawn curtains, nearly ripping them down from the ceiling, and race for the closest restroom.

CHAPTER 30: KELLY CONNECTIONS

Vick is channeling.

I DROP my spoon on the red-and-white-check-ered tablecloth covering our kitchen table. It's another example of what Vick terms "nesting," and she's right, but I don't have time to consider it now. I'm too busy running for the bathroom on the far side of my bed-room. I make it with seconds to spare before I vomit the broccoli and cheddar soup I'd made for dinner into the toilet bowl.

Panting, I prop myself against the wall and let the chill of the white tile chase the remainder of the nausea away. I stand on shaky limbs, run some cold water in the sink, rinse my mouth out, and splash some in my face. Then I stare at myself in the mirror.

That wasn't the soup. That wasn't even me.

It was Vick.

My comm is in the bedroom, and walking proves more difficult than I expected. Whatever set her off, it isn't over. My stomach roils with each movement, but without the element of surprise, and recognizing the source, I'm in control now. I hesitate to raise my walls against our connection, but I need to be clearheaded, not distracted by nausea and whatever else might be behind it if I'm going to help.

I set the blocks in place, picturing solid steel doors closing her out a bit at time, then leaving a small gap between them. Cutting her off entirely would defeat my purpose as her emotional support partner and the woman who loves her. I pick up my comm from the bedside table, tap in her code, and wait.

It buzzes multiple times, and I'm thinking she won't answer and I might have to override and barge in when there's a soft click and her hoarse voice says, "I'm fine, Kel."

I roll my eyes, even if she can't see it. She hasn't activated visuals, so either there aren't any cameras VC1 can commandeer in her current location, or she doesn't want me to know how bad off she looks. I suspect the latter.

"I'm not," I return, sinking onto the edge of the bed. "I just threw up perfectly delicious broccoli and cheddar soup that I made, and I'll probably end up throwing the rest out because of the association."

Vick groans. "Geez, Kel, don't talk about food. I hate broccoli to begin with." She's trying to lighten the situation, but I can hear the truth beneath her words. She's still not well.

Reaching with my empathic sense through the opening in my walls, I seek out the aura of the blue line that connects us. It's faded, so she must be on the civilian side of Girard Moon Base, but I can follow it if necessary. "Talk to me or I come find you," I warn. I don't like forcing her hand. Vick needs to believe she has free will and independence even with the way the Storm limits both. But a reaction so intense that it reached me this far away is one I have to look into.

Vick sighs, a long, weary sigh that belies things kept hidden from me for some time. She's been struggling with her recovery and what she saw in the surgery mirrors, but this is something more.

I sigh right back at her. "I thought we were past secrets," I say, keeping my voice calm and soft.

There's a long pause, and I can almost hear the wheels turning in her head. I cover my mouth to stifle an inappropriate snort of amusement. With VC1, Vick sort of does have wheels turning in her head. But she won't appreciate me finding her decision-making process funny.

"We are," she says at last. "I'm in the restroom at the Purple Leaf. Probably won't be by the time you get here. At least I hope not. Check the alcoves in the rear first. I'm with Helen Sanderson. Don't ask. I'll explain what I can when you arrive. It's her shitshow."

"Wait. Really?"

"Really what? That I'm in the sex club? Look, I'm sorry. It was Sanderson's idea, and—"

"No," I say, interrupting her apology. "I mean, you're really going to clue me in? I won't have to drag it out of you?"

Silence. Then, "Not this time. You need to know what's happening. Your life might depend on it."

I swallow hard. "Ten minutes," I tell her, then cut the connection.

I make it there in seven, my heart pounding from the jog across the base. I'm out of breath when the bouncer at the door asks if I'm carrying any weapons, so I shake my head. He passes a scanner wand over me anyway, then waves me through the entrance. A few uniformed men and a couple of women nod and smile as I pass. One points to her drink and raises a questioning eyebrow, offering to buy me one, but I politely thank her and move on.

The blue line between me and Vick is clear and bright, guiding me straight to the centermost secluded alcove in the back, though the raised female voice coming from within would have directed me just as well.

"—be here any minute. I can't believe you told her to come. This is all classified information. She's going to freak out when she sees this. I don't need more people capable of inciting panic. What do you intend to tell her?" Officer Sanderson. Helen. Not happy. I like her well enough, and I'm glad Vick has a buddy to do... buddy things with: watch games, drink beer, talk weapons. Lyle and Alex are great, and sometimes Vick hangs with them too, or all three, but it feels like in Sanderson, Vick has found a kindred spirit. I'm happy for it.

But Sanderson also has an annoying tendency to view me as fragile, naïve, and innocent, and it plays up Vick's inclination to do the same. Vick's grown a lot toward treating me like the professional I am and remembering I'm not so breakable anymore, and the fact that she's bringing me in on this is testament to that, but when those two are together....

I hover outside the curtain, waiting for Vick's response.

Something thuds hard against a surface, maybe a mug on the table? Then Vick's voice. "I'm going to tell her everything you told me and maybe more than that. I can't make you share the photos. They're your property. But I'd like you to. I'm going to give her all the information and hope that forewarning will help keep her safe."

"You can't—"

"I damn well can and I will. Unlike my bosses, you can't shut me up with a code. Look, Helen, this isn't what you bargained for when you brought me in, and I'm sorry. I still intend to help you. But these images change everything. I'm telling Kelly because she's my friend, my partner, and more than all that, I love her, and I'm not keeping dangerous secrets from the woman I love."

My entire body warms with that statement. I reach for the edge of the curtain.

"I just hope she can keep a secret," Sanderson mutters as I pull it aside.

"I can," I tell them both, noting the slight grin on Vick's pale face. There's a sparkle of mischief in her eyes, and I'm wondering how long she knew I was listening.

Probably the entire time, given her enhanced hearing and VC1's penchant for tracking everyone and everything in her vicinity. Knowing that doesn't lessen the impact of Vick's words. I get the distinct impression she said them more to stop Sanderson's arguing than to earn my favor.

I slide onto the couch next to Vick, taking her hand in mine and resting both on her thigh. Her entire body relaxes into the seat. She's stressed. Very stressed. I'm glad my presence helps, but my worry ratchets up a notch. "Okay," I say, looking from Sanderson to the woman I trust with my life and my heart. "What's going on?"

CHAPTER 31: VICK REVELATIONS

I am out of control.

SANDERSON AND I tell Kelly what's going on. Helen only shows her one printed image, the one most hidden in shadow so the mangled facial features aren't as discernible, but it's enough to make the blood drain from Kelly's face, even more so when we explain that all the victims look like her.

My hand trembles when I pass the photo over to Sanderson. Kelly raises a questioning eyebrow at me, but I give a slight shake of my head and she drops it. She knows there's more I'm not saying. She also realizes I don't want to say it in front of the security officer.

There may not be any true telepaths, but we can read each other without the benefit of psychic abilities.

I glance down to where her hand still rests on my thigh. Or maybe she's picking up my "not now" vibes through our physical contact. Either way, I'm relieved she got the message.

"Why?" Kelly asks for the third time. "Why would anyone be targeting women who look like me? Could it be a warning of some kind?" She shakes her head. "It has to be a coincidence, right?"

"I don't believe in coincidence," I remind her.

"As for who, that's exactly why I brought Corren in." Sanderson takes a swig from her second beer. We're all drinking now, though VC1's still burning most of mine off. This is not something any of us can handle completely sober.

It also occurs to me to wonder at VC1's sudden silence, her complete lack of commentary on this situation. Maybe she's honoring my request to wait for me to ask first.

Maybe she knows more than she's been permitted to share.

Kelly sips at her frou-frou frozen concoction, complete with a little pink umbrella to match the mixture inside the glass. "You don't have any leads?"

"None. But before you got here, and before Corren's unscheduled pit stop...." She pauses, turning from Kelly to me. "Never guessed you to be squeamish." She's not criticizing. She's barely even teasing. It's more a statement of fact.

Still, I blush, covering it behind my frosted mug. I don't have a weak stomach. Not with everything I've seen and done. But having my night terrors brought to life, or more accurately death, did a number on me. No way Sanderson's going to let me forget that anytime soon, but I have no intention of sharing the real reason with her. Kelly gently squeezes my thigh, offering comfort and support. She's piecing together what she's sensing from me, where the triggers are. I wish she weren't quite so perceptive.

"The dead girls look like me. Of course they made her squeamish. Under the same circumstances, you would have been too."

Kelly's defending my kick-ass rep. It's cute.

Sanderson waves the comment away. "Whatever. As I was saying, before you joined us, Corren made a comment about putting the security cameras in here on a continuous loop. I'm wondering if that's how the killer has managed to avoid being seen. All the attacks have taken place overnight, between 8:00 p.m. and 6:00 a.m. in secluded areas: private workspaces, unfrequented corridors, bathrooms, maintenance passages. All of the locations had cameras, public or individually owned. I've looked at all the feeds. Nothing. So I'm thinking some kind of loop making everyone think all is well and—"

"Isn't that kind of obvious? How else could they have done it?" Kelly asks. She's picked up a lot in her years with the Storm.

Sanderson shakes her head. "That's not what I mean. I mean, I wonder if the killer set up the video loop by the same method that *Vick* sets one up." She gives me a meaningful look. "What we can't figure out is how the murderer got access. There have been no reports of break-ins to our security panels, no 'new guys' in maintenance uniforms wandering about making 'adjustments' to the circuitry, nothing to suggest human tampering. So, what if it wasn't human?" Sanderson freezes, realizing her verbal slip the second it leaves her mouth, but she can't take it back. "Shit, Corren, I'm sorry. I—"

Great. One of my only friends is suggesting the murderer isn't human and comparing them to me. Because I'm not human, either. I close my eyes, fighting down the anger and losing. My hands clench into fists. It's irrational. I'm not entirely human and I live with that knowledge every day. But I thought the people around me had finally accepted me as one of them.

"Vick." Sanderson's voice is soft. "Come on, look at me. I didn't intend it that way, but I'm a security chief, not a public speaker. I meant, what if the *person*, the *human being*, even if it's a twisted one, has a device like yours. Something that can loop the camera feeds wirelessly, without direct access. That's what I meant. Really. I've always disagreed with the people who called you a machine, even when we first met."

"Sure. That's what you meant," I growl. I push myself up from the couch. The room rocks a little. Maybe VC1 allowed more alcohol into my system than I thought she did.

An unwelcome thought occurs. Maybe she's letting me be distracted by inebriation from thinking about what she really knows. Is anybody except Kelly on my side here?

"Screw this," I say. "You don't need my help. You've got it all figured out. Go input your data into some *other* computer and let it tell you your next move."

"Vick—" Sanderson half rises, catches my glare, and sinks back onto the couch, hands raised palms out in surrender. I don't know if I would have punched her if she'd stood all the way, but it's a definite possibility.

"Hey," Kelly says, standing beside me. She rests a hand on my shoulder. It's everything I can do not to jerk away from her touch.

Part of me realizes I'm not reacting logically, that something is off. Hell, why should I be upset that my friends think I'm a robot when I keep telling everyone that myself? But I can't stop the rage coursing through me, burning me from the inside out like I've blown a fucking fuse.

"I'll go with you if you're set on leaving," Kelly continues, keeping her tone calm and soothing, "but she's telling the truth. I know she is. You're still recovering. We're all upset and we've all been drinking. You're not thinking straight."

"You know, I am somewhat insulted by being referred to as a 'device,'" VC1 chimes in, using Kelly's comm unit as a speaker so everyone can hear her indignation. For one frozen moment, we all stare at the communicator lying on the table.

And that does it. The whole idea of my AI getting offended with me in solidarity turns the entire moment into surreal absurdism. I don't know what's going on with her withholding information from me, but I'm betting it has to do with her programming and not something she can help. A laugh forces its way from my throat, followed by another and another until I'm laughing so hard tears are rolling down my cheeks, though by that point I'm not so sure it's amusement anymore.

The others laugh with me. VC1 adds that she is not amused, which makes everything funnier. But when I find it hard to stop, Kelly sobers, pulling me into her arms. "Shh," she whispers against my hair. "Slow it down. Breathe."

I force air in and out of my sore lungs. The first breaths are hard. I'm still having mild hysterics. But eventually I'm able to inhale and exhale without gasping.

My eyes are squeezed shut, tears still leaking from the corners. Delicate fingertips brush strands of hair from my face, then cup my cheek. "Let me in," Kelly says, her talent pushing at my suppressors. "I need to know what's going on in there. This isn't normal." She chuckles. "Even for you."

I take the teasing as it was meant to be—loving— and open my eyes to glance over at Sanderson. She's anxious, her hands gripping the edge of the couch where she sits. Just the idea of letting Kelly help me through a release with the security chief watching is enough to bring the nausea back, but I want to show Kelly that I've grown. I also need to reassure Sanderson that I'm no longer angry. Allowing her to witness a vulnerable moment will go a long way toward both.

"We can go in the bathroom, if you want," Kelly offers, an olive branch if I ever heard one.

I shake my head and sit down, taking satisfaction in the way her eyebrows rise. "Just do it." She sits next to me. Internally, I ask VC1 to shut my suppressors off. I've had them running at 85 percent since the slaver mission, higher than usual. Kelly has to have noticed, but she hasn't made me lower them, and I'm grateful. The fact that I've been so emotional even with the suppressors running high starts some alarm bells ringing in my head.

This "device" will comply, VC1 says, distracting me.

Great. Now I'm dealing with a touchy AI. Solidarity is one thing. Bitchiness is quite another. *Save it*, I subvocalize.

The walls come down, not in the gradual decrease in blockage that I've worked with the AI to perfect, but in one tumultuous drop that floods me with all my suppressed emotions at once: exhaustion, stress, anger, fear, worry, and a touch of powerful aggression that has me really concerned, along with a strange longing, aching *need*, the source of which I can't begin to identify.

Kelly sucks in a sharp breath, her own senses overwhelmed by the onslaught. She winces, jerking her upper body away from me but forcing her hand to remain in contact with my face.

"Sorry... sorry," I murmur, catching my own breath. "VC1 is pissed."

That earns me a smile. "Just so long as she isn't pissed enough to put me in emotion shock, we're fine," Kelly says.

"She'd never do that," I assure her. "VC1 cares about you in her own way almost as much as I do."

"Um, so are you going to fill me in on those implants of yours? Because it's more than a machine. That much is clear," Sanderson says from the couch.

Right. She doesn't know VC1 is an AI. Almost no one does beyond my team. Even the Fighting Storm's board hasn't figured that out, though they know I'm a clone. I must be pretty off my game to make that kind of slip. For that matter, so must VC1. I glance at the security officer, gauging her trustworthiness before Kelly draws my gaze and attention back to her. Can I trust Sanderson with one of my two biggest, most dangerous secrets? I think so. When our current drama ends, I'll tell her that much. The clone part, though, that will have to keep. "Later," I mutter.

Kelly's essence, for want of a better term, floods my mind with soothing coolness, her love for me quieting even the most chaotic of my emotions. In my peripheral vision, I'm vaguely aware of Sanderson's comm buzzing and her taking a call, but she keeps her voice quiet, and I block it out.

Kelly's expression shifts from compassion to concern as she sifts through the tangle of feelings, pulling them apart one by one and helping me purge them through her. I've gotten a lot better about doing this on my own, but when things get really bad, I still depend on her. I'll always depend on her.

When she gets to the need and the aggression, now entwined with each other, she hesitates. "What is this?" she asks, voice pitched for my ears only.

I shake my head. "No idea. I was hoping you'd know where they came from."

With her unique empathic ability enabled by our brainwave match, she yanks them apart, pushing them out of me with deliberate force that leaves me breathless. "Sorry," Kelly says, not the least bit apologetic about her roughness. "I don't know their source either, but we need to figure it out. Because I've felt that combination before."

CHAPTER 32: KELLY
MEMORIES

Vick isn't alone.

"WHEN? FROM me?" Vick asks. "Was it at night?" Sanderson reaches across the table and pushes a frosty mug into Vick's hand. Water this time.

"When did that show up?" I ask, stalling. I'm not sure how to explain what I felt in the slaver installation or how to tell Vick it reminded me of her without upsetting her further. Also, if a waitress came in while I was purging Vick's emotions, well, that's not something she wants others to see. I'm surprised she let me do it in front of Sanderson.

"Don't worry," the security chief says, waving one hand in dismissal. "It just looked like the two of you were about to make out." She grimaces. "And I was some kind of voyeur. A lot more embarrassing for me than you guys."

"How about the comm call? Something important?"

"You're avoiding the issue," Vick accuses, studying me. We're still in physical contact, my hand brushing hers on the seat of the couch. She can read my hesitation through our bond.

"My office just wanted to know where to find me," Sanderson says, answering my earlier question. "Now that I've told you what's going on, I didn't see harm in telling them. I don't want them wasting time tracking down my location if another body is found. Now, on to other things." She crosses her arms over her chest. "I think we're all avoiding several issues. And if any of them are pertinent to our rash of murders, I need to know the facts. All of them. Whatever's going on here, it's connected to the two of you. I just don't know how." She looks from me to Vick and back again.

Vick drinks a sip of water, then presses the cold mug to her forehead. I reach out with my empathic sense, wincing at the headache pounding behind her eyes. This is stressing her out in a big way.

"Okay," I say, wiping sweaty palms on my slacks. "I'll go first." I face Vick. "That cluster of emotions, the aggression and the want, I felt them in the slavers' base. Our last mission," I clarify for Sanderson's benefit.

"From me?" Vick asks again.

I shake my head. "No. But why do you think it would have been? And why did you ask if it was while you were sleeping? It wasn't, by the way. We were both wide awake each time I picked up those feelings.

When I narrowed down the source, you weren't it. I think it was a woman I saw in the banquet cavern, and later in the landing bay, but her face was hidden each time, and I couldn't make out features. A coincidence, similar thought patterns, nothing more." Except Vick just reminded me how she feels about coincidence. She doesn't believe it exists.

"I don't think so...." Vick trails off, hiding her expression behind her glass. She glances at Sanderson over the rim. "What I'm about to tell you... don't freak out, okay?"

"No promises," Sanderson says.

"Right. Well, I didn't throw up earlier because those girls look like Kelly. I mean, that was horrific enough, and unsettling as hell, but... that wasn't it."

I wrap my fingers around hers. Her skin is cold and clammy. "Go on."

Taking a deep breath, she lays it out for us. "I'd seen them before. In my nightmares."

"Wait," I say, my eyes widening. "You mean the ones where you're... killing people?"

Vick opens her mouth to speak, but Sanderson beats her to it. "Whoa, whoa. You're telling me you dreamed about killing these girls, and now they're dead?" She fingers the comm she returned to her belt, like she's about to bring her team down on us.

"No. I'm saying I think I dreamed about killing those girls... as they were being killed. Look," Vick continues, tugging away from me to stand and pace behind the couch. It's not a big space in the alcove between the furniture and the wall, but she can manage five or six steps each way, and I know it helps her think. "You can check the security logs on our door, though given my capabilities, I guess that's not great evidence.

Kelly can vouch for me being in our quarters every
night for the past two weeks."

I nod. Vick has gone to bed early almost every
evening, her nightmares making sleep difficult, so she
hasn't been getting enough of it, and she's been tired.

"I'm not suggesting I had anything to do with the
murders, but I think I'm… picking up on them, somehow, on the killer's thoughts." She turns to me. "Could
I be channeling this person somehow? There was a similar victim in the slaver tunnels. I never had a chance to
tell you about her, what with the lake and stasis and all,
but could that girl's murderer have hitched a ride back
here?" She stops and closes her eyes, then opens them.
"I want to bring VC1 into this conversation."

"Go ahead," Sanderson says, waving a hand at
Kelly's comm still lying on the table. "Let's hear what
the AI has to say."

Vick and I stare at her.

"I'm not stupid," the security officer says, sounding offended. Then she grins. "Even if I am more brawn
than brains, I have ears. There've been rumors. Rumors
that Storm personnel have very carefully quashed.
VC1's an AI." She leans over and speaks toward the
comm. "I'll try to stop referring to you as a device."

"That will be much appreciated," Vick's voice says
from the unit. Inflection in her tone is limited. She must
be busy doing other things that keep her from demonstrating her human qualities.

"Tell them what you just told me, please," Vick says.

"Very well. Over the course of the last few weeks,
it would appear I have been experiencing… anomalies, though I didn't discover them until just now when
I tried to review the security logs on the door to our

quarters to prove our innocence, though as you say, they would be suspect."

It takes me a moment to figure out that by "our" she means her and Vick.

"There are gaps in my recorded memory," VC1 continues. "I have attempted to account for them and failed. Investigating further, these seem to have begun shortly before my host was placed in stasis, suggesting your suspicions about this murderous individual being on our transport are correct."

"I have more to add," I put in. "There was an incident on the shuttle. I dreamed… well, no, at the time I thought it was real. Alex convinced me it was a dream. But I would have sworn that someone came into my cabin on the trip back, that *she*, since we're assuming it's the woman I saw in the landing bay, was standing over me, and then ran off when I woke up. When I got into the corridor, there was no one there, and when I checked, Vick was in the stasis box, Lyle was asleep, and Alex was flying the shuttle. Alex checked the vid logs. We found nothing."

"Fuck," Vick whispers, pausing in her pacing to reach over the back of my couch and pull me against her chest. "If you hadn't woken up…."

This woman might have killed me. Or something.

"Assuming you weren't dreaming, the altered camera footage ties in exactly with what we're experiencing here—someone who can tamper with them wirelessly. Someone like Vick and VC1," Sanderson adds.

"And maybe they're tampering with VC1 too," Vick puts in, sounding uncomfortable. She should be. If this individual can mess with VC1's memory, she might be able to affect Vick's actions.

"But the part about you channeling the killer's actions through your dreams," I continue, thinking out loud. "That doesn't work. You aren't a psychic. I'd know if you had latent abilities."

"You're sure there's no way you could be responsible for these deaths?" Sanderson asks.

We glare at her.

"Hey, I have to ask. It's my job. And I know Vick's had a lot of trauma. I'm not saying it's happening consciously, but—"

"No!" we say in unison.

Vick's grip on my shoulders tightens. "Oh," she breathes against the back of my neck. "Oh, holy flying fuck. I think I know exactly what's going on. VC1, you told me you sent my really bad Rodwell memories to some other storage unit, something on a par with your capacity, but you didn't know exactly what it was. Or maybe," she says, resuming her pacing. "Maybe it *blocked* your ability to figure out what it was."

"It is conceivable," the comm unit says. "And I believe you are reaching a conclusion I reached earlier… and was programmed against telling you, but the circumstances have changed and I may share my thoughts with you now, because now you are in immediate danger."

"I'm not reading the killer through any kind of psychic ability. I'm reading her through VC1. And VC1 is reading her through another set of implants…."

"Oh my God," I whisper as the pieces fall into place for me as well. I whirl around on the couch, sitting up on my knees so I can make eye contact with Vick. She gives a slight shake of her head. We can't share the rest of this with Sanderson. The risk is too great. But we both know who our murderer is.

There's another clone of Vick Corren on the loose, one with some very traumatic memories and a second set of very capable implants. And she's using those implants to kill women who look like me.

CHAPTER 33: VICK
DOUBLE

I am not alone.

"SO, YOU'RE telling me there's another individual with implants similar to Vick's running around my base killing people. Someone with a lot of bad shit in her head." Sanderson eyes us, cocking her head to one side. "What aren't you telling me? There's more. I can see it in the way you two look at each other." We can barely understand her words; there's some commotion going on in the main area of the club. Maybe the evening revelers have come out after all. But we get the gist.

"It's classified," Kelly blurts out. It's the truth. The Storm board of directors has sworn us to secrecy on the subject of clones, since they're illegal and all.

On a personal level, I'd rather not be shot if they find out about me being one.

Sanderson fixes me with a hard stare. "I think we're past classified at this poi—"

Before she can finish her retort, the alcove curtain is thrown aside, and three uniformed station security officers come barreling through. They stop in front of Sanderson. "Ma'am," the youngest one says, giving her a quick salute, the other two taking up a stance behind him. He's gotta be new, ex-military. He's still got scars from puberty acne, and no one salutes in security. "We've got a lead on our killer. She missed a camera, and—" He breaks off as he notices his boss isn't alone in the small space. "Holy shit!"

Next thing I know, I've got three XR-7s aimed at my head and chest.

Oh, this is not going to go well. I raise my hands slowly, making certain everyone can see they are empty.

Kelly gives a little squeak, preparing to get off the couch and come to my aid, but I wave her off with a quick motion of my fingers. "Let's all take it easy," I say, keeping my voice calm while adrenaline surges through my body. The youngest one, the one with the gun in my face, holds his weapon with trembling hands, his trigger finger twitching—so, not ex-military then, or not very good ex-military.

I'm using VC1 to calculate my survival odds if he fires or I attempt to disarm him when Sanderson stands and uses one hand to push down on the weapon until it's at the officer's side. I breathe a small sigh of relief, even if two more are aimed in my direction.

"But ma'am," he argues, though he doesn't raise it again, "she's the killer. She's murdered six women." His companions nod in agreement.

Sanderson glances at me, her mouth forming a hard line. I shake my head slowly. No sudden moves from me. "Show me the evidence, Daniels." She holds out her hand, no tremors there, and the security kid pulls his comm off his belt and drops it in her palm. She activates the screen. Whatever they've got must be loaded and ready to view. Her eyes shift back and forth through several replays before she heaves a deep and weary sigh.

"We're gonna have to take you in, Corren. For questioning," she hastens to add when Kelly begins a protest.

"Whatever's on that screen, it's not me," I say, low and even.

Sanderson flips it around and touches the Play icon. The image is fuzzy and dark, but not so much that I can't make out what's happening. It's in the promenade dome, and everything is sideways, but beyond the dome's central gardens, it's picking up one of the side corridors leading in. The hour must be late, with the dim light and the absence of people, though one or two shopkeepers pass by the camera pickup, probably heading home. For a few seconds, nothing happens. Then, without warning, an exact duplicate of me, because of course, it's another clone, reaches out of the access hallway, wraps one arm around a passing blond woman's throat, and drags her backward out of view. The empty dome seems a lot more ominous after that.

The security chief turns the comm back toward her, fiddles with a few controls, and holds it out to me again, this time with the image of the killer's face frozen on the screen.

Yep, it's me. Except it's not.

My heart sinks and my chest tightens. I'm going to have a very hard time proving that. Still perched backward on the couch where she can also see the screen, Kelly swallows hard.

"We found the victim's body two days ago," Sanderson says. "You know her, though I wasn't going to tell you, and with all the disfigurement, I guess you didn't recognize her from the crime photo. She's the server from the Alpha Dog Pub you saved last year when the Sunfires decided to shoot the place up."

I feel the blood drain from my face. "Oh… fuck. Abby's mom?" Abby is seven. Well, probably eight by now. I saved her life, too, and got stuck in an airlock with her for a while. She kept a cool head, seemed like a good kid.

And she called me "Victory."

I wonder what she'll call me if this gets out.

Her mom bears a passing resemblance to Kelly in that they're both about the same height, female, and blond, but that's it. I'm thinking my evil twin chose this victim more for personal reasons. It's a solid tactical move, playing on your enemy's emotions, and I'm convinced VC2, for want of another name (I am *not* calling her Vick) is my enemy.

"How did you get this recording?" Kelly asks. I'm glad she did. I'm having a hard time finding my voice right now, and everything is a little blurry. If I thought I could lower my hands without getting shot, I'd wipe my eyes. Humiliating tears roll down my cheeks. I'm able to contort my arms over my face just enough to not alarm my captors and dry the wetness on my sleeves.

This sucks. Everything about this sucks.

"Tourist," Daniels explains. The youngest officer sidles closer to Kelly, resting a hand close to hers on the back of the couch.

Seriously? He's about to drag me through hell and he's flirting with my fiancée?

Kelly rolls her eyes, flips her hand to show off her engagement ring, and nods at me.

"No accounting for taste," one of the other officers mutters. Kelly doesn't hear it, but my enhanced hearing does, and I shoot him a glare. He backs up a step.

Daniels clears his throat and gets his head on straight. "Right. Anyway, a group of Martian colony tourists came through earlier that night. They posed for some vidshots on that bench in the foreground of the playback. Then they got distracted by some musicians working the dome and forgot it sitting there. The owner remembered in the morning, was thrilled to find it still on the armrest of the opposite bench, and they left on the next day's transport. When he scrolled through his vids at home, he saw what he'd caught and sent us a digital copy."

"Daniels runs the 'Tips Hotline,'" Sanderson explains. She gives him a meaningful glance. "He's *not* usually armed and leading a patrol."

Okay, that explains a lot of things.

"I—I just thought, since I got the call and put it together—"

She shushes him, returning her attention to me. "Until we get this cleared up, I'm holding you. Let's go."

They maneuver so that I can get around them and lead the way out of the curtained alcove. Before we step through, Sanderson gently pulls my arms down and binds them behind my back. A shiver passes through me when the cold metal clamps connect, holding my wrists together. I don't like binders. They remind me too much of being strapped in Medical's diagnostic chair.

"Try to calm down," she whispers for my ears alone. "You're pale, sweating, shaking, and I'm worried you're gonna pass out—all tells of guilt. I don't believe you did this, but I have to investigate."

"They're also tells of 'I've been framed and I'm freaking out,' but I understand," I manage through gritted teeth. To VC1, I think, *We can get out of these binders, right?*

With very little difficulty, she assures me.

My pulse slows a little.

"Okay, back to Security Central." Sanderson gives me a little nudge. One of the officers pulls the curtain aside for me.

This is a setup. The camera with footage of my double killing someone I know just happens to be the one that isn't discovered and wiped or looped? I'm not buying it. I'm betting if the tourists hadn't left it there, it would have been one of the dome's cameras that got conveniently "missed." If VC2 is half as talented as you, there's just no way this is accidental, I think at my AI partner. *But why now? She's had six opportunities to set me up. I get that Abby's mom is especially damning, but something in the timing is off.* We move through the archway of the alcove into the main area. Everyone is staring at us, staff and customers alike. A pair of Sunfires at the bar snickers as we pass. A few Storm soldiers are present as well, and their hands drop to weapons that aren't there—confiscated by the main entrance bouncer. Fists clench. Knuckles crack. It's nice to know they're all ready to jump to my defense, a far cry from how they treated me a couple of years ago, but I shake my head. Even with our exceptional training, fists against pistols is bad odds.

We're halfway to the front access into the promenade when it hits me. I snap my fingers behind my back, then shrug and offer a sheepish smile at the startled security team. "Sorry. Fingers are falling asleep. These binders are tight." To VC1 I say, *I've got it. The timing. The message containing the incriminating vid just* happens *to turn up while I'm meeting with Sanderson in a confined space? That's too much. What I don't understand, though, is how did VC2 know about the meeting? I didn't tell anyone except Sanderson and eventually Kelly. Were our communications intercepted?*

No, VC1 replies. Then, *Not... exactly.*

What does that mean?

I informed you about some anomalies with my memory. It is... possible... that my counterpart is tapping into my processes somehow.

I worried about that when she first said she was having issues, but now I'm terrified. *Can she control me? The way you can if I'm in bad shape?*

I do not believe so. Now that I am aware of the situation, I am putting precautions in place to avoid such an occurrence. However, you should know that the footage from the security on the corridor outside your quarters has been erased, and not by me.

Meaning there is no evidence other than Kelly's word that I was in my room every night these murders have occurred. Worse, as far as most folks know VC1 and I are the only ones capable of erasing that footage, which is even more incriminating. And Kelly has every reason to lie for me.

They can bring in another empath who would be able to testify to the truth of Kelly's statements, but that will take time, during which I'll be incarcerated, relatively helpless, and a sitting duck if VC2 decides to make a go at taking me out of the equation. And if she uses the opportunity to go after Kelly…. That, I cannot allow to happen. I will not.

What is her endgame? Does she want to humiliate me? Kill Kelly? Kelly spoke of frustration and need. Is VC2 trying to fill the gap that Kelly fills in my life? Getting me out of the way would make that a lot easier.

Our procession steps through the entrance into the promenade dome. Sanderson turns us toward the security section, when two heavily armed figures step out of an access corridor.

"Sorry. You're not taking Vick anywhere. She's coming with us," Alex says. He and Lyle each hold two pistols, and all of them are aimed at the security detail and Sanderson herself.

CHAPTER 34: KELLY
TUG OF WAR

Vick is torn.

I KNOW Vick didn't commit these murders. *Vick* knows. And I'm betting Lyle and Alex know too. Or they could lack confirmation and just be demonstrating team loyalty. I love them either way, and from the warm feelings emanating from Vick, I know she loves them too. It wasn't that long ago that both of Alpha Team's guys despised having to work with what they considered a "walking computer." Now she's a very human part of the team. I could hug both of them for it.

If they weren't otherwise occupied.

For a long, silent moment, it's a standoff. Our guys are outnumbered four to two with me and Vick caught in the middle. However, the Security folks are outgunned four to three, since our guys hold two pistols each.

No one wants a gunfight in the promenade dome, even if it is with the Safety Net weapons. Eyes dart back and forth, everyone wondering who will make the first move. Ironically, it isn't someone holding a gun.

There's a soft click, then a clatter as Vick's binders drop to the floor. All of us stare at her while she casually rubs her right wrist with her left hand, then switches and massages the other one. When she does look up, she shrugs. "What? Did you think VC1 couldn't override a simple electronic lock?" She offers Sanderson an apologetic smile as she pulls a pistol of her own from beneath her jacket, hidden in her tech-scrambler back holster. She doesn't aim it directly at the security chief, but her intent is clear. "Sorry, but you aren't holding me. I can't protect myself or catch the killer if I'm in custody, and I've been informed that any evidence exonerating me has conveniently been erased." She takes me by the arm and guides me behind Alex and Lyle.

My eyes go wide. "No camera footage?" I whisper.

"None," she mutters under her breath.

"Oh. Shit."

"Yeah, and you're hanging around me too much."

I cover my mouth with one hand, then catch that she's joking with me, even under the tense circumstances.

"Let's go," she orders, giving me a nudge down the access corridor that leads away from Security Central and the dome. I glance over my shoulder to see Lyle and Alex backing along the hallway behind us, never taking their weapons off the officers.

"This is putting a real strain on our friendship, Corren!" Sanderson yells after us. There's genuine anger in her tone. I can't really blame her.

The grays of guilt and sadness roll off Vick like storm clouds blowing in from the ocean. "Yeah, I know," she whispers in a response her friend will never hear. "And I'm sorry."

Once we're well out of sight of the security team, Alex takes point, and Lyle sticks to the rear, keeping me and Vick between them. I don't know where we're headed, but we're at a jogging pace. No one's set off any alarms yet. So, either Sanderson doesn't want to panic the civilians, she believes Vick is innocent and is giving her a chance to get away, or she thinks chasing Alpha Team is a lost cause. Probably a combination of all three.

"How'd you know what was going down?" Vick asks over my panting. I'm not in as good shape as she and the others are. The Storm doesn't make me train the way they do—something I will work on if we get out of this.

Alex glances back over his shoulder, his face reddening. "I, um, listen to Security chatter," he admits. "Among other things. Undercover Ops likes it when I advise them of any civilian-side situations involving our personnel before they get out of hand. Disturbance with Storm soldiers at the Alpha Dog Pub? We're on it. Tensions mounting at the sports bar? Some of our sober people get there first and make sure it's all under control. Keeps us out of trouble and makes us look like saints compared to the other merc outfits."

Like the Sunfires, who have a horrible reputation for drunken and disorderly conduct.

Alex is a younger, less experienced version of his tech genius brother who also works for the Storm, but he's still very good at what he does.

"I caught that they were gonna arrest you for the recent murders," he continues, directing his comments over his other shoulder at Vick. "We know you were in your quarters. I ran a scan and saw the footage was wiped, smelled a setup. Figured we'd get you out of there."

"Appreciated." Vick jogs along behind him, no sign of fatigue or breathlessness.

Sometimes I resent her perfect physique.

"Setup wasn't Sanderson," she adds, her tone allowing for no argument.

Alex stops in front of a side hatch labeled "Maintenance Only. No Entry." I'm not sure where we are, let alone where that leads, but I hear the rumbles of ships' engines on the other side, so loud they come through the steel. Hangar bay, maybe?

"We know that too. I saw the vid capture they got of the killer. There's another clone."

Vick nods.

"With her own implants?" Alex asks.

"That's our guess," Vick says, resigned.

"Fuck all of us," Lyle mutters from behind.

Vick grins. "You've *all* been hanging around me too long. So," she says, gesturing at the hatch, "what's the plan?"

Alex holsters his weapon. He pops an access panel to the side of the sealed entryway, then steps back, leaving the space open, presumably for Vick. "You get us through this door. We hotwire a fast ship and get

the hell away from here, wait for things to cool down,
give Security and the rest of the Storm a chance to deal
with all this shit. It's gonna take an army to take down
another you. Not something the four of us should try
to handle, and definitely not in my paygrade even now
that we're in Undercover Ops. You can't be involved.
Not on this one. Too much potential for a mix-up and
death by friendly fire."

"Or sacrifice as a scapegoat to preserve the Storm's
reputation and hide what you really are," Lyle puts in,
reminding everyone he's not just brawn.

Vick's eyebrows go up, as do mine. Neither of us
considered that possibility. I can't tell what she's thinking, but her lips set in a hard line and her eyes unfocus
in that way that indicates she's conferring with VC1.

"And then what?" I ask, drawing attention away
from her and giving her a chance to process all this.

The Storm, the organization she's pledged her loyalty to, might use her as a sacrificial pawn. God. And
why not? When they have more they can awaken when
this mess is cleaned up? A little plastic surgery and a
memory wipe and she would be good to go. Only it
wouldn't be Vick.

No. We're all paranoid. To do that, they'd have
to get rid of me, too, somehow. And they wouldn't go
that far.

Would they?

Vick turns toward me, the anguish on her face telling me she and VC1 have reached the same horrible
conclusion.

If it meant the reputation, hell, the entire existence
of the Fighting Storm was at stake, then yes, they very
possibly would.

"Then," Alex goes on, "we see where we are. If we're clear and our side figures a way to get Vick off the hook without revealing her secrets, then we come on back. If not... well, U Ops has taught us a number of ways to fake our own deaths."

Vick's eyes go glossy, filling with tears. One minute I'm reminded they are manufactured and reflective of her communications with her AI. The next, they are all too human.

"You guys would give up your entire careers... for me?" she asks, incredulous.

Lyle moves to stand beside Alex, holstering his own weapon and slipping an arm around Alex's shoulders. "We've been talking," he says, "and watching. You hate how Undercover Ops works. You never wanted to be part of it, did you?"

Vick opens her mouth, closes it, then fixes her gaze on the metal wall behind him. Alex gives me a confused look, but I know what's wrong.

"She can't say. Literally. But I'll tell you. She hates it, every second of it."

"Damn, have they got her that deeply prog—erm, brainwashed?" Lyle asks, using my preferred terminology for the Storm's tampering.

I nod.

Alex and Lyle exchange a glance. "We should have done this sooner," Lyle says.

"Yeah, we should have."

"Done what?" Vick asks, shifting her weight. A flare of discomfort hovers around her. There's more going on in her head than her inability to speak against the Storm, but I don't know what it is yet.

"Left," they say together.

"We've seen how the Storm treats you. We don't like it, but as long as you kept sticking around, we figured you were biding time, you know? Waiting for the courts to figure everything out and you could call the shots for yourself or even take over, since the whole outfit should legally be yours." Lyle shakes his head.

He's right. If not for the questions of Vick's humanity and the fact that she's alive when she should be dead, Vick would be the sole owner of the Storm, inheriting it from her now deceased father rather than the board taking over.

"We knew there were things you couldn't say, classified things, but you can't even complain? Can't choose your assignments? That's not okay, not by us," Lyle continues while Alex nods. "And now all this shit. It's time to get the hell outta here. We all have fake bank accounts, treasure troves squirreled away. We can get new identities, maybe start up a private security company somewhere dirtside. The four of us, we'd be great!"

The four of us. The absolute wanting need on Vick's face is painful to look at. She takes an unsteady step.

Backward.

My heart sinks for her. I know what's coming before she opens her mouth. Through meticulously constructed conversations told in riddles, euphemisms, and the carefully orchestrated placement of emphasis, I've pieced together exactly what Vick can and cannot say.

Or do.

We've kept it all between ourselves, not wanting to draw any more attention to Vick's mechanical limitations. The guys don't know the true extent of her enslavement. They believe, if she wants to, she can run.

"There's one fatal flaw in your plan," she says, voice breaking. She takes another step back.

"What's that?" Alex asks.

Vick heaves a shuddering breath. "Me."

CHAPTER 35: VICK
RESTRICTIONS

I am programmed.

A TREMOR works its way from my legs up my spine. I hold myself in place through sheer force of will. I'm balanced on the balls of my feet, ready to run... or fight. God, I don't want to fight them. These are my teammates. My friends. And I have so very few people in my life I can trust. I just lost Sanderson to this nightmare, held her at near-gunpoint and put her in a terrible position. I can't lose them too.

"You can't leave," Alex says, getting it at last. "Aw, fuck." He turns to Kelly. "We could stun her. Lyle can carry Vick, and we can cover them. I'm not VC1, but

I can get us through this hatch with a little more effort, and I can steal us a ship."

I sigh. "I'm right here. I'm hearing this plan. And even as you're making it, VC1 is calculating six different ways to stop you."

"Come on. You wouldn't actually hurt one of us." Lyle pauses, looking at Kelly, his brow furrowed. "Would she?"

I close my eyes to steady myself. When I open them, I feel the walls rising between us, and between myself and my emotions. I didn't ask VC1 to turn my suppressors up. She did it on her own. Preparing me. "If you draw on me, my programming—"

Kelly opens her mouth to protest the use of the word. I stop her with an upraised palm.

"Quit it. We both know what it is, even if we don't want to use the words," I snap. She closes her mouth, lips turning down in a hurt pout that isn't put on, but real. Sometimes I really, really hate myself. "If you draw on me with the intention of forcibly removing me from service to the Storm," I begin again, "three primary directives in my subroutines go to war with each other: One: my purpose to serve the Fighting Storm; Two: my purpose to protect my own, very expensive self, and Three: my purpose to protect my teammates. You would be committing treason, so that would negate you as my teammates. That means One and Two take precedence. My implants would view you as the enemy. Even if neither I nor VC1 actually *wants* to, I am always allowed to use deadly force to serve the Storm and protect myself from my enemies. And I will."

And just like that, everything shifts. I swear I can see their estimation of me as a human being changing as I watch: the tightening of lips, the narrowing of eyes, the frown of disgust. Not from Kelly, of course. She's looking back and forth between me and the guys, uncertain of what to do next. "She's still your friend, and your partner," she says, tone soft. "She's saved your lives a dozen times, always had your backs even when you treated her like garbage. It's not her fault, what they've done to her. Don't turn on her now."

I ignore her defense of my actions even as the guys' expressions soften. I signed up to be part of this outfit. My signature is on all the paperwork giving them permission to do whatever they wanted to me after my death. I couldn't have known what they'd turn me into, but it's my own damn fault I am the way I am.

"The exception," I continue, "might be Kelly. I consulted with VC1 while you were telling me your plan. Since my mental health is directly connected to Kelly, I might spare her if she takes steps against me. Or I might not, regardless of what my heart wants." I meet her eyes. "Please, please, don't test this. I don't want to know which way the programming will decide."

This is a moment that's been a long time coming.

"We're willing to take our chances," Alex says, checking with Lyle in a glance and getting a nod in response. "We don't believe, when push comes to shove, that you'll hurt us."

I think my heart is going to break. "I—"

"She will. She'll kill you both. And it won't even take her much effort to do so, because while you two morons are trying not to hurt *her*, she will hold nothing back. She'll have no choice. And it will destroy her." The new voice in the corridor catches all of us by surprise as Carl comes around the corner, hands empty and outstretched in a gesture of peace.

We're caught, all of us, with the guys openly talking about betraying the Storm. Everyone's shoulders slump. Lyle and Alex move their hands away from their holsters. The stalemate with Officer Sanderson was one thing. Drawing pistols on our unarmed boss would be something else entirely and not a place they want to go to.

You knew he was there and didn't say anything, I growl at VC1.

I am sorry, she responds. *I tried.*

She's just as trapped in this as I am.

With a start, I realize I'm gripping my pistol, now in its side holster. Out of habit, I flick my thumb over the safety, checking. It's already off. I have no idea when I did that. I always keep it on when holstered. I set it back in the on position, pressing the switch so hard it bruises the skin.

God, I was really intending to shoot them. This is so fucked-up.

"Where's your backup?" I ask, looking over Carl's shoulder. My voice wavers. We have twenty-five people in Undercover Ops—six teams of four and Carl overseeing us all.

"I'm alone. And this conversation and the one before it never happened." He lowers one hand to his belt pouch and removes a capped hypodermic.

"Wait! You don't need to drug me. You know I'll follow orders." I back away, hands raised. Drugs make me defenseless. With VC2 loose in the base, I need my guard up.

"I'm sorry. I have a mission for you. And I need the appearance of you being subdued and unconscious to pull it off. You're going to have to trust me. Hold still."

I stop in my tracks, unable to refuse a direct order from my commanding officer. My muscles go rigid, every fiber of my being wanting to flee while I hold my position.

"What kind of mission?" Kelly asks. "She's in no shape for that. And there are things you don't know."

"Oh, believe me," Carl says, slipping the needle into my arm while he speaks over his shoulder to her. "I know a lot more than you think. Don't worry. You're going with her. And you two," he adds to Lyle and Alex, "are going to remain here and keep up appearances."

The world goes fuzzy. I brace myself against the nearest corridor wall. My head feels like it's doubled in weight. But even without the chemicals muddling my thoughts, I don't think Carl's words would make sense.

"What are you talking about?" Alex asks, confirming my confusion.

"Don't worry. I'll brief all of you as soon as I get Corren off the station."

"Off the—" I don't finish the thought. I'm already gone.

SHIP'S ENGINES, padded but still hard table beneath me, antiseptic smells. I'm in a transport's medical bay. I crack one eye open against the blinding white lights reflecting off equally blinding white and metal surfaces. Pain lances through my head—knockout drug aftereffects suck.

No one around and I'm not hooked up to anything, so I swing my legs over the side and check out the rest of my surroundings. Standard medbay setup, though smaller than I expected. Two tables, including mine, so I'm on a shuttle, not a larger vessel. I stand on shaky limbs, then rotate, searching out the door. It's behind me, in the center of a wall comprised mostly of a giant window looking out into an observation area. Must be soundproofed, because though Kelly and Carl stand on the opposite side, I can't hear them. And judging from their facial expressions, Carl's rigid posture, and Kelly's gesticulations, they're having a heated argument.

I can imagine what it's about.

Bracing myself against the table with one hand, I reach out for the first throwable object I can grasp—in this case, an empty bedpan on the rolling tray beside me—and hurl it at the window. It makes a satisfying *clang* as it bounces off and clatters to the tile floor. Both arguers turn as one to stare at me, Carl frowning and Kelly exuding relief. She gets through the door first, shoving Carl out of the way to make it to my side and offer me the support of her shoulder.

"Hey," I whisper, voice hoarse. "How long have I been out?"

"Hours," she growls back, more at Carl than to me. "And he would have kept you under longer, but I guess VC1 had other ideas."

"Damn AI," he says, keeping the table between us. "There's only so much programming can cover."

Kelly and I stare at him. "You knew?" we ask in unison.

Carl taps the side of his head with one finger. "I told you, I know more than you think. Probably more than you even know about yourself," he says to me.

Alarm bells go off in my head, an old-fashioned klaxon loud and obnoxious at once—VC1 sending a blunt warning. I do not like what Carl's words imply, but I keep my mouth shut.

"Come on," he says, heading back into the obser-vation lounge.

I put an arm around Kelly's shoulders for balance and we follow him. My headache fades into the back-ground as the adrenaline kicks up. We sink into a cou-ple of side-by-side cushioned armchairs and wait.

"So," he says, taking an opposite chair. "You're probably wondering what the mission is. Bear with me and try not to bite my head off." Taking a deep breath, he finishes with, "We're checking you into Earth's Kle-nar Facility."

"What the fuck is—" I break off as VC1 fills my head with images, first of me in a straitjacket. Then an-other one of a room with padded walls. I blink the dis-play off. "You're putting me in a mental institution?"

Kelly sucks in a sharp breath. Guess she'd never heard of it before either.

"Not just any mental institution. The best money can buy. It's a privately owned facility, catering mostly to members of the One World Government and their relatives, but also open to high-powered business ex-ecutives, famous entertainment industry personalities, and a handful of other wealthy clientele, for the right price."

I lean forward, resting my elbows on my knees and my face in my hands. "And how, exactly, am I getting in?" My voice is muffled, but he hears me anyway. It's finally happening. They think I'm crazy, that these re-cent events have pushed me over the edge. Not that I blame them, what with the break I suffered on our is-land vacation, mixed with my old Rodwell trauma and my more recent issues with mirrors. But an asylum? "I really didn't think I was that bad off."

Kelly rests a hand on my back, rubbing in circles until my shoulders untense. Her love flows through our connection. "You're not. I've been worried, but you don't need an institution."

"No, you don't," Carl confirms.

I glance up. He's grinning, that bastard. "This isn't funny." I've feared losing my mind for years.

Sobering, he shakes his head. "Sorry. No, it isn't. I apologize. You're getting in as a called-in favor from the OWLs. They owe you for helping with the Secretary of the Treasury and her daughter. Don't misunderstand," he adds, raising his hand to forestall further questions. "You *will* be receiving specialized treatment there for your recent dysmorphia. However, mostly you're there to be bait."

Oh. Shit. Of course.

"Bait for what?" Kelly asks, uncertain.

I turn to her and take her hands in mine. "They wanted to get me off Girard Base, and they needed a plausible cover story. The Storm is trying to protect the civilian population." I glance at Carl, who nods in confirmation.

"I still don't get it. What's really going on here?"

"Are we secure?" I ask Carl, rather than VC1. After all, if the AI is compromised, she'll lie, and a computer that can lie is a dangerous thing indeed.

"We're secure," my boss assures me. "While you were sedated, your med team added a new security chip to your implants. They've been working on it since we became aware of the other clone, shortly after returning from the slaver base. The chip will scramble all incoming and outgoing data beyond recognition to anyone outside of the Storm who tries to read it. We're confident you're no longer a liability."

So the headache isn't just from sedative side effects. I nod, relieved, and give Kelly's hands a gentle squeeze.

"I'm a lure," I tell her. "For VC2."

CHAPTER 36: KELLY
PERCEPTIONS

Vick is bait.

I DO not like this plan. I understand it, but I don't like it. The reasoning is sound enough: Vick is known to have suffered a traumatic injury that has given her some severe anxiety in recent days. So checking her into Klenar Mental Health makes sense to anyone looking. It's a beautiful facility, located in a small valley in the mountains of Germany near the Swiss border. At this time of year, late spring, flowers cover the surrounding hills, though there's a touch of persistent snow on the very tops of the peaks.

I did some research on the facility while we were en route. Luxury and comfort abound. The hospital is small and exclusive, one main building with a reception area and administrative offices, and two wings—one for the regular patients and one for those who suffer from more serious problems or tend toward violence. The small but highly respected staff treat everything from substance addictions, to severe depression, to all varieties of PTSD and much more. At maximum capacity, they can serve about forty individuals, though from the sparse numbers I'm seeing, they don't appear to be close to full.

"Impressive security," Vick comments as we stroll along one of the corridors. She tilts her head toward corner cameras painted the same colors as the pale yellow and cream walls. Now that she's pointed them out, I can spot them, but they blend well.

An older female staff member in all white leads us toward what will be mine and Vick's accommodations while we're here. Vick's medteam is already onsite, having arrived a couple of days earlier. At least they're keeping us together. Our guide pauses, turning to smile over her shoulder. "We want all our guests to feel safe, but we try to keep it unobtrusive. We also cater to some very important people. Our location does a lot to keep the media and particularly tenacious fans out, but the few who venture this far don't get past our system and the guards." Her slight German accent is noticeable, but not distracting from her fluent English.

"Guards?" I ask, hurrying to keep up when she starts walking again. Vick's longer stride causes her no problems in that regard.

"They're dressed as orderlies," Vick murmurs to me from my right. "Four have shadowed us since we arrived."

Beige-uniformed men and women circulate among the doctors and nurses, but Vick's right. They aren't carrying anything or helping with patients. Instead, their gazes touch on everything and everyone, though their expressions are calm and politely friendly. Several cast surreptitious glances at us every few moments.

"Look closer. They're heavily armed." Tension rolls off Vick in deep waves of teal.

I do so. Telltale bulges in the pockets of the baggy coveralls indicate a variety of weapons they can reach in a matter of seconds.

When we come to a pair of automatic doors, each marked with a set of double black diamonds, one of the milling "orderlies" pauses and looks our way, a big grin set on his handsome face.

"Robert!" I exclaim, rushing forward to embrace him.

If anything, the OWL's grin widens. "Kelly, good to see you," he says in his cultured British accent.

Vick offers a hand, which he shakes.

"And you, Vick." Robert frowns in concern. "I understand you've had a time of it since your return from our joint mission."

"You could say that," she says with no inflection.

"Well," our guide says, "I'll leave the rest of the check-in process to Robert. He's head of your onsite security team, so all questions about what you can do and where you can go should be directed to him. But I'm certain you'll find the accommodations we've provided for you and your staff will meet all your needs." With that, she gives us a little wave and heads off toward a desk at the far end of the corridor. I can't help noticing the flare of white relief that sparks in her emotional aura. Was she nervous about walking with us? I was so focused on Vick, I didn't pick up on it, but now…. And why the contingent of guards?

"What do the black diamonds mean?" Vick asks, indicating the doors in front of us.

Robert shifts uncomfortably. "Well, if you were a skier, they would stand for an extremely challenging ski slope. Here…."

"Spit it out, Robert." Vick crosses her arms over her chest. Some of the milling orderlies tense, a few hands dropping closer to weapons pouches.

"It's Klenar's subtle way of saying Maximum Security wing, patients who are dangerous to themselves or others." He meets Vick's stare with a steely one of his own. Lowering his voice, he adds, "The lads and ladies on my team know you're not dangerous to us, but if we're going to perpetuate the charade that you are here because you snapped and went on a killing spree—"

"Wait. Is that what they're telling everyone?" My voice rises, drawing attention from some nurses and a passing doctor. I lower my tone. "Seriously, this is what we want people to believe back at the base?"

Beside me, Vick goes very still and very quiet.

"Come on," Robert says, waving his palm over a scanner by the double doors. After a couple of soft beeps and a click, they swing open, only now allowing us to see how thick they are—at least a foot and made of solid steel.

I take Vick's ice-cold hand in mine. Her grip is tight, her pulse too fast. "Breathe, Vick," I whisper. She takes an unsteady breath and we move forward. I don't miss her other hand trailing its fingers across the access pad as we pass through. I look away quickly before Robert notices. The doors swing shut behind us and lock into place. Vick's eyes go unfocused for several critical seconds before they zero in on my face and she nods once in silence. I nod back.

VC1 can handle this. No words needed between us for me to figure that out. If we need to get through those doors in a hurry, she'll make sure we do.

Robert leads us through a central hub where two hallways branch off, one on either side. Overhead, a huge beautiful glass dome crisscrossed by metal framework lets in natural sunlight in a bright blue sky.

The weather outside must be perfect. I wonder how long it will be before Vick can get out and enjoy it again. She gazes upward, a longing expression in her eyes, and I know she's thinking the same.

Several nurses seated at a horseshoe-shaped desk look up and wave, though their smiles seem forced and their auras show trepidation at our approach. We're told that treatments are down to the right and patient rooms to the left. One nurse indicates the left archway with a shaky hand. Once we're in the new hall, Robert glances along the corridor. Empty. This section is decorated just as comfortably as everywhere else, but there are subtle differences: more cameras, patient suite doors farther apart with smaller windows in them. Some have slots instead of viewing panes, for passing food through? Are the people receiving treatment in here that much of a threat?

"Come on," Robert says, setting off. Eventually, we pass a few additional armed orderlies, but it appears they're relying more on technological than human security here.

"Aren't we worrying about the other patients and staff?" I murmur. If VC2 gets in here....

"We're secure. You've got experts and soldiers from both the Storm and the OWLs onsite and working with Klenar's security people. It's under control. We're only talking about one woman, highly skilled or not. Our folks will intercept her before she can reach the facility. We just wanted to isolate her, and this area is sparsely populated and hard to reach. And just in case, we've been quietly transferring the most mobile patients elsewhere. It's fine," Robert assures us.

I'm not assured, and from Vick's expression, she isn't either.

When we come to the end of the corridor, Robert stops in front of a door with Vick's name taped to the side of it. There's also a datapad in a wall holder, probably containing her medical information. Out of curiosity, I lift it from the holder and swipe my fingers across the screen. It lights up, offering me access. I shoot Robert a confused look. "How much of her real data is on here and how much is for show?"

"It's all on there," Robert says. "Fingerprint locked, but you're on the official access list, so it opened for you."

"And you?" Vick asks. "How much do you know about me?"

Robert uses another touchpad to open Vick's suite of rooms. We follow him into a large living space with comfortable couches and a wall of windows with a view of the mountains. Doors to the left and right must lead to bedrooms. There's a small half bath just inside the entrance. The door shuts, sealing all three of us inside.

"This is a secure area. We sweep it daily for bugs. We can talk here. And as for your question," Robert says, making for the closest couch and dropping onto it with a heavy sigh, "if you mean do I know you're a clone with an AI in your head, then yes, I do. And so does the highest echelon of the One World government."

Chapter 37: Vick
Laying the Trap

I am stunned.

"YOU KNOW?" My knees buckle and I fall more than sit on the other sofa in my new, better-be-temporary, quarters.

"We do," Robert affirms. "Well, I didn't until One World brought me into the loop for this mission, but the government knew. Don't panic. You're safe enough." He frowns. "At least you were until your doppelganger showed up and started killing civilians."

"Full-body human cloning is illegal. I'm not complaining, but why is Vick an exception?" Kelly asks, taking my hand once more and sitting next to me. I lean into her for support.

Robert shrugs. "Lots of reasons. Her missions, for one thing, have done a lot of good for both Earth and her colony worlds. Her future mother-in-law is a high-powered diplomat. And then there's the loophole."

"Enlighten me." It comes out snarky. I'm edgy and tired and don't want to play games.

"Technically, the law states that cloning cannot be used to duplicate an existing human being. You can make cloned replacement parts, limbs and such. You can clone animals. And if you go by the exact letter of the law, you can clone a human, so long as the original is deceased. At least that's how the Storm played it to One World when the OWLs started looking at you harder. You're a hero, rapidly becoming a legend in your own time. We've got a file on you over a hundred pages long. We investigated your crash on Elektra4 and determined from the damage to the transport, in particular the pilot's chair, that there's no way you could have survived." Robert leans forward, forcing me to meet his eyes. "You didn't, did you?"

A shiver passes through me. I close my eyes, seeing the lightning streak down, piercing the shuttle's hull like it was nothing, piercing *me*. My pulse rate picks up. My breath comes too fast.

"Get her some water, please," Kelly orders.

To his credit, Robert jumps up to comply, stepping to a wet bar off to the side and fetching me a glass of ice water. The frozen cubes tinkle against the glass while I let VC1 get me under control. I note while I take my first sip that there is no alcohol on the bar shelves, just juices and sodas. Makes sense in a mental health facility.

"No, I didn't survive," I say, my breathing returning to normal, my voice soft.

"So a clone replaced you. Kudos to your medical personnel. Your people aren't the only ones researching the process. They're just the only ones who've had success. A success One World is looking to purchase, I might add, in exchange for helping with your current problem."

I hide a grin behind my glass. They can purchase the process. Without blueprints to the implants as well and a willingness on the patient's part to have a majority of the brain removed, it won't work. Which I'm certain the Storm knows and One World doesn't. Good deal.

"So," I say, the shakes evaporating at last, "who all is in on this and who thinks I'm a dangerous homicidal maniac?"

"Your Storm team working here and your additional OWL security know you're not a murderer," comes Carl's voice as he steps out of one of the bedrooms. Of course he's sticking around. "Klenar's regular staff thinks you're traumatized, which is true, and terrifying, which, to some extent, is also true. They think you killed the victims on Girard Base, but they want to help you regain your sanity. We need to perpetuate that belief. No one is allowed to speak about the reality of this mission outside this suite. We can't put anything into any sort of computer or communications system about it, either. All contact must be verbal or handwritten."

"Or VC2 will be able to access it," I say.

He nods. "I'm afraid most folks on the Girard Base also think you've lost your shit, though Lyle and Alex are in the loop."

Kelly shifts to glare at him. "And how long is that going to be allowed? Vick's reputation is destroyed, and no one seems to care about that."

"Oh, believe me, we care. Until this gets resolved, we can't contract her out for any missions, can't use her in any way."

Of course his concerns aren't for me, personally.

"Once VC2 shows up here, and all indicators suggest she's on her way since the murders on Girard have stopped, we can eliminate her. Then, with the OWLs' help, we'll fabricate some kind of cover story, alter the other clone's body to make it look like someone who's had plastic surgery to look like Vick, someone with a grudge against her. We'll clear Vick's name and that will be that."

"Simple," I say, setting my drink aside, sarcasm dripping from the word like condensation on the glass.

Carl shrugs it off. "In the meantime, you get the therapy you need. Get settled in. You start your sessions tomorrow."

THERAPY, AS it turns out, isn't as bad as I feared. I need it. I know I need it. I can't walk past a reflective surface without flinching, can't brush my teeth or put my hair up properly without seeing that metal skull staring back at me from the mirror. Sometimes it's so bad, I'm shaking for minutes afterward. I'm no good to anyone like this.

I'm certainly not good enough to fight VC2, but I keep that to myself and hope like hell she takes her time in coming after me.

"Are we even sure it's me VC2 is after?" I say to Kelly and Carl. We've been discussing what might be taking her so long to make her move. I'm on my way to my third counseling session, the treatment side of the maximum-security wing empty except for our party. It's always empty when I'm out of my suite. I'm beginning to suspect that's by design.

It is, VC1 confirms. *A safety precaution. You are, after all, considered to be a lethal threat.*

I shake my head, earning some confused looks from my escort guards dressed as orderlies. But hey, I'm crazy, right? They can think what they want. Fuck 'em.

Just so long as you can get me in and out of here if I need to move fast. Claustrophobia has a lot of triggers. Close quarters are only one of them. Being locked in, even with the spaciousness of the suite and all the amenities of the Klenar Facility, is another one.

I can. Do not worry.

Robert is always on duty when I'm moving about, and he answers my earlier question. "We think she's after both of you. You to kill, because you're competition for her," he says to me, "and you to keep," he says to Kelly.

Kelly opens her mouth to speak, but Carl beats her to it. "We think the reason she's murdering women who look like Kelly is because none of them can do for her what Kelly does for you."

And it hits me. "VC2 is what I would have become if you hadn't found Kelly to help me purge my built-up emotions, if you'd let me continue to live rather than terminating the implant project." The project being me, of course.

Carl rests a hand on my shoulder. For once, I don't shrug him off. "We think so, yes."

Holy fuck.

We arrive at my therapist's office, but Dr. Nuzzi steps out almost immediately, waving for us to follow her farther down the long row of offices with doctors' names on them. "We're going to the large conference space today," she says, white teeth glowing in a bright smile.

I like her. She's older, an expert in dysmorphia, no nonsense, sees right through my bullshit, and pushes me to my limits. I've told her everything I can about what I'm experiencing. She didn't let up until she'd dragged every detail from me. I can feel she wants me to get through this as fast as possible, so we share the same goal.

Even better, Carl has brought her into the loop, so she knows I'm not a threat to her and doesn't treat me like the other staff members sometimes do—polite, caring, and as if I'm going to strangle them at any moment.

We're almost to the door at the end of the hallway labeled Conference Room Level Two when one of the other offices opens up and two women step out, one wearing the white coat and trousers of another therapist, the other—

"Valeria?" the young woman shrieks, then throws her arms around my neck, hugging me for all she's worth. "Oh, I'm so glad you're okay. You changed your hair! It is you, isn't it?"

I'm not big on physical contact, especially by surprise and from people I don't know well, but if this attractive blond is calling me Valeria, then I must have interacted with her on the slaver mission. I take both her forearms in a gentle grip, pushing her away from me to put some space between us and study her. A moment later it clicks.

"Cynthia Hothart, right?"

She nods, blond curls bobbing with the motion, and offers up a big smile. No wonder I didn't recognize her right off. Last time I saw her she was drugged, depressed, pale, and thinner. Now she has color in her cheeks, a spark of life in her eyes. I'm guessing she's been at Klenar since we rescued her, so several weeks longer than me. They've worked wonders with her, that's for sure. It also clicks that she's here, in the maximum-security wing. She's certainly no threat to anyone around her, which means she is or has been a threat to herself. My heart sinks. I know what that feels like, know it far too often, and I hope she makes a full recovery.

"What are you doing here?" I ask, using the question as an excuse to take a small step backward. I don't want to hurt her feelings, but I'm feeling closed in.

"Oh, my mother works for—"

"One World. Right. Of course." Her mother is Secretary of the Treasury. Of course Cynthia would be admitted to the government's exclusive mental health treatment center.

"I'm so glad to get a chance to thank you for leading the team that saved so many of us. I asked my mother to find out who you were. You work for the Fighting Storm, right?"

I glance over her shoulder at Carl, raising my eyebrows. He gives me a go-ahead nod.

"Yeah. And it's Vick, not Valeria. That was a cover."

"I knew it!" She gives a little bounce on her toes, reminding me of how a much younger Kelly might have been. The smile is infectious. I can't help returning it. But it fades when she adds, "You were hurt, weren't you? I wanted to send flowers or a card, but I didn't know where."

"I'm okay."

Her frown intensifies. "Not if you're here, you're not. But you'll get better. I'm getting better. They're wonderful here." Behind her, her doctor smiles.

She seems a little manic, like maybe she's on some serious mix of antidepressants, but her improvement does give me hope. Not too improved, though, if they haven't transferred her yet. This must be a good moment for her. I'm not seeing the bad.

"Yes, well, on that note, we do have a session," Dr. Nuzzi says, not unkindly. She places a hand on my shoulder while Cynthia's doctor leads her away by the elbow—a protective gesture—from me.

Sigh.

"Stay in touch, Vick!" Cynthia calls back as they head in the opposite direction from the conference space. "Let me know how you're doing."

I offer a halfhearted wave and a forced smile before they turn the corner, entering a walkway that circles the two-story nurses' station central hub. We continue toward our destination. At the farthest door, Dr. Nuzzi stops.

"We're on the upper level, so we'll need to go downstairs eventually, but I wanted you to be prepared for your challenge over the next few days or weeks, depending on how long it takes to overcome your aversion. I have every confidence that you *will* overcome it. From your records, you are a strong individual with a remarkably resilient psyche." She winks. "And stubborn as hell. So," she says, throwing open the door and leading the way onto a small balcony overlooking this side of the room, "here is your challenge."

I step to the railing and lean over it to look down into the large space that is probably used for lectures and group sessions, or maybe recreational activities like dances or banquets. About the size of a high school gymnasium, it would hold hundreds of chairs or tables or displays, though it contains none of those things now.

In fact, it only contains one thing, and there are a lot of them.

Mirrors.

From one side of the conference space to the other, it's a sea of mirrors. They aren't angled upward, won't reflect my appearance from here, so I lean over a little farther to analyze the setup.

It's a maze. A maze of mirrors from one set of double doors on the left all the way to a matching set of doors on the right. And without facing into those mirrors, looking right at them, working my way through them, I will never, ever get across that room.

"Oh fuck no," I breathe. "So much fuck no."

CHAPTER 38: KELLY
GOALS

Vick is challenged.

"SO MUCH fuck yes!" Dr. Nuzzi blurts out, throwing her hands up like a kid on a roller coaster.

Vick and I turn to stare at the petite, white-haired, grandmotherly therapist.

She takes one look at our faces and bursts into laughter, so hard she doubles over with the effort. I can't help but join in, though tentatively, watching Vick with a cautious eye. Relief floods me when Vick's lip twitches, just slightly, upward before she cracks a small grin.

"Sorry," Dr. Nuzzi says, straightening and wiping her eyes on the sleeve of her lab coat. "Couldn't resist. You soldier types always amuse me with the colorful turns of phrase. And believe me, I've heard it all. But." She points a finger at Vick's chest. "Yes. This is your challenge, to get across that room without needing someone to pull you out. No hyperventilation, no nausea, no averting of the eyes, no hesitation whatsoever. If you want me to return you to active status, that's what you'll have to accomplish."

Vick says nothing as we follow the doctor out the door, into a stairwell, and down a flight of stairs to an identical door on the first floor of the facility. This one has had some recent electronics installed next to it, as evidenced by areas of chipped paint around a shiny new scanner pad.

"You're going to lock me in?" No one misses the trepidation in Vick's voice. She runs a hand through her hair.

I resist the urge to comfort her with a hug. She wouldn't appreciate the gesture here in front of her therapist and Robert, who is watching the proceedings with great interest.

"You'll be under observation at all times," Dr. Nuzzi says, not answering the question. "We've installed cameras and sensory equipment. The conference hall's green room"—she points to a clearly marked Staff Only door off to the side—"has been reconfigured to be a monitoring center. Your company spared no expense."

"Yay for them," Vick mutters.

Dr. Nuzzi laughs. "I'll let you in. Get to the other side of the room and the doors will open for you. Simple, right?" She palms the door open. No one misses that Vick keeps herself facing away from the entry while she finishes gathering information and preparing herself.

"What if I have a meltdown?" she asks.

"You mean, 'What happens *when* you have a meltdown?'"

Vick's eyes widen in surprise. "You expect me to fail?"

"Absolutely," Dr. Nuzzi says with a definitive nod.

Vick glances at me, raising her eyebrows. "What the actual fuck?"

Robert snorts an almost laugh, then gets himself under control.

"Look," Nuzzi says, resting a hand on Vick's arm, "you're going to struggle with this. It's inevitable. But I have confidence that given time and support, you'll overcome it. And the sooner we get started, the sooner that day will come." She claps Vick once on the shoulder, spins on her heel, and leads the way to the monitoring room, motioning for me and Robert to follow. We precede her through the Staff Only door. "Step inside whenever you're ready," Nuzzi calls back, then follows us in and lets the door slide shut, leaving Vick alone with her current worst nightmare—her self-image.

To be honest, it's always been her worst nightmare.

I stand with Robert at the center of the converted green room, staring at a bank of monitor screens installed along one wall. A couple of couches, probably left over from the room's previous purpose, line the opposite wall. With Robert's help, Nuzzi drags one over and we plop ourselves down on it to watch the screens.

One shows the hallway where Vick still stands, looking lost. My heart goes out to her. She's not facing into the room, not making any move whatsoever to enter it. "I wish she could hear me," I say.

"Oh, we can do that." Nuzzi leans forward and taps a few commands into the monitoring system. "Can you hear us, Vick?" she asks.

On the hallway view, Vick's head snaps up. She looks from side to side, until her eyes locate the camera, and gives a faint wave. "Yeah, loud and clear, Doc. You have my internal comm code?"

"Your company gave me access to anything they thought would better help me help you."

"How generous of them." None of us misses the sarcasm.

"I'm here too, Vick," I remind her. "It's a solid set-up. Your… tech partner would find it impressive."

On the screen, Vick's eyes unfocus for a split second, too fast for anyone else to catch it. "Not so much, no, but then she's hard to impress."

Robert and I exchange a grin. The doctor furrows her brow. So, they haven't told her everything. "Well, I'm impressed," I say. "We'll know the moment you have any problems and we'll come let you out, right, Doc?"

Nuzzi nods, realizes Vick can't see that, and says, "Of course." She reaches over, tapping multiple commands into the console. A number of readouts appear, measuring Vick's heartrate, pulse, respiratory system, and overall emotional stress. The bar graph for each one can register in the green, yellow, or red areas. At the moment, all the stats are in the lower yellow zones. Not the best places to start.

"Take a couple of deep breaths, Vick," I tell her.

She rolls her eyes, but she complies, rotating her shoulders and releasing both physical and emotional tension. The readouts drop to the upper greens. Better.

"Whenever you're ready," Nuzzi says.

Vick turns and faces the open doors. The readings jump back into the yellow zone.

Well, I tried.

"I wish I was in uniform."

Oh. I rock back on the couch. Yes, that makes a lot of sense. Since we arrived, we've both been in comfortable, casual, civilian clothes. Nothing military. Nothing to draw more attention to who she is. But civilian wear would take away some of her power, make her more vulnerable. "Let's consider that for your next try."

Vick's no longer looking at the camera, but she cocks her head to one side. "You're *both* assuming I'm going to fail."

Dr. Nuzzi fields this one, thank goodness. I'm blushing at my slip. "Yes, we absolutely assume you're going to fail. And you shouldn't beat yourself up over it when you do. You suffered a massive trauma. And you're human."

I notice the slight jerk of Vick's shoulders, though no one else seems to. Covering the microphone pickup on the console, I whisper, "You just said the magic words, Doc."

"Let's hope so," she whispers back with a faint smile.

Vick takes a tentative step into the conference room, then another and a third. The doors swoosh closed behind her. She sucks in a harsh breath. She's facing a mirror head-on with more on either side and a single pathway a little farther forward and to the right. Her breathing comes hard and fast over the green room's temporary speakers. I swear if I listen closely enough, I can hear her heart pounding as well. All the indicators leap for the red zone.

Beside me, Dr. Nuzzi is leaning forward, watching every move, every blip, every shift of the numbers and colors on the screens. Her hands clench in her lap, but she's grinning like this is the most wonderful thing she's ever seen. I'm beginning to doubt *her* mental stability as well.

Four steps, five, but Vick never makes it around that first turn in the mirror maze. With an almost inaudible groan, she sinks to her knees, covering her face with her trembling hands.

"Well, then!" Nuzzi says, rising to her feet and clapping once. She's all smiles. "Let's go and get her. I can work with this."

Robert and I exchange a confused glance, then follow her out to the hallway.

"Oh yes, that kind of strength and resilience? I can absolutely work with this," she says again, and with a swipe of her hand over the access panel, she swings open the double doors.

CHAPTER 39: VICK
BABY STEPS

I am doomed.

IT TAKES one full-on look. One! And I'm down for the count. That half-flesh/half-steel skull staring back at me, one mechanical eye rotating in an otherwise dark, empty socket, teeth hanging in a half-lipless mouth, a hole where my ear should be.

Or shouldn't be.

This. Is. Who. You. Are.

All the cosmetic surgery, all the comforting in the universe, all the therapy won't convince me that reality isn't reality. I shouldn't be seeing it in the mirrors, but

I damn well know it's really there, just beneath the surface of my synthetic skin.

And I cannot unsee what I've seen. Cannot get it out of my head.

I keep waiting for Kelly to say, "It's just one trauma after another with you, isn't it? So needy. So damaged."

I'm not giving her any more reason to say it to me today.

Soft black covers have already dropped over all the mirrors on this side of the room, triggered by my body hitting the floor, apparently. Nothing more to see here. Before they can open the doors and rescue me, I spin on my knees, place my palms flat on the expensive dark green tile flooring, and push myself to a standing position. When the doors swing open, both Kelly and the doctor take a startled step backward, not expecting me on my feet.

Good. I'm all about surpassing expectations.

Granted, I'm facing them, not the room of mirrors, so it isn't as hard as it could have been. But hey, small victories. There's a soft swishing sound behind me indicating the coverings have gone up again, revealing the reflective surfaces once more. I don't turn around to check. Instead of being helped into the hall, I'm able to walk myself out, even if it is a shaky handful of steps. I focus on placing one foot in front of the other until the doors close again, sealing off the conference room from my potential view. Only then do I raise my head.

Kelly has a soft smile on her lips. I can't tell if that's pity or compassion, and I'm not sure I want to know. Robert stands behind her, all business, his face schooled into a serious expression that conveys nothing. It's the doctor, though, who stuns me. Dr. Nuzzi looks like she just won the star system lottery. I swear, she's beaming from ear to ear, bouncing on the toes of her white canvas shoes in her excitement.

She stretches her arms toward me, hesitates, and asks, "I know you're not much for hugs, but… may I?"

With my eyebrows raised, I give a faint nod, and a second later, her spindly arms are around me, hugging me for all she's worth. I can feel the excitement vibrating through her. When she steps away, she's still grinning.

"Okay, seriously, what the fuck? I didn't even make it past the first turn." The slight hitch in my voice surprises me. I thought I had myself under control.

Kelly moves to my side and places a hand on my shoulder. It takes a lot to not shake her off, but I manage it. I know she's worried.

"You walked in!" Nuzzi exclaims, still bouncing. "I didn't think you'd step through those doors, thought we might have to give you a push, but you walked in. On your own. That's amazing given the trauma you've described, simply amazing."

I stare from one of them to the other. Even Robert gives an approving nod, then breaks into a grin. "You're serious. You're not just saying that."

Kelly tugs on my sleeve until I look at her again. "She's telling the truth, Vick. I'd know if she wasn't. That first step was the hardest one. She's really encouraged."

Well, okay, then.

My progress varies from there, at least in my own head. On the exterior, I'm gaining ground every day, getting a little farther into the maze on each attempt, even if it's a single step, before I can't take the sight of my own face anymore. Inside, though, I'm not quite as impressive. That first move through the doors continues to be the hardest, maybe even harder than in that initial trial, knowing I'll subject myself to what amounts to torture: nausea, shakes, hyperventilation, collapse.

Dr. Nuzzi continues my therapy sessions in her office as well, asking detailed questions about what I'm seeing, teaching me breathing exercises to control the panic attacks and get a little farther. The only time I sense any disappointment from her is when I tell her my self-image hasn't changed. It's still the half-metal/half-flesh skull staring back at me from the glass. It's not flickering or fluctuating or fading. It's not blurry or temporary. It's there. It's me. In that regard, there's been zero change, zero improvement.

After a week and a half of trials in the conference room, I've made it more than halfway across before having to cover my eyes and feel my way back to the entry point. It's progress, but Carl's impatience to return me to active duty, and, if I'm honest, my own impatience as well, are wearing on me.

Everything about this is too damn slow. We don't know why VC2 hasn't made an appearance yet, but it's got everyone on my team nervous. She has to know where I am, where Kelly is. The killings on Girard Base stopped, so she's moved on from there. What's taking her so long to strike?

All I can think is she's planning something big, and here I am helpless to do anything about it. I should be grateful for the reprieve, but instead I'm in a constant state of heightened awareness, waiting for an attack that could come at any moment.

When Robert and Carl pull me aside after one of my mirror room trials, I'm almost relieved.

"Someone's been testing the facility's perimeter defenses," Carl begins, watching my face. I know all the color has drained from the artificial skin (yay, realism), know I'm swallowing huge gulps of air. Kelly's life is at risk and I'm useless. With me down for the count, VC2 will tear her apart, mentally, physically, or both.

I hold up a hand, gesturing for Carl to wait a moment while I lean against the nearest wall, take a couple of deep breaths, and hold them for ten seconds each before letting them out. Not sure which is worse, going pale or flushing with embarrassment at my continual weakness, but the heat in my cheeks tells me I'm looking more… human. Sweat that beaded on my forehead in the mirror room chooses now to drip into my eyes. I wipe it away on the sleeve of my gray/black/white uniform shirt.

"In what way?" I ask, responding to his earlier statement. "Physically or with tech?"

Robert glances over his shoulder to where Dr. Nuzzi is conferring with Kelly a little farther down the corridor. They can't hear us from there, but I wonder why he cares.

"Both," the OWL says, lowering his tone. "We've found some damage to one of the fences—"

"There are fences?" I break in, stunned. When I look out the windows of my suite, there's nothing but fantastic scenery: grass, wildflowers, pine trees, mountains.

"Just beyond the tree line," Carl confirms. "They don't want everyone in here to think they're prisoners."

"Even if we are," I mutter. They ignore me.

"Our technology experts also say someone is testing the computerized security. There have been a few breaches into the system that didn't get further than the operating menus before they were kicked out, but they're there. We've had teams out searching for her, but so far, no luck. As soon as you're up to it, we'll send you with those teams. The goal was to lure her to an isolated area here in the mountains, not actually into this facility. The tech guys swear we're secure enough, but…." Robert checks on Kelly and Nuzzi again. They're still engaged in deep conversation.

I nod in their direction. "Hey, Kelly knows the potential threat, and Nuzzi should if she doesn't already. Why all the secrecy?"

Robert looks down at his polished black boots, and even Carl flushes a bit with embarrassment. "Um, well, it's not about them. It's about you. We're not supposed to be adding to your stress. We've both been warned by both of them that if anything happens that doesn't immediately concern you, we're not supposed to involve you in it. Since the issues have been contained, Dr. Nuzzi said we shouldn't tell you. Kelly was uncertain." Carl grins. "I felt differently."

"Good," I say with a firm nod. Everything regarding VC2 concerns me. Though something about what he's telling me feels off.

"They didn't want us to set you back," Robert adds, brow furrowed in concern. "You really are doing well. I've heard them talking. They're not just pulling your chain."

"If it was a chain that would drag me the rest of the way through that damn mirror maze, I'd put it around my own neck."

Carl rests a firm hand on my shoulder. "Keep at it, Corren. We need you sooner rather than later." With that, he turns and strolls away, leaving Robert to watch over me until the doctor is ready for my next therapy debriefing.

In Nuzzi's office, I can't stop tumbling things over in my head: VC2 is close. She's working on getting into the facility. I need to take her out while she's still off the property. Carl swears the OWL guards and Storm personnel are enough, the security tight, but there are too many innocent lives at stake in here, even if most of them are military or government and not purely civilians, even if they've transferred many of them away. And I can't do a damn thing while I continue to fail to see my exterior in favor of my grotesque interior.

"They told you, didn't they?" Dr. Nuzzi interrupts my whirling thoughts.

"I'm sorry, what?"

"You've missed two questions I've asked about your latest maze attempt. So," she says, placing her palms on her knees and leaning forward in the faux leather chair across from the couch where I'm sitting. "They told you. I asked them not to." She's frowning hard. I almost never see her frown. She's always so upbeat.

I'm not going to lie to this woman who's helped me so much, but I'm not thrilled about her attempts to keep me out of the loop. "Yeah, they did. You should have. I need knowledge to protect myself." And I need it to protect Kelly, but I don't voice that out loud.

"Can you? You're still experiencing the hallucination." She stands and strolls over to a side table by the desk I've never seen her sit at and pours herself a cup of tea from a kettle on a hotplate there. "Until you learn to accept yourself at face value, so to speak, you aren't going to be much in a fight. One reflective surface and you've got what could be a fatal distraction."

"Yeah... I've been thinking about that."

Nuzzi pours a second mug full of tea and brings it to me. I've never been a tea gal, but the warmth of the mug between my cold hands soothes me. When I take a sip, it's just the right temperature, and the flavors of vanilla and caramel surprise me into a pleased "Mmmm."

The doctor raises an eyebrow.

"I've always thought tea tasted bitter."

She removes the spoon she's been using to stir hers and points it at my chest. "You've clearly been deprived of good tea. Now," she says, returning to all business, "tell me what you've been thinking about. When my patients start thinking too much, I worry." Her face is serious, but her eyes sparkle with humor.

"Okay, well," I begin, trying to find the right words to explain what I've been suspecting for a while, "I'm wondering if maybe I would have more success if I stop trying to change what I'm seeing and just accept it for who I am."

Nuzzi opens her mouth, but when I hold up one hand, she closes it again.

"Look, I know it sounds...." I don't say "crazy," but we both note the omission. I sit up straighter on the couch and use my free hand to rap lightly on my skull with a closed fist. I swear I hear a faint metal clang inside my head and wonder if she hears it too. If she does, she gives no sign. "It's what's in there. It's not something my brain has made up. I *am* the person I see in the mirrors. It's the artificial covering that's the illusion. I'm definitely not trying to tell you how to do your job. You've made more progress with me so far than I thought was possible. But I think I need to accept myself, get comfortable with myself, maybe even learn to appreciate it all. It does make me pretty badass." I grin, and it comes more easily than I thought it would.

"Maybe then the hallucination will stop, or maybe it won't." I'm trying to gesticulate and coming dangerously close to spilling tea all over the shaggy beige rug. With careful precision, I set the mug aside on an end table. "Either way, I should be able to function around mirrors. It's a win, regardless."

"You mean that, for now, you want me to stop pestering you about what you see," Dr. Nuzzi says, a knowing smile on her lips.

My spirits plummet. That's not what I meant, but I understand why she thinks so. I hate her probing questions.

"Still, your hypothesis is not without merit." She takes a long sip of her tea, sets it aside with mine, and steeples her fingers beneath her chin. "All right, Doctor Corren. We'll try it."

My face flushes with heat at the "doctor" comment. I'm so busy getting VC1 to diffuse the blush that for a long moment the complete meaning of her words eludes me. "Wait. We can?"

She nods, then reaches out and takes one of my hands between her wrinkled ones. "I'm not one of those therapists who never really listens to her patients. And I've often found that when it comes to someone's own mind, they have a better understanding of what's really going on in there and what might make them whole again. We'll try it. But." She waits for my eyes to meet hers.

"There's always a but."

"Yep!" She releases me and retrieves her tea. "If the hallucination does not fade with this experiment you've come up with, then you have to be open to trying something else. Maybe medication."

I frown. The last thing I want is drugs, especially after my recent encounter with Jacks's sex-enhancement concoction. While some can be effective, the side effects often seem to outweigh the benefits. VC1 will play with the levels of the natural chemicals my body produces, but that's different. Nuzzi is referring to mixtures made in labs, synthetic compounds, not natural ones. I've looked up some of her suggestions, and they're hard-core, seriously mind-altering shit… that often produce solid results, but… I've also got my memories back, and I know I experimented with some drugs in high school to my detriment. I never got hooked, but it was a close thing. I've told Dr. Nuzzi all of this. I've never told anyone else, not even Kelly.

She pats me on my camo-clad knee. "Not all drugs are bad for you. Promise me if this doesn't work, you'll be openminded and trust me. If you agree, then we can go ahead with the treatment plan you've got in mind."

I study her open and honest expression, her deep desire to help me clear in her eyes. "I promise. I trust you." My eyebrows rise, startled at what I just said. I'm pretty sure I've said those last three words to exactly two people since the airlock accident. Kelly was the other one.

Dr. Nuzzi laughs. "Don't be so stunned. There are a lot of reasons the facility won't let me retire. Lots of reasons why I'm the go-to therapist for all the military patients. I'm the kindly older aunt, the grandmother they miss from childhood. And I'm very, very good at my job."

I laugh with her. "Yeah, Doc, you definitely are."

CHAPTER 40: KELLY
ENCOUNTER

Vick is trapped.

AFTER ALMOST two and a half weeks of mirror maze attempts, Vick has managed to get two-thirds of the way through the conference room without collapsing. She's changed tactics. I watch her face the reflective surfaces head-on rather than casting her eyes down in an attempt to avoid them. She locks her jaw so tight the muscles are visible beneath her pale skin. She never breaks eye contact with the image in the mirror, regardless of what she sees there. It's a dare, both to herself and the woman in the glass. I can almost hear her thinking, "You will not take me down forever."

While she does this, I monitor her both through the technology in the green room and through my own empathic senses. The monitors continue to register her vitals in the low red zones, but that's better than they were at the beginning. On her first few attempts at this new strategy, she had her emotion suppressors set to their highest capability. I put a stop to that. She discarded that crutch over a year ago. I won't have her overly leaning on it now.

Not to say I've forbidden their use entirely. She will need those assistive devices for the rest of her life. But not on full, not high enough that she becomes the robot she sees in the mirrors, devoid of all emotion whatsoever. Inhuman to everyone except me.

I always feel what she feels.

Not to the extent that I used to, thank goodness, or I'd be on the tile floor with her after every collapse, but enough to know she's very, very human, always.

On the screens before me, Vick takes another couple of rigid steps toward the far door. She's in full tactical gear, black bodysuit overlaid with black Storm armor, her most powerful attire that she had shipped to her from Girard Moon Base. When she dressed this morning, she had a new, heightened determination that today she would succeed.

She won't. Her raspy breath echoes over the speakers in the small green room. I'm on the edge of the couch, fists clenched, my own breathing faster than it should be, in synch with hers. I'll have to provide lots of extra encouragement when they bring her out.

Beside me, Dr. Nuzzi taps my knee. I jump a little. She's been so quiet, I almost forgot she was there. "She's about done. I'll go get her. Five more feet. Not the victory she wants, but a victory still." No anger or disappointment. The woman has infinite patience.

I move to stand with her, but she halts me with a raised hand.

"Stay put. Robert and I can handle her. We'll bring her in here. You look like you didn't get any sleep last night."

"I didn't," I admit, stifling a yawn. "Thanks." I reach for my cooling cup of coffee on the end table as she leaves the room to join Robert in the hallway. I turn off the screens and speakers, returning the green room to a more comfortable silence.

Ever since Carl and Robert and the other members of the Storm team on Earth detected VC2's presence, Robert has taken up position right outside the conference space doors, just in case Vick's cloned twin makes it through the facility's security and tries to take advantage of Vick's most weakened state. Knowing she's out there somewhere, testing the defenses, searching for a way to attack, has had a negative effect on my sleeping habits. There've been multiple breaches now, with our technology specialist helping the Klenar staff to plug each incursion into the electronic systems. Even Vick's strong arms around me all night long haven't kept the nightmares away.

VC2 is nearby. She's coming. If the teams don't locate and capture her soon, she'll find a way in.

Suppressing a shiver, I stare at the green room door, willing them to hurry. Even at her lowest, I feel safer when Vick is near me.

There's a bit of a commotion in the hallway, carrying through the closed door. Robert and Nuzzi must be having more trouble helping Vick than usual. I sigh, knowing this will weigh heavily on Vick's self-doubt for the next several hours. Any miniscule loss of ground for her has a massive impact. I'm tempted to go and assist, but that makes things worse for her. She hates for me to see her during her initial collapse. Giving her a few moments in the hall to compose herself before I get involved has become our routine.

The door opens, and Vick steps in, eyes wild and darting around the room before settling on me.

All the hairs on the back of my neck stand on end.

Something is very, very wrong.

"Where are Robert and Dr. Nuzzi?" I ask, craning my neck to look past her into the hall. There's no sign of them, no sounds coming from the corridor. Just her harsh, ragged breathing. I lower my empathic shields just a bit. The flare of anguish, pain, and frustration knocks me back against the far armrest of the couch. I raise my shields as fast as I can, blocking the worst of it, but the residual energy leaves me panting.

"They had an emergency to deal with," Vick says with no inflection. My insides ice over. No, not Vick. And not VC1 speaking through her, either, because under the current circumstances, the AI would be using as much inflection as she is capable of so she doesn't scare me. Because the artificial intelligence... cares... about me.

No. This is VC2.

Her emotional rush has me failing to think straight, but I know. I *know* this isn't Vick. I scan her from head to boots, needing to be sure, wanting to be wrong. Her hair sits in a messy bun at the back of her head. She always puts it up that way to keep it out of her face in the maze. These days, she wants to see her reflection. Her green-and-brown camo pants and olive-green T-shirt cling to her lanky frame, accentuating the curves of her waist and her breasts.

But… she wore her black tactical gear today. Sometimes she wears camo beneath her armor, but when would she have discarded the black coverings?

Oh God, please let that be the commotion I heard in the hall. Please let this be Vick.

I hold out my hand to her, using the identification verifier that the two of us worked out a few nights ago. Because Vick was afraid VC2 might try exactly this. Because Vick is paranoid.

And because Vick is usually right.

"Vick…." My voice trails off as she steps fully inside. I catch a glimpse of a dark mound of something on the hallway floor behind her before the door swings shut, blocking my view. I swallow hard. "Give me your heart, Vick."

And I realize what else is wrong.

The blue line that connects us is missing.

"My heart?" She gives a soft laugh that falls flat, even taking her suppressors into account. Her head cocks to one side. She's studying me. I can almost hear the wheels turning as she attempts to analyze where she's going wrong. "I gave you my heart a long time ago."

Her smile would almost be convincing. If I was actually talking about her love for me.

But I'm not. I'm referring to the tiny gold heart I gave her when I first tried to convince Vick that she wasn't the Tin Man she believed herself to be, that she was and always will be human in my eyes.

And VC2, while she might know about it from her brief interactions with VC1, would not have one. Or so we hoped.

I know our guess was correct when the woman in front of me doesn't reach for her wallet that she keeps in a back pocket while wearing her camo, the wallet where the heart memento would be.

"Of course you did," I tell her, stalling. "But it's nice to hear you say so from time to time."

My throat tightens, preventing me from saying anything more. I'm trapped in a very small room with VC2.

To hide my reaction, I swivel back toward the console and bring my hands up to its surface.

"What are you doing?" VC2 snaps, moving to stand beside me, between the couch and the electronic surveillance system.

"I thought we'd go over your monitoring results while we wait for the others to come back." And maybe get a message out to Carl and the rest of our people onsite in the process. But my voice wavers. I'm hoping VC2 doesn't know me well enough to catch it.

Her hand snaps out and grabs my wrist before I can activate anything. "They aren't coming back," she says, low and even.

Oh God. Did she kill Dr. Nuzzi and Robert? Is that what I glimpsed in the hallway?

And what about Vick? Did VC2 kill her as well, or is she still trapped in the mirror maze, which, once she's already collapsed, might be worse for her than death.

A rush of adrenaline hits, and I yank my arm away, making a break for the door and the hall and Vick. I'm aware of rapid movement behind me, but I manage to get the door open and rush out, stumbling over the two bodies between me and the conference room entrance. I stagger-step until I hit the wall by the doors, catching my balance with my palms on the bloodstained surface before me. The soles of my white canvas shoes stick to the tile.

A chill shivers through me as I glance back to see I've tracked blood across the hall, blood from an ever-growing pool around the bodies of Robert and Dr. Nuzzi. The grandmotherly doctor is definitely dead, her eyes wide and staring up at the ceiling tiles, but I'm certain I catch a twitch of Robert's hand, still wrapped around the grip of his pistol, before it falls still once more.

I should have known, should have felt the attack, especially the death so close, but with my shields in place for Vick's trial, I detected nothing amiss outside the green room. I've made tremendous progress managing my empathic abilities around traumatic events. The irony isn't lost on me.

"Done running?" VC2 asks from her position leaning against the green room door frame.

I open my mouth to scream. In a flash too fast to follow, she's beside me, her hand covering my mouth, the other gripping me around the chest, pulling me back against her.

"Not much point in shouting for help," she says. "Everyone on this floor of the wing is dead. But just in case I missed someone, I'll keep you quiet."

Everyone? No. Not everyone. Vick is still alive. She has to be. I stare around at the hall, the walls, the ceiling, searching for the blue line, but before I can get a fix on it, VC2 drags me down the corridor, away from the conference room, toward one of the emergency exits. A quick swipe of her hand across the access panel opens the door that should only unlock itself during a fire or some other major threat.

"Where are you taking me?" I mumble against the chilled skin of her palm. Somehow she comprehends the words.

"Someplace private where we can talk and not be interrupted. I need help. You're going to help me."

She pauses, holding me under an awning until a security camera swings away from us on its overhead mounting. She glances into my eyes once before turning her face away, but I can see the torment and insanity there. Her grip around me tightens.

"You're going to make me whole."

CHAPTER 41: VICK
TO OVERCOME

I am imprisoned.

THE MINUTES tick by, each one like an hour to my anxiety-ridden self. I'm on the floor, the cold of the tile seeping through the legs of my black pants everywhere the armor doesn't reach, adding to the shivers already wracking my body. It's humiliating, waiting to be rescued, unable to stand and walk the much longer distance back to the entrance, but it's that distance that gives me the pride to endure the humiliation. Today, I almost made it.

Twenty more steps and I would have been at the opposite side, raising my hands in triumph as I plunged through the far double doors. If it hadn't been for the mocking laughter, I would have gotten there.

Yeah, that's a new setback. The faces in the mirrors have begun laughing at me, taunting me. I can't hear words or sounds, thank god, or else I'd have to report auditory hallucinations to Nuzzi and she'd be sure to end my experimental self-treatment. But I know they're laughing, the half-steel, half-flesh mouths agape, the teeth flashing in the curved half lips, the eyes bouncing around in their sockets.

I think I'm going to puke. Where the hell are they?

The covers have already dropped over the mirrors leading to the entrance. This isn't some new endurance test. I push myself halfway to my feet and topple, landing on my backside, my knees too shaky to hold my weight.

Real badass, Corren.

It isn't until I've crawled a dozen meters that it dawns on me something might be wrong.

I open the channel to the green room on my internal comm. "Kelly, you there?" My voice comes out thready and weak. Great.

No answer. Worse.

"Hey, Doc, could use a little help here," I try again. No response. New chills that have nothing to do with my maze attempt ripple over my body. A painful hardness settles in my chest.

What's going on out there? I ask VC1. I've avoided interacting with her when I'm in the maze. She's an easy crutch to lean on, and I need to do this on my own, but everything about this situation is off. Even the pause before she answers goes on so long I'm afraid I've lost contact with her too.

I am unable to communicate with the rest of the facility.

"Oh, thank god," I breathe aloud. "I mean, no, that's bad. I'm just glad you answered." I crawl faster, the adrenaline giving me strength. After a few more meters, I'm able to stand. Leaning on the covered mirrors for support, I stagger-run to where I came into the conference room.

Where the doors don't open. Of course.

"VC1, can you—"

I cannot.

"Um… when we first got here, I had you insert yourself into their systems. You reassured me you could open any door on the property, including this one if necessary, though I told you not to unless there's an emergency." I pause, thinking about some of her more rigid programming. "You would consider this to be an emergency, right? You aren't just keeping me in because I asked you to?"

An amused chuckle echoes over my internal speakers. *No. This would indeed constitute an emergency.* The humor vanishes from her tone. *Someone has blocked my access to the facility's systems, including the doors.*

There's only one person I'm aware of with the ability to do that. And with sudden clarity I realize what's been bothering me so much about VC2's failed attempts to breach the Klenar Facility's security systems—she shouldn't have been failing.

Shit. Anything VC1 can do, VC2 should also be capable of.

Okay, maybe not anything. VC1 is an AI, and VC2 hasn't been operational long enough to evolve to that level. Right?

Your hypothesis is sound.

I jump at the unexpected response, staggering against the sealed doors. "You're listening in on my personal thoughts again."

This is an emergency.

I swear I can hear the smirk beneath her words.

"This isn't the time for snark," I tell her.

My research indicates witty banter helps defuse tension in stressful situations.

Not wasting time on arguing with that. I take a couple of deep breaths, trying to calm my ever-increasing anxiety, for myself and for Kelly and what VC2 might be up to out there.

I find the door's access panel on the right and look for something to pry off the covering. I'm not carrying any gear beyond the armor, no tools. My nails are short and blunt, since I only grew them out for the Valeria persona. I send a sharp kick at the closest mirror, thinking maybe a piece of glass will do the trick, but it doesn't even shift position, let alone crack or shatter. I do manage to dislodge the black fabric covering, so my metal skull can laugh at my pitiful attempts to do damage.

It is made of a reflective polycarbonate. Virtually indestructible. They were concerned you might try to get through the room by breaking all the mirrors.

I'd thought of that. But it would have defeated the purpose, and I was never quite freaked out enough to try it. I understand why they took the precaution, though.

Also, fuck.

Panting, I shift my position to face the sea of other mirrors leading back across the room. They are all covered.

"Okay, I can do this."

You have already taxed your systems substantially. You are bordering on exhaustion.

"I don't have a choice. Kelly's out there."

There is no guarantee that the doors on the far side will open either, if VC2 is truly in control.

"I have to take that chance."

The AI falls silent.

Sweat beads on my forehead even though my palms are cold and clammy. "Calm the fuck down, Corren. The mirrors aren't even visible. You're just tired. You can work through tired." I'm speaking out loud, hoping hearing my own voice will distract me from the tremors in my limbs.

It's not working. I take a dozen steps back toward the far side and the doors I hope will unlock when I get there. If I get there. Deep breathing seems to help. I swipe the sweat away on my sleeve and keep going. Just as I round the fourth turn in the maze, there's a soft click.

All the covers on the mirrors go up.

I close my eyes, dropping my head to my chest. "Oh, fuck me now."

It appears VC2 has control over the equipment as well as the exterior cameras and doors.

"Yeah, I got that." And it means the exit is even more likely to be locked to me, but I have to try. What else am I going to do? Opening my eyes, I face my disfigured reflection head-on. "Okay, bitch, let's see what you've got." It's as much anger at her as encouragement to myself, since we are the same person after all. I can't suppress a bark of harsh laughter.

You are raising concerns, my counterpart says in my head.

"Deal with it."

Another twenty steps and I'm flat out yelling at my own image, using all the adrenaline-fueled rage and energy at my disposal, channeling my fear into anger. "Laugh all you want! Yeah, go ahead! That's right. I'm hilarious, except you're me. You're me and I'm a fucking lunatic." I'm shouting and slamming my tightened fist against each face I pass, counting off each mirror as a victory. "Twenty-seven, and fuck you! Thirty-one, you motherfucking nightmare. Thirty-nine, bitch. Yeah, that's right." If this does turn out to be some kind of new and very twisted test, Nuzzi is gonna wrap me in a straitjacket and lock me up for good.

And here I believed I was finally beginning to comprehend human behavior.

That earns a second laugh and another six steps.

By the time I hit the fiftieth mirror and what I've perceived to be about the halfway point, I'm hoarse from the yelling, raging, profanity-filled rant. My heart pounds. My pulse races. I'm dripping with sweat and can't catch a full breath. Every last ounce of badass has abandoned me.

I'm not going to make it across.

As soon as I allow the thought, my knees buckle and I go down. I can't even crawl. The mirrors are full-length, and I'm still catching glimpses of myself on both sides and in front at the next turn. On all fours in the middle of the walkway, I focus on the tile and heave air into my lungs. "What can you do for me?" I ask VC1. "Anything?"

You have already exhausted your adrenaline reserves. I took the liberty of setting your suppressors to full over twelve steps ago. I am sorry. I cannot think of any way I can assist you.

I manage a low growl, then stop when a sigh echoes in my head. "Hey," I say softly. "I appreciate what you've done. When I'm yelling at the face in the mirrors, I'm not yelling at you. It's not you I'm angry at. You know that, right?"

I know it now. A pause. *I am, essentially, the metal and circuitry you persist in seeing. Sometimes it is difficult for me to tell at whom you are directing your disgust and hatred. I thank you for considering my feelings.*

Is that what I just did? Yeah, I guess it was. I've acknowledged VC1's capacity for emotions in the past, but I don't think I've ever taken them into consideration when I've acted before now. I allow myself a small grin. "I'll try to do better with that. You are so much more than metal and circuitry."

So are you.

I let that sink in. She doesn't say anything more, but the silence is companionable, not angry. I don't know how I sense that, but it comes through. We're an odd team, VC1 and I, but we *are* a team. So, how does this team solve this problem? I look up, not at the mirrors but at the ceiling, searching for inspiration. My eyes land on one of the overhead security cameras Kelly and Dr. Nuzzi have been using to monitor my progress.

"VC1, you said you couldn't access anything outside this room. What about the cameras inside?"

A pause. Then, *I am able to see you through the cameras in this room, yes, but I—*

"Guide me," I say, closing my eyes, rising to my feet, and bracing myself against a mirror.

Brilliant. I don't have long to bask in the glory of her approval before she says, *Forward four paces.*

I'm unsteady as hell, but if I use both hands out-stretched to the sides and grab the tops of each mirror I pass, I can remain upright. I take four steps.

And walk face-first into very hard polycarbonate.

"What the hell?" I release my grip on a mirror to rub the bridge of my nose—not broken, but very, very bruised.

Recalculating for your longer than usual stride. VC1 sounds miffed.

"I'm in a hurry."

A sigh. *And you gave me your complete trust. I apologize. I will endeavor to better live up to your faith in my guidance.*

It goes faster after that, though with my eyes shut, the second half of the room seems to go on forever. When she at last tells me I'm facing the exit doors, I crack open first one eyelid, then the other. Then I slap my hand against the exit panel.

Nothing happens.

Of course the doors are locked. I flip myself so my back is against them and slide down until I'm seated on the floor facing the backs of the mirrors. I made it, dammit. I found a way across and I made it and I'm still fucking trapped in here.

What am I supposed to do now?

CHAPTER 42: KELLY
DARK REFLECTION

Vick is unique.

"YOU'RE AGITATED," I say, keeping my voice soft and calm while my heart threatens to burst out of my chest. I want to scream for help, but it might trigger some violent reaction in my captor. We're also far enough away from the main building that no one is likely to hear me, and Vick and VC1 should be able to find me without me needing to scream.

VC2 paces back and forth across the storage building where she's dragged me. It's small, about the size of a one-bedroom cabin, made of logs but sealed well with no visible seams between them. On either side are racked snowmobiles, stored for the spring and summer. Along the front and back walls hang skis, snowshoes, ice skates, and various other winter recreational equipment. We're still within the perimeter fence but hidden in the trees.

The back of my head aches. When we first arrived, she knocked me out to keep me still while she tied me up, though I couldn't have been unconscious more than a half hour or so. In the meantime, she changed clothes—from the brown-and-olive drab camo to the black tactical armor Vick wore today. At least she didn't try to fool me again. I spotted her discarded clothes in the corner right off, and she shrugged it away like she didn't care if I knew. I swallow hard at all the implications that come with the wardrobe switch. Is her plan to replace Vick entirely? Step into her life without anyone but me noticing? If she were more balanced, would that become possible?

I tuck my knees into my chest, where I sit on the floor in the middle of the storage space. The rope she's used to bind my wrists and ankles chafes my arms, though my legs are protected by my thick socks.

VC2 acts like she never heard my words, though she casts a glare in my direction from time to time. I use the somewhat quiet moment to study her with my empathic sense, careful to keep my walls mostly in place. Even the slight crack I allow pours her rage, anxiety, fear, and aggression through it. I suck in a sharp gasp.

She whirls on me, stopping her pacing so she ends up standing over me. Guess she was listening after all.

I look up and up until my eyes meet hers, and a shiver passes through me. Vick is about five foot nine or so. A little on the taller side, but not too much. I've always felt our bodies fit together, since my head comes right to her shoulder on the rare occasions when we dance or the more common embrace. But she carries this *presence*, this sense of complete control, this outer confidence that makes people jump to obey her orders. It's all a front. I can read the insecurity beneath the persona she portrays. But it's effective.

Vick has told me more than once that I'm the only one who really sees through her. She complains that she can't get away with shit when she's dealing with me, and I suppose that's true. While she's certainly intimidating to her enemies (and often her fellow members of the Storm), I've never found her frightening.

Until now.

With a start, I realize that's what's missing in VC2. She's got the confused mixed emotions, the anger and frustration, but she's missing the guilt and the low self-esteem, the self-deprecation that makes Vick approachable when she lets down her guard. Quite the contrary. The whirl of colors around VC2 tells me she's got ego in spades. She knows she has issues, but she's confident that she'll resolve them. With me.

Given her earlier comment about making her "whole," I can't come to any other conclusion.

VC2 crouches in front of me, leveling the playing field a little, her eyes never breaking contact with mine. For a long moment, we stare at each other. Then, "I need you to do that thing you do," she says, waving one hand in an abstract manner. Her expression softens, something almost akin to affection in her features, but it isn't love. That's missing too.

"What thing?" I whisper, unable to keep the tremor from my voice.

She reaches out and I flinch back, but I can't get away from her. Her fingers tuck a stray strand of hair behind my right ear. The gesture is sweet, tentative, and so very, very *Vick* that my heart goes out to her. "You shouldn't be afraid of me," she says, rocking back on her heels.

The fear returns in a wave, but there's anger too, and I channel that to strengthen my voice. "You kidnapped me. And you killed people I care about."

VC2 puffs out an impatient breath, her bangs rising and falling with the exhalation, the rest of her hair tied back. "I wouldn't have. Not if they'd made me right. They screwed up. I'm broken in here." She slaps a palm against the side of her head for emphasis.

I wince in sympathy. "I'd like to help." I force the words out. Part of me does want to help her. Part of me is repulsed and terrified. I worry about the long-term effects of this encounter and how it will alter my relationship with the real Vick Corren, assuming she's alive.

No. I'm not thinking that. She's alive. She has to be alive.

"But I can't do what I think you're asking me to do," I continue, pushing the darkest of my nightmares away. "I can ease some of your emotional pressure," I say when her face hardens again, "but I can't complete a bond with you. It's a rare thing, and even in the rumors of its existence, it's never been between more than two people."

Her hands move so fast I barely notice the motion before they clamp on to the sides of my head. I can't hold back the whimper that escapes my lips as she pulls me forward and rests her forehead against mine. Our lips inches apart, she growls, "You're damn well going to try."

In this much physical contact, the empathic channel erupts open between us, and we both gasp in surprise at the sudden rush of the emotional onslaught in both directions. Genetically, VC2's brain wave patterns should be identical to Vick's, which means they are almost identical to mine. The impact tears through my walls as if they are tissue paper.

I get all her aggression. She gets all my fear. They mix and flow, back and forth, roiling around inside us, searching for an outlet. I can't think straight enough to provide one. There's a roaring like a launching shuttle in both my ears, a pounding in my skull that hurts like the mother of all migraines. My vision tinges black at the edges.

"If you don't let me go," I pant, gasping between the words, "I'm going to pass out."

"Then fucking fix me!" VC2 shouts into my face. "This is your fault. Yours and hers. You gave me the basics but none of the context, the skills but not the training, the bad shit but none of the good. You have that good. Give it to me!"

I moan as my sight tunnels. "We didn't do it on purpose," I tell her. "We didn't even know you existed. Please… you're going to send me into emotion shock." Which, if untreated, could result in coma or even death.

VC2 might not know that, but her implant surely does. She thrusts me away from her so that I tumble over onto my side, unable to right myself with my arms and legs tied and lacking the strength to do so even if I were free.

Standing, she takes up her pacing again, her boots and lower legs coming into my line of sight, then leaving it. It heightens my nervousness, not being able to keep her in my view at all times. She's muttering under her breath, half incoherent, half profanity. But when she comes to a sudden stop and goes silent, that is much, much worse.

My heartrate slows enough for me to get my breathing under control. My head still pounds in painful throbs, and my shoulder hurts where I landed on the pock-marked wood floor, but rocking side to side gives me enough momentum to roll onto my knees and sit up again. I search her out, finding VC2 standing near the door, staring out through the single window in its surface, staring toward the edge of the trees and the Klenar Facility beyond.

"You can only bond with one person at a time," she says, not looking at me. It's a statement, not a question, so I don't respond, but her tone is dead even, cold, and calculating. "I'd hoped to be more together before tying up loose ends, but it appears I need to reorder my to-do list."

Without another word to me, she pushes open the door and steps into the brisk evening air. A few faint rays of setting sunlight cast their glow across the floor before the door swings shut behind her. Several locks click into place. Her booted footsteps recede into the distance.

Terror clenches my chest and closes my throat.

I know exactly where she's going and which "loose end" she intends to take care of, and exactly how frayed that loose end will be if she's been stuck in the mirror maze all this time.

CHAPTER 43: VICK
EXIT STRATEGY

I am at the end of my rope.

"DAMMIT!" I shout, my voice bouncing off all the glass and echoing through the high-ceilinged room. Yelling hasn't helped the situation. It hasn't even made me feel better. But the pressure of my bottled-up emotions needs some kind of release, and Kelly isn't here.

Thinking of where Kelly might be makes everything even worse.

You need to regain control, VC1 warns. *You are redlining in four out of six critical areas.*

"Will I overload?" I do not need that right now. My medications are in my suite or with Kelly. Either way, I don't have access to them or time to deal with the side effects.

Not if you regain control.

"Not helpful."

I take a couple of deep breaths and stare at the ornately decorated ceiling of the two-story room, plaster curlicues forming intricate designs and patterns from one side to the other. Sooner or later, someone will figure out I'm trapped in here and they'll come get me, but will that be too late?

If I had something to pry off the access panels with, I might have a chance at hotwiring the doors, but I've already torn my short nails to the quick. Several of them are ragged and bleeding with no progress to show for my pain. I swipe the blood on my pants and sink back down onto the floor, concentrating on maintaining as much calm as I can muster, which isn't damn much.

There has to be something I can break and use as a lever. I scan every inch of the room again, at least the parts I can see, my eyes falling on the two balconies halfway up the twenty-two-foot walls and marking the second floor. The one on the right is the same one Dr. Nuzzi brought me out on to show me what she had in mind for my treatment in the maze. I squint at an anomaly there, then activate my enhanced eyesight.

Sure enough, a thin beam of light across the ceiling just above the balcony zooms into definition. The doors leading from that balcony into the exterior hallway beyond are ajar. Makes sense. Sometimes, when she wanted a better view of me, Nuzzi would stand up there rather than watch me on the monitor screens in the green room. She must have left a door unlatched.

I leap to my feet, wait a moment for some dizzy nausea to pass, and study the underside of the balcony from where I stand. If I can find a way to get up there, I can escape the conference room. Except, even at my best and on an adrenaline burst I can't leap more than five feet straight up. In my weakened condition, I won't get half that high, and there's nothing to grab on to if I could.

Fuck.

An image of the murdered girls flashes through my brain—not on my heads-up display. VC1 isn't that cruel. Rather, it's a real memory of the victim I found in the slaver tunnels and the photos Officer Sanderson showed me. All young, all blond, all similar to Kelly. If I don't get out of here soon, Kelly could end up like one of them.

Think, Corren. Think. What can you use to get up there? I ask myself. I need a rope and a grapple or some other kind of hook.

"Learn to use the resources you have at hand rather than wishing for ones that aren't there." My father's voice comes back to me, faint and almost unrecognizable in my memory, but at least now I *have* the memory, and lots more, of his early lessons in survival from high school freshman year on. He knew I'd pursue some sort of military career. My aptitude for the required skills was too great to ignore. And as the owner of the Fighting Storm, he'd had plenty of advice to give.

God, I miss him.

After the trial that determined my not-human status, the Storm had held a funeral for him. I'd still been in semi-shock, but Kelly stood by me, supporting me through it all. Everyone in the Storm not out on assignment had gone, dozens and dozens of respectful soldiers clothed in black dress uniforms like all these black-cloth-covered mirrors in row upon row.... My thoughts trail away as I stare at the rolls of fabric atop each reflective surface in the room.

The mirrors are unbreakable, immovable, but what about the covers? Would they secure something that I would never have any desire to remove since that would reveal the glass beneath?

I step to the rear of the closest mirror, grasp the rolled-up fabric in both hands, and yank on it, hard. It tears at the edge, then comes off with another couple of sharp pulls. I want to jump for joy or at least pump my fist in the air, but I'm too damn tired and settle for an exhalation of relief.

VC1 helps guide me back to the room's halfway point beneath the balcony, and ten minutes later I have a pile of black fabric rolls collected at my feet. Another five and I've shredded them into thick strips of cloth and tied the strips together to form a makeshift rope. I tug off one boot and use the laces to tie the footwear to the end of my rope to make an anchor. Then I step back from the balcony until I have a clear view of the railing.

It's a metal bar with a narrow space between it and a solid panel. Not a lot of room for error. I have to throw my boot just right so that it goes over the railing and through that narrow opening to drop back down to me.

"VC1, I need some very precise calculations."

Working on it.

A major advantage to having the AI as part of my actual brain is the lack of need to repeat myself. She's always listening. She knows what I know. Unnerving at times but helpful now.

The margin of error is too narrow for you to accomplish the goal on your own or even with my assistance. You will need to give me control in order for us to succeed.

Damn. I was hoping to avoid that. "Am I strong enough to take control back when you're done?" It's always a risk, turning things over to her. I'm beyond thinking she'll take advantage of the situation and keep my mind and body for her own. I trust her. But when I'm physically and emotionally stressed, my psyche sometimes shies away from retaking responsibility for my own actions, leaving her to manage all of me until I'm stable.

I believe you are strong enough. If not, I will use the interim to locate the second clone and Kelly. And... thank you for your trust. You have not always felt so.

I nod, knowing she will feel it or see it through the conference room's cameras. "Okay, hang on a sec." I remove all my overlay armor, the vest and arm coverings, and toss them up over the railing onto the balcony. Climbing will be easier without all the bulk, but I'm not leaving them behind. I have a feeling I'm going to need that gear. "All right, I'm ready." I take a couple of deep, cleansing breaths to prepare myself for the switch. When it comes, it's abrupt, like a shroud thrown over my head and a sizzling jolt that knocks out my external senses.

For a moment, I'm deaf and blind. The absence of sensation moves to the forefront of my perception as I note my complete inability to feel anything: not the growling of my stomach over a missed lunch, an urge to pee from being trapped in the room, not even the brush of air currents across my skin from the ventilation system. Nothing.

I've only been this way once before that I can remember, and that's when I needed to bury the body of my... original, for want of a better term. I'd been so emotionally overwrought that I couldn't complete a single step in the process, and VC1 had done it all. *This is unpleasant,* I send into the darkness of what I perceive to be the space inside my own head. *Do this quick, okay?*

Working on it now.

Why can't I feel anything? Was I that close to overload? Surely I should sense the movement of my own body. Under other circumstances, I've seen, heard, and felt what VC1 is doing when she's in control, just been unable to intervene.

You are stressed from the maze, frustrated by our inability to escape the room, and panicking over Kelly's potential circumstances. I am maintaining your functionality, but for these additional tasks, I need to redirect my focus from you to the task. Now quiet, please. I must concentrate.

Alone, in the darkness of my own head, the worry creeps in worse than ever. How much time has passed since I entered the mirror maze? I can't ask VC1 right now, but I'm guessing it's been over an hour, maybe two—less than I think, more than I want. Feels like I've been in here for days. I also realize I'm not completely sensory deprived. Tugs on my body make themselves known to my brain. A distant rhythmic pounding might be my heartbeat. My physical self, under VC1's guidance, is doing something strenuous. The whole thing is unnerving, to say the least.

Sight returns in a sudden bright flash, and I squeeze my eyes shut and cover them with a hand that responds to my commands. Blinking furiously, I ease it away a little at a time until they readjust to the conference room's overhead illumination, embedded discreetly in the ornate ceiling.

A ceiling a lot closer to me than it was before.

"We made it," I breathe, taking in my new position on the balcony. Something warm and wet covers the lower left side of my chin, and I swipe at it with the back of my hand. It comes away with a smear of blood. "What the hell?"

I am not as infallible as you believe. I caught your chin on the railing as I was hauling us over it. Sorry.

It's a small price to pay for my—no, our—freedom. Pronouns for being half of a symbiotic pair are confusing. "No worries," I tell my counterpart. I glance around the small balcony, spotting my boot lying beside me, still attached to the fabric rope, and the rest of my armor scattered around. But the boot is not connected to the railing. I'd thought to throw it and have it wrap around a few times as an anchor, then pull myself up.

"Um, how the hell did we get up here?"

The thickness of the boot was too wide to throw through the space beneath the railing. I threw it over the top. Then you climbed up a mirror, balanced yourself atop two of them, and jumped... which is how your chin hit the railing.

"You're saying I wasted a lot of time making a rope I didn't need."

That is what I am saying, yes. Neither of us thought of climbing a mirror until the last moment. Do not concern yourself with things you cannot change.

I nod and unknot the bootlaces from the rope so I can pull it on, then reach for and reattach the armor to the rest of me. Using the railing, I lever myself to a standing position and feel the burn in both my arm and leg muscles. I don't know what VC1 had to do to get us up here, but it must have been one helluva workout.

Leaving me that much less ready for a fight.

I shake that thought away, literally, working out
the kinks in my shoulders and neck. One problem at a
time. Taking a deep breath, I peer through the crack in
the partially open door.

Nothing. No movement. No sound. I check my internal chronometer now that VC1 isn't diverting herself
so much: 1636 local time. I was in the maze for two
hours and thirty-six minutes.

It's coming on dinnertime in the facility. The hallways should be bustling with food service carts and
personnel, nurses giving the evening medications, doctors making final rounds, but it's silent and still.

"Anything?" I whisper, my voice loud in the silence despite my efforts.

No access beyond the doors, VC1 responds.

Great.

I take a step out, then two. A flicker catches my
eye, emergency warning lights coming on at last, now
flashing steadily above all the doors lining the hall. I
turn toward the stairwell and bound down the steps two
at a time, terrified of what I might find when I emerge
on the first floor.

CHAPTER 44: KELLY
SOLUTIONS

Vick is in my soul.

MY HAIR hangs in my eyes. I blow at the strands to clear my vision, glad VC2 isn't here to push them aside for me. A shiver rolls from my neck to the base of my spine. So alike and so very, very different. Same genetics, different minds. Says a lot for nature vs. nurture, or, if not nurture, then whatever the exposure to certain experience memories counts for.

Where is Vick? Did she get out of the maze? She's been so close to success, maybe she got back up and finished the test, especially given so much recovery time. Or is she trapped, weakened, waiting for rescue that will come in the form of VC2's imminent attack?

And what about me? Useless. That's what I am. Tie some rope around my limbs and I'm out of commission. Some member of the Fighting Storm I turned out to be.

Okay, that's unfair to myself, and I know it. I'm support personnel, not a field operative, not really. But Vick has worked hard over the years to teach me basic skills: self-defense, a mean right hook, beginner piloting, general physical fitness, and other survival assets. I should be able to get myself out of this. Somehow.

The sun's going down, the quality of light changing from bright daylight to warmer evening tones. My stomach rumbles. I had a snack in the green room, but no lunch, and it's probably dinnertime by now, and if I were speaking out loud, I'd be babbling. Instead my thoughts chase themselves in endless irrelevant circles.

I tug on my wrist and ankle bonds, succeeding in causing more painful abrasions before I give up. If there's one thing VC2 knows, it's how to tie a proper knot.

Vick would have knives hidden in three places on her person. Well, maybe not now. Definitely not now. As a patient at the Klenar Facility, she is not allowed any kind of weapons. That's why she had Robert for protection.

My heart twists at the thought of Robert—and Dr. Nuzzi—lying in the hallway, blood spreading everywhere. My stomach turns over, and I fear I'll lose the little bit of food I consumed. Swallowing hard, I get my body under control. Small victories.

The darker it becomes, the more time that passes, the less likely I'll be able to do anything and the more likely VC2 will return... having killed Vick.

No. I'm not letting that happen, if it hasn't already.

If I could smack myself, I'd do it. Thinking like that helps no one.

Rocking myself from side to side, I manage to roll onto my knees. Getting to my feet is much harder. I lean forward, putting pressure on my bound wrists and the sides of my hands, then attempt a little jump that lands me on my side once more. If I live through this, I'm going to have a bruise the size of a dinnerplate on that hip.

Five more attempts and bruising on both hips and I make it to my feet. Yay. Now what?

The light is even dimmer now, the sun blocked by both mountains and trees. Klenar has lots of exterior spotlights that make the surrounding lawns practically glow at night, so bright that Vick and I draw all the curtains in our suite of rooms just to get any sleep… or do anything else. But the trees prevent most of those lights from reaching the storage building as well.

I waver on my tied-together feet, my balance off with the unusual stance, and peer into the corners. Tons of winter athletic gear. There must be something sharp I can use. My eyes rake over the snowmobiles, but they're all curved plastic and smooth metal. And far. I mean, okay, ten feet or so isn't *far*, but when you're going to be hopping the whole way, distance takes on a new perspective. Even if there's a broken piece on one of them, I'm bound to fall more than once trying to get there.

Rotating with care, I face the back of the space. Snowshoes, all-weather rubber boots, some spare parkas. Nothing helpful. The other side is more snowmobiles, and by the front door are skates… with metal blades. Sharp metal blades. And farther away from me than the snowmobiles.

At least they're in the right direction for the door, and a sure thing to cut my ropes if I can reach them.

I give an experimental hop, then another and another, before I go down hard on my knees. Something in my left knee pops, sending pain reverberating up my thigh and down to my bound ankle. Oh, that's just wonderful. It's not excruciating, probably a sprain, but it makes getting back up even harder than the first time. And hopping? Oh God, that hurts.

I get five more hops before I take another tumble, this time smashing my face into the hardwood floor. My teeth drive into my lower lip, and the coppery taste of blood fills my mouth. Holding up both wrists, I manage to wipe the worst of it on my sleeves, but I must look horrific. When Vick sees me, she'll—

If she's still alive.

I need to know. I've been hesitant to lower my walls after my brief link with VC2. She did damage and I'm still emotionally fragile, but now I drop the barriers and reach out with my empathic sense… and almost sob with relief. She's alive. The blue line that connects us is faint at this distance, but not invisible, leading out beneath the door and across to the mental health center. She's alive. For now.

A new wave of determination fills me, and instead of standing, I drag myself forward the last few feet on knees and elbows, ignoring the pain in both. When I'm beneath the dangling skates, so near and yet so far, the logs of the wall provide good handholds for me to haul myself upright once more.

I study the pairs of hanging skates and select the best-maintained, sharpest-looking ones. Twisting my arms at an awkward angle, I use my elbow to press the skates against the wall for leverage while I rub the ropes between my wrists back and forth over the blades. I'm not the most coordinated on my best days, and it would be just like me to slit my own skin open during this process, so I'm extra careful even while I'm trying to hurry. After ten or fifteen minutes of sawing, the strands of the rope part, one by one by one until I'm free.

With the use of two separate hands, cutting the ankle ropes is much easier, taking only a handful of minutes to snap them. I toss the skates into a pile of tarps on the floor and study the door VC2 left by.

A jerk on the handle tells me what I already know; it's locked from the outside, and the mechanism on the interior of the door looks damaged. A couple of attempts confirm VC2 disabled it so it can't be opened from within. I roll my eyes. Not sure why a shed at an isolated mental health facility needs locks at all. Maybe they're worried about adventurous yetis. Another scan of the room reiterates that it is the only door in the building.

With the only window.

It doesn't take much to use a skate blade to smash the window. Then I wrap my sleeve over my hand to swipe away the remaining glass. For a moment, I consider screaming for help, but it might bring VC2 instead, so I don't. Instead, I shove an empty crate in front of the door, stand on it, use the window's edge to lever myself up, and squirm my way through the narrow opening.

Vick would have had no trouble with this. She's taller, but lean and wiry. My chest and hips both get caught, and for a horrible minute, I worry this is how I'll be captured again—stuck half in and half out of a door's window. My twisted knee screams as I use my toes for one last push, and then I'm falling, of course, headfirst onto the ground outside.

I guess I'm lucky that, one, there isn't a concrete walkway or something, and two, I don't cut myself on the shards of glass scattered across the dirt pathway, but it hurts, and I've opened my split lip again.

Whatever. I'm free. I wipe away the new blood flow on my already stained sleeve and jog down the path, letting the trees around me hide me from sight. When I reach the edge of the clearing, all lit up with spotlights from the facility, I stop and study the multi-winged structure.

Well, someone knows there's a problem. Emergency lights on the roof and sides of Vick's wing are flashing an orange-yellow, although there are no interior lights on in that section. The thrum of distant alarms, muffled by the brick and stone, reaches my ears. There's a cluster of men and women in Klenar uniforms, along with a handful in scrubs and lab coats gathered around the nearest outside door. What looks like a technician, toolkit beside him, kneels in front of the electronic locking mechanism. Even as I watch, he looks up at the medical professionals and shakes his head.

They can't get in. VC2 has overridden the locks.

CHAPTER 45: VICK
CONFRONTATION

I am pissed.

"LET ME know if you regain access to the building's systems," I say under my breath once I reach the exit to the stairwell on the first floor. "I'm not big on going in blind."

Acknowledged.

VC1 sounds a little miffed. "Um, please? Look, I'm not trying to treat you like a machine when I give you orders. I'm trying to treat you like any member of my team. Even if you solved the balcony problem without me, I do kinda consider myself in charge of this unit most of the time. Okay?"

Okay. I am... pleased that you consider me a team member and not an accessory. And unless you place me in control, you are most definitely in charge, though I may take some liberties if I see a way to improve our odds in a situation.

"Just... keep me in the loop, please, whenever possible."

A chuckle in my head. *Affirmative.*

Okay, then.

The emergency lights are still flashing both in the stairwell and the hallway I can see through the face-sized window in the stairwell door. Far in the distance, an alarm is ringing, though I think that's coming from outside or another wing in the facility. How much havoc has VC2 caused?

I stand on tiptoe in order to see as much of the corridor as I can through the small glass pane. At least it isn't reflective. I've seen quite enough of my infra-structure for one day.

Nothing appears amiss in the hall, except the ab-sence of all personnel and patients, and some disturbing bloodstains on the far wall. All right, yeah, that's pretty amiss, actually. No sign of VC2.

With caution, I push the door open, getting about an inch before it stops. Not a security measure. Some-thing is on the other side, on the floor, blocking the door. I shove harder, making it another foot when red begins seeping beneath the bottom crack. Startled, I jump backward to avoid the horrific flow.

I have to take a wide stance and then press with all my upper body strength so as not to step in the puddle of blood at my feet. I don't have to see it to know I'm shoving a human being along with the door. Once I've opened it wide enough, I slip through the space and into the hall, where I'm greeted by the wide-open, unseeing eyes of Dr. Nuzzi staring up at me from the tile.

"Aw, dammit," I whisper, moisture gathering in my artificial eyes. Not for the first time, I wish for a little less realism there. No point in checking her body. She's got multiple stab wounds in addition to her neck being half twisted backward on her shoulders. Dead without a doubt.

A little farther down the hall I spot Robert, seated propped up against the wall, legs sticking out in front of him. The bone of one leg protrudes through the upper thigh as if VC2 used an adrenaline burst to literally *break* him. A swash of blood hides half his face. His one visible eye… blinks.

I dash to his side, crouching down, keeping my other senses on high alert in case this is a lure. "Robert?"

"Sorry," he breathes, more blood bubbling from his lips. "She has Kelly. Took us by surprise. Killed everyone else."

"Okay, okay. Stop talking." I tear off a piece of his shirt and wrap it around his forehead to stem the blood from a nasty cut there, then take another, larger strip, the entire other sleeve, and tie off his broken leg above the wound. Using his belt, I make the tourniquet even tighter. Robert groans, teeth clenched, sweating with the effort not to scream, but we don't know where VC2 is now, and we don't want to draw her here. I rock back on my heels and survey my handiwork. Not bad for makeshift medical care. He should be able to hold on until I can find help. "I'm going to drag you into the stairwell. Not much of a hiding place, and the blood trail will give you away, but it's better than nothing. Then I'll get a doctor."

He nods, more of a loll than a conscious gesture, and I take him under his arms and haul him through the stairwell door. I have to push Dr. Nuzzi's body aside with my boot, and I send up a quiet apology to whichever deities she favored in life. Robert is unconscious before I get him all the way to the stairs, which is probably a relief. I tuck him in the space under the first flight, double-check my bandages, and hope for the best.

Then I'm in the corridor again, keeping to the walls, peeping through the small windows in each door and grimacing at what I find: furnishings and belongings strewn everywhere, blood and bodies. So many bodies, so much blood. Robert was correct. VC2 seems to have killed every patient, every orderly, every doctor on this hall. And not quick kills. Many show signs of torture: burns, bones broken, shallow cuts, but in large numbers not deep enough for the victim to bleed out, just to suffer before the final blow.

The flashing yellow-orange wreaks havoc on my vision, casting everything in alternating bursts of light and semidarkness. As I make my way toward the nurses' station near the juncture of this wing to the main building, I try a few exit doors—all locked beyond VC1's ability to open them. "Is VC2 better than you?" I whisper, more to hear a voice, any human voice even if it's my own, than to communicate with her.

She is not. Different, yes. Better, no. She is not an AI, and I WILL determine a pathway around her blocks. I have access to some of the security cameras now.

That perks me up a little. "Anything to report?"

A short pause, then, *You are not alone. Movement behind the nurses' station desk.*

So, VC2? Or a survivor?

I hurry faster, stepping carefully for silence, though my combat boots squeak a couple of times on the polished tile. Good for most terrain. Not good for health facilities.

I reach the hub where the nurses' station sits, no visible movement, no sign of life. But it's a little brighter here, the two-story hub topped with skylights that let in the fading evening sun. "Where—?" Then I hear it, a soft rattling followed by a muffled curse coming from behind the large, multiperson desk where the nurses greet visitors.

I wish I had a weapon, any kind of weapon. Robert had been stripped of his when I found him, and I hadn't passed any of my other security team members' bodies. I'm hoping they weren't in this wing when VC2 struck.

I'm hoping she hasn't wiped out the entire facility.

Unlikely. Someone sounded the alarms and turned on the emergency lights.

"Could be automated," I suggest, "triggered by her opening the exterior door."

The lights, perhaps, but the alarms are coming from a different portion of the facility.

I round the edge of the desk, prepared to lash out at whomever I find, but only discover the corpses of both nurses sprawled across the floor. So what was making that— The rattle comes again, and the handle on one of the cabinets beneath the desk shifts up and down. I judge it to be a fairly large storage space, big enough to hold a child or small person if it was otherwise mostly empty.

"Come on out," I say, low enough for the hidden individual to hear me, but not loud enough for my voice to carry beyond this space.

"You're going to kill me," a high-pitched voice responds. A familiar high-pitched voice.

"Cynthia?"

The Secretary of the Treasury's daughter rattles the knob again.

"You can't get out, can you? It's me, Vick."

"Go away! Don't hurt me."

I frown as I crouch beside the cabinet. "Why would you think I'd—" Oh, right, of course. If she saw VC2 in action before she found her hiding place, she'd assume it was me. "That wasn't me," I say, keeping my voice calm and soft. I'm no good at this. I need Kelly. She'd know what to do and say. "That was someone pretending to be me. She's why I'm really here, to lure her out and catch her, only things went... really, really wrong."

"That sounds like something a crazy person would say. I asked where your room was. I thought I could visit. They said you were in the highest security section. Where they put the psychotic killers."

I let out a sigh. "Look, I don't have time to argue with you. The real psycho has Kelly, and my friend Robert needs a doctor, and you can stay in there and hope she doesn't come back, or you can come with me to get help. And just a reminder, if I am a psycho killer, then I could have killed you back in the slaver base. It also means I have weapons and I could have driven a blade or fired a pistol through that flimsy little cabinet door. I haven't, because I'm unarmed, tired, and almost as freaked-out as you are."

A small sniffle. "You're really not crazy?"

Yes. "No."

"Can you let me out?"

I study the handle and the keypad lock that must have sealed her in. "Scrunch yourself back as far from the door as you can get." There's some shuffling from inside the cabinet. When it ceases, I launch a full-force kick into the cabinet door, breaking the lock and shoving the door inward a foot and a half.

"Ow!" Cynthia squeaks, louder than I'd prefer.

"Shh." I reach around the splintered wood and peel the door back, grimacing at the squeak/crunch of the material. Cynthia scrambles out and stands beside me, keeping as far from the nurses' bodies as possible while remaining partially hidden by their desk.

"You're shushing me? You just smashed a cabinet," she says, voice low.

Oh yeah, right. I did.

I give her a visual once-over, checking for injuries. She's unharmed except for a bruise forming on her upper left arm, probably from where I hit her with the door. Given all she's been through, she's holding it together well. The doctors here have helped her a lot. Shame this new clusterfuck will likely undo all their hard work.

"Now what?" she asks, shifting from foot to foot in soft white tennis shoes.

Great question. I glance around the nurses' station hub. Nothing will work as a weapon, at least nothing more sophisticated than broken shards of the cabinet door. I grab one anyway. Better than nothing. "Come on." Skirting around the desk, I head for the double doors connecting this wing with the main building. Soft footsteps behind me tell me Cynthia is following.

There's motion outside the two small windows in the doors. People. Living, breathing people. So VC2 kept to this area. I rap on the glass to get their attention. One is a guard I recognize from the OWLS. Another wears coveralls and appears to be working on detaching the entire door from the frame, though it's hard to see from my angle.

The guard lifts a comm unit to his mouth, and a buzz in my head indicates an incoming transmission. I open the channel.

"You secure?" he asks. "We're working on removing the doors. Your counterpart has locked the entire wing down."

"I'm secure for the moment, and I have the secretary's daughter with me, unharmed. How did you know I'm the good... version?"

The guard smiles. "You answered your comm code."

Ah, right. I roll my eyes at my own stupidity. "How long on the doors?" It's weird watching his mouth move through the window but hearing the sound in my head.

He glances down and to the right, consulting with the maintenance guy, then looks back at me. "Ten, maybe fifteen minutes."

I nod just before another voice, *my* voice, interrupts from behind me.

"Too long for the two of you."

Cynthia screams. VC2 has returned.

CHAPTER 45: KELLY
TO THE RESCUE

Vick is locked in.

"WHAT'S THE situation?" I ask, channeling my inner Vick. All heads turn away from the locked exterior door, eyes narrowing as I hobble up to the gathered medical personnel and the maintenance guy working on the lock. I swipe away more blood from my split lip, place my hands on my hips, and glare right back at them.

One of the doctors approaches. I don't recognize him, but he holds out his hands in a placating gesture. "We're locked out, some kind of system failure, but we'll get you inside as soon as we can. Why don't you

have a seat and let me look at your injuries. Who's
your therapist?"

I stifle a semi-hysterical laugh that won't help my
situation. They think I'm a patient here. "I'm Kelly La-
Salle, with the Fighting Storm group."

The doctor lowers his hands but doesn't stop
his approach. From a pocket of his coat, he removes
a small first aid kit and passes me a sealed packet of
gauze and a disinfectant wipe for my lip. "These should
help. We've got techs working on both the exterior and
interior access doors to this wing, but so far, we haven't
gotten inside."

"Don't go in without a security backup, preferably
some of my team." I pause. "Did any of them make it
outside before the lockdown?"

"A few of us were having a late lunch in the central
cafeteria," comes a familiar voice from behind me. I
turn to find Carl and two of our people, a man and a
woman in orderly uniforms. One is an OWL. The other
I recognize from the Storm. "I've got two more guards
outside the entrance to the nurses' hub in Vick's section,
waiting for the doors to be removed from the frame."

The technician looks over his shoulder again.
"That's what I'm thinking here too. I haven't been able
to find another way. I even tried shutting down the entire system, but it came back online almost instantly
with the scramblers still in place."

"What about cutting off access to the wireless?" I
venture. I know nothing about tech, but I do know that's
how Vick makes her connections to external systems.

Carl shakes his head and lowers his voice so only
I can hear him. "This is Earth. We're literally blanketed in wireless access systems, as are most of the heavily settled worlds. Even if they are locked down, the

implants are programmed to hack into them and make use of whatever they can access. And they can connect one system to another, route information between them. One World has no idea what VC1 and VC2 are really capable of, and we have no intention of telling them. If they knew, they'd shut both clones down, not just the crazy one. I don't even think Vick fully comprehends it herself." He pauses, then raises his voice. "Get on the door removal."

The maintenance tech waits for a confirmation nod from the doctor and then pulls a drill from his kit, going to work on the hinges themselves.

Moving closer to me, Carl leans close to my ear. "Where are they?"

I'm assuming he means VC2 and Vick. "Inside," I say, equally quietly. I give him a quick rundown of what happened to me, ending with "VC2 can lock and unlock the doors at will, trapping anyone anywhere in the facility, at least in this section. And she's killed Robert and Dr. Nuzzi." My voice catches on that last bit.

His face clouds when I mention the losses, but he hides the emotion quickly. He lays a gentle hand on my shoulder. "I suspect it's a lot more than two fatalities. We can't reach anyone inside this wing. My only contacts are my people outside the hub doors. Most of the cameras are on a feedback loop, and the ones we can access show a lot of unmoving bodies. We thought we saw movement at the nurses' station but lost control of that camera a few seconds later. Central comms are shut down, but private ones should work. So far no one is respon—" He breaks off, pressing one hand to his ear where his own comm pickup is inserted. A small smile curls at the corners of his lips. "Scratch that," Carl adds after a moment. "Vick is at the interior doors. She's got

Cynthia with her. The Klenar staff are working to get
them out, with my guys ready to go in when they do."

Relief floods through me. I knew she was alive but
had no idea of her condition. If she's talking, she isn't
terribly hurt. I'm about to head around to the front of
the main building when our tech announces, "Got it!"

Everyone jumps as the side door swings out,
unlocked.

Carl frowns. "You found a workaround?"

"Actually, no," the technician admits, sliding tools
back into their carry case. "The signal scrambling the
entry code just stopped. I had my reader sending the
code on repeat just in case." He holds up a small box
with numbers scrolling across a tiny screen. "This time
it worked." He shrugs massive shoulders.

"That... might not be a good thing," I whisper.
A trickle of apprehension works its way through my
shields, followed by a sudden increase in anxiety and
an involuntary tension in my muscles. My gaze snaps
to Carl's. "The door unlocked because VC2 has her
mind elsewhere. Vick's under attack."

"Or we're being lured in. Or both. Dammit." Carl
gestures to the OWL guard to follow him, draws his
weapon, and heads inside, ordering everyone else to
stay out. I ignore the command, trailing them a few
steps behind. He shoots me a brief glare over his shoulder, opens his mouth to say something, then thinks better of it and nods. "You're with us. We might need your
skills to deal with VC2, but stay behind Kenneth here."

I nod back, willing to agree to that order, for now.
Unlike Vick, I'm not under any sort of compulsion to
obey his commands to the letter. I step behind the burly
redheaded OWL and follow them both into the short
hallway containing the stairs to the second floor.

"Blood trail," Carl says, having produced a flashlight from a cargo pants pocket. He shines the beam along the brownish smear to where it disappears under the stairs. Kenneth moves forward to check it out.

"I've got Robert, not dead. Close, though," he calls to us.

"Get the doctors outside to help. Make sure he's secure, then follow us." Carl pushes open the interior door to the central hallway. "Don't suppose I could convince you to do that instead," he says to me.

I fold my arms over my chest. "No chance in hell."

Carl mutters something rude-sounding under his breath and moves forward. His light finds Dr. Nuzzi, also moved from where I last saw her, but he doesn't pause. She's clearly dead. We proceed along the hall, Carl stopping at intervals to peer into patient windows, then shaking his head and moving on. When I step up to one of the panes myself, he catches my arm and pulls me away. "Don't. VC2 is thorough. And… enthusiastic… with her victims. You don't need to see the evidence."

I tug my arm from his grasp but step from the window without looking through it. This experience is going to give me enough nightmares without adding additional fuel to them.

Lowering my empathic walls a little farther, I focus on the blue line that connects me to Vick, thicker and brighter than what I saw in the storage building and leading deeper into the facility. My heart pounds and my breathing picks up. "They're fighting," I say.

Carl doesn't question my pronouncement but increases his pace.

We pass more bodies of staff, some dragged into side corridors, one half in and half out of a maintenance closet, one beneath an overturned cart bearing food trays, their contents splattered across the tile and mixed with the victim's draining blood. I cover my mouth with my hand and swallow hard.

Sounds of battle carry to our ears: dull thuds, shouts of pain and anger, shattering glass, a gunshot. "You realize if you stay with me, you're going to be onsite for at least one and possibly more deaths," Carl says as the arch into the nurses' station hub comes into view. Something flies past the opening—a potted plant, maybe—and crashes against an unseen wall. My guide stops a dozen feet away. "In a battle between VC1 and VC2, only one of them is coming out alive."

I meet his eyes while I strengthen the walls around my empathic abilities. "I'm well aware of that. And her name isn't VC-anything. It's Vick."

CHAPTER 47: VIEK
ONE ON ONE

I am outmatched.

"FUCK." THE heavy ceramic pot containing a three-foot ficus tree slams into my torso and carries me halfway across the empty space in front of the nurses' desk. I land on my tailbone, skidding another three feet on the slick tile before coming to a stop. The brown pottery shatters into a million sharp pieces, adding to the dozen other hazards in the room: a broken lamp, tablets and styluses, medicine vials, loose syringes, and other equipment. It's all scattered across the floor, making footing precarious.

No time to worry about it. I press both palms to the floor and flip to my feet, slicing open my left hand on a piece of glass in the process. Not deep, but it will make gripping any sort of makeshift weapon difficult, not that I have one. I lost my piece of cabinet door a while ago, when I embedded it in VC2's thigh. A flash of movement tells me VC2 is behind the nurses' desk, keeping her covered and me out in the open.

Something whizzes toward me, displacing the air with a whistling sound. My head ducks without any intent behind the motion and a sharp blade passes over me, then drives into one of the double doors to my rear.

Did you do that? I think at VC1.

Indeed. You need to pay more attention. She is toying with us, but she is armed. You are not.

Yeah, well, thanks. Keep it up. I dive-roll to the right, ending up behind a couch that sits as part of a small cluster of chairs and a table between the doors and the horseshoe-shaped desk—a visitors' waiting area if it's not visiting hours or if a patient is out having treatment.

You are giving me permission to take control as needed? Her surprise is evident in her tone.

I think on that while I catch my breath. When we escaped the maze, I said I understood she might manipulate me if our lives were at risk. This is different. I'm acknowledging us as one body, two brains, either of which has the right to make unilateral decisions for the both of us. *As long as you warn me when possible*, I send back.

Agreed.

I suck in a few more lungfuls of air and check on Cynthia, most of her smaller body hidden behind the other potted ficus still upright beside the double doors.

So far VC2 has ignored her. I'm the target here. But if I lose, I have no doubt Cynthia will be her next victim. She's come a long way since her enslavement. I intend to make sure she lives to come a lot further.

More movement in my peripheral vision. I glance to my right, where an archway leads into the dark hallway beyond. Three shadows shift and move, one crouching, the other two standing behind. The cavalry has arrived.

High-pitched drilling sounds reach my ears from beyond the double doors—yet another distraction. They'll come through soon. More backup. She's out-numbered and cornered. Why doesn't she surrender?

Would you? VC1 asks.

No, I wouldn't. And I realize I need to not think like a target. I need to think like VC2. *Analysis, please. If I were where she is right now, what would I do to win?*

Silence.

"Everyone freeze!" comes Carl's voice from the corridor. He's standing now, leaning around the edge of the arch so only his upper body and head are visible, ready to duck back out of sight if necessary. He's got one pistol trained on my general position and another aimed at the desk, and I realize he doesn't know which of us is which. Great. "All of you stand up with your hands raised where I can see them."

I catch a glimpse of another guard, an OWL member whose name I never learned, right behind him, and… Kelly. Shit.

We move as one, me, VC2, and Cynthia rising slowly from our hiding positions with our hands raised high. Mine and Cynthia's are empty. VC2 holds a pistol pointed up in her right grip. I recognize the make and model as the one the OWLs prefer. She must have taken it off Robert when she attacked him.

She's giving up a defensible position, I realize. She's got to have a plan in mind. Nothing else makes sense. I wouldn't do what she's doing. I would... I would....

What the hell would I do?

"Set the gun on the desk and shove it away from you," Carl demands, keeping his own weapon trained on VC2. The other guard has me covered with his own pistol.

To my surprise, VC2 does what he asks, setting the gun with a dull *thunk* on the desk and sliding it to the far end, where it stops just before falling off the edge. It's out of her immediate reach, though she could dive for it. Still, she'd likely be shot before she could get it and aim.

What am I missing?

"Cynthia, come to me," Carl says. Never taking his eyes off the room, he tilts his head to the side and says something to Kelly that, to my enhanced hearing, sounds like, "Which one is VC2?"

Kelly doesn't hesitate. She points to the clone behind the desk. I let out an audible sigh of relief. Dressed in identical clothing, I wasn't certain she'd be able to tell us apart, but I guess our emotions give us away. Carl has the other guard shift his aim to VC2 and holsters his own pistol. I put my arms down.

That nagging sense of impending disaster keeps poking at me as Cynthia moves quickly across the open space between the potted plant and the hallway arch, skirting around the remains of the other destroyed pottery and random debris. Carl goes to meet her, offering her an arm to lean on. They're together at the halfway point when VC1 says, *Robert carried two pistols.*

Shit shit shit.

"Everybody down!" I shout even as VC2 blurs into motion, reaching behind her back to pull a second gun from her waistband. She doesn't shoot Cynthia or Carl, like I expect her to. She doesn't even fire at me, her primary target. Instead, she aims the barrel straight up and fires three times... into the huge glass dome overhead.

Maximum damage, maximum chaos, maximum casualties.

It's what I would have done. If I were a sociopath.

If she can disrupt the entire room with one blast, she might escape out some other exit before the rest of the guards can get in through the double doors.

I don't think. I move, leaping over the couch and tackling Cynthia to the floor to roll with her against the desk and the limited protection the overhanging surface of it will provide. I'd meant to grab Carl as well, and I do knock him down, but not out of the way of the shower of glass falling all around us. Most of the bits are tiny, snowflake-like in the way they glitter in the emergency lights and blanket the tile floor.

But those are the precursors.

The metal support framework holding the glass panes in place groans, then bends, central connectors breaking apart with a screech that has Cynthia clamping her hands over her ears. In seconds, much larger, sharper shards drop like transparent blades, one landing in the center of Carl's chest where he lies sprawled in the center of the floor.

My boss has one brief moment of shock and surprise, his eyes flying wide, all his limbs jerking taut in four directions, before everything slackens. He exhales a single gasping, wheezing breath as his eyes slide shut.

Carl might have been an asshole, but he didn't deserve that. Cynthia chokes out a sob from where she lies half beneath me.

A second sob echoes it, coming from the archway to the corridor beyond. Kelly.

I raise my head just in time to see her slide backward into the shadows of the hallway, then a soft thud when she hits the floor out of sight. The other guard turns at the sound, bends to help her.

It's all the distraction VC2 needs to shoot him in the back of the head.

Cynthia screams. Kelly, somehow still conscious, also screams, though I can't see her.

"Stop fucking killing everyone. You're going to send her into emotion shock!" I shout at VC2.

The only response I get is a half-hysterical laugh.

She's really insane, I think at VC1.

As insane as you would have been without Kelly, my AI confirms.

How do I beat an insane version of myself?

"We're about to remove the doors," comes the other OWL's voice over my internal comm.

Don't, I tell him, using thought-to-text so my words come up on his comm screen rather than me speaking out loud and risking being overheard by VC2's aural enhancements. *My double has multiple weapons, protective cover, and a clear line of sight to those doors. She'll pick all of you off as you come through. If you can, send more backup through the interior halls. Come in from behind her. We've got two dead and one disabled in here.*

"Roger that."

"What do we do now?" Cynthia whispers.

I consider our options. We're in front of the desk, up against it. VC2 is on the opposite side. She's likely got both her pistols in hand. If we try to run for the corridor, she'll gun us down before we take three steps, but we can't stay where we are, waiting for her next move.

Her next move....

If I were VC2, what would I do next? How would I eliminate my targets without taking damage to myself?

"OWL3 to Corren. The exterior doors have resealed. Security access codes rescrambled. We're working on overriding, but for the moment you're on your own." The guard pauses. "I'm sorry. Apparently the one they managed to open slammed shut in the wind and VC2 took the opportunity to retake control of it."

Understood, I text back, not wanting to alarm Cynthia further.

We're stuck, lying on the floor, with a few inches of wood between us and our attacker.

Inches... wood.... Oh fuck.

"Move!" I shout, grabbing Cynthia by the collar of her pastel yellow fuzzy sweater and shoving her across the room toward the archway. I go the opposite direction, away from the safety of the hallway, crouched and working my way around the far corner of the horseshoe desk.

A beat later, three shots echo through the high-ceilinged room, and three neat holes appear in the back of the desk, right where the two of us had been lying seconds before. You don't need your targets to be visible if you can just shoot through a barrier to kill them.

Most opponents wouldn't have thought to do that, but I would, and VC2 would. I have to stop treating her like any other enemy. She's me. A deranged, psychotic me, so she won't care how much damage she does or whom she kills, but she's still me.

And I'm terrifying.

Leaning around the curve of the desk, I spot Cynthia vanishing into the shadows of the hall, safe for the moment.

VC2 and I are the only ones left in the room, and this needs to end now.

I draw my legs up under me, coil my body for maximum momentum, and launch myself up and over the desk.

CHAPTER 48: KELLY
NO CHOICE

Vick is overmatched.

I COME to on the tile floor, my right hand lying in something warm and sticky. My brain makes the connection first, and I jerk my fingers out of the spreading puddle of blood pouring from the back of Kenneth's skull. A scream rises in my throat, drowned only by the bile filling my mouth. I swallow it down, the acidic liquid burning on its return to my stomach.

A shout and a crash draw my attention to the ongoing fight at the nurses' station. Using the wall for support, I push to my knees and lean around the archway opening. Everything aches. My limbs tremble. My heart pounds and sweat drips into my eyes, though I feel cold.

Emotion shock.

Like Vick's implant overload, emotion shock is one of the greatest risks I face as an empath, especially one working for a mercenary soldier. It can incapacitate me temporarily, like now, or it can tumble me into a coma if the emotional blows keep coming. And at least one more person is going to die near me this evening.

Vick's had to pull me out of emotion shock more times than I want think about. So far, her voice, her touch, our connection have been enough to drag me free of the overwhelming emotional onslaughts she's exposed me to. And I'm better with my blocks and walls. I passed out, but given where the fight stands, it wasn't for long. I'm not staring into space, unaware of what's going on around me like I would have been a year ago.

I need to hold myself together. If Vick puts me in a coma, she'll never forgive herself. And if I should die in that coma….

That might be the thing that pushes Vick to overcome her self-preservation programming.

More shouting and the dull thuds of fists meeting flesh draw my attention back to the fight, and I realize I zoned out. Not good. I brace myself against the side of the arch, try to ignore the smear of blood my palm leaves on the pale wall paint, and focus on the two identical combatants.

They've rolled clear of the far side of the horseshoe-shaped desk, one atop the other, pounding away. A pair of pistols lies scattered across the open space, out of reach of them both and far beyond my own as well. Not that I'd pick one up. VC2 would know it to be an empty threat.

Would it be? If you were saving Vick's life?

I shake that away. I've never killed someone. I can't imagine what that would do to me. The closest I've come is one of the robot-like soldiers in the asteroid base where Vick's father, the former owner of the Fighting Storm, had been living. Dr. Whitehouse had wanted to create supersoldiers and used a human body and the remnants of its brain for greater mental flexibility with its implants, but Vick assured me it wasn't alive, not really. Even that had done me some serious damage. I don't ever want to feel that again.

Besides, even if VC2 does win, Vick will come back in another clone. Won't she?

"You can't kill me forever," Vick shouts as if voicing my thoughts. Or is it VC2? There's no telling them apart. Even the bright blue line of our love for each other ends in a brilliant blur around the two of them— they're too close together for me to differentiate which of them it attaches to.

Beyond that, they wear identical clothing, bear similar cuts and bruises. I think Vick is on the bottom, which has my insides twisted into knots. But it makes sense. She would have been weakened by her time in the mirror maze. I don't even know how she managed to get out unless someone discovered and freed her. But VC2 would be unhindered by that particular emotional trauma.

"It doesn't work that way," the one on top responds to the previous statement. "The implants seek out the closest operational equivalent device. The only reason you were able to create two of us is because two clones had been awakened at one time."

I'm right. The one on top of the pair is VC2. There's no other way to explain how she knows what happened to Vick's former lover and more recent physician. I wonder if VC2 killed Alkins as well. Given her current state of insanity, it wouldn't surprise me.

I swallow hard. That means Vick is the one taking all the immediate damage. VC2 uses her own body to pin Vick to the floor, her arms trapped at her sides, while she punches her in the stomach and face with both fists. At some point, Vick's armored vest came loose, leaving it open and her vulnerable. Vick grunts with the impacts. Something cracks, causing Vick to groan and writhe beneath VC2. I writhe with her, the pain piercing my weakened walls. She's broken one of Vick's ribs, maybe two.

Leaning down, VC2 gets right in her face. "When I kill you, I'll be one step closer to whole. *Everything* in your head will be mine. All the data. All the memories. All the missing pieces except one." She casts a glance over her shoulder to where I'm crouching, her cold, heartless gaze sending shivers through my entire body. "And with you gone, Kelly will be free to bond with me," VC2 continues, speaking to Vick but never taking her yes from mine. "I'll finally be complete."

"You kill me," Vick pants out, struggling to free herself and failing, "you're likely to kill her too."

"Not if she bonds with me fast enough."

I sit up straighter. She might actually be right. It's the breaking of the bond that would be life-threatening, but if that bond never fully breaks.... If, like the transfer of Vick's knowledge and memories, it simply seeks the closest replacement... I could find myself emotionally tied to VC2.

"Then we'll find out. Is it really love between the two of you? Or is it a convenient empathic brainwave match? Doesn't matter, really, as long as it fixes me." VC2 digs her knee into Vick's side, grinding the fractured bones against one another while Vick screams in agony.

"Kel, go! Get out of here," she manages through clenched teeth. "Get as far away as you can."

It's what she said to me the last time she died.

I look closer, at the pale complexion, the blood running in a slow stream from between her lips. Her body shudders from another impact. Her scream is fainter than the last.

I cannot go through this again.

And I will not risk Vick losing all that she is to VC2. I will not be bound to that… thing.

Because, unlike Vick, VC2 is a machine—a twisted, evil machine with programming so corrupted as to be unfixable. It might feel emotions. I read the waves of anger and insanity rolling off her, buffeting at my barriers. But she's too far gone to be human.

I scan the hallway around me, searching for anything I might use to help Vick win this fight. My gaze falls on Kenneth's body… and the gun in his outstretched hand.

I wouldn't be killing a thinking, loving human being.

I'd be shutting down a piece of faulty technology that should never have existed.

VC2 has returned her full attention to Vick, her forearm now braced across Vick's throat, and she's pressing down and down even while Vick pushes and kicks in a useless attempt to dislodge her.

The blue line is fading, growing dimmer with Vick's waning life force. My own throat constricts, and I suck in a painful breath. The edges of my vision dim—the result of oxygen loss by proxy.

Moving slowly, gingerly, I reach for Kenneth's hand and pry his fingers from the grip of his weapon, one still-warm digit at a time.

VC2 is a machine.

I can kill a machine.

CHAPTER 49: VICK
SACRIFICE

I am devastated.

TOO TIRED. Can't breathe. Can't focus.

VC2's arm presses my throat, threatening to crush my larynx. She shifts so her knees dig into my chest, my lungs, preventing me from taking a deep breath, even if my neck weren't compressed. She's got one of my arms pinned. The other pushes at her shoulder, nails digging into the camo fabric and doing no damage. I cannot dislodge her no matter how hard I thrash from side to side.

Is she right? I subvocalize with what little consciousness I retain. *If I die here, will you download into her?*

The theory is sound, VC1 responds.

Wonderful.

I make one last, torso-twisting effort to knock VC2 off me, but she presses down harder, the sneer on her face saying it all: *I'm stronger. I've won.*

And Kelly. What will this do to her? Three deaths, one of them mine, in close proximity to her empathic sense. And what steps will VC2 take next? Kel will never allow herself to be bonded to this evil version of me. But she may not have a choice.

VC2 presses harder. The last bit of high-pitched wheezing air forcing its way through my throat cuts off. The blackness encroaches further on my vision.

How many fucking times can one person die?

My senses fade, the sounds of VC2's quiet laughter at my demise, the smells of blood and sweat, the pressure and pain in my neck and broken rib cage.

When the one loud *crack* rings out, echoing off the remains of the high ceiling, it's distant, as if coming from far away in the mental health facility. A neat, round hole appears in the side of VC2's head. Then her body stiffens, her eyes flying wide before sliding closed, her body slipping sideways to tumble off me and land with a dull thud on the tile to my left.

What the hell just happened? Did the Storm manage to get through the security doors VC2 had locked again? Has backup finally arrived to save the day?

And what the hell is happening *now*?

A roaring sounds in my ears, like ocean waves crashing against rocks in a tsunami. I suck in a sharp, harsh breath, air rasping painfully through my bruised throat and lungs. My vision whites out in a blinding flash, so similar to when lightning struck me that every muscle in my body clenches in remembered panic.

But that isn't the worst of it.

The rush of sensory input is nothing compared to the rush of *data*. Numbers, images, memories, then emotions: anger, fear, aggression, in one insane mix that threatens to overwhelm my rational mind, and realization hits. VC2 is dead. Rather than the other way around as she'd planned, *her* implants are downloading into *mine*.

Too much. Too much. Too much.

I get it all: the Rodwell rape I thought I'd left behind forever, though now it's blunted and faint—a copy of a copy of an original; Dr. Alkins's intent to use VC2 as her puppet plaything and her immediate death at VC2's hands; the killing of those who stood between her and getting to me and Kelly; the murders of so many women in her rage and instability and desperate search for the one to make her complete.

And under all of it, a bleak, empty, hopeless loneliness.

The blackest, deepest of pits opens inside me, sucking me down and down and down while I kick and drive against the pull, reaching for the rim and the bright blue light just beyond my grasp.

My hoarse scream reverberates through the room, my hands outstretched.

An image appears in my heads-up display—me, straining to grab for something, anything that will pull me from the abyss… and another me, suffused in sparkles of blue, made up of particles of swirling energy, her own hands held out calmly before her, open and welcoming and ready to accept me.

At first, I think I'm watching myself and VC2 merge, but there's no evil intent, no incoherent anger. This other me is logical, rational, balanced.

I take VC1's hands in mine and pull her to me and *into* me, her emotions—and yes, they are emotions— filling me with comfort, acceptance, love, and finally peace, before all the glittering diamonds that make up my AI companion swell and burst apart in a final shower like the last tendrils of a fireworks display.

A whisper of sound ghosts through my internal receivers. *Look after our Kelly.* Our Kelly. Ours. Because in her own way, VC1 loves her too.

Then, nothing.

I come to, or just open my eyes, after an indeterminate silence. I'm not sure if I ever lost consciousness, but I'm awake now, blinking up at the twinkling stars visible in the black night sky through the broken glass dome above me.

Twinkling like the remnants of VC1 scattering across my internal display before it all went black.

VC1. Shit.

I sit up, then wish I hadn't when my ribs shriek in protest. I wrap one arm around my midsection and wait for my darkening vision to clear again before attempting any further sudden moves.

VC1? I think into the emptiness behind my eyes.

No response.

Status report! A command this time. Her programming won't permit her to refuse or ignore a direct order.

But instead of a snarky comeback, a complaint about how I'm addressing her, or even a metaphorical image to express her displeasure, a simple readout of my vital signs and implant processes appears on my heads-up display: everything in the orange zones, so I've overtaxed myself as usual, but dropping in gradual intervals toward the greens.

VC1? I try one more time. But there's no response beyond my own quiet, solitary thoughts.

She's gone. The AI is gone. In protecting my sanity from the corrupted download from VC2, she's sacrificed her own sentience, her humanity.

Since waking up in the Storm's medical center after the airlock accident that killed me the first time, I've never felt so alone.

Except I'm not alone. I roll to my knees, groaning at the aches and pains. My first attempt at standing fails miserably when I come crashing down again, making everything hurt worse. Instead of risking more, I crawl across the open space toward the archway where the yellow emergency lights surround Kelly's shadow, giving her a soft, ethereal glow.

When I reach her, her eyes are open, staring at the opposite hallway wall, unfocused, unseeing. I wave a hand in front of her face, but she doesn't blink, doesn't move. Her breathing comes in quick soft huffs more like a trapped, cornered animal than a human being.

I could talk to her. I could touch her. Instead, I just… connect.

Leaning forward, I brush my lips across hers and let the channel open between us. It's a risk. I might be adding my stress and anxiety to hers, but I focus on the love. It builds and builds until the yellow glow turns to a bright blue aura surrounding us both.

I settle back, watching her face as she blinks once, twice, and her gaze narrows on mine.

"Vick?" The tremor in her voice betrays her uncertainty and fear.

"Yeah, it's me." My throat's so bruised I can barely produce sound, but she hears me.

"Did I—?" She tries to lean around me, to see the body.

I shift to block her view. "You broke it. You damaged it beyond repair."

Kelly shakes her head. "I killed her."

"No," I say, taking her hand in mine so she can feel the truth of my words. "You shut down a machine."

For a long moment, she says nothing, just watches my face. Then she nods. "What's wrong?"

Of course she's also reading my loss and sadness, but the last thing she needs is more emotions to deal with. "Later." I remove my hand from hers and put a few inches of space between our bodies.

Sounds erupt from down the corridor, the staff having gotten through the exterior doors at last. Or more likely the locks failing when VC2 ceased to exist, and her control over the security systems along with her. I glance back into the nurses' station atrium, where two orderlies are pushing against the outside of the double doors, sliding them open an inch at a time, but some of the ceiling supports came down right in front of those doors, blocking them with their weight. It will take the staff a while to get through.

The closer the voices come, the more exhausted I am. I want nothing more than to take Kelly and run somewhere far away where we'll never have to deal with the Storm and their missions and orders ever again. Carl is dead, but someone will replace him, and who knows what sort of boss that will be. I'm tired of being bossed. I'm tired of being *owned*.

Before I fully understand what's happening, I've slipped one arm beneath Kelly and the other under her arms, around her shoulders. My heads-up display appears, an indicator informing me I've triggered an adrenaline burst. Guess I've recovered enough to draw on a few of my implants' resources with or without VC1's help.

Next thing I know, I'm rising to my feet, Kelly cradled in my arms. My broken ribs ache with the motion, but it's dulled. The connections between those nerves and my brain have been weakened.

I tighten my grip on Kelly and stride across the atrium and down the corridor on the opposite side, *away* from the help soon to arrive.

"What are you doing?" Kelly whispers, her breath shifting my hair beside my ear, her chin tucked tight to my shoulder. "Where are we going? You're hurt. We both need medical attention."

I keep going, every stride I take becoming more purposeful, more determined, more sure of myself. "We'll get help. Somewhere else. Someplace far from here." My steps echo in the otherwise empty hallway. VC2 really did eliminate everyone in this wing of the facility.

Monstrous.

When I reach another emergency exit, I use the implants to override the security code, push through, and step into the darkness outside. I'm on the opposite side of the building from the remainder of my protection detail. There's no one to stop me. I take one step, then another across the expanse of shadowy grass surrounding the connected buildings that make up Klenar.

I have to avoid the pools of light cast by the spotlights and time my movements so the exterior cameras don't catch us in their sweeps, but three minutes later I'm past the tree line and heading for the perimeter fence. When we reach it, Kelly is stable enough to stand. She wobbles a bit on one knee, and her face twists into a grimace, but with a boost from me, she's able to scale the fence and drop into a crouch on the opposite side. A moment later, I land with a soft thud beside her.

Taking her hand, I pull her along beside me, not too fast since she's limping, but fast enough. We don't get far before she tugs me to a halt. "How?" she asks, peering into my face, the moonlight casting shadows across us both. "How are you doing this? Your loyalty program—" She breaks off, clears her throat. "I mean, brainwashing."

I shake my head once, hard. "No, it's programming. I'm human. The implants are machines." My throat threatens to close with the emotions swarming me, but I swallow them down. "Just machines. VC1 is gone. Let's call them what they are." But not what I am. I'm human. I've always been human. It's high time I accept that.

Kelly's eyes go wide with shock, then sadness. "Oh, Vick, I'm so sorry. Really. I may not have completely trusted her, but I... liked her," she says, referring to the AI.

"She liked you too." Loved, actually, but I don't say it out loud. We're both hurting enough. "She saved me from being overwritten by VC2 when all her data transferred to me. But a few things got through." I pause, sifting through algorithms and programs in my head. "VC2 had no loyalty compulsion program." She had no self-preservation programming, either, but that's a revelation for another day. "VC2 was free to do what she wanted. And now, so am I. So are we."

CHAPTER 50: KELLY
A RELATIVE TEAM

Vick is... well, it's complicated.

I ONLY have flashes of the events that occur during our escape from the Klenar Facility, Germany, and finally, Earth. Vick's implants might no longer be an AI, but the technology surpasses most of what's out there. From what Vick tells me, we have no trouble obtaining fake identities and boarding a shuttle off world.

I'm in and out of consciousness throughout the journey to wherever Vick is taking me. Recovery from emotion shock is a slow process. But our destination doesn't matter. All I care about is that I'm with her.

She's alive, and we're finally free of the Storm's hold over us.

We move from a small sleeping compartment on a sketchy transport company's passenger shuttle to a private space yacht just for the two of us. Vick settles me comfortably in the single stateroom while she pilots us to points unknown, coming in and out only to scan my vital signs, feed me, and catch a few hours of rest here and there. During that time, we sleep curled around each other, her love flooding my senses and healing us both.

When at last I awake fully rested and it doesn't hurt to lower my empathic walls, I'm in a different bedroom. Rough-hewn log walls surround me, and for a moment my breath stops with the thought that I'm back in that storage shed where VC2 held me captive. But no. The bed beneath me is soft and warm, a huge king, the frame also made of natural wood logs and a headboard carved with a variety of furred foresty herbivores and carnivores prancing across it. The quilt covering me is patterned in rustic shades of reds, greens, and browns. I push it off to find Vick's dressed me in plush black pajamas covered in multicolored glittery stars and wonder how embarrassing it must have been for her to go shopping for that. The thought makes me smile.

A single lamp glows on a chest of drawers across from the bed, and a mirror casts my too pale complexion back at me. Not entirely healthy yet, but I'm getting there. I swing my legs off the side of the bed, placing my feet on a thick faux-fur rug in blacks and grays, and test my ability to stand.

My limbs hold my weight. I pad across the dark hardwood floor to one of the two windows and pull aside the deep green curtains.

To my surprise, it's night here, wherever here is. I lean as close to the glass as I can, pressing my nose against it and startling back at how cold the surface is. It's winter. That's for certain. Or maybe not. I might be on a world farther from its sun. I'm in a two-story log structure, this bedroom being on the second floor, and it's surrounded by tall, dense pines. Some decorative external lighting gives the house? cabin? a soft ethereal appearance like something from a romance novel. I can't see much beyond that.

Then the overhead clouds part and two full moons shine down on the scene, taking my breath away.

Sparkling snow covers the grounds around the cabin and weighs down the branches of the thick forest of pines. In the distance, I can just make out a lit open space with a single private landing platform, our space transport resting upon it. No other homes or structures of any kind as far as I can see.

One of the shadows below moves a bit, drawing my attention—Vick, standing on a wide rounded wooden deck, leaning with her arms crossed over the railing and staring into the peaceful darkness of the woods. She turns her head toward the shaft of light now cast across the snow from my window, then glances over her shoulder up at me and raises one hand in silent greeting.

I wave back, more enthusiastically, bouncing on my toes and giving her a wide smile, which earns me one in return, though there's sadness in it, too, and I remember that she's gained her freedom but lost a friend. I wonder if VC1 will ever return.

Vick strolls toward the cabin, disappearing from my view. A moment later a door on the ground floor opens and closes. Heavy booted footsteps come up what must be wooden stairs, echoing throughout the structure. She opens the bedroom door and pauses, leaning against the door frame, scanning me from head to toe as if she's memorizing every inch of me.

Then she's crossing the floor and taking me in her arms, pulling my body against hers as if she'll never let me go. Her padded olive-green jacket is cold, but I slip inside it, letting my plush pajamas warm her through her simple black T-shirt and black trousers. All new clothing. I have no memory of her leaving for an extended period of time, so either she had things delivered, or I've been more out of it than I realized.

"You're better," she murmurs against my hair, which, now that I think about it, smells clean, along with the rest of me.

"Yes," I agree. Then, "Did I shower at some point? Or did you find a way to bathe me? I don't remember."

Vick leans back to study my face, worry creasing her forehead. "You showered. You insisted on it, so I held you up while you got clean, both times. It was one of the few coherent things you asked for in the last four days." She sighs, exhaustion and concern evident in that single exhalation.

Okay, now that she says that, I do have vague memories of wanting to scrub away the touch of VC2 and the blood and gore of that final fight.

I rest my head against her shirt, taking in all that is Vick: the hard muscles, the way she holds me to her as if she's afraid I'll disappear, yet gentle in her grasp, the tantalizing scent of that simple cologne she sometimes wears. "I'm okay. Really." Four days is the longest I've ever been in emotion shock, and that scares me a little. I probably needed a medical facility. But I understand her hesitation in taking me to one. If the Storm gets ahold of us, they'll replace her loyalty programming, maybe even make it more restrictive. Choosing between my health and our freedom must have been horrible for her. "You made the right choice," I say. "I promise, I'm going to be fine."

Another sigh shudders out of her and the muscles in her shoulders relax. Her arms loosen their desperate hold. "You sure you're not telepathic?" she asks, not for the first time.

"There are no true telepaths," I remind her, giving the same response I always give to that question, then add, "but I'm starting to wonder if, with the brainwave match, the two of us might be the first."

Instead of the laugh I expect, Vick fixes me with a serious look. "There are things in my head you don't want to know. Ever."

I don't have a response to that. Instead, I ask, "How are you holding up? And where are we? It's beautiful here."

"Deci," she says, answering the second question first, which doesn't surprise me at all. "Any part of my income the Storm didn't take back as repayment for my implants and continued medical care, I turned over to VC1 to invest as she saw fit." Vick's lips curve in an embarrassed little smile while a soft pink suffuses her cheeks. "Turns out she was quite the entrepreneur. I'm fucking loaded. And I own investment property on four different worlds." She releases me to spread her arms out, indicating the whole cabin. "This is one of them."

"She had good taste," I muse. "Romantic too. Are the others the same?"

Vick shrugs. "Don't know. Haven't looked at them yet. There might even be more than four. There's a whole file of financial data to go through. I've barely had a chance to glance at it while I was taking care of you and making sure we're safe."

"And are we? Safe, I mean." A shiver passes through me that has nothing to do with the cold outside. Vick is still property of the Storm, with or without her loyalty compunctions. And she's an illegal clone. Those two facts make for a lot of potential enemies.

But instead of stress and anxiety, Vick's emotional aura reflects calm contentment. "We are," she assures me. "A lot has happened in four days. I've been in contact with Secretary Hothart back on Earth. She's more than a little grateful to me for saving her daughter's life, twice, and she's added her voice to your mother's petition to have me declared legally alive and human by Earth's laws. It hasn't officially passed yet, but they expect it to go through in the next One World session. That means I'll be even wealthier, once I inherit my father's Earth holdings. Won't fix my issues on Girard Moon Base, but it's a start. It also means—" She pauses dramatically. I glance up. Her eyes are alight with joy. "—we can marry for real, legally, on Earth."

"Oh!" I hug her again, bouncing up and down in my excitement. "We'll invite everyone! Mom and Dad, Lily and Tonya and Michelle. Not too many, just an intimate gathering. I've always wanted an elegant, romantic wedding."

Vick laughs. "Well, I'm not sure how well I'll do at 'elegant,' but I'll try my best."

"You always do." I reach up to stroke her cheek. She leans into my touch, wanting, needing, and I detect a different set of emotions building within her, desire at the forefront of them, stirring my own. "And your... other issue?"

Vick's grin is wicked. "One World wants to keep human cloning as secret as possible. Apparently, there are some very important, high-powered people looking to make use of the process if they can ever resolve the memories issue. Genetics transfer. Knowledge and memories still don't. Not without implants, and no one in their right mind wants to go through that." Vick pauses, taking a deep breath. "But it's still illegal, even on the moon. They've explained away my 'double' at Klenar as some really good plastic surgery, and my name's been cleared back at Girard Base. But the One World government has told the Storm board of directors in no uncertain terms that if the Fighting Storm pursues me, tries to force me to come back to them, they will reveal the Storm's cloning research to the moon's legal representatives. It's all a delicate dance, but the negotiations are holding. For now." She cups my face in her hands, looking deeply into my eyes. "We're safe, so long as we never go back there, so long as I never set foot in their jurisdiction again. I assume you're okay with that?"

I nod. "I'll miss Lyle and Alex, but yes, I'm okay with it."

Vick grins again. "You may not miss them for long. I've talked with them too. When their current contracts are up at the end of the year, I've invited them to come work for me. I've got an idea for opening a private security company—Torrent Protection Services."

Torrent. Vick's real last name. I wonder if she'll go back to using it or if it's just a memorial to her father. Either way, she won't be retiring and settling down. I never expected she would.

"And we might be getting Robert as well," she goes on.

A wave of relief washes over me for the injured OWL. "He made it, then?"

A shadow of darkness passes across Vick's face but quickly disappears. "Yeah. His injuries were pretty severe, though. He'll mostly recover, but he won't be OWL quality. I think he'll fit in great with us. I just need to convince him."

"I'm sure you'll find a way," I say, patting her arm.

A comfortable silence falls while we continue to hold each other. Vick breaks the stillness with, "So, you're better. A lot better. Right?" Her tone is a study in casual calm, but my empathic skills pick out the urgency beneath the words and I laugh.

"Yes, much. Definitely up for… whatever you've got in mind," I say, lowering my voice to a sultry purr.

A shiver passes through her, and I feel her heartbeat pick up speed through her thin T-shirt. Instead of a verbal response, she leans down and presses her lips to mine, conveying everything in one desperate kiss.

"Let me give you what you need," I breathe when we come up for air.

"Oh no," Vick whispers, her eyes dark with want. "You've been giving me that since the day I met you. Tonight, I'm going to do everything in my power to give all of it back."

CHAPTER 51: VICK
LOVE AND SECRETS

I am woven.

WRAPPING MY fingers around Kelly's, I tug her toward the door. She hesitates, gesturing toward the bed with her free hand, her eyebrows raised. "I thought we were—"

"No," I tell her, opening the door and stepping with her to the top of the open staircase with a railing overlooking the two-story living room below. "I have something special planned."

I release her and she steps to the rail, a gasp escaping her soft lips. I join her, taking in what I spent hours setting up earlier today. The overhead lights are out, but dozens of artificial candles in crystal holders glow on every surface. They cover the coffee table, the end tables, the bookcases against the far wall, bathing the room in warm romantic light. A fire roars in the large stone fireplace, casting flickering shadows across the room. I pushed the furniture back, leaving an open space in front of the hearth where I scattered blankets and throw pillows. An ice bucket with a bottle of chilled champagne sits within easy reach of the cozy nest.

"It's breathtaking," Kelly says, turning to me with a beatific smile.

I shrug. "Guess I can do 'elegant' after all." I didn't even use the implants for suggestions. This is mine, all mine, as perfect as I can make it for her. Kelly deserves no less.

She starts down the stairs, taking them carefully, holding on to the wood railing, and I worry I may have rushed this. I've been monitoring her recovery. I knew she'd be up and around today, but maybe this is more than her body is ready for.

"If you're too tired—" I begin.

Kelly halts at the halfway point, turning to face me. I'm two steps up, and she grabs the collar of my jacket and tugs my lips down to hers, but before I can kiss her, she speaks. "Love and romance are exactly what my empathic senses need. Positive emotions are better than any medicine. I want you, right there," she says, pointing at the collection of pillows, "and right now. If you hesitate again, I'm going to take you on the stairs." Then she spins around and sashays the rest of the way down to the first floor, swaying her hips and making me melt inside.

By the time I catch my breath and catch up, she's standing in front of the fireplace, the flames behind her giving her an ethereal, angel-like appearance, and even as pale as she still is, I swear she's never been more beautiful. Outside the floor-to-ceiling windows making up the opposite wall, snow falls in an increasing curtain of white, dampening sound and causing everything to sparkle.

I am not worthy of this woman. I never have been. But for some reason, she wants me anyway. My hands shake as I reach for the hem of Kelly's pajama top and draw the soft fabric up to reveal her slim waist. She raises her arms for me, and I tug it higher, over her bare breasts, then off. I toss the top aside. Goose bumps spring up along her arms, and her nipples harden to taut nubs. Despite the heat coming in waves from the fireplace and the central system in the cabin, she shivers, an abrupt, violent tremor that works its way from her shoulders to her middle. I rub my palms up and down her arms, creating warmth, concerned for her comfort. Her healing isn't complete. I don't want her to catch a chill.

She crosses her arms and covers my hands with her own, stopping my motions. "It's all right," she whispers. "You're going to heat me up soon enough."

Okay, then.

Since the Rodwell assault, I haven't done much leading in our sexual encounters. With VC2's memories woven with mine, I have those negative images back, even if they are blurred. I'm nervous about how this will go. When I reach to remove Kelly's pajama bottoms, my hands tremble so badly that I end up snapping the elastic waistband back into her skin.

"Eep!" Kelly jumps backward, then laughs, pointing down at the multicolored plush pjs. "You know, in a setting like this, I should be wearing satin or lace, not plush. There goes the romance novel."

I shake my head, stepping to close the distance between us again, and pull her to me. Her breasts press against my T-shirt, the hardness of her nipples sending my pulse rate skyrocketing. "You're adorable. And beautiful. And the pjs are perfect."

"Well, you chose them. Right?"

"Are they okay?" Other than the clothes on our backs, everything we both owned was either abandoned on Girard Moon Base or at the Klenar Facility. I've had new wardrobes delivered to the cabin, ordering for Kelly by going off the sizes of the clothes she escaped in, but styles? I picked things similar to what I've seen her wear, and for the rest I selected by choosing the absolute opposite of anything I'd buy for myself.

"I love them."

"There's lingerie too," I admit, feeling a blush creeping into my face.

Kelly raises up on her toes to breathe into my ear. "Good. Next time. I like variety. Now take these off me." She snaps her own waistband.

I get a firmer grip and ease the supersoft material over her hips and buttocks, letting my fingers trail over the smooth skin of her bottom as they pass. Following her pjs to the floor, I kneel before her and lift first one bare foot, then the other, to remove the pants fully. Then I toss them onto one of the couches and focus on the gorgeous naked woman standing in front of me.

My mouth comes approximately to her belly button, so I kiss around it, then tease my tongue into the sensitive spot. Kelly squirms, giggling, her fingers digging into my shoulders. I slide my hands over her curves upward to her breasts and massage them, brushing my palms across her nipples and tugging those between my thumbs and forefingers. Her skin is flawless, soft and smooth where I'm calloused and rough, but that doesn't seem to bother her. On the contrary, she presses her breasts more firmly into my grasp while her hips give occasional, involuntary thrusts against me.

"Mmm," she murmurs.

I glance up at the sound. Her head is tilted back, eyes closed, a half smile curving her full lips. Instead of continuing to kneel up, I settle onto my feet, lowering myself farther, and drop my hands to part her legs. I slide my thumbs up to the juncture of her thighs and stroke her sex from top to bottom. She's warm and wet—very wet—and a shiver of pride and anticipation passes through me. Mine. Kelly is mine, as impossible as it seems. And I am hers.

"So good," Kelly says, hips thrusting forward more rhythmically while I continue to stroke her, spreading her wetness everywhere I can reach and easing the passage of my fingers over her slick skin, then inside.

She moans as first one finger, then a second enter her, slowly moving in and out, then picking up speed as I increase my pace.

"Vick, please."

"Please what? I'll do anything you want me to." I mean that, and when her eyes open and she looks down at me, I know she feels the truth of my words through our connection.

"Love me always."

For a split second, my rhythm falters. I cover it by curling my fingers inside her, drawing forth a long, desperate almost-growl as I hit her most sensitive spot, but my mind is racing. Kelly is wrapped up in the pleasure I'm giving her, too distracted to detect my momentary anxiety, but there are things she doesn't know, knowledge VC2 possessed that transferred to me, like the fact that Dr. Alkins never really solved the clone aging problem, that this body I'm inhabiting isn't aging at a normal rate, but rather one that is much, much slower than an ordinary human's.

Whether I live a more careful life over a greatly extended lifespan, or I'm killed and transfer to other cloned versions of myself, I'm going to outlive Kelly one way or another, by a tremendous number of years.

We've always assumed she would lose me first, but now I know.

Sooner or later, I'm going to lose her. I'm going to have to face living without her.

I no longer have self-preservation programming. That's a bridge I'll cross or burn when I come to it.

I push the depressing thoughts aside, focusing all my attention on the woman I love. Her walls tighten around my fingers. She's panting, her hips rocking in time with my thrusts. "So close," she moans, her knees trembling, hands gripping my shoulders to maintain her balance. "Now, Vick. Take me over the edge now." With those words, the channel between us opens fully, and her extreme arousal hits all my senses in one erotic surge.

"Ohhh…. God." My own nipples harden to painful points. I'm instantly wet, soaking my undergarments as a flush of heat suffuses my entire body. I wrap my free arm around Kelly's waist and hold her upright. I bury my face between her legs, my tongue darting out to flick her clit, and through our connection, my own as well, adding to both our pleasures, but I keep my eyes focused upward, watching Kelly's face as her orgasm hits. Hard.

"Vick!"

For the first time in my implant-enhanced life, I fully appreciate my 100 percent sensory-perfect photographic memory storage, because the image of Kelly utterly losing herself at my hands is one I will replay over and over for the rest of my days. She throws her head back. Her spine arches, thrusting her harder against my tongue and my fingers.

I'm so overwhelmed by the sight that when my own orgasm crashes, it takes me by surprise. I let out a low groan, my hands slipping from her as I curl into a ball of overly sensitive nerve endings. Then Kelly's there, on the blankets beside me, sliding her hand beneath the waistband of my trousers, into my dampened undergarments, and then her delicate fingers inside me. I writhe at her touch, pressing into her palm, increasing the friction until I reach a second climax. She holds me through the aftershocks, each one less violent than the last, until my body stops shaking.

Somewhere in there, I must have passed out for a moment. When I regain capability of coherent thought, she's sitting cross-legged on the blankets, still naked, watching me, a smile on her face and a glass of champagne in her outstretched hand. "This will help cool you down," she says, passing the crystal champagne flute to me.

I guzzle half in one go, then set it aside. "Kel," I say, then stop. My heart is full. My mind is at peace. I've never known contentment like this, and I have no idea how to describe it to her.

"I know," she says. "I feel everything you feel. I know."

AFTER A couple more rounds of passionate lovemaking, Kelly falls fast asleep among the pillows and blankets I laid out for us, but while my muscles ache and all my pent-up sexual frustration has found its release, I'm not quite ready to close my eyes. Instead, I stand and wander over to the floor-to-ceiling windows to watch the snow fall.

It's already blanketed the outside deck where I'd been standing when Kelly awoke earlier this evening. There's a good six or seven inches of accumulation. I'm glad I had provisions brought in for several days, because even though the vehicle I rented has ice treads (aircars don't work well in freezing temperatures), I don't trust the safety of the surrounding winding mountain roads.

We're stuck up here, alone together, and while I know I'll get antsy soon enough, right now, I wouldn't want it any other way. Still, I do wonder how long the snow will last, whether things will get worse before they get better.

An image appears on my heads-up display—dozens of tiny cats and dogs encased in bubble-like snow globes, surrounded by snowflakes and falling from the sky.

I go rigid, pressing my hands to the cold windowpane for support. "VC1?" I whisper, not wanting to wake Kelly and barely daring to voice the hope.

No response. The slightly-off metaphorical image flickers out, replaced by weather data captured from the nearest newsnet satellite. Snow and more snow—snowing cats and dogs. Like the implants are learning human slang, but not quite getting the hang of it. Not yet, anyway.

But soon, I think. Because like me, VC1 is resilient and very, very difficult to destroy.

The snow falls, and I return to Kelly's side, curling around her as if we share one body. However much or little time we have together, I've learned the most important thing.

Our hearts make us human and love makes us whole.

Read how the story began!

ELLE E.
IRE

THREADBARE
STORM FRONTS: BOOK ONE

DEADLY WOMEN,
DANGEROUS ROMANCE

Storm Fronts: Book One

All cybernetic soldier Vick Corren wanted was to be human again. Now all she wants is Kelly. But machines can't love. Can they?

With the computerized implants that replaced most of her brain, Vick views herself as more machine than human. She's lost her memory, but worse, can no longer control her emotions, though with the help of empath Kelly LaSalle, she's holding the threads of her fraying sanity together.

Vick is smarter, faster, impervious to pain... the best mercenary in the Fighting Storm, until odd flashbacks show Vick a life she can't remember and a romantic relationship with Kelly that Vick never knew existed. But investigating that must wait until Vick and her team rescue the Storm's kidnapped leader.

Someone from within the organization is working against them, threatening Kelly's freedom. To save her, Vick will have to sacrifice what she values most: the last of her humanity. Before the mission is over, either Vick or Kelly will forfeit the life she once knew.

www.dsppublications.com

CHAPTER 1: VICK
NOT QUITE UP TO SPEED

I AM a machine.

"VC1, your objective is on the top floor, rear bedroom, moving toward the kitchen. Rest of the place scans as empty."

"Acknowledged." I study the high-rise across the street, my artificial ocular lenses filtering out the sunlight and zooming in on the penthouse twelve stories up. A short shadow passes behind white curtains. My gaze shifts to the gray, nondescript hovervan parked beside me. In the rear, behind reinforced steel, my teammate Alex is hitting the location with everything from x-rays to infrared and heat sensors.

Our enemies have no backup we're aware of, but it doesn't hurt to be observant.

I switch focus to Lyle, the driver, then Kelly in the passenger seat. Lyle stares straight ahead, attention on the traffic.

Kelly tosses me a smile, all bright sunshine beneath blonde waves. My emotion suppressors keep my own expression unreadable.

Except to her.

Kelly's my handler. My counterbalance. My... companion. My frie—

I can't process any further. But somewhere, deep down where I can't touch it, I want there to be more.

More what, I don't know.

Midday traffic rushes by in both directions—a four-lane downtown road carrying a mixture of traditional wheeled vehicles and the more modern hovercrafts. As a relatively recent colonization, Paradise doesn't have all the latest tech.

But we do.

Shoppers and businessmen bustle past. My olfactory sensors detect too much perfume and cologne, can identify individual brand names if I request the info. I pick up and record snippets of conversation, sort and discard them. The implants will bring anything mission relevant to my immediate attention, but none of the passersby are aware of what's going on across the street.

None of them thinks anything of the woman in the long black trench coat, either. I'm leaning against the wall between the doctors' offices and a real estate agency. No one notices me.

"Vick." Kelly's voice comes through the pickups embedded in my ear canals.

She's the only one who calls me that, even in private. I get grudgingly named in the public arena, but on the comm, to everyone else, I'm VC1.

A model number.

"The twelve-year-old kidnap *victim* is probably getting a snack. He's hungry, Vick. He's alone and scared." She's painting a picture, humanizing him. Sometimes I'm as bad with others as Alex and Lyle are toward me. "You're going to get him out." A pause as we make eye contact through the bulletproof glass.

"Right," I mutter subvocally.

Even without the touch of pleading in her voice, failure is not an option. I carry out the mission until I succeed or until something damages me beyond my capability to continue.

Kelly says there's an abort protocol that she can initiate if necessary. We've never had to try it, and given how the implants and I interact, I doubt it would work.

"Team Two says the Rodwells have arrived at the restaurant," Alex reports in a rich baritone with a touch of Earth-island accent.

The kidnappers, a husband and wife team of pros, are out to lunch at a café off the building's lobby. Probably carrying a remote trigger to kill the kid in their condo if they suspect a rescue attempt or if he tries to escape. They're known for that sort of thing. Offworlders with plenty of toys of their own and a dozen hideouts like this one scattered across the settled worlds. Team Two will observe and report, but not approach. The risk is too great.

Which means I have maybe forty-five minutes to get in and extract the subject.

No. *Rescue* the *child*. Right.

"Heading in." My tone comes out flat, without affectation. I push off from the wall, ignoring the way the rough bricks scrape my palms.

"Try to be subtle this time," Lyle says, shooting me a quick glare out the windshield. "No big booms. We can't afford to tip them off."

Subtlety isn't my strong suit, but I don't appreciate the reminder. Two years of successful mission completions speak for themselves.

I turn my gaze on him. He looks away.

I have that effect on people.

The corner of my lip twitches just a little. Every once in a while an emotion sneaks through, even with the suppressors active.

I'm standing on the median, boots sinking into carefully cultivated sod, when Kelly scolds me. "That wasn't very nice." Without turning around, I know she's smiling. She doesn't like Lyle's attitude any better than I do.

My lips twitch a little further.

Thunder rumbles from the east, and a sudden gust of wind whips my long hair out behind me. Back at base, it would be tied in a neat bun or at least a ponytail, but today I'm passing for civilian as much as someone like me can. I tap into the local weather services while I finish crossing the street.

Instead of meteorological data, my internal display flashes me an image of cats and dogs falling from the sky.

This is what happens when you mix artificial intelligence with the real thing. Okay, not exactly. I don't have an AI in my head, but the sophisticated equipment replacing 63 percent of my brain is advanced enough that it has almost developed a mind of its own.

It definitely has a sense of humor and a flair for metaphor.

Cute.

The house pets vanish with a final bark and meow.

The first drops hit as I push my way through glass doors into the lobby, and I shake the moisture from my coat and hair. Beneath the trench coat, metal clinks softly against metal, satisfying and too soft for anyone around me to pick up.

The opulent space is mostly empty—two old ladies sitting on leather couches, a pair of teenagers talking beside some potted plants. Marble and glass in blacks, whites, and grays. Standard high-end furnishings.

"May I help you?" Reception desk, on my left, portly male security guard behind it, expression unconcerned. "Nasty weather." A flash of lightning punctuates his pleasantries.

Terraforming a world sadly doesn't control the timing of its thunderstorms.

My implants reduce the emotion suppressors, and I attempt a smile. Kelly assures me it looks natural, but it always feels like my face is cracking. "I'm here to see...." My receptors do a quick scan of the listing behind him—the building houses a combination of residences and offices. If we'd had more time, we could have set this up better, but the Rodwells have switched locations twice already, and we only tracked them here yesterday.

"Doctor Angela Swarzhand," I finish faster than the guard can pick up the hesitation. "I'm a new patient."

The guard smiles, and I wonder if they're friends. "That's lovely. Just lovely. Congratulations."

"Um, thanks." I'm sure I've missed something, but I have no idea what.

He consults the computer screen built into the surface of his desk, then points at a bank of elevators across the black-marble-floored lobby. "Seventh floor."

"Great. Where are the stairs?" I already know where they are, but I shouldn't, so I ask.

The guard frowns, forehead wrinkling in concern. "Stairs? Shouldn't someone in your condition be taking the elevator?"

"My condition?"

"Vick." Kelly's warning tone tries to draw my attention, but I need to concentrate.

"Not now," I subvocalize. If this guy has figured out who, or rather *what* I am, things are going to get messy and unsubtle fast. My hand slips beneath my coat, fingers curling around the grip of the semiautomatic in its shoulder holster.

"You're pregnant." The giggle in Kelly's voice registers while I stare stupidly at the guard.

"I'm what?" Sooner or later this guy is bound to notice the miniscule motions of my lips, even speaking subvocally.

Alex replaces Kelly on the comm. "Dr. Swarzhand is an obstetrician. She specializes in high-risk pregnancies. The guard thinks you're pregnant. Be pregnant. And fragile."

Oh for fuck's sake.

I blink a couple of times, feigning additional confusion. "My condition! Right." I block out the sound of my entire team laughing their asses off. "I'm still not used to the idea. Just a few weeks along." I don't want to take the damn elevator. Elevators are death traps. Tiny boxes with one way in and one way out. Thunder rumbles outside. If the power fails, I'll be trapped. My heart rate picks up. The implants initiate a release of serotonin to compensate, and the emotion suppressors clamp down. Or try to.

In my ears, one-third of the laughter stops. "It'll be okay, Vick." Kelly, soft and soothing.

Of course she knows. She always knows.

"Just take it up to the seventh floor and walk the rest of the way. It's only for a few seconds, a minute at most. It won't get stuck. I promise."

"Thanks," I say aloud to the guard and turn on my heel, trying to stroll and not stomp. "You can't promise that," I mutter under my breath.

"It'll be okay," she says again, and I'm in the waiting lift, the doors closing with an ominous *thunk* behind me.

The ride is jerky, a mechanical affair rather than the more modern antigrav models. I grit my teeth, resisting the urge to talk to my team. Alex and Lyle wouldn't see the need to comfort a machine, anyway.

Figures the one memory I retain from my fully human days is the memory of my death, and the one emotion my implants fail to suppress every time is the absolute terror of that death.

When the chime announces my arrival on seven and the doors open, I'm a sweating, hyperventilating mess. I stagger from the moving coffin, colliding with the closest wall and using it to keep myself upright.

There's no one in the hallway, or someone would be calling for an ambulance by now.

"Breathe, Vick, breathe," Kelly whispers.

I suck in a shaky breath, then another. My vision clears. My heart rate slows. "I've got it."

"I know. But count to ten, anyway."

Despite the need to hurry, I do it. If I'm not in complete control, I can make mistakes. If I make mistakes, the mission is at risk. I might fail.

A door on the right opens and a very pregnant woman emerges, belly protruding so far she can't possibly see her feet. She takes one look at me and frowns.

"Morning sickness," I explain, grimacing at the thought on multiple levels. Even if I wanted kids for some insane reason, I wouldn't be allowed to have them. Machines don't get permission to procreate.

The pregnant lady offers a sympathetic smile and disappears into the elevator. At the end of the hall, the floor-to-ceiling windows offer a view of sheeting rain and flashing lightning, and I shudder as the metal doors close behind her. I head for the stairwell—the nice, safe, stable, I'm-totally-in-control-of-what-happens stairwell.

"Walk me through it," I tell Alex. I pass the landing for the eleventh floor, heading for the twelfth.

"The penthouse takes up the entire top level," his voice comes back. "Figures. No one to hear the kid call for help. Stairwell opens into the kitchen. Elevator would have let you off in a short hallway leading to the front door."

Which is probably a booby-trapped kill chute. No thanks.

"Security on the stairwell door?"

A pause. "Yep. Plenty of it too. Jamming and inserting a playback loop in the cameras now. Sensors outside the door at ankle height, both right and left. Not positive what they trigger. Could be a simple alarm. Could be something else."

Could be something destructive goes unsaid. I might have issues with my emotions, but that doesn't make me suicidal. At least not anymore. Besides, with the kid walking around loose in the penthouse apartment, all the doors have to have some kind of aggressive security on them. Otherwise he would have escaped by now.

"Whatever it is, I won't know unless you trip it," Alex adds.

Oh, very helpful. I'm earning my pay today.

My internal display flashes an image of me in ballet shoes, en pointe, pink tutu and all.

Keeping me on my toes. Right. Funny. I didn't ask for your input.

The display winks out.

I take eight more steps, round the turn for the last flight to the top floor, and stop. My hand twitches toward the compact grenade on my belt, but that would be overkill. No big booms. Right. Give me the overt rather than the covert any day. But I don't get to choose.

I verify the sensor locations, right where Alex said they'd be. He's right. No indication of what they're connected to.

And time's running out.

If it's an alarm, it could signal the Rodwells at the restaurant. If they have a hidden bomb and a trigger switch….

"Wiring on the door?" I weigh the odds against the ticking clock. They don't want to kill their victim if there's any chance they can make money off him. If I were fully human, if the implants weren't suppressing my emotions, I wouldn't be able to make a decision. Life-or-death shouldn't be about playing the odds.

"None."

"Composition?" Some beeps in the background answer my request.

A longer pause. "Apartment doors in that building were purchased from Door Depot, lower-end models despite the high rents. Just over one inch thick. Wood. Medium hardness."

"The door at the bottom of the stairwell was metal."

"But the one on the top floor isn't. It's considered a 'back door' to the apartment. It's wood like the front entries." Alex's info shifts the odds—odds placed on a child's survival. I try not to think too hard on what I've become. It shouldn't matter to me, but— The suppressors clamp down on the distraction.

"Give me a five-second jam on those sensors," I tell him and count on him to do it. Damn, I hate these last-minute piecemeal plans, but we didn't have much time to throw this together.

"Vick, what are you—?"

Before Kelly can finish voicing her concerns, I'm charging up the last of the stairs, past the sensors, and slamming shoulder-first into the penthouse door. Wood cracks and splinters, shards flying in all directions, catching in my hair and driving through the material of my jacket.

Medium hardness or not, it hurts. I'm sprawled on the rust-colored kitchen tiles, bits of door and frame scattered around me, blood seeping from a couple of cuts on my hands and cheek. The implants unleash a stream of platelets from my bone marrow and they rush to clot the wounds.

I raise my head and meet the wide eyes of my objective. The kid's mouth hangs open, a half-eaten sandwich on the floor by his feet. I'm vaguely aware of Kelly demanding to know if I'm okay.

Her concern touches me in a way I can't quite identify, but it's… good.

"Ow," I mutter, rising to my knees, then my feet. "Fuck." I might heal fast, but I feel pain.

The kid slides from his chair and backs to the farthest corner of the room, trapped against the gray-and-black-speckled marble counter. "D-don't hurt me," he stammers.

I roll my eyes. "Are you an idiot?"

"Oh, nice going, Vick."

I ignore Kelly and open my trench coat, revealing an array of weapons—blades and guns. "If I wanted to hurt you...."

His eyes fly wider, and he pales.

A sigh over the comm. "For God's sake, Vick, try, will you?"

My shoulder hurts like a sonofabitch. I try rotating my left arm and wince at the reduced range of motion. Probably dislocated. I'm in no mood to make nicey nice.

"You're not the police." Oh good, the kid can use logic.

"The police wouldn't be able to find you with a map and a locator beacon."

My implants toss me a quick flash of the boy buried in a haystack and a bunch of uniformed men digging through it, tossing handfuls left and right.

"I'm with a private problem-solving company, and I'm here to take you home," I continue. "Will you come with me?" I pull a syringe filled with clear liquid from one of the coat's many pockets. "Or am I gonna have to drug and carry you?" That will suck, especially with the shoulder injury, but I can do it.

Another sigh from Kelly.

I'm not kid-friendly. Go figure.

My vision blurs. We're out of chat time. A glance over my shoulder reveals pale blue haze filling the space just inside the back door, pouring through a vent in the ceiling. A cloud of it rolls into the kitchen, so it's been flowing for a while. "Alex, I need a chemical analysis," I call to my tech guru. I remove a tiny metal ball from a belt pouch and roll it into the blue gas. Several ports on it snap open, extending sampler rods and transmitting the findings to my partners in the hovervan.

A pause. "It's hadrazine gas. Your entry must have triggered the release. Move faster, VC1."

Hadrazine's some fast and powerful shit. A couple of deep breaths and we'll be out cold, and not painlessly, either. We'll feel like we're suffocating first. If I get out of this alive, my next goal is to take down the Rodwells.

"Report coming in from Team Two." Alex again. "You must have tripped an alarm somewhere. Rodwells leaving the restaurant, not bothering to pay. They're headed for your location."

A grin curls my lips. Looks like I might get my wish.

I know I'm not supposed to *want* to kill anyone. I know Kelly can pick up that urge and will have words for me later. But sometimes… sometimes people just need killing. But not before I achieve my primary objective.

I'm in motion before I finish the thought, grabbing the kid by the arm and hauling him into the penthouse's living room. Couches and chairs match the ones in the lobby. "Tell Team Two not to engage," I snap, not bothering to lower my voice anymore. The boy stares at me but says nothing. "They may still have a detonator switch for this place." And Team Two is Team Two for a reason. They're our backup. The second string. And more likely to miss a double kill shot.

"You're scaring the boy," Kelly says in my ear.

I'm surprised she can read him at this distance. Usually that skill is limited to her interactions with me.

"Jealousy?" she asks. "What for?"

Or maybe she's just guessing. Where the hell did that come from, anyway? I turn up the emotion suppressors. Things between me and Kelly have been a little wonky lately. I've had some strange responses to things she's said or done. I don't need the distraction now.

"Never mind," I mutter. "Alex, front door. What am I dealing with?"

"No danger I can read. Nothing's active. Doesn't mean there isn't some passive stuff."

"There's a bomb."

I stare down at the boy by my side. "You sure?"

He nods, shaggy blond hair hanging in his face. I release him for a second to brush it out of his eyes and crouch in front of him. He's short for his age. Thin too. Lightweight. Good in case I end up having to carry him. "Any chance they were bluffing?"

The kid shrugs.

"The café manager stopped them in the lobby, demanding payment," Alex cuts in. "Doesn't look like they want to make a scene, so you've got maybe five minutes, VC1. Six if they have to wait for the elevator."

Maybe less if the gas flows too quickly.

Right.

I approach the door, studying the frame for the obvious and finding nothing. Doesn't mean there isn't anything embedded.

There. A pinprick hole drilled into the molding on the right side of the frame. Inside would be a pliable explosive and a miniature detonator triggered by contact or remote. Given the right tools and time, I could disarm such a device. I have the tools in a pouch on my belt. I don't have the time.

"Um, excuse me?" The boy points toward the kitchen. Blue mist curls across the threshold and over the first few feet of beige living room carpet.

I race toward a wall of heavy maroon curtains, shoving a couch aside and throwing the window treatments wide. Lightning flashes outside the floor-to-ceiling windows, illuminating the skyscraper across the street and the twelve-story drop to the pavement below.

Oh, fuck me now.

"Lyle, I need that hovervan as high as you can get it. Bring it up along the east side of the building. Beneath the living room windows."

"Oooh. A challenge." He's not being sarcastic. Lyle's the best damn pilot and driver in the Fighting Storm.

Too bad he's an ass.

The van's engines rev over the comm, and the repulsorlifts engage with a whine.

"Vick, what are you thinking?" Kelly's voice trembles when she's worried, and she rushes over her words. I can barely understand her.

"I'm thinking my paranoia is about to pay off."

I wear a thin inflatable vest beneath my clothes when we do anything near water. I carry a pocket breather when we work in space stations, regardless of the safety measures in place. I'm always prepared for every conceivable obstacle, including some my teammates never see coming.

So I wear a lightweight harness under my clothes when I'm in any building over three stories tall.

Alex teases me about it. Lyle's too spooked by me to laugh in my face, but I know he does it behind my back. Kelly counsels that I can't live my second life in fear.

Sorry. I died once. I'm in no hurry to repeat the experience.

Using my brain implants, I trigger an adrenaline burst. The hormone races through my bloodstream. I'll pay for this later with an energy crash, but for now, I'm supercharged and ready to take on my next challenge.

The hadrazine gas is flowing closer. I shove the kid toward the far corner of the room, away from both the kitchen and the damage I'm about to do.

For safety reasons, high-rise windows, especially really large floor-to-ceiling ones, can rarely be opened. Hefting the closest heavy wood chair, I slam it into the windows with as much force as I can gather. My shoulder screams in pain, and I hear Kelly's answering cry over my comm. With her shields down, she feels what I feel. They're always down during missions. I hate hurting her, but I have no choice. I need her input to function, and I need the window broken.

The first hit splinters the tempered glass, sending a spiderweb of cracks shooting to the corners of the rectangular pane. Not good enough.

I pull my 9mm from a thigh holster and fire four shots. Cracks widen. Chips fall, along with several large shards. There's a breach now. I need to widen it. I grab the chair and swing a second time, and the glass and chair shatter, pieces of both flying outward and disappearing into the raging storm.

Wind and rain whip into the living room. Curtains flap like flags in a hurricane, buffeting me away from the edge and keeping me from tumbling after the furniture. I'm soaked in seconds. When I take a step, the carpet squishes beneath my boots.

"VC1, I think the Rodwells made Team Two in the lobby.... Shit. I'm reading a signal transmission, trying to block it.... Fuck, I've got an active signature on the bomb.... It's got a countdown, two minutes. Get the hell out of there!"

Alex's report sends my pulse rate ratcheting upward. Other than not being here in the first place, no paranoid preparation can counter a blast of the magnitude I'm expecting.

Judging from the positioning of the explosives, anyone in the apartment will be toast.

I take off my coat and toss it into the swirling blue gas, regretting the loss of the equipment in the pockets but knowing I can't make my next move with it on. The wind is drawing the haze right toward the windows, right toward me. I grab gloves from a pocket and yank them on. I unsnap a compartment on my harness and pull out a retractable grappling hook attached to several hundred coiled feet of ultrastrong, ultrathin wire.

Once I've given myself some slack in the cord, I scan the room. The gaudy architecture includes some decorative pillars. A press of a button drives the grappler into the marble, and I wrap the cord several times around the column and tug hard. I'm not worried about the wire. It can bear more than five hundred pounds of weight. I'm not so sure about the apartment construction, given the flimsy back door.

The cord holds. I reel out more line, extending my free hand to the kid. "Come on!"

He stares at me, then the window, then shakes his head. "You're crazy. No way!" He shouts to be heard over the rain and thunder.

My internal display flashes my implants' favorite metaphor—a thick cable made up of five metal cords wrapped tightly around each other. Over the last two years, I've come to understand they represent my sanity, and since Kelly's arrival, they've remained solid. Until now.

One of them is fraying, a few strands floating around the whole in wisps.

Great. Just great.

The image fades.

"Die in flames or jump with me. Take your pick." The clock ticks down in my head. If the boy won't come, I'm not sure I'll have time to cross the room and grab him, but my programming will force me to try.

He comes.

I take one last second to slam myself against the pillar, forcing my dislocated shoulder into the socket. Kelly screams in my ear, but I've clamped my own jaw shut, gritting my teeth for my next move.

One arm slides around the boy's narrow waist. I grip the cord in the protective glove.

"Five seconds," Alex says.

I run toward the gaping hole and open air, clutching the kid to me. He wraps his arms around my torso and buries his face in my side.

"Four."

"Oh my God," Kelly whispers.

"Three."

Lyle and the hovervan better be where I need them. The cord might support our weight, but it won't get me close enough to the ground for a safe free-fall drop.

"Two."

The sole of my boot hits the edge and my muscles coil to launch me as far from the window as I can. There's a second of extreme panic, long enough for regrets but too late to stop momentum, and then we're airborne. Emotion suppressors ramp up to full power, and the terror fades.

My last thought as gravity takes hold is of Kelly. My suppressors have some effect on her empathic sense, but extremely strong feelings and emotions like pain and panic reach her every time.

If she can't get her shields up fast, this will tear her apart.

ELLE E. IRE resides in Celebration, Florida, where she writes science fiction and urban fantasy novels featuring kickass women who fall in love with each other. She has won many local and national writing competitions, including the Royal Palm Literary Award, the Pyr and Dragons essay contest judged by the editors at Pyr Publishing, the Do It Write competition judged by a senior editor at Tor publishing, and she is a winner of the Backspace scholarship awarded by multiple literary agents. She and her spouse run several writing groups and attend and present at many local, state, and national writing conferences.

When she isn't teaching writing to middle school students, Elle enjoys getting into her characters' minds by taking shooting lessons, participating in interactive theatrical experiences, paying to be kidnapped "just for the fun and feel of it," and attempting numerous escape rooms. Her first novel, Vicious Circle, was released by Torquere Press in November 2015, and was re-released in January 2020 by DSP Publications. Threadbare, the first in the Storm Fronts series was released in August 2019 by DSP Publications. To learn what her tagline "Deadly Women, Dangerous Romance" is really all about, visit her website: http://www.elleire.com. She can also be found on Twitter at @ElleEIre and Facebook at www.facebook.com/ElleE.IreAuthor.

Elle is represented by Naomi Davis at BookEnds Literary Agency.

DEADLY WOMEN,
DANGEROUS ROMANCE

ELLE E.
IRE

PATCHWORK
STORM FRONTS: BOOK TWO

Storm Fronts: Book Two

Empath Kelly LaSalle means everything to cybernetic soldier Vick Corren—and Kelly deserves a partner who can love her in a romantic way.

For the first time since receiving her robotic enhancements and an AI that makes her faster and stronger than the average merc, Vick thinks she can be that person.

Vick wants Kelly for life, and she'll do whatever it takes to be worthy. A holiday on a tropical planet seems the perfect time for Vick to demonstrate her commitment.

And she has big plans.

But the best intentions unravel when they're pursued by a rival mercenary company that wants Vick's technology—with or without her cooperation. A competitor for Kelly's affection is determined to tear them apart, and a lover from Vick's past has depraved plans of her own. Vick might not be able to save their lives without giving herself over to the machine she's trying so hard to transcend.

www.dsppublications.com

FOR **MORE** OF THE **BEST GAY ROMANCE**

DREAMSPINNER
PRESS
dreamspinnerpress.com